THE WEIGHT OF INTERFERENCE

THE RUPTURED KINGDOM
BOOK 3

ALLAN N. PACKER

LUMINANT PUBLICATIONS

THE RUPTURED KINGDOM SERIES

The Hard Edge of Magic (Book 1)
The Riven Land (Book 2)
The Weight of Interference (Book 3)
Waking the Dragon (Book 4)

Companion Novelette
The Renegade: A Prequel to The Hard Edge of Magic

~

Other epic fantasy by Allan N. Packer

THE STONE CYCLE SERIES

The Stone of Knowing (Book 1)
The Cost of Knowing (Book 2)
The Stone of Authority (Book 3)
The Struggle for Authority (Book 4)
The Stone of Vitality (Book 5)
The Hope of Vitality (Book 6)

Companion Novelettes
The Seer: A Prequel to The Stone of Knowing
The Rending: A Prequel to The Cost of Knowing

To Ivy
In celebration of the way you complete us.
Looking forward to walking the journey with you, whatever the future may hold.

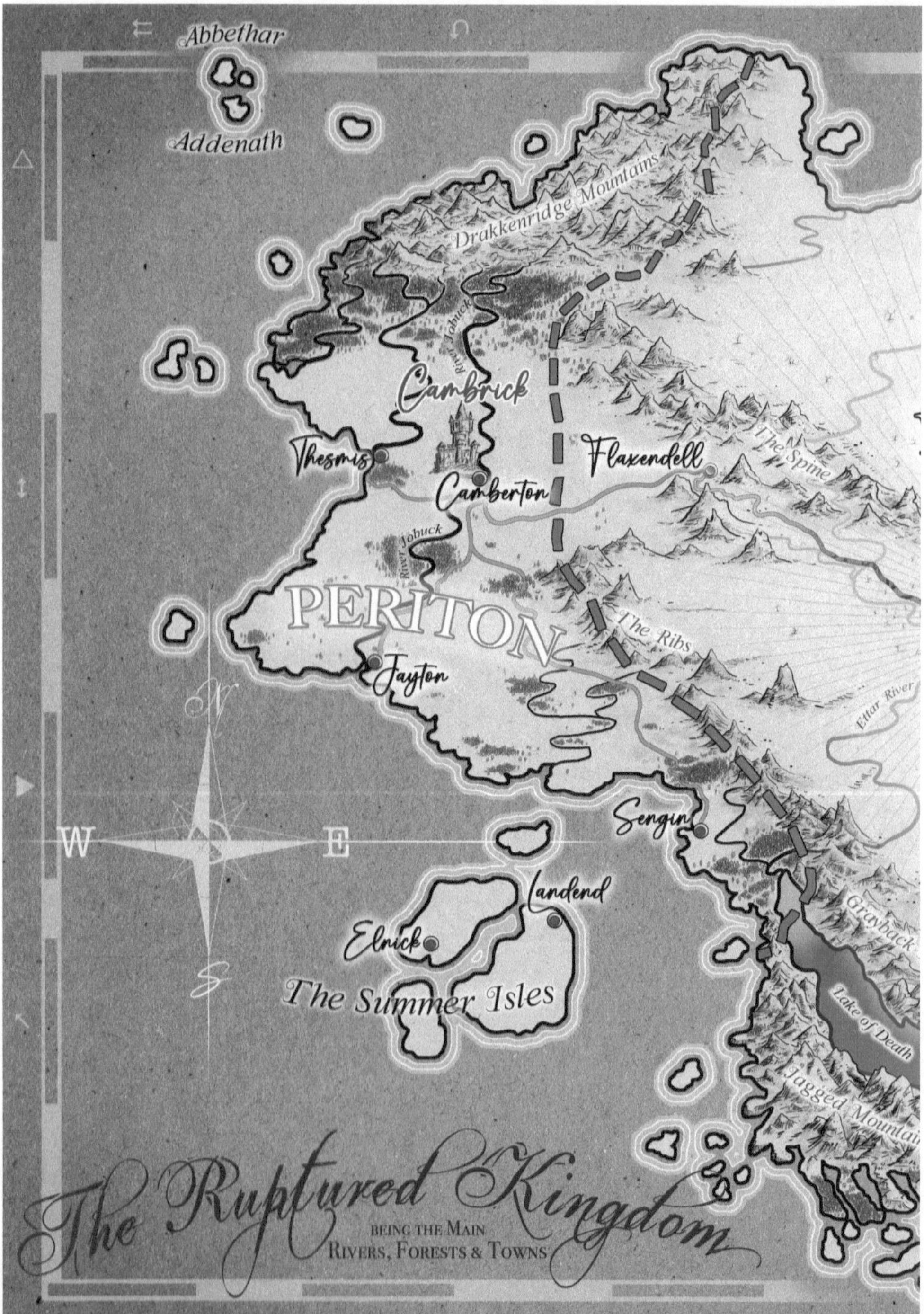

Abbethar
Addenath
Drakkenridge Mountains
River Jobuck
Cambrick
Thesmis
Camberton
Flaxendell
The Spine
River Jobuck
PERITON
Jayton
The Ribs
Ettar River
Sengin
Landend
Elnick
Grayback
The Summer Isles
Lake of Death
Jagged Mountains
N
S
W
E
The Ruptured Kingdom
BEING THE MAIN
RIVERS, FORESTS & TOWNS

Northport
Forshem
METHESIA
Ruined Kingdom
Ettaran
Ettar River
Souther
Bane Mountains
Mountains
TANTEL
Antilin
Firetip Mountains
Brynford
Brynburn River
River Antil
Shelmar
Dynsdale
Naird H'Sulp • Royal Cartographer & Geographer • High Street • Cambrick

VOLUME 1—EXILES

PROLOGUE

Casting about untiringly for the best path forward, the creature scrabbled over the uneven terrain, its antennae questing back and forth in the darkness. Guided by its keen sense of smell, the young land crab clambered on, eager for a meal.

Although its path led ever downward, it had no reason to fear either enclosed spaces or the dark. Nor was it likely to encounter predators in such a place. Rightly wary of larger crabs, it would soon be large enough to discard the broken coconut shell it used to protect its soft abdomen. Then it would fear no predators besides the dangerous and ever-hungry humans.

The crab had been moving steadily, yet the tasty treat it anticipated was proving unexpectedly elusive. And now, far from the surface and everything familiar, uncertainty was slowly building.

It was accustomed to minor irritation as its growing exoskeleton stretched and thickened. But it was becoming aware of a new kind of discomfort—a nagging unease that grew as time passed.

Had the robber crab been favored with greater mental capacity, it might have understood that something was preventing it from abandoning its quest and retracing its steps. It was being drawn—in ways and for purposes it could never hope to grasp.

Having long since wearied of its search, the crustacean at last found itself approaching the epicenter of the discomfort. Dragging itself forward with increasing reluctance, it finally found its way blocked. A tiny fissure in the rock was all that remained of its path. After a moment, the crab became aware of something shiny inside the crack. Reaching out with a pincer, it grasped and examined it.

Dimly deciding to keep the shiny thing, the creature reached back and nestled it into the coconut shell on its back. Then it promptly forgot about it.

Bemused at having found itself in such a forsaken place, it turned about and scrabbled upward in search of a more congenial habitat.

Wandering among coconut palms not far from the ocean, the eye of a young mage was caught by an unusual glitter. Closer examination showed it to be a small object about the size of a fingernail, loosely attached to the outer surface of a broken coconut shell. The half shell might have been used as a portable home by a robber crab in the juvenile stage of its life cycle, much as hermit crabs co-opted mollusk shells to cover their fragile abdomens.

The object was an item of considerable value. After glancing around quickly to be certain prying eyes had not witnessed the discovery, the mage picked it up, hid the prize in an inner pocket, and hurried away.

CHAPTER 1

Aimless and alone, a weary figure stumbled along a path that stretched away to a featureless horizon.

The traveler paused, yielding to a lethargy he didn't understand. Where was he? Why was he there? Was this place real, or was it a dream?

Glancing down at himself in the semidarkness, it occurred to him he wasn't even sure who he was. He'd had a name once. At least he thought he did. If so, it was lost to him now.

Soft voices tugged at the edge of his awareness. If the words were intelligible he couldn't grasp their meaning.

Questions pressed in on him, tumbling over each other endlessly. Every one of them defied answers.

Confounded, he lowered his gaze and plodded on.

~

LOST IN HER THOUGHTS, Dannah paced the healing hall in her slow, methodical way. Although she had retained much of her vigor, she no longer darted about restlessly as she had in her youth. Her energy levels had slowly diminished as she aged.

She had at least acquired patience as the years progressed, and she knew she was a better healer for it. If patience had eluded the young Dannah, it was largely because she had little interest in it. Now it guided her work every moment of the day, in both subtle and obvious ways.

Approaching the slab that supported her newest patient, she peered down at him. He remained prostrate in spite of her best efforts, and the sight of him stirred her compassion anew.

The youth, identified by the dragon as Kalmithien, occasionally made slight movements but otherwise betrayed no hint of awareness. His injuries had been catastrophic. Magical examination had shown evidence of acute trauma to multiple body systems. Fractured ribs and a punctured lung were immediately obvious, and he had suffered a number of other fractures as well. His spleen was severely bruised, although thankfully the splenic capsule was still intact. While there were no signs of skull fracture, Dannah had seen clear evidence of a traumatic brain injury.

When Elef'nissar brought him, she initially assessed his case as hopeless. But he had surprised her. For days he lay at the threshold of death. Thus far, he had not crossed it.

He was alive only because of the dragon's intervention, of course, and the thought brought a wry smile to her lips. Dragons were supposedly prohibited from interfering. They had never been shy about pointing it out. If a case like this wasn't interfering, she didn't know what to call it.

Her experience suggested another possible explanation for his unresponsiveness. The severity of his trauma might have prompted some part of his inner being to withdraw from the world in an attempt to preserve his sanity.

She sighed. He wasn't suffering pain—of that she was confident. They could thank the dragon's interference for that as well. The boy had been a mage, not that it helped him. No human mage could call upon magic powerful enough to deal with a situation like this. Nothing but dragon magic would suffice.

His bones would mend in time. She even expected his internal organs—including his bruised spleen and punctured lung—to make an eventual recovery.

His spirit was another matter. Perhaps the day might come when it rallied, but it was impossible to predict.

She nodded to one of her assistants. Needing no instruction, he began carefully spooning fluids into the young man's mouth.

It was an ongoing frustration to Dannah that fluids needed to be administered so inefficiently. There had to be a better way.

If a more efficient approach could be found, perhaps her own granddaughter, Marielle, would find it. Like Dannah, she was a mage, well suited to healing thanks to her mage touch capabilities. She was also ingenious and unorthodox. Junior she might be, but she showed considerable promise.

A voice interrupted her musings, calling her name.

"Dannah! You are needed! A child has been brought in. He appears to have broken his leg."

She hurried away, happy to be presented with an injury she could treat effectively.

AFTER ANOTHER BUSY day treating the sick and injured, Dannah headed for her quarters more weary than usual. Rewarding as the day had been, concern for Kalmithien had been niggling away at the back of her mind. She felt confident his body was continuing to heal, yet he showed no sign of regaining consciousness. She was at a loss to know what to do about it.

Sensing a shadow passing across the sun, she glanced up to the sight of a dragon gliding in. She groaned inwardly. Gifted with mage hearing, she had always welcomed the arrival of a dragon with delight. On this occasion a tinge of discomfort mingled with the pleasure. She had glimpsed enough of the dragon's coloring to identify it, and she had little doubt about the reason for its visit. It would fix its unnerving gaze on her, and she would have nothing encouraging to report about her patient's progress.

With a sigh she headed for the healing rooms.

Kalmithien was lying in a huge hall that had never previously been used to house patients. Lacking an outer wall, it was readily accessible to winged visitors. It was therefore not surprising that Elef'nissar had taken him there.

The hall had been built into the side of a mountain. The Artoran exiles discovered it generations earlier during their flight southward when their ships first made landfall on an island off the northwest coast of Periton. The most northerly island in a cluster of three, their new home, which they named Abbethar, technically belonged to Periton, although Peritonians never came there. As far as she knew, dragons were the only living beings aware of the now thriving Artoran community.

Unusually broad and with a roof that towered high above the stone floor, the hall was part of a much larger structure with many rooms, all carved out of rock. Some asserted that the entire edifice had been fashioned for the use of dragons. She didn't doubt it. On their rare visits, the majestic creatures always seemed at home there—so much so that she sometimes felt like an intruder.

This particular dragon had not contented itself merely with depositing its human burden in the hall. From the beginning, it had used its magic to dull the young man's pain. That came as a great relief to her. Given the extent of his injuries, she knew of no easy way for her team to ease his suffering over a protracted period.

But Elef'nissar had done much more than that. Dannah stumbled upon two of its more momentous contributions entirely by accident.

When first alerted to Kalmithien's arrival, she had hurried to the hall to find the critically injured young man on a rock slab. Two identical slabs had always lain side by side in the hall. It would never have occurred to her to use them as beds for the sick or injured. She had always supposed they were ornamental in purpose, a notion that baffled her since she saw nothing vaguely attractive about them. It seemed logical that the dragon had used the slab solely for its accessibility.

Elef'nissar had still been present when she arrived.

"I'll move him to a more suitable resting place as soon as I can arrange it," she promised. "We'll find a soft bed that isn't exposed to the elements."

Hearing it, the dragon's orbed eyes had whirled disconcertingly. "You wish him to be uncomfortable?"

She had frowned at the creature in puzzlement. "Why would a human be comfortable on an unsheltered stone slab?"

When its demeanor hadn't changed, she climbed onto the other slab and stretched out on it. Trying out the slab allowed her to show she was taking the dragon seriously, although she was honest enough to acknowledge to herself she wanted to make a point. The experience left her speechless. The rock did not change its appearance—she checked more than once—yet to her astonishment her body sank gently into it as if it had been designed precisely for her contours. Never in her life had she experienced a bed so comfortable, so perfectly molded to her form.

Just as surprisingly, the stone slab was not cold to the touch.

It was only then she noticed the air temperature inside the hall. She had subconsciously shed a layer of clothing as she arrived. The atmosphere there was noticeably more pleasant than outdoors, even with the hall exposed to the open air and with rock walls on three sides.

A long moment passed before she finally found her voice. "How is it possible?" she breathed.

The dragon had simply stared at her. "Humans ask peculiar questions," it informed her.

Now, with her initial surprise behind her, it was easy to understand the dragon's reaction. A child could have answered her question. 'Possible' took on a different meaning when you had dragon magic at your disposal.

She couldn't shake the conviction that the creature could have healed Kalmithien with ease. There was a reason why it didn't, of course. It would have reminded her that interference was not permitted. Her face twisted in frustration at the glaring inconsistencies in draconic behavior.

•　•　•

PUTTING the past from her mind, she hurried to the hall. She found Elef'nissar at the side of Kalmithien, eyeing him with its inscrutable gaze. With a quick bow, she offered a greeting. The mighty creature returned one of its own.

Sucking in a deep breath she delivered the bad news. "Our best healers have worked tirelessly on his injuries, and his body has been mending. But I can see no change in his condition." After a pause she added, "I don't know what else to do for him."

Elef'nissar studied her dispassionately. "Perhaps it is time."

Her eyebrows furrowed. She couldn't begin to guess what it meant.

Not bothering to offer an explanation, the creature dipped its head to her. Then twisting slowly around, it shuffled forward a step or two before spreading its wings and gliding into the air.

She stood watching silently until it was out of sight. Then with a sigh she returned to her quarters.

TRUDGING SLOWLY ONWARD, the lost traveler dimly became aware of another presence off to one side. He kept his head down, doing his best to ignore it. Apart from keeping pace with him, whomever or whatever it was showed him the same disregard.

The silence stretched on. He vaguely registered that in a past time he might have seen such silence as companionable. He couldn't summon the energy to think it through.

Time continued to pass without change, except that gradually the other being moved closer. They were soon side by side, although neither made any attempt to engage.

Eventually the fellow traveler seemed to have blended into the landscape. They plodded on together.

Then he heard a groan.

It could only have come from his companion. He paused, trying to make sense of it. The effort was too much for him. Bowing his head once more he took another mindless step forward.

Before long he heard another groan. It sounded louder this time.

He came to a halt. Lethargy tugged at him, and his thoughts

refused to untangle themselves. Even so, he couldn't shake the feeling that some kind of response was demanded of him.

Overwhelming as the effort seemed, he somehow managed to turn his head toward his companion. He found himself face to face with a dragon. It stared back at him impassively.

A flicker of memory told him he knew the creature, impossible as it seemed.

"Are you...hurt?"

Incredibly, the words had come from his own mouth. The awareness shook him to the core. Becoming involved would steer him onto a different and unknown path. Such a road surely had to be perilous. How could he find his way back to safety?

The dragon's mouth opened. "I am not."

He frowned in confusion. "Why...?"

"Why did I groan?" It gazed calmly at him. "That was not me. The groans came from you."

His mouth dropped open. Whatever could the creature mean?

The minutes dragged slowly by as they stood staring at each other.

Eventually the dragon spoke again. "It is you who are hurt, Kalmithien."

His brows puckered in confusion. Hurt? How could he be hurt? He felt no pain, and a brief glance down at himself revealed no sign of injuries.

Yet something deep within told him it was true, in spite of every appearance to the contrary.

The creature had called him Kalmithien. Could that be his name? It didn't feel right. Nevertheless, something stirred faintly in his memory. He had heard the word before—he felt sure of it.

Snatches of the past were slowly returning to him. This dragon had a name. He struggled to retrieve it, but it remained out of reach.

The dragon hadn't moved. It seemed content to patiently watch and wait. For what?

He peered around in an attempt to recognize his surroundings. Where was he? *Who* was he?

Something told him that answers would only come at a cost. With a sigh he decided he was willing to pay it. He had been wandering help-less, hopeless, and lost for too long.

Elef'nissar's mouth had fallen open. Was it smiling?

Elef'nissar?

"Your name is Elef'nissar!" he cried. "And I'm Kylen! Kalmithien is the name you gave me."

He frowned again. "Kalmithien. The other dragon used that name for me too. Was it trying to kill me? When the library collapsed?"

"It had no real interest in you, although your death would have pleased it. It has other purposes. The end it strives for transcends the fate of any individual. It craves the annihilation of humankind."

He wasn't quite able to make sense of that. "Where am I?"

"In a mind prison."

"Created by the other dragon?"

"You created it."

He shook his head in bewilderment. "Why would I have done that?"

"To protect yourself."

"From what?"

"From madness. Humans are fragile creatures. You were about to die, and the agony was unbearable."

"Am I dead, then?"

The dragon's orbs spun in a way he remembered.

He nodded slowly. "If I'm in a mind prison, I suppose I can't be dead."

It offered no response.

"How do I get free from the prison?"

The creature appeared to have lost interest in the interaction. "It is your prison," it rumbled.

It offered a final warning. "A difficult path lies before you, Kalmithien."

Then it was gone.

CHAPTER 2
ABBETHAR

"Welcome back, Kalmithien."

Kylen lay still, gazing up at the face of an old woman. His eyes seemed to be working properly, but he felt weak and disoriented. He made no attempt to move. He currently had no pain, but he wasn't willing to take risks.

"I'm Kylen," he said. His voice sounded thin to his own ears. "Kalmithien...that came from the dragon. Elef'nissar."

"Ah." She nodded. "I understand."

He was struggling to marshal his thoughts. She didn't seem to be in a hurry.

"How long?" he managed.

"You've been here eight weeks," she replied.

When his eyebrows went up in surprise, she added, "You're beyond fortunate to be alive. Your injuries were catastrophic. Without Elef'nissar's help, both at the time of your accident and since, you would certainly have died."

"Interference..." he murmured.

"Is not permitted," she finished for him with a wry smile. "Or so the dragons insist."

She searched his eyes. "I'm greatly encouraged to see you awake. I wasn't certain you would ever return to consciousness," she told him frankly.

He closed his eyes for a moment. "It was the dragon."

He opened them to confusion on her face.

"I was lost. Elef'nissar found me," he murmured.

"I'll be very interested to learn more about that. Not now, though. It's important not to wear you out."

He blinked slowly a couple of times, hoping it might convey gratitude.

WHEN KYLEN'S eyes opened again he realized he'd been asleep. Properly asleep, with no dreams and no trace of mind prisons. Best of all, he seemed capable of thinking straight again.

Noticing he was awake, the old woman reappeared.

"I haven't introduced myself," she said. "My name is Dannah. I'm a healer in this community. I'm also a mage, like you."

This time he managed to dip his head a little in acknowledgment. It didn't seem to hurt too much.

"Where am I?"

"You are on Abbethar, the island of the exiles."

"Exiles?"

"Artorans, to be more precise."

Unable to make sense of that, he changed topics. "How long have I been asleep?" His voice still sounded strange.

"You've slept ten hours since we last spoke."

He gazed back at her wide-eyed.

"You seem alert," she said.

He offered a small nod.

"Do you have any pain?"

"No," he replied.

"Good. You can thank Elef'nissar for that."

She gazed at him thoughtfully for a moment. Then she nodded to herself, apparently having come to a decision.

"There are a few things you need to understand before you make any attempts to exert yourself," she began.

He felt his brows twitching. She was speaking as though he intended to exert himself. The idea hadn't occurred to him.

Perhaps she'd noticed, because she continued, "You won't recover just by lying there. You need to move."

She shook her head in wonder. "You had more broken bones than I've seen in one person." Then her face lightened. "But your bones have slowly been knitting. Your internal organs have been healing, too. I think it's time for a new beginning."

Her voice softened. "That means Elef'nissar's pain relief will need to be eased back. You can't stay numbed forever."

When he didn't respond, she added gently, "It isn't going to be easy. I'm sorry to be the bearer of bad news."

He released a long sigh.

"You might have noticed you're very thin," she said. "We can at least do something about that."

Glancing down at his arms, he winced. He'd always been thin. Gaunt would be a better word for it now. It wasn't surprising if he'd been lying there for eight weeks.

"We've been feeding you broth. It's very nutritious, but now you're awake we'll reintroduce solids into your diet."

That idea at least sounded appealing.

"Before you attempt to walk again, one of my assistants will work with you on strengthening your muscles. He'll give you exercises to do. You won't enjoy it, but you won't recover unless you're willing to make an effort."

At that moment a younger woman appeared with a bowl of something that smelled good. Dannah stepped away so she could reach him.

"You look like you might be hungry," the newcomer said with a smile. Putting down the bowl, she tore off a chunk of bread from a loaf and dipped it into the broth. Then she gently placed the bread into his mouth.

It was warm, moist, and it tasted delicious. He closed his eyes and chewed slowly, savoring every morsel. When he stopped chewing and flicked his eyes open again, she repeated the gesture. After only a few mouthfuls his stomach felt full.

Never before in his life had he considered turning away food. Nevertheless, when she offered more, he told her, "That's enough. Thank you."

With a nod and a smile, she picked up the bowl and departed.

Dannah stepped forward again, slowly sucking in a deep breath as if bracing herself.

He eyed her uneasily. Something about her demeanor didn't look encouraging.

"There's one other thing I need to tell you," she said frankly. "When you first arrived we operated extensively on you. Resetting your bones was mostly done with magic, but some of the repair work would have been impossible without incisions. At times in the past we have found it necessary to transplant bone fragments from elsewhere in the body to help repair badly fractured bones."

He screwed up his face involuntarily at the thought of it.

"You needn't worry. We've found the results to be very positive," she assured him. "In your case, the procedure was unusually challenging because of the extensive damage to your body. Elef'nissar was visiting at a moment when we urgently needed a suitable piece of bone." She colored slightly. "We used a small sliver the dragon provided from one of its own claws. It was a generous gift. I understand that extracting it would have caused Elef'nissar considerable pain."

Not at all sure what to make of it, Kylen said nothing.

"Since then I have used mage touch to examine the site—without needing to make an incision. My investigations suggest the transplant has been effective."

"Is that surprising?" he asked.

She shrugged. "It was a most unusual transplant, using material that wasn't bone, and from an entirely different species. Perhaps this particular procedure might be likened to the agricultural practice of stem grafting, where a shoot from one plant is grafted onto the trunk of a different kind of plant."

It sounded bizarre.

"The point is that the long-term effectiveness of such a transplant is unpredictable," she continued. "And no one knows the implications of having draconic material in your body."

Did that mean he was part dragon now? "What do you think might happen?" he asked.

"I can't be certain. And for that reason I owe you an apology. Under normal circumstances I would never consider doing anything so unconventional without first gaining consent, either from the patient directly or from one of their loved ones. It wasn't possible in your case."

"If that's the only thing troubling you, then please relax. You saved my life, and I'm grateful to you for that."

She nodded tightly.

Finding himself conversing with someone who had experience of dragons, a stray thought came into his mind. "Have you ever seen baby dragons?"

"I haven't, although they must exist. If you're asking whether dragons are male or female like other creatures, then the answer is yes."

Seeing his puzzled frown, she smiled. "I referred to Elef'nissar as 'it,' and you're probably wondering why."

He waited patiently.

"Dragons only ever refer to another dragon as 'it.' We simply follow their lead. I think of Elef'nissar as a male, but I don't know for certain. Dragon gender isn't something they talk about. Not with humans, anyway."

His eyelids were beginning to droop again.

"That's more than enough for now. I'll leave you to rest."

He was asleep almost before she finished the sentence.

LEANING HEAVILY ON HIS CRUTCHES, Kylen stood beside the slab that had become his bed, staring out across the horizon. Both Dannah and Elef'nissar had warned him that a hard road lay ahead. They had not been exaggerating. The healers insisted he was making progress, but at times even the most basic control over his limbs seemed out of reach.

Most miserable of all, pain accompanied every attempt at movement. It had become his constant companion, wearing away at his resilience and sucking much of the joy from life.

Pushing his woes from his mind, he tried to focus once more on the vista before him. Having been built into the side of a mountain, the hall commanded a magnificent view across the island and to the sea beyond. The larger of two neighboring islands was clearly visible in the distance.

Marielle, Dannah's granddaughter, buzzed around him as always, taking observations.

"Is that island inhabited?" he asked her.

"You ask a lot of questions," she grumbled.

He knitted his brows in frustration. "I'm not planning to betray your community!" He felt like he was constantly doing the wrong thing when she was around, and he couldn't understand why.

"If you must know, then yes. It is inhabited. We call it Addenath. Our people have long since outgrown this island."

It still surprised him that foreign refugees had remained hidden for generations within easy reach of the Peritonian mainland. Wanting to acknowledge the capabilities of the community, he said, "It's impressive that no one knows of your existence after all these years, even after your expansion."

"Which is why it's obvious that no alien should ever have been allowed to come here. Obvious to everyone except a dragon, that is!" Her eyes flashed.

Why did she believe he was so intent on exposing their secret? He would have been willing to honor their secret even if they hadn't saved his life. But he'd assured her of it more than once, and she apparently refused to be convinced. He rolled his eyes.

Unfortunately for him, she shot a glance in his direction at the wrong moment. Noticing his gesture, her own eyes narrowed.

"From the way you prance around speaking our language, you seem to be under the impression you're one of us. You're not! It's offensive to speak another language without having made the tiniest effort to learn it. And you understand nothing of our customs!"

He stared at her, speechless. He was hardly prancing around. Even with his crutches he could barely shuffle. It was true that he spoke her language effortlessly. And it was no less true that if she ever wanted to speak his language, or any other, she would be forced to learn it the hard way. It was monstrously unfair, and he was painfully aware of it. But he couldn't help having mage hearing when she didn't.

He could think of nothing to say in response. Suddenly weary, he turned slowly toward his slab. Frustratingly clumsy as always, he lost control of one crutch. Crashing to the ground, he lay there helpless and in considerable pain.

"Look what you've done now!" she groaned.

Calling loudly for assistance, she waited impatiently until another healer appeared. Then, with surprisingly gentle hands, she helped him onto the slab.

Marielle baffled him. She was ideally suited to her calling as a healer. Although her magical awakening had taken place relatively recently, she was already showing strong mage touch capabilities. And he had witnessed plenty of evidence of her compassion, even toward him.

There was so much to admire about her. Frustratingly, for reasons he couldn't understand she seemed to find him intensely annoying.

The last thing he glimpsed as he closed his eyes was her face. It was flushed, no doubt from the exertion of lifting him. Flushed or not, she troubled his dreams.

WAKING FROM A NAP ONE AFTERNOON, Kylen was startled to find an intimidating visage peering down at him.

A rumbling voice issued from its gaping mouth as the creature settled. "Greetings, Kalmithien."

"Greetings, Elef'nissar," he managed.

He sat up carefully. "I haven't thanked you for rescuing me from Ettaran."

"You were content to be rescued?"

He stared at the dragon quizzically. "How could you ask such a question? If you hadn't rescued me I would be dead."

The dragon huffed. "Human lifespans are brief. Why would it matter?"

Kylen's lips curled in a wry smile. "It matters *because* our lives are so brief."

Elef'nissar said nothing.

"Why did you want to know whether I was happy to be rescued?"

No response was forthcoming.

Acting on a sudden insight, he asked, "Does it have something to do with interference? Am I right in thinking it might have counted as interfering if I wasn't glad to be rescued?"

A whiff of smoke escaped the creature's nostrils.

Kylen shrugged. "Your prohibition against interfering with humans makes no sense to me. But I do understand one thing. You ignored my short lifespan and rescued me anyway. And you brought me to the one place where my injuries could be treated effectively. I am very grateful to you for that."

The dragon dipped its head. "You have proven yourself worthy of honor."

He dipped his head in return. "Dannah told me you also donated a piece of claw. She said it's knitted into my bones."

"Does that concern you?"

He raised his hands helplessly. "Should I be concerned? I don't understand what it means."

Elef'nissar leaned forward and breathed on him. Curiously, his breath smelled of musk.

"What did you just do?" he asked curiously.

"I have just hidden your 'dragon talisman,' as human mages like to call such things."

"So I have a talisman, but one that isn't visible to other talismans?" he asked in surprise.

The dragon regarded him with its orbed eyes. "It will be of little use to you unless you activate it."

During the crisis in the observatory the other dragon—the evil one —had pressured him to grant the Amulet of Zinth access to his inner being. It would undoubtedly have enhanced his power. But for what purpose?

"I suppose I need to grant it access to my inner being," he said uncertainly. "Is that a good idea?"

"It came from me. Do it only if you trust me," the dragon replied dispassionately.

This situation wasn't like his brief encounter with the Amulet of Zinth. He was not being pressed—he was being offered a choice. And while there was plenty about the dragon that made no sense to him, he had witnessed more than enough to understand its intent. He didn't doubt it abhorred evil.

Kylen's thinking had undergone a profound shift since first he met Elef'nissar. It had involved itself in both of the crises he had faced, and in a way that left him trusting the creature implicitly. Reaching inward, he sought out the talisman. Once he located it, he freely offered it access to his inner being.

It settled in without attempting to intrude on his will. Instead, it filled him to overflowing with power, while offering him possibilities he could never have dreamed of—new ways of expressing magic, all of them within easy reach whenever he might need them.

Abruptly remembering his benefactor was still present, he tore himself away from the shining vistas before him. He stared up at the dragon. "Thank you!" he breathed.

If the creature had thoughts about what had been happening inside him, it chose not to verbalize them. Rising slowly to its feet, it spread its wings. "Fare well, Kalmithien."

"Before you go," he asked hastily, "do you know what became of Dalthinir and the others?"

The creature grunted. "Humans are as the morning mist. I pay them little heed."

Without another word it spread its wings and took to the air.

"Fare well, Elef'nissar!" Kylen called.

How had he attracted the dragon's notice? He had been fortunate indeed.

"My thanks twice over!" he bellowed after it.

CHAPTER 3
ABBETHAR

After the latest round of exercises, Kylen pushed through the curtained partitions that now enclosed his slab. With the privacy offered by the partitions, it felt as much like home as many places he had lived.

Climbing up awkwardly, he stretched himself out with a deep sigh. He felt weary beyond belief. It was one thing to be told there could be no gain without pain. It was another thing entirely to experience the reality. Even he could see that he had improved over the past weeks, but genuine freedom of movement seemed more like an impossible dream than a soon-to-be emerging reward.

"May I enter?"

He recognized the voice immediately. "Please come in, Dannah."

She appeared, moving to his side with concern in her eyes. "You look worried, Kylen. Have the exercises been too difficult?"

Maneuvering himself painfully into a sitting position, he gazed into her face, grateful she was a person he could truly relax with. "I've been wondering about the future."

She placed a gentle hand on his shoulder. "I know it must seem like a long journey. Don't give up! You *will* get there in time. Your progress has actually been quite encouraging."

"That isn't what I meant." He took in a steadying breath. "Will I be allowed to leave this community?"

Her brows knitted together. "What prompted that?"

He sighed. "Marielle seems to have convinced herself I'm going to tell the world about you all."

"I see." She stared back at him, her expression unreadable.

"It isn't true! Please believe me, Dannah—I would never betray your presence here!"

"I do believe you, Kylen. I'm sure you must be aware that you are here solely because Elef'nissar holds you in very high regard. And the dragon is an unusually good judge of character."

He felt a blush rising up his cheeks.

She gazed at him thoughtfully. "Your arrival has definitely raised questions. We're not accustomed to outsiders visiting these islands. And no one has ever been brought here by a dragon before."

"Don't fishermen occasionally visit Abbethar?"

She shook her head. "There are few places where it's safe to land, and our settlements are not visible from the sea. We intentionally built them out of sight of the coast. The smallest of the three islands in this cluster is uninhabited, and it has an accessible beach and plentiful fresh water. Fishermen tend to go there if they have need."

"Don't you all find it strange to avoid the sea when it's so close at hand?"

"We've become accustomed to it. As you've probably heard, we have a crater lake in the middle of the island, and people use it for swimming and boating as well as fishing. There are no sandy beaches around the island to tempt us, and plenty of sharks are lurking offshore. So it doesn't feel like a sacrifice."

"Haven't there ever been shipwrecks?"

"There have," she acknowledged. "We regularly patrol our shores by boat. If ever we find shipwreck survivors, we pick them up and take them to the mainland. They have no way of knowing where their rescuers are based. We let them think they were found by foreigners who happened to be in the right place at the right time."

He was impressed. They left nothing to chance.

"There have only been two occasions when someone from outside found their way to one of our settlements. They had no desire to leave. In each case they married and became part of our community."

To his annoyance, he felt his face coloring.

Either she didn't notice, or she chose to ignore it. "Are you eager to return home?" she asked.

His face twisted in a wry smile. "I don't exactly have a home. Since my magical awakening I've been a renegade in Periton, and I've spent my life wandering. I do have friends, though—others like me. And I very much want to know what's become of them."

"Perhaps it would be helpful if you have a conversation with some of our elders, the leaders of our community. I'll see if I can arrange it. There's probably no urgency, though. I doubt that you'll be physically capable of going anywhere in the near future."

He thanked her sincerely. After excusing herself, she left him to rest.

FIVE MONTHS HAD PASSED since Kylen's conversation with Dannah. While he still had a long way to go, he was able to walk about as long as he was careful. A couple of healers of a similar age had offered to show him around the island when they weren't working, and he had eagerly accepted the offer. Thus far, he had spent two mornings and two afternoons wandering around Abbethar with a guide.

To his eye the people seemed prosperous and content. To his amazement the community showed no evidence of poverty and reported very little crime. His guides explained that there was no king and no nobility. Community elders were chosen by secret ballot, with every adult member of the community casting a vote. The concept was new to him, and it took him some time to make sense of the way it worked. But they assured him the people approved of it.

He had lived in poverty in his early years in Periton's capital, Cambrick, and later witnessed firsthand the plight of the poor and sick during his travels throughout the kingdom. One thing was becoming abundantly clear to him: people on Abbethar enjoyed a better quality of life than all but the most privileged in Periton. The more he saw of the community, the more impressed he was by it.

His fourth guided tour had taken him entirely by surprise. He had been expecting to go with a cheerful and energetic young healer whose company he always enjoyed. However, the guide visited him briefly late in the morning to say he was being unexpectedly called away that afternoon. He had instead arranged for another guide to take his place. He had hurried away without saying anything further.

Marielle had arrived at around noon.

"I hope you won't mind if your work is interrupted soon, Marielle," he told her tentatively. "I'm expecting someone will arrive any minute to show me around the island."

"There won't be any interruption," she replied evenly. "I will be your guide."

Too surprised to respond, he followed her out of the building and out into the open air.

Once outside she compounded his amazement by turning a sunny face to him. "It's time I introduced you to some of our local delicacies."

With that she steered him to one of a number of outdoor food markets where people had gathered for their midday meal. On the way she checked more than once to make sure their pace was not too difficult for him. After depositing him at a small table, she waited in line at a couple of different food carts before returning with her arms full and a beaming smile on her face.

Kylen didn't know what had come over her. He saw her frequently in her role as a healer, and since the memorable day when she made it clear he didn't belong, she had been more careful in what she said. But she had never made any particular attempt to be friendly. He felt as if he was seeing her for the first time.

Both of them washed their hands in bowls placed on the table for the purpose. Then, after artistically laying out the food on two wooden plates, she handed him one with a smile and invited him to eat.

Both of them fell silent as they set to.

"This food is delicious, Marielle!" he enthused. "What is it?"

She pointed. "The fish is one of a number of varieties caught in the crater lake. We call it *wengi*. It's hard to come by, and it's my favorite.

We call the greens *viteny*, and the orange vegetable *reena*. All of it is served on a bed of rice and garnished with a lightly spiced sauce."

From the moment he returned to consciousness he had been served nutritious and tasty food, but never anything as delicious as this. They followed it up with milk fresh from a coconut, mixed with some kind of flavoring he couldn't identify.

When they first sat down together he had been too nervous to talk. He recognized that he was clumsy around her, and he had no desire to say or do anything that might shatter her mood. But her antipathy toward him seemed to have melted away, at least for the moment. She chattered away freely, and after a while he was drawn in as well. She told him about her childhood, and especially about her father, who had passed away unexpectedly the day after her fifteenth birthday. He had been a greatly respected community leader, and she had loved him dearly. She described how Dannah, her grandmother, had stepped in to provide extra support for her mother.

Kylen responded with stories about his time with Dalthinir. Tears of laughter rolled down her cheeks when he described the more outrageous antics of the twins and the despairing responses of his mentor.

He had always thought of her as prickly. The warm and engaging person before him was a revelation. From the moment they met he'd recognized her as unusually attractive. But a smiling and animated Marielle was nothing short of breathtaking. More than once he had to tell himself to stop staring at her.

When they had finished eating, her face turned serious. "How did you come to be so badly injured?"

"We were in Ettaran," he began hesitantly.

"The old capital of the ruined kingdom?" she asked, her eyes wide.

He nodded, feeling suddenly miserable. "We were pursued by a group of Tantellan mages. We confronted each other in the ancient library building, high up in a massive domed room they called the observatory. The Tantellan leader was planning to do something unimaginable." A shadow passed over his eyes. "We were able to thwart those plans, but the building collapsed. I remember nothing after that." He bowed his head. "I think my friends got clear. But I don't know what has become of them." The terror and agony of the dome's final collapse had come roaring back. His breath hitched, and he buried his face in his hands.

Leaning across the table, she gently placed her hands on his arms. "I'm so sorry," she said contritely. "I should not have asked you about that!"

After a long moment he recovered himself with an effort. The compassion on her face inspired him to summon up a tight smile.

"I have something else planned that might be helpful," she told him. "Please come with me."

Taking his arm, she steered him past the stalls and onto a road that led in the direction of the crater lake. She set an unhurried pace, but even so he was forced to ask for a rest break more than once.

Every part of him ached. And physical pain was the least of it. Revisiting the disaster in Ettaran had been traumatic, and a dark mood had descended on him. The intensity of his distress had taken him by surprise, and he was barely holding himself together.

He wanted nothing more than to offer an excuse and retreat to the safety of his curtained space. But with Marielle being so uncharacteristically kind and considerate, he felt obligated.

As they drew closer to the lake, she told him about the deep fulfillment she was finding in her role as a healer. Something in her tone had changed after his revelations about Ettaran. She shared vulnerably about mistakes she had made and how much she still had to learn. Uncertain what to say in response, he contented himself with listening.

The lake came into full view at last. The sight was stunning. The colorful sails of small boats provided a picturesque contrast to the deep blue of the water. Large numbers of swimmers were taking advantage of the pleasant weather.

Handing him a small bag, Marielle led him to a pair of sheds. She directed him to one of them before disappearing into the other. Stepping inside, he found an open space with low benches around the walls. A couple of men had just finished changing into swimming outfits. Nodding pleasantly to him, they left, carrying their discarded clothes with them.

Inside the bag Kylen found a pair of swimming trunks. After eyeing the trunks uncertainly, he shrugged and changed into them.

Looking down at his legs, he saw how shriveled his muscles had become. His muscles were in better shape than when he first tried to walk again, but it was nevertheless confronting. He decided not to closely examine the many scars that crisscrossed his bare flesh.

With a sigh of resignation he headed outside.

Marielle was waiting for him. At the sight of her his heart skipped a beat. Modest as her swimming costume was, it showed her curves to maximum effect. He had never set eyes on a girl who came close to matching her beauty. He discovered he was struggling to breathe.

His reaction was not lost on her. With a teasing grin, she glided forward and took his hand. Then she tugged him toward the water.

Immensely grateful that Dalthinir had insisted on teaching him to swim, he followed her in, gasping as the icy water rose over his legs. Shivering with the cold, he eyed the lake unenthusiastically. The idea of fully immersing himself held no appeal whatever.

Then a stream of cold water hit him, accompanied by a peal of laughter from his companion. It took only a moment before he was doing his best to respond in kind. His efforts were quickly rewarded by loud squeals from a thoroughly drenched Marielle.

Worn out by the exertion, he flopped into the water almost without thought. As he had often experienced in the sea, he no longer felt unusually cold.

"I think you won that round!" Marielle told him with a grin. "You did cheat, though! You used magic to help you in that last dousing, and don't think I didn't notice it."

It was true he'd resorted to mage touch when his own strength had run out. But he'd only done it once, and he'd been sparing. Thankfully, the sparkle in her eyes suggested she hadn't minded.

Then her face became more serious. "Let's see if you're up to some gentle swimming. Try to avoid supporting yourself with mage touch if you can." She set off slowly along the shoreline, looking back encouragingly.

He followed tentatively, mostly to please her. To his delight, it proved to be easier than he expected. His muscles were soon protesting, but the water helped to support his weight.

After a while, she paused. "How are you managing?"

"I'm able to exercise without putting strain on my joints!" He smiled sheepishly. "If I'm honest, I'm enjoying it much more than I expected."

She nodded in satisfaction. "I felt sure that time in the water would help your recovery. You should try to do it regularly!"

Her words brought him up short. It suddenly occurred to him that this whole outing might be nothing more than a healer exploring creative ways to treat a patient. The idea was unexpectedly deflating.

He reminded himself that she hadn't needed to share so honestly with him. Whatever her motive, though, it served as a warning that he shouldn't read too much into what had happened.

They spent more time doing gentle exercises before they left the water. Kylen found clean towels in the changing sheds, and he dried himself thoroughly before emerging.

Neither of them had a lot to say on the long walk back to the healing hall, although the silence felt comfortable rather than awkward.

When they arrived, he turned to face her. "Thank you, Marielle! I can't remember when I last enjoyed myself so much. You truly are becoming an outstanding healer!"

She cocked her eyebrows. "Is that all I am?" Gazing at him seriously, she said, "I'm glad you enjoyed yourself. I did, too. Thank you for telling me some of your story. I'm ready to hear more whenever you're willing to share it."

He returned a smile and a nod.

Turning to leave, she added, "I know you'll be meeting with the community elders sometime soon to discuss your future. I hope it goes well."

And with that she was gone.

CHAPTER 4
TANTEL

Lokan sat alone in a corner of the tavern, sipping at his mug of ale as he surreptitiously scanned the room. To a casual onlooker he was just another worker relaxing after a heavy day of labor. He appeared to be minding his own business. In reality he was anything but indifferent. He was there for a reason.

On that particular occasion his attention was focused on a stranger who had recently entered the tavern. Strangers were not common in Brynford. Situated in the far north of Tantel, the town was a long way from anywhere, and people didn't come there without a purpose. Lokan knew all of the locals and most of the itinerant traders, at least by sight. He made it his business to know such things.

Having never previously seen the newcomer, Lokan studied him carefully. He must have been in his early twenties, of average height, and well-built without being intimidating. But it was the newcomer's restless gaze that captured his attention. Lokan wouldn't exactly call the eyes calculating, although they were definitely intelligent. Unearthing background on the stranger had just become a new priority.

To his surprise, the young man stood up and headed purposefully in his direction.

Lokan carefully masked his surprise. He was unusually skilled at remaining inconspicuous—surely he couldn't have given himself away. Taking a slow breath he steadied himself.

The stranger's eyes were fixed on him. "You appear to be someone responsible," he began respectfully.

For a moment Lokan was too taken aback to respond. Finally, he managed, "You're new here."

Nodding a tight affirmative, the man lowered himself onto a vacant stool. He clearly didn't intend to stay there for long. "I've just arrived in Brynford. My name is Deemis."

"Where are you from?"

"From a farm west of here."

Lokan nodded an acknowledgment. Discovering the stranger's background might prove easier than he expected.

"At the northern end of the Firetip Mountains," Deemis added distractedly.

Lokan's eyebrows went up. "Near the border with Methesia?"

The newcomer's mind was elsewhere. "Aren't you concerned about the weather?"

"The weather?" frowned Lokan. "Why should I be?"

Deemis stared back at him in surprise. "You need to go outside! You'll see for yourself!" He appeared agitated. "I've seen similar signs on the farm. A storm is heading this way, and before long it's going to hit this town like a sledgehammer! Someone needs to warn people!"

Lokan had witnessed big storms rolling in from the sea, and some of them had done a lot of damage. But this wasn't the season for storms. A quick glance around the tavern confirmed that no one else seemed perturbed.

Nevertheless, there was something unsettling about the earnestness of the young man. Getting up, he headed for the tavern door, Deemis hurrying along behind him.

Emerging into the open he glanced up into a lowering sky. There was a heaviness in the air that didn't feel right.

People in the streets were pointing to the northwest. Dark clouds had spread out across the horizon like a ragged curtain, mantling the upper half of the sky and obscuring the sun. Below them he saw unevenly lit clouds stretching down vertically. He had never seen anything like it.

The signs were definitely not good. And the storm had appeared so quickly. The sky had been clear a couple of hours earlier.

"We need to do something!" urged Deemis. "There isn't much time!"

As if to emphasize his words, a flash of lightning lit up the clouds, a loud crack of thunder following it almost immediately. Lokan's eyebrows furrowed. It surely wouldn't be long before the storm was upon them.

The wind had picked up, whistling ominously, and scattered drops of rain were beginning to fall. People still in the open were becoming visibly unnerved.

"Wait here!" he told Deemis. The newcomer couldn't have known it, but he'd found his way to one of the few people capable of doing something about the situation. Hurrying back into the tavern, Lokan approached the proprietor. "A huge storm is almost on us! You need to secure your building. And tell everyone to get home immediately." He hurried outside without waiting for a reply.

Deemis had waited for him.

Lokan waved him toward the stables. He found his horse trembling nervously. Its unease removed any lingering doubt about the likely severity of the growing storm. Swiftly pulling open the door of the animal's stall, he led it outside, speaking to it quietly. There was no time for a saddle or bridle. Vaulting onto its back, he waved Deemis up behind him. The young man didn't hesitate.

Lokan urged the horse onto the street. Big raindrops began splashing onto his face the moment they emerged into the open. Buffeted by the wind and brushing water from his eyes, he guided the horse toward the municipal building in the center of town.

Lokan was dripping wet and disheveled by the time they arrived. Leaping from the horse's back, he turned to his companion. "You'll find a stable behind this building. Could you please take my horse there?"

Deemis agreed readily. Leaving him to find the way himself, Lokan hurried into the building.

A group of people stood clustered in the entranceway, staring out at the growing tempest through the open doors.

Pushing through them, he demanded, "Where's the governor?"

"In his office," a junior official replied. Seeing where Lokan was heading, he yelled, "You can't just go in there!"

Knowing he would be granted access with or without an appointment, Lokan sprinted down the corridor and burst into Governor Tunney's office.

The official had followed in his wake. "My apologies, Your Excellency!" he sputtered. "This man slipped past us!"

The governor waved the underling from the room. "Leave us!" he ordered firmly.

Bowing awkwardly, the official backed out of the door, closing it behind him.

Tunney cocked an eyebrow. "You look about as wild as the weather, Lokan."

Before he could respond, scattered hailstones hit the glass, drawing the eyes of both men to the window. He jerked his head in the direction of the clouds. "This isn't just a bit of wild weather, Tunney! A huge storm is brewing! We need to get people and animals under shelter!"

Leaving his desk, Tunney went to the window and peered up at the sky. It only took a glance. Hurrying to the door, he called for his officials. In response to his flurry of orders, people were soon scurrying in every direction.

Lokan allowed himself a steadying breath, grateful that for once the king had appointed a governor capable of handling a crisis.

Abruptly remembering the newcomer who alerted him to the danger, he headed for the building's main entrance in search of him. Witnessing the conditions up close left him glad he was undercover. He shook his head, still struggling to understand how the weather could have changed so abruptly.

There was no immediate sign of his companion. Then he spotted an old man on the opposite side of the road, struggling to make headway against what was rapidly developing into a howling gale. He hadn't been the only one to notice the man. Deemis appeared at his side. With his help, the old fellow soon found shelter in a house further down the road.

Driven before the gale, the newcomer scrambled back to Lokan at the entranceway of the governor's building.

Lokan dipped his head. "That was well done."

The young man showed no interest in dwelling on his approval. "There must be other people who need help!" he pressed.

A new hailstorm reinforced his concern. Hailstones quickly covered the surface of the ground, and Lokan eyed them doubtfully. "I'm not sure it's safe out there right now."

As he spoke he heard a distant crash. It appeared to be coming from the direction of the river.

"That sounds like a building collapsing!" exclaimed Deemis. Without waiting for a response he sprinted off in the direction of the noise. The hailstones appeared to be getting bigger, and the hurrying figure had no hope of avoiding them.

Lokan watched wide-eyed, more uncomfortable with every minute that passed. He didn't want to expose himself to this storm. Was he a coward? Coming to a sudden decision, he stripped off his leather jacket and positioned it over his head, hoping it might provide at least a minimum of protection. Then he dashed after the younger man, wincing as icy missiles sought out every exposed inch of his body. Running, at least, was not difficult. The blustering gale drove him in his chosen direction.

After a few minutes the hail eased, replaced by a heavy downpour of rain. Thoroughly drenched, he pressed on. Even though he was soaked, it scarcely mattered, especially considering the bruises that must be covering his legs and arms.

Turning a corner he was confronted by a chaotic sight. A large wooden building had collapsed into the road, spilling debris in every direction. From its appearance, the building's structural integrity had probably been questionable even before the high winds sprang up.

Deemis was poised in front of the building. Spotting Lokan he waved him forward urgently. Then he began climbing onto the collapsed structure. Lokan moved closer, joining a few other bystanders nearby. None of them made any attempt to join the young man climbing slowly but steadily over debris that was groaning ominously beneath him.

As he watched, Lokan discovered the reason why the newcomer had been willing to risk his safety. A hand could be seen above the ruins, waving a piece of cloth. And over the noise of the wind he could faintly hear the plaintive cries of a child, calling from somewhere within the wreckage.

Reaching the waving hand, Deemis began pulling at pieces of wood and casting them aside. Soon the figure of an old woman emerged. Leaning heavily on his arm, she clambered slowly and feebly downward toward safety. The moment she reached the ground, a couple of people sprang forward and embraced her. One of them led her away with evident relief.

"I need your help," Deemis told Lokan, pointing into the ruins where the voice of the child had gone quiet.

"You can't be serious!" he protested. "It isn't safe!"

"I know that," the other replied. "But we can't leave a child in there to die alone!"

So saying, he scrambled boldly back onto the groaning wreckage.

Other bystanders were casting sidelong glances at Lokan, watching to see what he would do. He frowned darkly. These people surely had to be neighbors of the victims. Why couldn't one of them help?

Eventually he could bear it no longer. Throwing up his hands in resignation he climbed carefully onto the ruined structure.

Remarkably, the wind had subsided to little more than a gentle breeze. It was beyond fortunate. Keeping his feet was challenging enough without being thrust back and forth by gusts of wind. Even the rain had eased to light showers.

He was soon acutely aware that he was carrying too much body weight. No matter how gingerly he tried to move, or how carefully he chose his footholds, every time he transferred his weight the debris below him shifted and creaked threateningly.

Deemis must have reached the child, because whimpering had resumed—louder than before. He was pulling frantically at the wreckage in an attempt to break through. Catching sight of Lokan, he urged him on. "We need to hurry! This whole thing is about to collapse!"

Pushing the risk from his mind, Lokan stepped hastily forward. He had almost reached the younger man when the structure beneath him collapsed. Plunged suddenly into the debris, he tried to grab at a wooden beam to break his fall. His weight dragged the beam downward, slowing his descent enough to spare him serious injury. He landed on what must have been an inside wall of the house.

At a warning shout from Deemis he ducked instinctively. He wasn't quick enough to escape a glancing blow from another falling beam. After touching his forehead, his hand came away covered with blood.

Dazed, he glanced around. A little girl was staring at him wide-eyed. When he caught her eye, she began crying in earnest. She was trapped beneath a sofa.

Getting down on his knees to spread his weight, he crawled to her, ignoring the pain in his head. As he approached her he saw that the sofa had fallen across her without crushing her. She seemed more stunned than injured.

Even if he could summon the strength to lift it, he wasn't sure what might happen as a result. "Come to me," he urged.

After staring numbly at him for a moment, the child slowly began to crawl forward.

He beamed at her. "That's the way! Keep going!"

In a few moments she was clear of the sofa.

"Well done!" called Deemis. "Lift her up!"

Putting his hands under her armpits, Lokan hoisted her as high as he could.

He heard a grunt of satisfaction as his arms relinquished the weight. "I've got her!"

As he prepared to climb out himself, he was interrupted by a loud creaking and a child's scream. Both Deemis and the girl came crashing through the wall he was standing on. Only the upper half of each of them was visible when they came to a rest.

Shouts of alarm could be heard from the bystanders. Then, after a stunned silence, a mad laugh burst from Deemis. "That was exciting!"

He calmed down long enough to examine the girl. "Neither of us appears to have been injured."

It was all too much for the girl, who began crying loudly.

At that moment Lokan's nostrils twitched. Glancing around he noticed a trail of smoke coming from the ruins. Building debris had been ignited, most likely from a cooking fire. Faster than he could have believed possible, he heard the steady crackle of flames.

"We need to get out of here!" he called.

There was no longer time to be careful. Both men began scrabbling upward desperately in an attempt to break free of the wreckage. Their efforts were repeatedly frustrated. The moment they succeeded in struggling to the top of the rubble they stepped on the wrong piece of wreckage and came crashing down again.

The fire was rapidly becoming a roaring blaze, and Lokan could feel the heat beating on his face. Even though the rain had resumed, heavier than before, it made little difference. The fire had too much of a hold.

Clambering on all fours to spread his weight, Lokan inched closer to the onlookers, some of whom were ready to grab him as soon as he came within reach.

"Take the girl!" called Deemis.

Glancing back, Lokan saw the fire drawing dangerously close to his companion. Encumbered by the child, the other man had made noticeably less progress.

"Take her!" Deemis called, frantically thrusting the child toward him.

Leaning forward as far as he dared, Lokan narrowly grasped her little hands and pulled her close. Then, twisting around, he threw her with all his might toward a waiting bystander. The man caught her, to a chorus of cheers from the growing crowd.

Lokan faced the fire once more. "Take my hand!" he urged, stretching out as far as he could. Gathering himself, Deemis leaped toward the offered hand. The wrists of the two men locked, and with a mighty effort Lokan retracted his hand, dragging the other man with it. With a final spurt, both of them crawled desperately forward into the grasp of many outstretched hands, reaching safety even as the heat from the fire was becoming unbearable. A new round of enthusiastic cheers followed them as they were helped away from the hungry flames.

Everyone was talking at once. The mother of the child had appeared, and she was hugging the little girl fiercely, tears running freely down her cheeks. The child's father stood beside them, his arms around them both as he stared dejectedly at the ruin of their home.

A hand gripped him by the arm. "That was a near thing!" gushed an animated Deemis.

Lokan shook his head. "I've never been that close to death."

"But we made it! All of us—the girl and the old lady too. No lives were lost here today."

"It was your doing," insisted Lokan. "I'm man enough to admit you shamed me into it."

"Motivation isn't important," Deemis replied with a grin. "Not if you do what you need to do."

Excited faces swung into view, and Lokan was separated from his companion. A woman appeared with a bandage and attended to his bleeding head. He barely had time to thank her before he was surrounded. It seemed that every witness to the rescue wanted to congratulate the two men.

The evening was drawing on by the time they finally succeeded in moving away.

"Do you have somewhere to stay?" asked Lokan.

Deemis shook his head.

"I'll arrange something. We can't leave Brynford's new hero out in the open on such a night."

"Thank you—I'd welcome some shelter," Deemis replied, waving away any suggestion of heroics.

"What brought you here? What are your plans for the future?"

A sober look came to the younger man's face. "I'm only passing through here on the way to the capital."

"What takes you to Antilin?"

"I need to deliver a message."

Lokan's eyebrows went up inquiringly.

"An urgent message," Deemis added evenly. "To the king."

CHAPTER 5
TANTEL

After two days in the saddle, Lokan and Deemis were still a long way from Antilin. Two armed soldiers had accompanied them, in spite of Lokan's protests. To him the likelihood of encountering brigands seemed small, but Governor Tunney had insisted and he had reluctantly agreed.

Lokan could have requisitioned soldiers, of course. Technically he outranked every royal official in the northern provinces, and he had the authority to issue orders if the occasion arose. In practice, he rarely found it necessary to pull rank on them.

Lokan's role was an unusual one. He did not appoint the governor, and Tunney did not report to him. The king reserved such roles for himself. It suited Lokan perfectly. The idea of being weighed down by a bureaucracy held no appeal for him.

Attempting once more to draw out Deemis on his mission, Lokan asked, "What prompted you to leave home and head for Antilin?"

"I will explain that to the king when I meet with him," Deemis replied gravely. Then his lips parted in a broad grin. "I can scarcely believe my good fortune in connecting with a person who has direct access to His Majesty. Your standing with him is a great credit to you!"

Lokan's frustration over this topic had been growing, and he made no attempt to summon a smile in response to Deemis's flattery. Although he had set out without knowing why his companion needed to meet the sovereign so urgently, he had expected to extract the information before long. He had been wide of the mark. Every attempt to draw the newcomer out, directly or indirectly, had been deftly parried. It was unsettling to be kept in the dark, not least because he was risking the king's displeasure in escorting Deemis to the capital.

Lokan had not forgotten the bravery of the young man during the storm, nor that he had been the one to raise the alarm in the first place. The governor had received enough warning—barely—to spread his people throughout the town. They had been in place when they were most needed.

After it was all over, Lokan felt that the town owed Deemis. It was the only reason he offered to take him to the king. The governor must have felt obligated, too, given his eagerness to contribute guards to the expedition.

Nevertheless, Lokan was under no illusion about the potential outcomes. The king might be furious with him when he learned he had abandoned his post without royal approval. And there might be consequences for both of them if he decided Deemis had no compelling reason for disturbing him.

The simplest solution was to turn back, allowing Deemis to proceed on his own if he was foolish enough. He was, after all, the one taking the biggest risk. Lokan wasn't willing to do it. Irritated as he was by Deemis's tight-lipped responses, he recognized something remarkable about him. Young as he was, he had behaved with unusual maturity in difficult circumstances at Brynford. No one could reasonably describe his actions as inconsequential.

Lokan's gut told him Deemis had good reason to meet with the king. And if the king saw it the same way, he should view Lokan's involvement favorably.

Weighing it all up, it was worth the risk.

All of that aside, his companion was turning out to be surprisingly good company. An attentive listener, he had shown considerable interest in Lokan's history, and had soon teased out his role on behalf of the king in the northern reaches of the kingdom.

In return, apart from the one notable exception, he had freely responded to Lokan's probings. He had chattered with some animation about his adventures growing up. He had also spoken warmly about the small community that nurtured him.

Perceptive as he was, Lokan learned a lot from what was said, and almost as much from what wasn't said. The picture emerged of a youth brought up in a strict but caring environment who had emerged wanting much more. A plodding future in a forgotten corner of the world could never satisfy the energy and ambition of someone like Deemis. That he would someday emerge from his isolation was inevitable. It had only been a matter of time.

As the afternoon wore on, their path had been taking them steadily upward. Ahead of them, the main road to Antilin led directly toward the Firetip Mountains.

Drawing his horse alongside the guards, he asked, "Have you ridden this way before?"

Both of them shook their heads.

"Then I should warn you," Lokan told them. "The road will continue to climb for a while, then we'll ride through a narrow opening. It's known as Howling Pass." Seeing their eyebrows rise, he added, "It takes its name from the eerie sound made by the wind racing through the gap. You'll hear it for yourselves soon enough."

Both men shifted restlessly in their saddles.

He ignored their reaction. "I've traveled this route many times, and it isn't the wind you need to worry about. On this side of the summit, the road has been cut into the side of a cliff. Not surprisingly, it's quite narrow."

The men were looking increasingly uncomfortable.

"We'll be fine as long as we stay close to the rock face," he assured them. "There is one other thing, though. If we're going to encounter brigands at any point on this journey, this is as likely a location as any. So stay alert."

Their hands moved instinctively to their sword hilts, and they sat taller in the saddle.

Lokan smiled to himself. He thought the threat of brigands might serve a useful purpose. Human foes were easier to face than the mindless eccentricities of nature.

One of the guards now took the lead, with Lokan riding close behind. The other guard brought up the rear.

As the Firetip Mountains drew closer, their path led them toward a narrow gap between two peaks. When the mountains filled their vision, the road began to rise above ground level, hugging the side of a mountain as it went. It must have taken prodigious effort to construct the road. Lokan couldn't imagine anyone doing it without the assistance of magic.

Ahead of them a rock face now towered to the left of the road. The ground fell away steadily to their right, leaving an increasingly precipitous drop down the mountain. Seeing it, the leading guard came to an abrupt halt.

Lokan couldn't blame him. He still found it unnerving himself. Nevertheless, this was the only way across the mountains. "Keep moving!" he called.

Bending low over his horse, the guard patted its neck. Then he guided it slowly forward onto the road.

At its narrowest point the path ahead of them was reputed to be broad enough for a wagon. Lokan hadn't seen a wagon driven over the pass, but there wouldn't be much margin for error.

True to his warning, the wind began to howl as they climbed ever higher. Having heard it before made it no less unnerving.

At last they approached the top of the pass. The yawning chasm to their right gradually narrowed as the peak opposite the road drew closer. Once they passed the summit, walls of rock would close in on both sides of the road.

Travelers heading in the opposite direction, north from Antilin, would have traveled with peaks on either sides of them. Then, at the summit of the pass, the way before them would have emptied abruptly into a terrifying plunge to the rocks far below. It was at this point that the path turned aside to become the road cut into the cliff face.

Since they were heading the other way, south toward Antilin, the unnerving stretch of road with a sheer drop along its right side was about to end for them. They would soon find themselves on the stretch of road enclosed by mountains.

Reaching the enclosed section of road, they heaved a sigh of relief. But even as they dismounted and led their horses forward, they found themselves confronted by a new challenge. With a precipice at their backs, they faced a headwind that seemed determined to push them over the brink. Rushing up the narrow passageway between the two peaks, the wind reached its maximum strength as it roared out across the gap. It was called Howling Pass for a reason. The wailing sent tingles up his spine.

Leaning into the gale, they plodded forward as quickly as they were able.

The trailing guard had barely set foot on the safer stretch of road when four men sprang out ahead of them. Armed with hide-covered shields and thick clubs, they faced the travelers menacingly.

"Put your valuables down on the road and step back from your horses! If you're smart, we might let you live!" called a harsh voice.

In response, the rear guard pushed forward to join his fellow soldier. Lokan moved up beside them. He was armed, and he knew how to fight.

It was Lokan's place to offer a response. He instinctively glanced behind them, unable to ignore the terrifying drop that lay directly at their backs.

Irritatingly, the brigands had good reason to be confident. When it came to numbers, the two groups might have been closely matched. But in practice, the odds were very much against Lokan and his companions.

If it came to fighting, the brigands had no need to overcome them. They only needed to drive their victims backward until they fell to their deaths on the rocks far below. The horses would go over with them, which would benefit no one. The robbers were apparently counting on them being smart.

Before he could decide how to respond, Deemis stepped into view. "They're the least of our problems!" he called to his companions, jerking his head in the direction of the brigands. "Listen to the wind! It's about to get dangerous here."

Completely taken aback, Lokan frowned at the younger man.

"Follow me!" Deemis called commandingly, leaping into the saddle. Swinging the horse around, he urged it carefully back the way they had come. The two guards took off after him with barely a hesitation.

Lokan abruptly found himself alone. With no other choice, he hastily remounted. More than a little annoyed, he followed the others back onto the road cut into the mountain side. In taking matters into his own hands, Deemis had not only put the entire group at risk, he had failed to respect Lokan's seniority.

The others had come to a halt a short distance down the road. "Get off your horses, and don't let go of them, whatever happens," Deemis called.

The two guards obeyed immediately. For a few moments Lokan remained in the saddle obstinately. Then, buffeted unmercifully by the wind, he gave in and slid to the ground. He belatedly realized why the others had positioned themselves with the rock wall on one side and their horses on the other. Lokan himself had nothing between him and the sheer drop on the other side of the road.

It was too late to change position now. The situation was too precarious.

Deemis had been right about the wind picking up. The howl had transformed into a roar. The brigands, pursuing on foot, were thrust forward by it. When the first of them reached the point where the road turned aside to become the road cut into the mountainside, he hesitated. With a sheer drop immediately before him, it was almost a fatal mistake. Pushed by a sudden gust, the man behind him smacked into his back, nearly sending both of them into the void. They barely recovered in time.

There was no turning back now for the brigands. Bending low, the first two made it onto the exposed section of road, working hard at staying close to the cliff face. As the other two began to follow, a new gust of wind sent them to the brink. The man in front frantically tried to pull back to safety, only to find his passage blocked by the man immediately behind him. Lokan watched in horror as he tottered helplessly on the edge. Then he disappeared into the depths, his screams of terror swallowed by the wind.

Losing his nerve entirely, the fourth brigand threw himself to the ground, looking on helplessly as his club, freed from his grasp, tumbled over the cliff. His life now depended on reaching the stretch of road cut into the mountain. Inching slowly forward, he somehow managed it.

The other two brigands had lost all interest in their victims. Both of them were crouching on their knees, absorbed by the drama confronting their surviving comrade. Having regained his feet, the hapless fellow stumbled forward with arms spread wide in an attempt to join the others.

A new gust, more forceful than ever, sent him sprawling at the moment he reached them. The effect was catastrophic.

As a child, Lokan had sat on a low hillside watching ducks come in to land on a frozen river crowded with birds. Instead of skidding to a stop as they would in the water, the new arrivals slid across the ice, bowling over any birds unfortunate enough to be in their path. It was a comical delight he had never forgotten.

There was nothing amusing about the situation that now unfolded before him. The newly arrived brigand crashed into both of his companions before coming to rest on the very edge of the road. Realizing he was about to fall, he grasped the heavy coat worn by his nearest companion. The other man tried desperately to pull free, even resorting to the use of his club.

The grip of the desperate man could not be shaken. Inch by inch he slid off the road until only his connection to the other brigand prevented him from falling.

The other man in turn was now being pulled slowly but irresistibly toward the edge. He also tried to grab the remaining brigand to arrest his slide. Slithering frantically out of reach, his companion eluded him, hanging back as both of the others fell screaming to their deaths.

Having arrived last among his party, Lokan was positioned closest to the remaining brigand. He stared wide-eyed as the man began to crawl toward him. Determined not to suffer the same fate as the brigand's companions, Lokan drew his sword threateningly. To the frantic brigand it made no difference.

The man crawled closer. He had come within reaching distance before Lokan realized he was not the target—the brigand wanted his horse. Trying to forestall him, Lokan swung his sword at the man's arms. But a gust of wind caught him at the wrong moment. Overbalancing, he fell heavily to the ground.

Taking advantage of the situation, the brigand grasped hold of the horse's reins. Abandoning his sword, Lokan sprang at the intruder. Lashed by the wind, the two men grappled fiercely, trying to keep away from the edge.

As they struggled, Lokan momentarily had his back to the drop. Seizing the opportunity, the brigand shoved him toward the edge. Grabbing the front of the other's coat, Lokan fell onto his back. Pulled forward by the momentum of his own thrust, the brigand sailed over Lokan to his death.

Poised on the brink himself, Lokan slid slowly toward the abyss.

At that moment Deemis appeared, reaching out boldly. "Grab my hands," he urged.

Desperately clutching the offered hands, Lokan came to a momentary halt. But his relief was fleeting. Like the brigands before them, both men slowly began heading for the edge.

"Let go!" gasped Lokan. "Save yourself!"

Deemis ignored him.

Intervening almost at the last possible moment, the guards pulled both men to safety.

Lokan scuttled to the cliff and planted his back against it, shivering with shock. For a while he lost all sense of time. Eventually he became aware that the wind was easing.

It was Deemis who took command of the situation. "Make your way across the pass onto the safe stretch of road," he told one of the guards. "We'll follow."

With a nod of acknowledgment, the guard set off to do his bidding.

They moved out leading their horses. Lokan could hardly bear to look as they approached the summit again. He hadn't fully mastered himself until mountains towered on both sides of the road. By then they were well beyond the point where they first encountered the brigands.

When they next halted for a break they had almost reached the end of the pass.

Lokan sought out Deemis. "You saved my life!" he breathed. "And almost lost your own in the process."

A grim smile momentarily twisted the lips of Deemis. After slapping Lokan amiably on the back, he turned away without further response.

Deemis's reason for seeking out the king remained a mystery. But in that moment Lokan determined he would do whatever it took to help him fulfill his purpose. He owed it to him.

CHAPTER 6
TANTEL

Chief Master Kharkin stood restlessly in the reception room of King Garneth, waiting for the monarch to appear. Standing for any length of time these days left him aching all over. He didn't dare to sit, though. Not when the king could burst in at any moment.

After Pernilla's failure in Periton he wondered why the king still tolerated him. Technically it wasn't possible for the king to remove him, of course. The Compact was independent of the crown, and no king would dare to interfere with the head mage. Not openly. Given his health, though, his death could hardly be viewed as untimely whenever it took place. And whatever his age and condition, he didn't doubt that the king could arrange for an accident to befall him, one that left no evidence of foul play. Garneth could insist, for example, that Kharkin meet him in the garden with the evil reputation. No subject of the king would dare to refuse, chief master or not.

The loss of Pernilla and her team had weakened the Tantellan Compact, and its chief master in particular. She had been sent to Periton to kill Trisanna on the king's behalf. Kharkin had also secretly given Pernilla a second goal: to recover the Amulet of Zinth and to return it to him.

He had later learned Trisanna was not the only illegitimate child of

King Garneth's father. A son, also born of a mage, had been sent to Periton as an infant, and he was presumably still there somewhere. The king would surely want him dead as well. That meant Pernilla's team would soon have acquired another task.

She had fallen without achieving any of her objectives.

He had never ceased wondering what became of her and her team.

In spite of vigorous efforts to uncover the details, his best sources had provided little useful intelligence. All he knew for certain was that she had led the other mages in her team deep into Methesia. He felt certain that at some point she must have decided to pursue an objective of her own.

Agalar had reportedly been the only survivor of the mission, and Kharkin would have dearly loved to get his hands on the mage. Agalar would provide answers, even if they had to be wrung out of him. It was an impossible dream, though.

His grim thoughts were interrupted at last by the arrival of the king.

"Kharkin," said the king indifferently, as usual omitting the honorific that was a chief master's right.

"Your Majesty," he replied with an equal lack of enthusiasm.

"I often ask myself why I bother with you, Kharkin. You have been a constant disappointment! Nevertheless, I have decided to give you another chance. One final chance, you might say." The king's lips drew back, revealing his teeth in an unpleasant semblance of a smile.

Kharkin bowed his head to hide his glowering face.

"I am going to entrust an important mission to you. I want you to personally escort a group of people to Ettaran."

The head mage's head snapped up. "That is impossible! Your Majesty is surely aware that anyone traveling in Methesia beyond the border region will quickly go insane."

"Don't dare to claim it is impossible! According to the Peritonians, Pernilla and her mages reached Ettaran."

"What makes you certain the Peritonians were telling the truth?" sputtered Kharkin.

"Your team reached Flaxendell before heading for Ettaran. My sources confirmed it."

Before Kharkin could respond, the king added, "And don't try to pretend to be surprised! I'm well aware your own sources gave you the same report."

The chief master was not willing to give up. "Even if they did make it as far as Ettaran, we don't know what state they were in when they reached it."

"You are conveniently forgetting that Agalar returned from his little visit to Ettaran. Your sources will have made it clear to you that he did indeed return. According to all accounts, he was entirely in his right mind. That assessment is reinforced by the fact that he later escaped from the Peritonian mages. If he managed all that, how can you call it impossible?"

Kharkin's mind was spinning.

"I will give you four weeks to prepare. After that you will lead a team into Methesia. You will include two other mages of your choice, and I will provide five soldiers to accompany you. None of you will return until you have reached Ettaran."

Kharkin was completely confounded. "What is the purpose of this mission?"

There surely had to be a purpose of some kind. If the king merely wanted to dispose of him, he had no need to throw away seven other lives to achieve it.

"You must be aware of my current focus on Periton. The simplest and most direct route to it is through Methesia. I wish to explore the practicality of using that route. Beyond that my reasons need not concern you. You have preparation to do—I suggest you get started. Consider yourself dismissed!"

The king strode from the room, leaving Kharkin to wallow in his thoughts.

WELL AWARE THAT once he entered Methesia he had no way of preserving himself, much less an entire team, Kharkin acted at once.

He had been told that two mages would accompany him. The identity of one of them at least was immediately obvious. Since the loss of Pernilla, Jaizor had stepped smoothly into the role of his right hand.

Taking him aside, Kharkin outlined the king's demands. "I'm taking you into my confidence because you will be accompanying me to Methesia."

Jaizor paled, but he nodded tightly.

Kharkin was relieved by his reaction. There were reasons why he had promoted Jaizor to the role of his deputy. Beyond his magical abilities, the mage was competent, steady, and capable of thinking for himself. He also possessed another essential personality trait—he was loyal to a fault.

The chief master had decided to be collaborative and respectful in dealing with his new right hand. He was honest enough to admit he'd been neither with Pernilla. Perhaps he was growing soft in his old age. If so, he didn't care. Chief master or not, he was more vulnerable than ever before. It made sense to surround himself with people he could depend on. Jaizor had earned the right to be held in high regard, and loyalty went both ways.

"Everyone understands what will happen if you spend time in Methesia," Kharkin told him. "However, it might be possible to defend ourselves against madness using a dragon talisman."

Having once been told in a vision that the Amulet of Zinth would provide him with such protection, he knew it to be possible. And if the amulet offered a way of staying sane, it seemed reasonable to suppose that other dragon talismans might also be capable of it.

He remembered Pernilla carrying a trinket reputed to be a piece of a dragon's claw. Perhaps it had been the reason she and her team reached Ettaran.

She must have gone there in pursuit of Trisanna and the amulet. Whether she had done it on his behalf or solely for her own benefit he would probably never find out.

Jaizor cut across his thoughts. "A dragon talisman? Like the Amulet of Zinth?"

Kharkin started. His deputy might have been reading his mind.

His surprise quickly turned to anger. The amulet had supposedly been a closely guarded secret.

"Yes, like the amulet," he growled in irritation.

Pernilla was not the only person who knew about it—other mages had been sent in search of it to the farm where Trisanna grew up. But every one of them had followed Pernilla to Periton, which meant the secret should have ended with them. Word had spread more widely than it should have.

His final vision of the ruined city had suggested the amulet was lost, presumably when the library had been destroyed. Taking a deep breath to recover himself, he acknowledged it was time to put it behind him.

"I don't want to hear another word about the amulet," he said sharply. "I instructed Pernilla to recover it, and she failed. We can safely assume it has been lost forever."

"What do you propose we should do?"

"You can begin by searching the Compact library. I've scoured the place on more than one occasion. Some sections of it are not well organized, though. I might have missed something."

He had also spent more than enough time avoiding the prying eyes of the Compact's librarian. Jaizor could take a turn at it.

"What do you want me to look for?"

"Anything you can find about the madness in Methesia. Look especially for any evidence that dragon talismans can protect against it."

"How will that help us if we don't have a dragon talisman? Do you know of others?"

"I know of none. But if there are others out there, I intend to find them. That's what I will be working on."

His deputy's eyebrows went up inquisitively, but Kharkin had no intention of indulging his curiosity. "There isn't time to waste, Jaizor. Get started immediately."

Kharkin wasted no time himself. He clearly remembered the vision's depiction of Pernilla and her team. If it was authentic, things had ended very badly for them. Crossing the border into Methesia without the protection of a talisman didn't bear thinking about. He intended to pursue his own plans with all the energy he could muster.

Hopeless as any search for dragon talismans might seem, the Amulet of Zinth—the most powerful of them all—had lain hidden in

Tantel for generations. Why shouldn't there be other forgotten talismans lying unrecognized?

After considerable thought, he decided the most promising approach would be to seek out antiquated relics. As many as possible. He would offer to pay people for their old trinkets.

Kharkin was well connected. Leveraging some of those contacts, he let it be known there was money to be made for old objects. He made it clear that the payment might be significant for the right object.

He began accumulating coin in preparation. As a wealthy man, it was no great sacrifice to sell off a few assets for the purpose.

It wasn't long before a flood of trinkets came his way. He rejected almost nothing—he saw no reason to be picky since most items cost him very little. He willingly paid generously for items with even a vague chance of proving useful. Occasionally he examined an object very closely before settling on a price. The pile grew steadily.

He spent the next few days sifting through it all.

Predictably, almost all of it was junk. Occasionally a valuable object appeared, encrusted in decades of dust and grime. Such unappreciated treasures would enrich him significantly if he lived long enough to benefit from them. He soon saw he would more than recover his costs.

ALMOST A WEEK after Kharkin's fateful interaction with the king, he met with Jaizor again.

"I searched the library thoroughly, and I found nothing particularly useful," Jaizor reported. "The madness afflicting travelers to Methesia since the fall of the kingdom is well documented, and I came across references to dragon talismans in a number of older scrolls and papers. But documents that combine the two topics don't seem to exist. Not in our library, anyway."

Kharkin grunted an acknowledgment. "Then I'm sorry to say you've wasted your time, Jaizor. I needed you to do it on the chance you'd find something I've missed." He sighed. "Our understanding of magic has diminished since the heyday of Methesia. The most authoritative ancient commentaries on dragon talismans preceded its fall.

There was no reason for them to discuss the madness. It didn't exist when those documents were written."

Jaizor looked despondent. "So there's no way we can know if a dragon talisman will protect us."

"The only way to be certain is to get our hands on one. Then we can answer the question for ourselves."

"I've heard you've been inviting people to sell you old trinkets. That was a clever move. Have you found anything useful?" He didn't sound hopeful.

"Not so far," Kharkin admitted. "There's a small mound of items I haven't examined closely yet, and people are still bringing more in. So I'm not entirely without hope. Not yet."

"Would you like me to help?"

"No. I want you to track down any mages who've been to Methesia. I know of at least two. Find out anything you can from them. Be discreet about it. I don't want to stir up a lot of questions. If anyone wants to know why you're doing it, refer them to me. And if you think there's any chance they'll actually try to speak to me, tell them I'm in a very bad mood."

Jaizor grinned. "I can do that."

THE CRUCIAL BREAKTHROUGH CAME UNEXPECTEDLY. A farmer had brought in what appeared to be a small lump of metal. He had inherited it from his great-grandfather, who claimed it was valuable, although he didn't know why. No further details had survived.

A brief examination by Kharkin suggested it was worthless. As was his practice in such cases, he offered a small payment in exchange for the item. He was almost certainly wasting his money, but the flow of trinkets would dry up if he sent people away empty-handed.

When the farmer grew red in the face, he offered to double the amount. The man left contented only after Kharkin quadrupled his original offer.

Upon closer examination, Kharkin began to suspect that the lump of metal had been crudely formed to encase an object of some kind. If he was right, someone must have regarded the object as worthy of special protection. Willing himself to remain patient, he carefully set about removing the walls of the little prison.

The task proved to be more challenging than he expected. He wasn't surprised when he noticed signs that others before him had made similar attempts. Apparently his predecessors had given up without succeeding.

A master craftsman could have completed the task more quickly, but he decided secrecy was more valuable than his time.

In the end, an entire afternoon of painstaking labor lay behind him before the final pieces of the metal casing came away. He gazed in awe at the tiny object he had exposed. It appeared to be a small piece of tooth. It was a dragon talisman—he was certain of it. The scent of magical power hovered at the edge of his consciousness.

Was there something he needed to do to gain access to its full benefits, or did he simply need to carry it with him? The longer he thought about it, the more unlikely it seemed that physical access alone would unlock its potential. If its power was solely based on proximity, any mage close enough to the talisman should benefit. That idea ran counter to the little he knew about talismans.

After asking Jaizor to urgently carry out further research on the way talismans worked, they reconvened the following morning.

"There was a reason for my request," Kharkin said, trying to contain his elation as he showed Jaizor the talisman. "Can you sense it?"

His deputy shook his head. If he was envious, he was hiding it well.

The chief master's eyebrows drew together. "That's odd. I've been aware of it since the moment I recognized what it was."

"Perhaps it has somehow attuned itself to you."

"Perhaps. What did you learn about the way talismans work?"

"I went back to the library and smuggled out a document. Getting it past the librarian wasn't easy. She was nosing around the whole time I was there. Asking why I was there, what I was looking for, on and on."

"What did you tell her?" asked the head mage anxiously.

"Nothing! What I'm researching is not her business."

Kharkin nodded in satisfaction.

"According to this document, a dragon talisman enhances the strength of a mage's existing abilities, and allows the mage to use those abilities without becoming weary. It also offers ways of responding to situations. Sometimes unexpected ways. Further, it makes the bearer aware of the presence of other talismans."

"I haven't sensed any other talismans. I suppose that means the other trinkets I acquired are all worthless. It doesn't matter, of course. Not now I have a talisman. What else does the document say?"

"That the full benefits are only available after the talisman has been activated by the bearer."

Kharkin frowned. "How is it activated?"

"It doesn't say. The writer seems to treat activation as common knowledge."

"I'll figure it out somehow," said Kharkin determinedly. "And once I have, Methesia will hold no terror for us."

CHAPTER 7
ABBETHAR

Accompanied by Dannah, Kylen entered the main civic building on Abbethar for his scheduled meeting with the community elders. He had set out well before the meeting time, not wanting to arrive worn out from the walk. Even after taking it slowly he arrived in plenty of time. As a result, he found himself waiting with the healer for many minutes on a bench seat outside a pair of large wooden doors.

"As you're aware, I've been given permission to attend the meeting with you," Dannah told him in a whisper. "That isn't what usually happens, but this situation is unusual. I pointed out that no one could reasonably expect you to be fully aware of our history and customs. It seems I was suitably persuasive."

"Thank you!" he breathed. He was grateful beyond measure for her support.

"When they first ask you a question, don't forget what I suggested you say before you answer it."

He nodded tightly, grateful for her guidance.

As time crawled by he couldn't stop himself from fidgeting restlessly. Eventually the doors opened and an aide appeared, waving them into the room.

Dannah got up, taking his arm with an encouraging smile.

Clambering to his feet and walking slowly into the room, he saw about a dozen men and women sitting around a polished wooden table.

A woman stood and greeted them in a neutral tone. "Welcome, Dannah, Kylen. Please take a seat."

She pointed to a pair of empty seats at the near end of the table. No welcoming smiles were on offer, but no one appeared hostile. Kylen probably had Dannah's presence to thank for that.

Another of the elders addressed him after introducing himself as Rydel. "We understand you have been asking about leaving these islands. Could you please explain your reasons?"

Kylen looked at him nervously, acutely aware he was poorly equipped to face a formal inquiry. Dalthinir would have known how to handle it, and thinking of his mentor brought a lump to his throat.

Glancing at Dannah, he saw an expectant smile on her face. He gathered his courage and took a breath.

"Before I answer, I'd like to say how grateful I am for the care I have received here. I would have died without the efforts of Dannah and the other healers. I am also grateful that you've permitted me to be here at all. I've been told it's very unusual for anyone to come here from outside."

He was relieved to see some of the faces relaxing a little.

"In answer to your question, I'm not ready to leave. I don't think I could go anywhere, even if I wanted to. I can't walk far without discomfort. I have no great desire to return to Periton, and even less to Methesia. But when Elef'nissar brought me here, I left my friends in great danger. No one in Methesia can keep their sanity for long without magical protection. I would very much like to find out what became of them."

They apparently had no interest in discussing what he wanted to do. "Elef'nissar communicated little or nothing of your story," another of the elders told him. "It isn't surprising—we have never found dragons to be a satisfying source of information. We are aware of what you told Marielle about your situation."

He felt his face coloring at the mention of Marielle, and a rapid glance at Dannah left no doubt that she had noticed it. But he pushed any thought of her aside. He could not afford to be distracted.

"She insists you were in Ettaran at the time of your injury. That is difficult to believe. How did you come to be there?"

He groaned inwardly. How could he convey all that had happened? And how could he possibly expect them to believe it?

"I did not go there willingly," he began. "I was with a small group of friends in Flaxendell, a deserted town in Methesia not far from the border with Periton. We were searching for information in the old library. I was captured by a group of Tantellan mages. They had come there to find and kill a young woman from Tantel who was traveling with us. They hoped to use me as leverage."

"Who is this young woman, and why did they want to kill her?"

For a moment he wondered if the information might be sensitive. But it was hard to imagine what harm it could do to share it.

"Her name is Trisanna. If she is still alive, she is a mage who is also the half-sister of the king of Tantel. He sent the other mages to kill her."

They exchanged glances, but he pressed on.

"She also had a powerful dragon talisman they wanted."

Several eyebrows went up.

"Does she still have it?"

He shook his head firmly. "It was destroyed when the library in Ettaran collapsed." He felt certain the amulet had been destroyed, although he couldn't be sure how he knew.

"So the Tantellan mages followed this Trisanna to Ettaran, taking you with them?"

"Yes. There was also something they wanted to do there. If they had succeeded, it would have ended life in the world."

Some of them didn't try to hide their disbelief. Dannah got in before any of them could speak.

"Incredible as this account seems," she ventured, "it does tally with the little we learned from the dragon. Elef'nissar confirmed that a terrible disaster had been averted and also made it clear that Kylen played a key role in preventing it. According to the dragon, Kylen had earned great honor for his valor and his sacrifice."

"Whatever the dragon might have said, the story is hard to take seriously," asserted one of the elders.

"The known facts are no less difficult to take seriously," Dannah countered. "How many of you would have believed it possible that a dragon would ever bring a human to us to care for? It is unprecedented! And you already know that it contributed a small piece of its own claw toward the mending of Kylen's bones. That is even more remarkable! I find it hard to imagine that such things have ever occurred before."

"What do you have to say to this, Kylen?" Rydel asked. "Is it true that you prevented a catastrophe?"

"It wasn't just me," he insisted. "Trisanna and Dalthinir were involved, too. And the twins! Every one of them risked their lives."

"What was the response of the king of Periton to this situation?"

"He had no way of knowing what was happening in Ettaran. Some of his mages came to Flaxendell, but they didn't follow us to Ettaran. I'm sure they knew they would go mad if they did."

"Why didn't you go mad?"

"Because of the dragon talisman."

"So why don't you want to return to Periton?"

"In Periton I am regarded as a renegade."

Seeing some dark looks, he added, "Not because of anything I have done or intend to do. It is only because my magic was awakened independently of the Compact. By their laws, that makes me a renegade."

"Why did you choose to remain a renegade after your magic was awakened? Why didn't you join the Compact?"

"Joining isn't an option in such cases. The Compact won't accept anyone they haven't trained. In their view, renegades are unpredictable and need to be destroyed before they do any harm."

Muttering broke out among the elders. Finally, one of them spoke. "We are finding this difficult to accept."

Kylen shrugged helplessly. "The Compact's position on renegades is common knowledge among mages. Any mage from Periton or Tantel will readily confirm it."

"Confirming your claims is not straightforward," the leader

replied. "As you are aware, neither kingdom is aware of our existence. We have no direct interaction with them."

He turned to Dannah. "You will both need to leave us for a short time. We will call you back after we have discussed the situation."

An aide was called in, and a couple of the elders spoke quietly with him. Then he ushered the two of them from the room.

Rather than leaving them on the bench seat outside the room, the aide led them to a small but pleasant room where food and drink was laid out. Then he left, closing the door behind him.

"You must be hungry," Dannah said with a smile.

He made no move toward the food. After what had just happened, eating was the last thing on his mind. His stomach was clenched too tight.

Eyeing him knowingly, she placed a gentle arm on his shoulder. "Don't take it personally, Kylen. They haven't faced a situation like this before. They're as anxious and uncertain as you."

"Why?" he asked. "I mean them no harm!"

"The safety and protection of the community is their highest priority, and they have no way of being certain you would preserve our secrecy if they let you leave. How could they be sure? They don't know you."

When he remained silent, she added, "It isn't surprising they consider you a potential threat. Yet in spite of that they are still doing their best to consider you and your wishes."

Something didn't make sense to him. "In all the time the community has been here, surely there must have been unhappy people who didn't want to stay. If any of them sailed to Periton or Tantel, it wouldn't be long before your presence was exposed."

"It's true," she acknowledged. "Some members of the community were disaffected in the past, occasionally to the point where the community eldership council needed to act. But I have no idea how those situations were resolved."

Kylen had the feeling she knew more than she was saying. "Have people ever been allowed to leave Abbethar or Addenath and move to Periton or Tantel?"

She looked uncomfortable. "I can't be certain. Details like that are not known to me. But I doubt it."

He ran a hand across his face. "They're never going to let me leave," he said miserably.

Concern furrowed her brow. "You mustn't assume that, Kylen! Every situation is different."

Apparently eager to change the tone, she pointed at the food. "It's important to keep your strength up. Have something to eat."

He didn't move. He felt too miserable to eat.

She eyed him curiously. "Would it be so bad to remain in our community? Is there nothing here that appeals to you?"

The previous afternoon came abruptly to mind. Was it possible that Marielle had been under instruction to be nice to him? Had she been trying to dangle a lure before him as an inducement to stay? It was unexpectedly painful to consider the possibility that her actions had meant nothing more than that. She had certainly seemed sincere at the time, even though her behavior was so out of character.

He acknowledged he didn't know her well enough to be certain.

He gazed with new suspicion at Dannah. Was her kindness just a tactic, too? The thought of it was crushing.

An overwhelming longing to see Dalthinir and the others welled up within him. Where were they?

True friends—people who acted with integrity—were not just wishful thinking. Since his magical awakening he had walked through life beside people he could trust. Even more remarkably, he'd been befriended by a dragon. As far as he could tell, Elef'nissar had only ever acted in his best interests.

Dannah was still waiting for an answer. He stared fixedly at her for a long moment.

"What's the matter, Kylen?" She seemed genuinely perplexed.

In a sudden flash of insight, he recognized that she at least had been unwavering in her care and concern for him. From the beginning she had shown herself to be genuine. She didn't deserve his mistrust.

He did his best to deliver a smile.

"I am grateful to you, and to your community. But I can't just ignore my friends. Perhaps they didn't make it out of Methesia. I won't know without searching for them. If they're gone, perhaps my future might look different."

He sighed. "It isn't just my friends, though. I'm not sure what I would do if I remained here."

"Your abilities as a mage would make you very useful," she assured him. "There would be no end to the ways you could contribute."

"Perhaps I could be useful. But that isn't the same as being needed. It's dangerous for renegades in Periton, but it never prevented us from helping people, especially in remote areas. They scrape out a living, often only barely. They live hard lives, and most of them have never sighted a mage from the Compact. They get no help from the king, either. We were able to use magic to do things they could never have done for themselves."

He waved a hand toward the window. "I haven't seen any hint of people in desperate need here. What you have achieved is impressive! But I have a feeling any contribution I make would be limited to making a good thing better."

He made no reference to the climactic events he had been caught up in. Perhaps some might see saving the world as more glorious than helping poor people. He saw nothing glorious about it. On the first occasion, with the schemes of Lars and Petria thwarted and the danger supposedly behind them, he had come close to bringing on disaster himself, in spite of everything.

On the second occasion, with the amulet in his grasp, he had faced a similar temptation and resisted. It hadn't helped him—he was going to die whatever he did. Both times he had escaped only because of the dragon's intervention. He had no interest in confronting any new crises.

Moved by his words, Dannah responded in a way he hadn't expected. "What you've been doing is remarkable, Kylen. I truly mean it! The people you're talking about must surely have medical needs that aren't being met. This suffering is almost on our doorstep. I can only wonder what I'm doing here."

The words had barely left her lips when the aide returned.

He addressed Dannah first. "The elders are requesting your presence." Then he turned to Kylen. "Please remain here. I will return for you shortly. In the meantime, please enjoy the refreshments."

Then she was gone.

Kylen hoped she wouldn't repeat to the elders what she'd said about wanting to help the needy in Periton. They would never release her, and it would only convince them he was stirring up trouble.

He sighed. There was no point in worrying about it.

No more interested in eating than before, he glanced indifferently at the display of food and drink. There was nothing he could do except wait.

Lowering himself into a chair, he tried to smooth his tangled nerves. He held out little hope of success.

CHAPTER 8
ABBETHAR

Dannah arrived in time to hear a strident warning from one of the elders. "Even in the unlikely event that this young man is telling us the truth, his presence among us threatens our very existence!" he exclaimed loudly.

"That's a bit of an overreaction, surely," Dannah interjected. She didn't like where this might be heading.

"What if he learns what we're capable of?" demanded another. "We cannot risk our secrets being exposed."

"How is he going to discover our secrets?" asked Dannah reasonably. "Very few of our own people even know we have anything to hide."

One of the elders eyed her narrowly. "Loose talk is how he could discover it, Dannah."

She stared back calmly. "If you think there's the slightest chance my tongue will wag, you're worried over nothing."

"It isn't you we're concerned about," came the reply.

"My granddaughter?" asked Dannah incredulously. She shook her head, frowning. "Marielle may be many things, but she is no fool."

"People behave in inexplicable ways when they're in love."

Dannah's brows drew together. "What makes you think she's in love with Kylen?"

"They've spent a considerable amount of time together during his recovery. And their outing yesterday was beyond friendly."

Anger welled up inside her. "You've been spying on Marielle?!"

Rydel and a couple of others looked uncomfortable, but most of the faces remained hard.

"A great deal is at stake here, Dannah. These are unusual circumstances."

Another of the elders interjected earnestly. "It isn't necessarily a bad thing if they're in love," she said. "The situation will be so much easier to contain if he chooses to remain here of his own free will. Do whatever you can to encourage a relationship, Dannah—for both of their sakes!"

Sucking in a deep breath, Dannah fought to calm herself. "Kylen didn't come here with an agenda. He was injured and vulnerable, and we nursed him back to health. Why? So we could keep him here against his will? All based on the bad excuse that he might discover our secrets?"

"There could be worse outcomes for him."

Her anger bubbled over. "Listen to yourselves! Our forebears fled their homeland to escape tyranny. They established this community as a haven! What are we becoming?"

A couple of them looked uncomfortable, but her passion hadn't swayed them.

One of them looked her in the eye. "We have been appointed to act in the best interests of the whole community. We make no apology for that."

She'd heard enough. Without waiting to be dismissed she left the room and headed back to Kylen.

It FELT like an eternity before Dannah reappeared, although it couldn't have been more than an hour.

"What happened in there?" Kylen asked.

"They were considering what you told them and weighing options," Dannah replied vaguely.

Kylen didn't press for more information, and she offered nothing further.

It wasn't long before the aide arrived once more. "The elders request both of you to join them," he announced.

The aide set off briskly, Dannah at his heels. Kylen trailed behind them, well aware that the elders had issued a command rather than a request. He felt as if he was about to be dragged before a court to receive a sentence.

The elders weren't smiling when they arrived.

"It's time to conclude our discussions around the situation of this young man," one of the elders began, waving a hand toward Kylen.

"With respect," Dannah retorted sharply, "he has a name, and he is here in the room with us."

Kylen's jaw hung open. Such things could never have been said to nobles or to a king. Yet the speaker not only received the rebuke, he began again, this time looking Kylen in the eye.

"We have been discussing your situation, Kylen. We cannot permit you to leave. Steps will be taken to confirm what you have told us. That is going to take time."

Dannah stepped in on his behalf. "And if you are able to confirm it? Will you consider allowing him to leave then?" She didn't sound hopeful.

"Such questions are premature," Rydel told her. "We will need to wait." He faced Kylen. "In the meantime, continue to heal. Perhaps when you are well enough, you can find ways to put your magical abilities to use for the benefit of the community."

Kylen dipped his head slowly in acknowledgment. He didn't trust himself to speak.

After the aide had ushered them from the building, they set out for the healing rooms. Aching all over, Kylen was reduced to traveling slowly. He had to pause more than once before they arrived.

During one of the rest breaks, Dannah eyed him closely. "You seem tense, Kylen."

He shrugged, not caring if he looked glum. "I've never been

comfortable with officials." He held up his left hand to show the missing little finger. "It didn't go well for me the last time I was brought before them, either."

She offered no comment, so he continued, struggling to keep his voice even. "I was captured by a group of Tantellan mages in Methesia. It was very traumatic. Now I'm a prisoner again, even if I don't have chains this time."

She appeared discomforted by his words, but she still chose not to reply. Both of them remained silent when they resumed their journey.

As they were entering the healing rooms, Marielle came upon them.

"Have you met with the elders?" she asked eagerly.

Dannah nodded.

She turned to Kylen, "Did it go well?"

The sight of her smiling and animated face caused his heart to pound in his chest. He wanted to tell her what she was hoping to hear, but he couldn't. Not after what he'd said to Dannah.

"They won't let me leave the islands," he said, as inexpressively as he could.

Her smile had faded a little. "Is that so bad?" she asked.

He avoided her question. "They weren't convinced by what I told them. Yesterday when I told you what happened to me, did you think I was lying?"

"Of course not!" she retorted. "Why would you ask that?"

"I...I wasn't sure why you were being nice to me."

She frowned. "Are you suggesting I wasn't being sincere?"

Belatedly deciding he'd said far too much already, he clamped his mouth shut.

"You thought it was an act?" She stared at him in disbelief.

Having transitioned from happy to confused, her face now shifted to furious. Turning on her heel, she stormed off without another word.

His heart sank.

Dannah had been watching the interaction with a bemused frown. Now she studied him knowingly for a moment. "You thought she might have been acting under instruction, didn't you? And when they sent us out of the meeting, you were wondering the same thing about me."

He could not prevent himself from wincing.

A wry smile twisted her lips. There was no humor in it. "Now you know the truth. Oh, Kylen. If you don't know who your friends are, it's time you figured it out." She shook her head.

Burying his face in his hands, he groaned miserably. When he looked up she was gone.

KYLEN HAD BARELY SLEPT when the sun rose. All night he'd tossed and turned, wondering what he could do to repair things with Marielle. Daylight found him none the wiser. And it wasn't just her. He kept seeing the disappointed look in Dannah's eyes. No matter which way he looked at it, recovering the situation seemed an impossible dream.

Both of them appeared to be avoiding him in the days that followed. Other workers in the healing rooms treated him the same as they always had, but even so he began to feel isolated. His longing to see Dalthinir and the twins and Trisanna was more intense than ever, but he had no idea where they were, or even if they were still alive. Even if he had a way of getting to Periton, the elders had forbidden it. It felt as if he were adrift at sea, entirely alone.

He kept reliving the events of the previous days in his mind, trying to make sense of everything that had happened. While he couldn't understand the reasons behind Marielle's initial dislike of him, he had no doubt she had been genuine and open during their outing together. It was beyond astonishing, and it made it all the more excruciating that he had later managed to alienate her so thoroughly.

As for Dannah, he couldn't ignore the consistent good will she'd shown him, or the effort she'd put into preparing and guiding him in his meeting with the elders. She hadn't needed to put herself out as she did, and it must have been galling when he'd been suspicious of her motives. He was sorry for ever doubting her.

At the same time, he had the feeling she knew a lot more than she was telling him. Understandable as it was for the community to want to remain hidden from larger and potentially more aggressive neigh-bors, he wondered if there might be more to it than that.

He decided to make more of an effort to learn about the commu-nity. It might raise alarms if he asked too many questions, so he decided to limit himself to observing.

His mage smell offered a place to start. From the moment he first regained consciousness after being deposited by the dragon, his farsense had highlighted the presence of other mages. It made sense that mages, especially those with mage touch abilities, would be concentrated in the healing rooms. But once he focused his attention, he quickly found he could detect other mages elsewhere, as well as bursts of magical power.

The islands were far enough from Periton for mages to remain undetected, although he wondered what would happen if a Peri-tonian or Tantellan mage sailed close to the islands. Even for a seafaring mage unable to sense magical auras, it would be difficult to miss the bursts of power from the islands as mages went about their business.

He had the impression the population might include a higher proportion of mages than in Periton. There was no way to be certain, though, both because there were too many mages on Abbethar to easily count, and because he had no idea how many people were living there.

It occurred to him to wonder if magical abilities like mage hearing or mage sight were as rare on the islands as they were in Periton. Someone like Dannah would probably know, but he decided it would be wisest not to ask.

An obvious place to learn more about local mages was the healing rooms. It seemed unlikely he would learn anything of great interest there, but there could be no harm in keeping his eyes and ears open.

With nothing better to do, he decided to take more of an interest in healing. Mage touch ability was used extensively by healers, and he possessed that ability, even though he had never attempted to apply it to healing. He held out hope there would be no objection. Especially since the elders had encouraged him to use his magical abilities for the benefit of the community.

~

"I'm truly sorry for ever doubting you and Marielle, Dannah. You didn't deserve it—neither of you."

Kylen peered at her hopefully. It hadn't been easy to get an opportunity to talk to her. He'd seen almost nothing of her since their visit to the community elders, mostly because a less senior healer had been assigned to his care. He'd been told that such a change was to be expected at this stage of his recovery. Although he was undergoing ongoing therapy to rebuild his physical strength, he had reached a point where little or no expert intervention was necessary. A healer as highly skilled as Dannah was needed elsewhere.

Helped by his ability to track her glimmer, he had carefully chosen the right time and place to intercept her. When she appeared he'd slid into position. Even though he'd resorted to scheming, he knew her to be a kind and gracious person, and it hadn't been difficult to convince himself she would receive his apology.

And now here she was, staring back at him without speaking. She studied him inexpressively for long enough that he felt color creeping up his face. Suppressing a groan, he turned away in defeat, muttering further words of regret as he began to move away.

"Wait!"

Her words stopped him in his tracks. Twisting slowly around, he faced her uneasily. He had no idea what to expect.

"For my part, I am willing to accept your apology," she told him. "Marielle will need to speak for herself."

"Thank you," he managed.

"Was there something more you wanted to say?" she asked. She sounded stern, although her face had softened.

"The elders suggested I use my magical abilities to help the community," he told her. "Since I'm in the healing rooms, I was hoping I might begin learning how to apply my mage touch abilities to help the healers."

She eyed him thoughtfully. He had almost abandoned hope when she finally replied. "I will give it some thought."

Turning on her heel, she left him to his uncertainties.

• • •

THE DAY after Kylen's apology to Dannah a young woman called Aleira breezed in. Kylen had met her before and knew her to be a mage with considerable skill as a healer. Her abilities might not have been as exceptional as Marielle's, but she was highly regarded. "Dannah has asked me to give you some tuition on the use of mage touch in healing," she announced brightly.

Kylen didn't try to hide his delight. Apart from the promise of having something useful to do with his time, Aleira's arrival suggested that Dannah had truly forgiven him. It would have been nice if Marielle had been assigned the task of tutoring him, of course, but he knew it had never been likely. The two of them hadn't exchanged as much as a word since he managed to alienate her. He was still at a complete loss knowing what to do about it.

Fortunately, there was no time to stew on past mistakes. "Come with me," Aleira said. "You'll need to begin with lessons on anatomy, so I've arranged for you to be placed in a class. It will be a steep learning curve, and the other students are all younger than you, but I'm sure you'll manage."

Arriving at the classroom, she introduced him to the instructor. "Kateren, this is Kylen. As you know, Dannah has approved him to be tutored in healing. Your introductory anatomy class should provide a perfect starting point."

The instructor, a woman in middle age, was less than excited about his arrival, and she made no secret of it. "I've heard of him. He's a foreigner, and most of the terminology I use in this class is very specialized. He won't understand a word we're saying."

"He has mage hearing ability, so there won't be a language barrier," Aleira replied calmly.

Kateren still wasn't convinced. "He's clearly older than the other students. I won't have anyone putting themselves above the others!"

She couldn't know it, but Kylen had doubts of his own. They were mostly related to the classroom style of teaching. He had only ever been tutored one-on-one before, first by Olatiren and later by Dalthinir. Trying to concentrate while surrounded by other students was not his first choice of a learning environment. Nevertheless, he wasn't being offered a choice.

"Just give him a chance," Aleira was saying. "I'm sure it will all work out."

The instructor, who apparently had no more authority over it than he did, yielded, if reluctantly.

Standing right beside Aleira, Kylen had heard every word the instructor said. It didn't seem to bother her at all.

It was hardly a promising start.

All he could do was suspend his own hesitations and try to learn whatever he could.

CHAPTER 9
TANTEL

Road traffic had been increasing steadily the closer Lokan and his party drew to Antilin. A seemingly endless stream of people trudged along the main road in both directions, weaving between farmers with carts, people on horseback, and nobles in carriages.

Soldiers represented an unusually high proportion of the traffic, marching two abreast or riding horses. At one point Lokan noticed a company of foot soldiers performing maneuvers on a ridge to the east, their banners waving boldly in the breeze. His brows furrowed in puzzlement. What was the reason for the sudden increase in military activity?

It brought to mind a quiet conversation with Governor Tunney in Brynford a couple of weeks previously.

"I've noticed a lot of young men marching north of late," Lokan had observed. "They were led by army officers, but they looked completely green, as if they were newly conscripted into the army. What's going on? Is there trouble I haven't heard about?"

The governor shrugged. "I've been ordered to raise new levies for the army. I haven't been given a reason. The men are heading north with the intention of taking ship to the capital."

If the recruits had been delayed for a few days, Lokan and Deemis might have been able to sail with them. It would have avoided the long ride south, not to mention the trouble in Howling Pass. Permission might have been refused, of course. That in itself would have been revealing.

It made little difference. Once he reached Antilin he would find out soon enough what was afoot.

A telling sign was the mood of the people they passed. After closely studying their faces and demeanor, Lokan realized he hadn't heard a laugh or seen a single smiling face.

Something had changed since last he visited the capital. King Garneth's people were anxious. Perhaps not sufficiently anxious enough to cause trouble, but they seemed to be carrying burdens that sapped their energy and joy.

He glanced across at Deemis. The young man was taking in the sights and sounds with wide-eyed curiosity. Lokan guessed he had never seen so many people before. His face bore no hint of uneasiness. If trouble lay ahead, he didn't seem to be anticipating it.

It would be easy to write him off as young and naive, except that Lokan had seen too much evidence of his intelligence. In a situation of crisis, he demonstrated clear thinking and took command effortlessly and effectively. There was a great deal more to him than met the eye.

He pulled his horse alongside Deemis's. "What do you know of King Garneth?"

"Just that His Majesty has been ruling the kingdom for many years."

"Do you know anything about the way he operates?"

Deemis shook his head. His expression suggested he'd given no thought to the question.

Lokan frowned. "Have you considered that the king might not look upon you with favor?"

The other shook his head. "I'm sure he will make me welcome."

"What is your confidence based on?!" asked Lokan, barely managing to conceal his exasperation. He had seen enough of the king to know he could be harsh and unyielding at the best of times. Empathy had never been a quality he was known for. At his worst he could be heartless and cruel.

With no answer forthcoming, Lokan tried again. "How can you be confident the king will take you seriously?"

Deemis returned a smile but didn't otherwise answer.

Lokan shook his head. He'd thought to prepare Deemis for the meeting, but he was wasting his time. If Deemis had no interest in his advice, then so be it.

Nevertheless, he couldn't shake off a feeling of impending doom. Over the years he had seen the king in a range of contexts with many different people. Never once had he witnessed the kind of amiable interaction Deemis seemed to be anticipating.

A wave of uneasiness assaulted Lokan as the walls of Antilin finally towered over them. It was too late for second guessing now, though. He'd set his course. Pushing down his apprehension, he led them through the city gates and on toward the royal castle perched on the highest hill within the city walls.

"It's so...extensive!" breathed Deemis. "And so full of people!"

Lokan rolled his eyes. Deemis had probably seen Brynford the same way about a few days ago. "You get used to it," he grunted, trying not to sound jaded.

The newcomer didn't seem to notice his reaction. He continued to gaze about him, wide-eyed. The palace soon filled their vision, pennants snapping in the breeze atop its many towers. Its thick walls and the sturdy buildings shielded behind them spoke of unyielding strength. It was a dwelling befitting a powerful monarch, one who spared little consideration for elegance.

When they drew near the palace's heavy iron gates, Deemis asked, "Will we go straight to the king?"

Lokan frowned. "It doesn't work like that. I will report to one of the king's aides. He will decide when the king will see me. When that happens, I'll pass on your request."

"Thank you." Deemis seemed entirely satisfied. He appeared to see the process as simple and straightforward.

Recognizing he was probably wasting his effort, Lokan added, "The king will have plenty else on his mind. Don't expect to see him anytime soon." Then he added pointedly, "You'll do well if he agrees to see you at all."

Deemis appeared undismayed. "I'm in no hurry," he assured Lokan.

Ignoring him, Lokan turned to the guards. "You've delivered us safely to the capital. We're grateful for your help, and not least for saving our lives!"

Both of them dipped their heads.

"I won't be needing you again until His Majesty sends us back to Brynford. I can't guess when that will be. In the meantime, report to the head guard once we're in the palace, and tell him I sent you. He will arrange for you to be accommodated and fed. He might assign you some tasks, but I don't expect them to be too demanding."

As they rode up to the gate, the guards challenged them stiffly. Then a smile split one of the faces.

"It's Lokan!" called the guard. "So you finally got tired of Brynford, eh? Or did some angry husband chase you out of town?!"

The other guards laughed heartily.

Lokan wasn't at all put out. "I've missed your ugly mug, too, Antone! I'll see if I can arrange some interesting guard duties for you all if you like. If I remember correctly, you're happiest when barrels full of rotting eels are involved!"

Antone and his friends howled in protest, but there was a good deal of laughter in it too. The little party was waved through with ready smiles.

"A couple of my friends here will be spending some time with you," Lokan told the guards. "Look after them for me!"

"We will! In return you can put in a good word for us with the king!"

He waved in response, to a chorus of hoots.

Passing through the gates, Lokan steered them toward the palace stables. "We can leave our horses here," he told the others, handing his reins to a junior groomsman who had hurried up to them.

After the interaction at the gate his companions from Brynford were staring at him with something akin to awe. Lokan set very little store by it. He had always made a point of cultivating contacts from a wide variety of backgrounds, and he derived energy from many of the resulting connections. But he never allowed himself to lose perspective. People like Antone didn't determine his destiny. The only thing that mattered was the king's reaction to his arrival.

~

Leaving Deemis to fend for himself for a few hours, Lokan sought out Lord Crinholm.

A visit to the nobleman was his usual practice whenever he visited the capital. Having connected under unusual circumstances many years previously, they had quickly discovered many values and perspectives in common. On occasion each of them had helped the other in the years that followed, and they had become firm friends. The nobleman's mansion within the city walls had become a familiar haunt for Lokan.

After exchanging greetings, they headed outside to a secluded area where they would not be disturbed.

"I presume the timing of your visit is not accidental," Crinholm ventured. "You clearly have a nose for trouble."

Lokan's eyebrows went up. "I've noticed that people are restless, and I've seen an unusual amount of military activity. I know no more than that."

"Have you met with the king yet?"

He shook his head. "I've only just arrived. I imagine he will find time for me sooner or later."

"Later, if you're fortunate," suggested the noble.

"Is it that bad? What's causing the unrest?"

Crinholm lowered his voice. "People are anxious about the future, particularly with the way the army is conscripting recruits. The king hasn't acted yet, but it's whispered that he is preparing for war with Periton."

"What! Why?"

At the outburst the noble winced, motioning downward with both hands. He immediately stood up and double-checked the area to confirm they were alone.

After muttering an apology, Lokan continued more quietly. "It certainly accounts for all the soldiers marching about and the extra levies being raised in the north. But why?! The two kingdoms have been at peace for longer than anyone can remember."

"I haven't heard any hint of a reason yet. I imagine one will surface eventually. It might sound compelling, but I doubt it will qualify as a good reason."

Lokan groaned despondently. "Wars between peaceful neighbors are almost never started for good reasons." He ran a hand over his face. "I haven't heard the smallest hint of this."

"In Brynford?" snorted Crinholm. "That hardly seems surprising."

"Don't forget that even in Brynford I sometimes receive valuable information from unlikely sources. That far from the capital, travelers seem to think no one can hear what they say."

His friend shrugged. "I haven't forgotten. It's no doubt a key reason why the king keeps you there. This is no ordinary matter, though. As you know, it isn't easy to keep anything secret for long in a palace, and you'd have to be blind to miss the military buildup. But details are unusually sparse. The king must have made some dire threats to keep his intentions this quiet. As you can imagine, he's in an even more difficult mood than usual."

"I appreciate the warning," Lokan told him grimly.

"I haven't asked what brought you to Antilin."

"A young man from the north. He wants to speak with the king, and he won't say why."

"You brought him here based on nothing more than that?" The nobleman whistled softly, shaking his head. He stared at Lokan. "Thus far you seem to have enjoyed a charmed life with the king. I sincerely hope that run will continue."

Lokan could find nothing to say in response, and both men fell to brooding.

Crinholm broke the silence. "Perhaps something of value can be extracted from this situation," he suggested. "If the king agrees to see this young man, I can guess where it might take place. I could try to arrange for someone to eavesdrop on their conversation."

"Is that even possible?"

"Almost anything's possible if you don't care what it costs. It isn't without its risks, but I have access to a person who has shown unusual creativity in similar circumstances."

"I can't pretend I'm not interested. There will be consequences for me if Deemis has nothing of substance to say. And given what you've told me about the king's state of mind, it could be worse than I feared."

The noble nodded soberly. "I will make the arrangements. These are perilous times, and extraordinary efforts must sometimes be made to ensure we are well informed."

SHIFTING HIS FEET UNEASILY, Lokan stood before King Garneth in one of his private reception rooms.

"What are you doing in Antilin?" the king asked him bluntly.

Having long anticipated the question, Lokan had a ready answer. "I came to escort a young man whose name is Deemis. There are matters he wishes to discuss with you."

"Who is he, and where does he come from?"

"He is from a village in the far north, at the feet of the Firetip Mountains. I know only what he has told me about his background."

"What matters does he want to discuss with me?"

"He refused to say. He insists he will tell only you."

The king scowled at him. "You abandoned your post without permission simply because you met a nobody with nothing to say. And you expect me to waste my time with this fool?" He surged to his feet in anger. "Tell me why I shouldn't just execute the pair of you!" he bellowed.

"Only because Your Majesty might miss out on hearing something of advantage," Lokan replied, feigning a confidence he didn't feel.

The sovereign eyed him narrowly. "You're bold, Lokan, I'll give you that." Then he added coldly, "But I hadn't previously thought of you as stupid."

Abruptly he turned away, as if bored by the interaction. "You are dismissed!"

CHAPTER 10
TANTEL

A restor stood motionless in King Garneth's private garden. The most careful observer looking directly at him would see a shrub slightly taller than a man. A master of disguise, the young Tantellan felt that he had outdone himself on this occasion.

He had been approached through a third party, on behalf of an unknown noble. The noble, almost certainly Lord Crinholm, clearly did not want to risk exposure if anything went wrong with the assignment. Arestor had not hesitated. The payout promised to be particularly generous, although that hadn't been the only reason he accepted. High risk occupations held a particular appeal to him. He wasn't stupid, though. He was well aware that this assignment was unusually hazardous, even for him.

The location was a favorite haunt for the king, especially as a venue for meetings of an unusual nature. The meetings were regarded as unusual because some guests had never been seen again.

Not surprisingly, the garden had developed a sinister reputation. Arestor found it intriguing—irresistibly so. His theory was that guards were concealed in the shrubbery, ready and willing to do the monarch's bidding.

His unknown employer was interested in the outcome of a particular meeting. Undoubtedly with the help of a hefty bribe, the noble had learned that the meeting was scheduled for that morning. Arriving well before dawn, Arestor had woven his way through the constant patrols of palace sentries and installed himself in the garden. He was in place as the sun was rising.

Smirking irreverently, he tried to imagine the king's reaction if he knew how easily his private meeting place had been compromised. Busily complimenting himself on his almost effortless success, he was astonished to discover a guard almost on top of him. Somehow keeping his head, he remained stiff as a statue, scarcely daring to breathe. His peripheral vision alerted him to other guards quietly moving through the garden. Whoever was responsible for the king's security was proving more vigilant than he had expected.

To his credit, the guards failed to discover him. And then, inexplicably, they were gone. So much for his theory that the guards lurked in the garden during the king's meeting.

Before long a youth arrived. Having been admitted to the garden, he was left there alone, presumably to wait for the king to arrive. Arestor watched with considerable interest as he wandered about, familiarizing himself with his environment. The stranger's calm demeanor both surprised and impressed him. Then it occurred to him that the youth might not have heard the stories about this garden.

His musing was interrupted by another arrival. The king had deigned to make an appearance.

The youth apparently recognized him. "Your Majesty," he said, bowing low. "My name is Deemis."

He received nothing more than a grunt in return. It didn't appear to discompose him.

After a long moment of silence, the king spoke. "Well? What is it you want to talk about?" he barked. "For your sake, it had better be worth my time!"

Deemis nodded. "I thought it might be to Your Majesty's advantage to become aware of two inhabited islands off the coast of Periton."

The king scowled. "I don't need you to tell me about the Summer Isles." He was sounding increasingly impatient.

"The islands I'm referring to lie off the northeastern coast of Periton."

"Why should I care if a few fishermen have established a settlement on some remote island?"

"The inhabitants are not fishermen. They are fugitives from another continent who have been there for generations. They are numerous and well established."

If the king was taken by surprise at the news, he didn't show it. "Are the Peritonians aware of these people?"

"They are not."

"Why have you come to me with this?"

Deemis bowed. "I am a loyal subject of Your Majesty. I see it as my duty to report such information."

"I want to know how you learned of this," growled the king. "And you have yet to tell me why I should care."

Deemis dipped his head. "Of course, Your Majesty. I will gladly answer your questions."

Before he could make a beginning, King Garneth added in a harsh voice, "I trust you are aware of the consequences of trying to deceive me. Any such attempts have always ended badly for those fool enough to attempt it."

The warning did not seem to alarm the young man. He began speaking at once. Clearly and succinctly he laid out all that he had learned. Occasionally the king interrupted him with questions, but his demeanor indicated he was absorbed and increasingly energized by what he was hearing.

The eavesdropper was himself listening in growing astonishment. In spite of the hefty fee he had negotiated for his services, he had little doubt his employer would see the information as well worth the cost.

In time the interaction came to an end, and the king bustled his informant out of the garden. Everything went quiet.

By now Arestor was aching to move, but he had no way of knowing if guards might do a final probe of the area once the king had left. Just in case, he decided to remain still for another five minutes.

The time dragged interminably, but a moment finally arrived when he was willing to risk movement. Even as he began to stretch, something touched his ankle, almost startling him out of his wits. Glancing down, he saw to his horror a serpent gliding between his legs. Seeing its alternating yellow and black stripes, he broke out in a cold sweat. This species had a bad reputation. It was known to be both aggressive and highly venomous. The king's final sweep of the garden was being carried out by an assassin more silent and deadly than any guard.

Hampered frustratingly by his disguise, Arestor sprang away from the snake. He had come armed, and he swiftly drew his sword and repositioned himself to aim a blow at it. Quick as he was, the serpent was quicker. It had struck his exposed legs twice before he landed a killing blow.

A careful scan of the area revealed no hint of other threats. Breathing heavily, he turned his attention to the bite marks, staring down at them with dismay. There was no time for regrets. He needed to go. Realizing that a dead snake would make it obvious the garden had been compromised, he picked up its broken body before limping away. The toxin was already taking effect, and he knew that vigorous activity was the last thing he should be doing. But he had no choice.

Somehow he made it clear of the area without being spotted by patrolling guards. By then he could go no further. Slumping to the ground among a stand of trees, he trusted in his disguise to keep him hidden while he waited for help.

The reason for the garden's fearsome reputation had been exposed at last. For Arestor, the knowledge had come too late.

UShered into Lord Crinholm's study, Lokan found the noble grim and brooding.

"Is there a problem?" he asked uneasily.

"I arranged for someone to eavesdrop on the king's conversation yesterday with your friend. I'm sorry to say the enterprise ended in abject failure, in spite of the not inconsiderable cost. Worse, the young man engaged on my behalf did not survive."

Lokan stared at his friend in alarm. "Was he captured?"

Crinholm shook his head. "It seems the king protects his private garden with venomous serpents. One of them bit my spy. He managed to escape the area, carrying the remains of the snake with him. My people tracked him down and spirited him away before the guards could find him."

"Were you able to learn anything from him?"

"No, nothing at all. He was incoherent and near death when they reached him. He survived no more than a few minutes."

Lokan was appalled. "This is horrifying!"

His friend nodded. "I'm no less devastated. Up to this point the young man in question appears to have led a charmed life, and I sincerely regret playing a part in ending that. We can at least be grateful that neither of us has been exposed in the process."

"I am grateful, of course! But I cannot ignore the fact that a man has died as a direct result of my foolish curiosity!"

Crinholm frowned. "Do not be deceived, Lokan. There is a great deal more at stake here than your curiosity. Many in the Conclave of Nobles view any notion of war with Periton as reckless and ill-advised. None of us can afford to be uninformed about the king's intentions."

"And you know nothing about why the king wants a war?"

Exasperation creased the noble's brow. "It's well known among the conclave that a few months ago the chief master sent a group of mages to Periton, supposedly as a delegation. The group included at least a dozen mages. A delegation of that size is unprecedented. They were not just any mages, either—the group was led by Master Pernilla, who had quite a reputation, as I'm sure you are aware. The chief master sent them at the king's request. None of them returned. The Peritonian king claims they pursued someone to Ettaran, and that all but one of them perished there. The only survivor has supposedly gone renegade."

"Ettaran?! How is that possible?"

"Apparently King Garneth had a similar reaction. He blames their demise on the Peritonians. He describes it as an intolerable provocation. The truth is far from clear, of course. Sending such a formidable group of mages to Periton would itself have been seen as provocative by the Peritonians. It was done for a reason of some kind. They may have been sent to assassinate someone."

Lokan's eyebrows went up in surprise.

Crinholm continued without pause. "Information has leaked out that King Garneth's father sired no less than two illegitimate offspring. At least one of them is reputed to be a mage, and both of them are supposedly hiding in Periton. The king seems to have concluded that Periton is harboring pretenders to his throne."

"A mage can't sit on the throne! There are laws preventing it."

"That hasn't stopped the king from becoming paranoid."

Lokan frowned. "Things would be a lot more straightforward if he had an heir," he muttered.

Crinholm grunted his agreement.

"It sounds like the king has no shortage of possible excuses," Lokan concluded. "But you have no idea of his real reasons?"

"None at all. They remain a closely guarded secret." Crinholm shook his head sadly. "These matters might be used as convenient pretexts for war. If the king believes he has legitimate grievances, though, whatever they might be, he should formally present them to the Peritonians. War should be a last resort. To my knowledge there has been no attempt at negotiations."

"Your information is very disturbing," said Lokan. "Nevertheless, I appreciate being made aware of it."

"Speaking of information, you might be interested to hear that the man you brought from Brynford is not only still alive after meeting with the king, he has taken up residence in the palace. Further, the king is reported to be in a rare good mood this morning. Finding out about their conversation yesterday has become more important than ever. Anything at all you can learn from your new friend would help."

SUMMONED before the king once more, Lokan entered the reception room with considerable apprehension. Would the king's reputed good mood extend to him?

"Ah, Lokan!" The king's face was creased with a smile.

Lokan had never before received such a welcome. He hid his astonishment in a low bow.

"I congratulate myself on recognizing your instinct from the beginning," the monarch asserted. "It is, of course, the reason I appointed you as my senior representative in the north. You have done well! All I ask is that you continue to repay my trust."

Lokan was too taken aback to respond.

"There will be no need for you to escort Deemis to Brynford. He will be remaining here. You are also to remain in the capital until further notice. I might have need of your services."

"As you wish, Your Majesty," he managed.

The king waved a hand airily. "You are dismissed."

CONNECTING with Deemis had proven unusually difficult. Lokan had no idea where he was staying, and he knew of no one who had access to him. He was reduced to hanging around the palace in the hope of catching sight of him. Thus far he had spotted him twice. On both occasions he had been in the company of the king. Lokan knew better than to interrupt the sovereign, whatever mood he might be in.

By now it was obvious that Deemis had been right about the value to the king of the information he had to convey. Lokan had never heard of anyone becoming a favorite so quickly. He was conscious that it was still early days, though. Favorites rarely retained that status for long.

A meeting eventually came about entirely by accident. The two men came upon each other suddenly while both walking the streets of Antilin.

"Lokan! What a happy coincidence! I've been wanting to speak with you for days, but the king rarely sees fit to release me."

"You seem to be high in his favor," Lokan observed.

"So are you, Lokan, I assure you! I made it clear to His Majesty that I would not be here without your support. And your extraordinary efforts. I'm sure I would never have arrived if I'd attempted the journey alone."

"I appreciate it," Lokan told him. With the pleasantries out of the way, he decided there was no reason to act coy. "Now that you've had your conversation with the king, what can you tell me about it?"

Deemis winced. "Nothing at all, I'm afraid. I'm truly sorry, Lokan, but the king was most particular about the importance of discretion."

It galled Lokan to know that the king had instructed a newcomer to be discreet in his conversations with an established official. But what could he do?

"It's been good to see you again, Lokan! I wish we could talk for longer, but the king is expecting me. I need to go." Deemis's smile looked awkward.

Lokan shrugged, working hard to appear nonchalant. "No matter—I have things to attend to as well. I wish you all the best, Deemis!"

The two of them immediately went off in separate directions.

Lokan had been sincere in wishing Deemis well. Whether the young man realized it or not, any new favorite of the king attracted enemies like a dead fox attracted flies.

CHAPTER 11
METHESIA

Dalthinir strode forward doggedly, determined to reach the hidden valley near Flaxendell before nightfall. The anticipation of a reunion with his wife kept his weary legs in motion.

The fact that a wife would be waiting for him was still a source of wonder to him. Why had he left it so long to resolve matters with Inga? He shook his head, bemused by his own thickheadedness. Even more astonishing, before long there would be another little person to capture his attention. He still couldn't get his head around it.

Reaching absently into a hidden pocket in his robe, his hand touched a smooth piece of silk. Wrapped within it was a necklace—a gift for Inga. After consulting with Trisanna, he thought he could picture the kind of ornament Inga might like, and he was determined to find something suitable. He had eventually stumbled upon an itinerant trader. Buying it had been a risk. In the past he had been careful to avoid contact with people who might one day report him. On this occasion he'd decided he didn't care.

Buying a trinket hadn't been his main purpose in leaving the valley. Months had passed since they hid themselves away there, and he felt the need to know what might be capturing attention in the wide world.

He had discovered news aplenty. Relieved as he was to discover that no one was talking about renegades, he found the topics of conversation no less troubling. They might be safe in their little cocoon, but others they cared about were not.

Keeping his head down, Dalthinir picked up his pace. He was making good time. With no expectation of meeting other travelers, he had decided it was safe to use the old main road that led to the ancient capital of Ettaran. As a result, Periton soon lay out of reach. He was well within the borders of Methesia, the ruined kingdom.

Focused entirely on reaching his home, he failed to notice the faintest of glimmers from a mage trailing him on the same road.

He was spotted first by Trisanna. "It's Dalthinir! He's back!" she called excitedly. She hurried to greet him, the twins not far behind.

He returned their greetings distractedly—he only had eyes for Inga. She looked very different from the day he had married her. How could she not, with her rounded belly and her glowing countenance? In his eyes, an inner tranquility had always characterized her. Now it seemed to have settled over her whole being. She was content, and it was more than enough for him.

Marigold appeared with her grandparents, Sorren and Vennia. Soon everyone was talking at once.

After a few moments Dalthinir held up a hand for silence. He needed to clear his throat significantly a couple of times before it eventually descended. "Can I please have a few quiet minutes to greet my wife? After that I will gladly answer all your questions."

Sorren laughed cheerfully. "Of course! Ring the bell whenever you're ready."

Dalthinir led his wife to their little dwelling as the others scattered. "Are you well?" he asked her anxiously.

"I am very well," she replied with a laugh. "More so than you, if the look on your face is any indication."

"I do have news to share," he told her. "But first, I have something for you."

Taking the piece of silk from his robe, he unwrapped it and presented her with the necklace.

"It's beautiful," she breathed. "You shouldn't have! Buying something like this is much too risky!"

"Nonsense," he returned. "If you like it, it was entirely worthwhile."

As they talked quietly about life in the valley, Dalthinir felt the troubles of the world beginning to ease away. He knew it couldn't last. It was Inga who brought the conversation to an end. "You promised the others," she reminded him.

Getting up with a sigh, he took her hand in his and headed outside. There was no need to ring the bell. The others had clearly been waiting fretfully for his reappearance.

Once all of them were assembled in the community dining room, he faced them grimly. "After leaving here I headed southwest, then south. The moment I came within sight of the main road between Cambrick and Sengin, I spotted many fugitives, all of them heading north. After a while I approached a small family group. They told me that Tantellan soldiers have taken over the Summer Isles. King Durvaryn has responded by sending soldiers and mages south."

A collective gasp greeted this news. As he expected, Inga was the person most alarmed by the development. "Is Sengin under threat from the Tantellans? It must be, if so many people are fleeing north!"

"It's difficult to know for certain. As far as I could tell, there's been no declaration of war from King Garneth. And the Summer Isles are not part of the Kingdom of Periton, of course. Since the destruction of Methesia they have been independent."

Inga's face was twisted with concern. "I'm worried about my aunt! And my cousin and her family!" She cast imploring eyes on Sorren and Vennia. "Could we bring them here?"

Dalthinir spoke before they could answer. "I've given that a lot of thought," he told her cautiously. "I'm not sure it would be wise to expose this place to a wider group of people. Considering we're renegades, it wouldn't be good for them, either. It isn't safe for normal citizens to have anything to do with us, whatever the reason."

Seeing the look on Inga's face, he added hastily, "That doesn't mean we can't help them, of course! Short of bringing them here, we need to do everything we can." He turned to Sorren and Vennia. "All of that is only my opinion, though. This is your community, so your opinion matters the most."

"I think you're right, Dalthinir," agreed Vennia. "It shouldn't be necessary to bring refugees here to help them."

"This isn't just our community anymore," Sorren insisted. "It belongs to all of us! Unfortunately, we don't have the resources to help everyone affected by strife in the world. But that doesn't mean we should stand by and do nothing. Reaching out to family members would be a good place to start."

"Thank you!" said Inga. "You are very kind."

"Right now we have little more to go on than rumors," Dalthinir told them. "We can only guess what might happen next. We need more information. I would like to travel closer to Sengin to assess the situation." He gazed at Trisanna. "I would be grateful for your help if you're willing to offer it."

"It's too risky!" exclaimed Inga at once. Then she paused, closing her eyes and taking a deep breath. "I'm sorry! I know I'm being selfish. When we came here I thought we would be able to shut out the world. But I've always known in my heart that it would never be that simple." She set her face hard. "Do what you need to do. You haven't failed the kingdom when it's needed you in the past, and I won't be the one preventing you from doing it this time. I'd go myself if my condition allowed it."

"I'm willing to go," said Trisanna. "You might need to hide from my countrymen as well as from mages."

"You'll need someone resourceful with you," said Jonno.

"Which means we'll be going, too," finished Bella.

More than one person rolled their eyes, but no one disagreed.

"You've only just arrived, Dalthinir," said Inga firmly. "Any departure can wait until tomorrow morning!"

· · ·

THE COMING of the dawn ended a restless night for Dalthinir. He knew he had not been alone in his wakefulness—sleep appeared to have eluded Inga as well. Why hadn't they been able to relax and enjoy the tiny window of peace available to them?

She gazed at him anxiously. "I can't bear the thought of you heading into danger again."

"What about your aunt and your cousin?" he asked. "You'll never forgive yourself if we don't do something to make sure they're safe."

"I know, I know," she acknowledged miserably.

"There's no need to worry about me," he assured her. "Trisanna and I are well able to protect each other. We've done it before."

He did the only thing he could, drawing her close and enfolding her in his arms.

"There's so much that could go wrong," she murmured into his shoulder. "But there's nothing I can do, and worrying won't help anyone. I just need to accept the situation for what it is."

He continued to hold her tight, trying to somehow etch the moment permanently into his memory.

THE LITTLE COMMUNITY had assembled to see the travelers off. Dalthinir and Trisanna would be accompanied by Jonno and Bella. The mage had his reservations about including the twins, but they had been bursting for some excitement. And they'd played their part before, no matter how dire the situation had been.

Marigold looked almost as conflicted as Inga. The spirited youngster would have joined them if her grandparents had allowed it. She had quickly backed down when she saw real distress on Vennia's face. Even so, Dalthinir had the feeling she might not be so easily dissuaded once she was a little older.

"Hopefully this will prove to be nothing worse than panic started by groundless rumors," Dalthinir told them. "Either way, we will try to make contact with Inga's Aunt Jemilla. I promise we won't be gone a moment longer than we need to be."

After warm embraces and more than a few tears, the four travelers set out.

Once they had left the hidden valley, Dalthinir called them together.

"I will hide our glimmer as I did in the past," he told Trisanna. "I'm hoping you will hide us both. There will be times when it's wise to hide the twins as well, such as when we're going somewhere that might raise questions. Initially, though, it might be useful for them to interact with refugees."

"When do you want me to start?" asked Trisanna.

"Immediately," he told her. Seeing her surprise, he added, "There's no way of knowing when we'll first encounter other people. Mages may not be easy to spot, either. Illusion is more widely used now, not to mention garments designed to hide magical auras."

Trisanna nodded her agreement, and the party resumed their journey, hidden both from mages and from prying eyes.

THE OBSERVER on a nearby ridge had escaped the notice of the little party entirely. He had witnessed their approach with considerable satisfaction.

With his glimmer hidden by a stolen garment, the intruder was close enough to see them clearly but too far away to hear what they were saying.

Then they disappeared entirely.

It was interesting. Very interesting indeed.

PERITON

WITH METHESIA BEHIND THEM, Dalthinir and his friends skirted the foothills of The Ribs, heading south toward the main road that ran from Cambrick in the north to the town of Sengin in the southeastern corner of Periton. As soon as they came in sight of the road, they saw it was crowded. Refugees were heading north, and only companies of soldiers were marching south. It didn't bode well.

Passing a greensward beside a stream that showed signs of previous campfires, they settled down to wait for evening. Even before the daylight began to dim, it became obvious they had chosen well. Several groups of travelers moved in to set up camp. They were soon pitching tents and building fires.

"Those cooking smells wafting around are making me hungry," grumbled Jonno.

"Looks like it's time for us to become fugitives ourselves," Bella told Dalthinir and Trisanna with a grin. "Make sure you both stay close so you don't miss the fun!"

Dalthinir slowly shook his head. If the twins noticed they chose to ignore it.

"We're the only ones visible, right?" asked Jonno.

"That's correct," Trisanna confirmed. "Only Dalthinir and I are hidden now. If you want to become silent and invisible again, just throw up your arms."

"We'll be nearby at all times," Dalthinir assured them.

Emerging from the trees, the twins approached a campfire, peering carefully at the people around it. "Hello," said Bella. "We seem to have lost our parents."

"Sadly, there are many such tales to be told," sighed an older woman. "Where are you from?"

"A tiny village to the northwest of Sengin," Jonno told her mournfully. "I never thought much of it when I was there, but I'm missing it now."

"Well you did the right thing getting out, now that the Tantellans have invaded," the woman continued.

"You mean they've actually landed soldiers in Periton?" asked Bella in dismay.

"That's what I've heard," she confirmed.

"Nonsense!" grumbled an old man. "Facts and rumors aren't the same thing."

"You were just as willing to leave as the rest of us!" insisted the woman.

"I could hardly run the farm on my own," he retorted.

Jonno decided to change the subject. "You did well to bring food with you," he observed, nodding toward the bubbling contents of the large pot over the fire.

"Our parents brought food too. It's miserable that we don't know where they are!" lamented Bella.

"You poor things!" responded the woman. "Sit down and share a bite with us."

"You're very kind!" said Jonno. "I can at least contribute something in return," he added modestly, thrusting out a large bag. "I've been lugging this around for my parents."

The woman barely hesitated before she yielded. Loosening the string securing the neck of the bag, she peered inside. "Flour!" she exclaimed. "I won't deny it will be useful."

"Where did you steal that from?" howled Dalthinir despairingly. "The pair of you will be the death of me!"

Thanks to Trisanna's illusion, he knew the others around the campfire wouldn't hear a word he was saying. He also knew the twins could hear him well enough.

Both of them ignored him completely.

The old man was peering at them shrewdly. "What are your parents going to say about giving away their flour?" he asked.

"They won't mind at all," said Bella confidently. "Their cart is overloaded with food. That's why they asked us to carry the bag. I would have carried something more useful if I'd known we'd become separated. Flour is no good if you have no way of baking it."

Nodding in satisfaction, the woman nimbly stashed the bag of flour out of sight and waved the twins to a seat around the fire.

They sat down gratefully and wasted no time devouring everything she offered them.

The woman stared at them open-mouthed. "Oh, my! You two clearly haven't eaten for some time!"

Jonno deftly changed the subject. "What else can you tell us about the Tantellans?"

The conversation sputtered on, with nothing useful being added.

As soon as they'd finished eating, both of them climbed to their feet. "We need to keep looking for our parents!" explained Bella.

"Thanks for the feed!" exclaimed Jonno. "It was delicious!"

Then, with a cheery wave, they were gone.

Dalthinir and Trisanna were hard pressed to keep up with them as they weaved their way among the people clustered around their campfires. The moment they were out of sight of their first benefactors, they approached another family group.

"Could you use some food?" ventured Jonno, holding out a new bag he had somehow pilfered from another unwary traveler.

"It isn't much use to us," added Bella mournfully. "We've been carrying it all day for our parents, but we somehow seem to have lost them."

Watching on as the two of them settled down for another feed, Dalthinir could only groan in dismay. Seeing Trisanna winking at him sympathetically, he raised his eyes heavenward, shaking his head.

Once more they soon had their hosts talking freely.

"Any news on what the Tantellans are planning?"

"Everyone has opinions," said the mother of the family. "It all seems to be guesswork, though."

"I spoke with a fisherman who had just fled the Summer Isles," replied the father. "His name was Zeke, if I remember rightly."

Trisanna started at this news. Dalthinir leaned forward with new interest.

"He said he hadn't been living there for long, so he decided to get out when the Tantellans arrived. Can't say I blame him. Apparently there was no resistance at all when they took over, yet he said new boatloads of soldiers were arriving every day. You can be sure the soldiers are there for a reason, and it won't be a good one!"

"You can't believe anyone from the Summer Isles!" scoffed the woman. "My father always said so."

The twins had shown no reaction at all to the mention of Zeke, but they hurried away the moment they could do so without being rude.

Moving away from the campfires and into the trees, the twins waited for their companions to rejoin them.

"All of us are invisible now," Trisanna informed them.

Before Dalthinir could berate the twins for their pilfering, Bella burst out excitedly, "Zeke is in Sengin! We need to find him!"

"What are we waiting for?" asked Jonno.

The three of them set off before Dalthinir could open his mouth.

CHAPTER 12
PERITON

Dalthinir's party had halted for a break by the side of the road. Thanks to Trisanna, if the refugees streaming north ever glanced in their direction, they looked right through them.

Trisanna was sitting slumped on the ground.

"How are you holding up?" Dalthinir asked her.

"I'm finding it very tiring without the amulet," she admitted. "I didn't realize how much it was boosting my abilities. It isn't easy to maintain the illusions for any length of time without a talisman."

"Then we need to find somewhere for you to take a proper break."

"Thank you," she murmured.

After a brief hunt they rested in a copse of trees. The road was barely visible through the foliage, but they could still faintly hear the cries of frustration.

"Get out of the way! You're taking up the entire road!"

"You almost ran me down with your cart! Take it across country!"

Dalthinir shook his head. "We're going to need to travel at night," he told them. "The road's crowded during daylight hours. And when we're visible we're attracting attention. No one else is heading toward Sengin apart from soldiers. From now on we'll stay completely away from other people."

"But how will we talk with the fugitives?" protested Bella.

"You won't!" he replied. "We rarely learn anything of value from them. And you've done enough mischief already!"

"Our mission is more important than a few items of food," said Jonno solemnly. "Besides, we only ever forage from people who have plenty."

Dalthinir rolled his eyes. He was fighting a losing battle, and he knew it.

They eventually reached the outskirts of Sengin without incident. It quickly became obvious that the town was under martial law. No one was going anywhere without permission. The only exception applied to people fleeing north from the trouble. The authorities seemed happy to allow the common people to depart. Presumably civilians were more of a nuisance than a benefit in a war zone.

"Do you detect any mages?" Trisanna asked him.

"There are faint hints of glimmer, but nothing more. The mages must be using garments to hide their auras."

"Is there anyone you recognize?"

"Master Kothlar is here." He smiled grimly. "He probably wouldn't be surprised to know I've arrived. He seems to have decided that trouble and I have a mutual attraction."

"He might be glad to know you're here. None of the recent crises would have been resolved without you."

"It makes no difference. I have no intention of trying to find out what he thinks."

Trisanna sighed. "Kylen should be here with us," she murmured.

Dalthinir didn't respond. He didn't trust himself. The tight knot in his stomach had reappeared when they left the valley, and he was doing his best to ignore it.

"Let's find Inga's aunt," he said.

"I remember the way," Bella assured them.

Skirting the town and making their way to the home of Inga's Aunt Jemilla was not difficult with Dalthinir and Trisanna's protection. They approached the house from the rear.

"It might be wise to let Bella and Jonno make contact," suggested Dalthinir.

"They're visible again," confirmed Trisanna.

Jonno knocked boldly on the back door. It opened a crack, then swung wide to reveal Aunt Jemilla with Zeke hovering protectively behind her.

After putting a finger to her lips, Jemilla opened her arms wide. Bella rushed forward with a muted cry of delight.

"Is Inga here?" asked the older woman hopefully.

They shook their heads. "Just Dalthinir and Trisanna."

"Go fetch them," said Jemilla quietly. "Then you'd better all come inside."

Dalthinir nodded to Trisanna.

At their sudden appearance Jemilla barely suppressed a cry of surprise. "I don't think I'll ever get used to mages!" she whispered. "Come on in!"

Once they were all inside, Bella turned to Trisanna. "Can you hide our voices?"

"Certainly. It's done," she replied.

"Hooray!" said Jonno loudly. "Now we can make as much noise as we like!"

Both Zeke and Jemilla winced, but they soon relaxed.

Jemilla bustled about, slicing cake and preparing tea. "How is Inga?" she asked over her shoulder.

"She's well," Dalthinir assured her. "She was very worried about you."

"Oh, that's sweet of her. I hope she's someplace safe."

"She is! She would have come, except she's pregnant!" cried Bella excitedly.

After putting a hand to her mouth in surprise, Jemilla came to Dalthinir and took his hands in her own. "Congratulations!" she said. "I'm delighted!"

He felt himself blushing, but he didn't care. "Thank you!"

Meanwhile, Trisanna had embraced Zeke fondly. "It's so good to see you again, Zeke! Or should I say Father?" she asked with a grin. "Unlikely as it must sound, a traveler told us you'd fled the Summer Isles and come here."

"I was concerned for Jemilla," he said soberly. "And, to be honest, I had reasons of my own for leavin'. Sooner or later the Tantellans would've heard I wasn't a local, and it wouldn't have been good for any of us if they found out everythin' that's happened." He smiled down at Trisanna. "I must say it's good to see you again!"

"Do you know what the Tantellans are planning?" asked Dalthinir.

Zeke shook his head. "I can only guess. But they had a lot of soldiers at Landend and more arrivin' all the time. I imagine they'll end up in Periton sooner or later."

"Our own king has been sending soldiers here," said Jemilla. "And mages, too. It's become impossible to go anywhere in Sengin. A lot of people decided to leave while they could."

"Why haven't you left?" asked Trisanna.

"I'm too set in my ways," Jemilla replied. "Besides, where would I go?"

"What about your daughter, Felicia, and her family?" asked Dalthinir. "And what's become of your sister? I heard she moved in with you."

"My sister still lives here. She's visiting a neighbor. My daughter decided to stay as well. Her husband isn't a man who panics easily. He isn't convinced the Tantellans will land at Sengin at all. He says there's plenty of undefended coastline between here and Jayton. Or between Jayton and Thesmis for that matter. What if we flee north only to find ourselves in the middle of an invasion?"

"One thing is clear to me," said Zeke. "If the Tantellans invade Periton, it won't be like the Summer Isles. The invasion will be opposed, and there'll be plenty of bloodshed. Soldiers will die on both sides, and local farmers and their families are not going to escape unscathed. The countryside will be destroyed."

Dalthinir's brows drew together thoughtfully. "Perhaps I should have a conversation with Master Kothlar after all."

BENDING FORWARD, Dalthinir whispered, "Would you be interested in a brief conversation, Kothlar?"

The senior mage almost jumped out of his skin. "How long have you been spying on me, Dalthinir?!" He didn't look happy.

Dalthinir nodded to Trisanna. As previously arranged, she created a new illusion and moved Dalthinir and Kothlar into it.

Kothlar's eyes narrowed when he saw the renegade standing before him. "Are we visible to anyone else?" he asked irritably.

"No," replied Dalthinir calmly. "This interaction is private. No one else can see or hear us."

"Apart from the Tantellan renegade who's providing the illusion, presumably."

"Her name is Trisanna. And you're right, she can see and hear us. But I trust her discretion completely."

"Why should I trust any of you?" snorted Kothlar.

Dalthinir sighed. "Apart from having the effrontery to be a renegade, have I ever given you reason to doubt my integrity?"

Kothlar grunted, but he didn't respond.

"If every mage in Periton had acted with integrity, I would never have needed to become a renegade in the first place."

"And what about Inga? Has she joined your little party too?"

"I'm not here to talk about Inga."

"Then why are you here?" growled Kothlar. "There must be a reason for this cozy little chat."

"There is. If King Garneth does invade Periton, the Compact will be under enormous pressure."

"I hope you didn't come here just to tell me that! Get to the point if you have one!"

"Mages are needed more than ever during times of war—to protect farms, properties, and especially non-combatants. If they don't, enemy soldiers will be able to roam the countryside burning and destroying fields and villages. Even if Periton wins it will take years to recover. Yet while a war is raging, Adrastas will still insist on tying down resources in an attempt to deal with your renegade problem."

"And I suppose you have a solution to propose," grunted Kothlar.

"Stop chasing us and work with us."

"Are you offering to kill enemy soldiers?"

"Don't be absurd! We're renegades only according to your definition, not because of bad behavior. None of us has ever attempted to harm living creatures. I've known mages who have, and they were all members of the Compact—members in good standing! People like Lars and Petria, and Banadin. Banadin is long gone, but Lars and Petria are still out there somewhere. They're renegades themselves, now. Why aren't you wasting your energy on them?"

Kothlar ignored his jab. "You don't need to be a member of the Compact to help defend Periton."

It was Dalthinir's turn to snort. "If we appeared anywhere, it would be the responsibility of every mage and soldier to execute us. Or at least to try." He grinned. "No one has succeeded yet." He grew serious again. "We'd just be a distraction."

"So what are you asking me to do?"

"You can do whatever you like. I'm not delusional—I know how Adrastas will react to this conversation. The only outcome that will satisfy him is our deaths. But I wonder if the king sees it the same way. Especially at a time of crisis like now. He might be able to recognize that all of us—including Trisanna, who grew up in Tantel—have only ever wanted to see Periton thrive."

Kothlar had fallen silent. After a nod to the invisible Trisanna, Dalthinir broke off contact.

They left him gazing distractedly into the distance, a thoughtful look on his face.

ROUGH HANDS startled Vennia awake as something was aggressively forced over her head. Sitting up with a start, she glimpsed in the darkness the dim outline of a figure at her bedside.

"Easy, now!" commanded a quiet voice. "I've just put a magical noose around your neck. If you pull away, you'll choke to death. And I'll pull it tight myself if you don't obey my instructions instantly! Behave nicely, and this will soon be over with no one getting hurt."

Even before she sent a shaky hand to her neck, she could sense the foul violation of the cord on her skin.

The intruder gave the other end of the noose a sudden tug, and she gagged, gasping for breath. Almost at once it went loose again.

"You see how it is," he hissed. "Wake up your husband. Carefully! Don't try anything clever!"

Shaking Sorren unsteadily, she sat trembling as he slowly became alert.

"Your lady has a magical noose around her neck," growled the voice. "Don't call out, and don't try anything. If you do..."

He tugged again, causing her to sputter painfully. Then the cord went loose again.

"Who are you, and what do you want?" asked Sorren.

His voice was calm, but she could sense the undercurrent of anger.

"It makes no difference who I am," came the gruff reply. "What I want is your dragon talisman."

"I can't give you that!" Sorren protested.

Vennia instantly began choking again.

"All right! Let her breathe!"

"Give it to me now!"

Lifting the talisman reluctantly from under his bedclothes, Sorren slipped its chain over his head.

The intruder thrust out his hand demandingly.

Sorren hesitated.

"Do it now, or I'll choke her!"

With a grimace he handed it over.

"Good. Now explain what I need to do to activate it."

When there was no immediate response, the noose was pulled again, more viciously this time.

The sight of his wife gasping for air was too much for Sorren.

"You have to reach down into your gut and draw the talisman in!" he cried in alarm.

Even as Vennia continued to gag, she knew that Sorren was risking his life by handing over the talisman. Some part of her mind registered that if she was dead he wouldn't need to do it.

But it was too late. The pressure eased at last. The flush of triumph on the intruder's face made it clear he had followed Sorren's instructions and activated the talisman.

Hearing a thud, she twisted her head around to see Sorren collapsed on the bed. Leaning over him instinctively, she felt the noose choking her again.

"There'll be time for you to help him later," growled the voice. "Until I'm clear of this place, you're coming with me."

In spite of the pressure on her throat, she hung back, unwilling to abandon Sorren.

The intruder was becoming impatient. "The quicker we go, the quicker you can return to him!"

Yielding against her will, she clambered out of bed.

"Keep it quiet if you know what's good for you!"

Hurrying out of the house, they emerged into the almost complete darkness before dawn. Grabbing her arm, the intruder raced away, dragging her with him.

Everything was a blur until she reached the entrance to the valley. Then suddenly her captor was gone.

Ignoring the noose still positioned around her neck, she ran as fast as she dared in the darkness toward her home.

Bursting inside, she raced to the bedroom.

"Sorren!" she called.

Placing her ear before his mouth, she felt rather than heard his breathing. It was weak, but it was steady. She took a deep breath to calm herself, then she lit a candle and examined him more closely.

Touching him gently, she reached out with her healing ability. She could discover nothing to account for his collapse, however hard she tried.

Finally she slipped into Marigold's room and shook her awake. "Please get Inga up, as quickly as you can! Tell her to come to our bedroom."

Marigold didn't waste time asking questions. She instead hurried away to do her grandmother's bidding.

All of them had soon gathered in the bedroom.

"What's that around your neck, Vennia?" asked Inga, frowning.

"It's a magical noose," she replied bitterly. "Can you get it off me?"

Inga tried to loosen it. "There's a knot preventing me from widening it. Tell us what happened while I'm undoing it."

"An intruder appeared, and he used it to force Sorren to hand over the dragon talisman." Anger twisted her face. "A Tantellan mage called Agalar did the same thing to Kylen in Flaxendell. Dalthinir handed him over to the Peritonians. Somehow his monstrous invention lives on!"

"Was it Agalar who did this?" asked Inga.

Vennia shook her head. "We traveled with him on our way back from Ettaran. If it had been him I would have recognized him."

"I've managed to remove it," reported Inga. She threw it aside with disgust.

Marigold interrupted them. "I'm worried about Grandpa! What's wrong with him? He's unconscious."

Vennia moaned. "Your uncle did a lot of research on dragon talismans before he went to Ettaran. He warned your grandpa never to give up his talisman under any circumstances. Giving up a dragon talisman is harmful, however it happens."

"It didn't seem to affect Trisanna too much when she got rid of the amulet," said Inga.

"I understand she gave it up not long after she activated it," Vennia replied. "Apparently a separation becomes more harmful the longer someone's had a talisman."

"We have to get it back, then!" said Inga. "How long ago did this thief leave?"

"Only a few minutes," Vennia replied.

Inga frowned. "I can't detect his glimmer. Was he wearing something under his cloak?" she asked.

"He was," Vennia confirmed. "A heavy garment of some kind."

"Then he has a garment that masks glimmer," Inga groaned. "Maybe he found one discarded by the Tantellans."

"Whatever magical abilities he has will be enhanced by the talisman now. So we don't know what we'd be facing if we pursue him," said Vennia miserably.

"We can't stay here, Grandma," piped up Marigold. "Without the protection of the talisman, we'll need to leave the valley."

Vennia aimed a sad smile at her granddaughter. "You always were the one to think ahead."

She was right, of course. "We can't afford delay. Could you please set the animals loose, Marigold? I don't want to leave Sorren's side."

She glanced at Inga's bulging abdomen. "Do you think you could manage to gather some supplies, Inga?"

Both of them were gone in a moment. They would be busy.

There was so much that needed to be done. What would become of them all? Shaking her head grimly, Vennia returned her attention to her stricken husband.

INGA SCURRIED ABOUT RESTLESSLY, gathering supplies. The task was overwhelming. Gathering everything they needed would have been challenging enough for a team of able-bodied workers. Instead, only a young girl, a pregnant woman, and an aging grandmother were available. They did at least have a donkey cart, even if its capacity was limited.

They had Sorren to think about as well now. Leaving the valley with a comatose man was going to be a major problem. There was more to it than that, though. How could they help him recover from the loss of the talisman? Was a recovery even possible?

Pausing for breath, she shook her head in misery. She couldn't imagine how it would be possible to transport everything they needed.

They were going to miss Trisanna, too. The moment they crossed the border into Periton they would be exposed. Marigold would be spared if they were caught, but there would be no mercy for the mages. With dark clouds of war looming on the horizon people were less likely than ever to be tolerant.

Why did this have to happen while Dalthinir and Trisanna were away?

Why did it have to happen at all?

She shook her head. Dalthinir and Trisanna had left for the right reasons. She could only hope they weren't in the middle of an invasion at that moment.

The little community couldn't afford to lose anyone else. Dalthinir still hadn't recovered from the loss of Kylen. He probably never would.

And yet Trisanna believed that Kylen was still alive. If it was true, where was he?

"Kylen, we need you!"

It was a cry of the heart she hadn't intended to express out loud. Somehow it happened of its own volition.

Not that it made any difference. Even if he was alive, he had no way of hearing her.

VOLUME 2—MANEUVERINGS

CHAPTER 13
ABBETHAR

Fortunately for Kylen, the instructor had been willing to be proven wrong about her new student. At the end of the first day, Kateren complimented him on his even-tempered manner and willingness to learn. He could see that the other students were beginning to look up to him, and that she was aware of it. By the end of the first week, she was blatantly using his enthusiasm to inspire and motivate the entire class.

Quickly captivated by what he was learning, Kylen used every available moment after classes to absorb the extensive medical texts made available to students. His mage hearing ability allowed him to understand them without difficulty, even though they were written in the Artoran language. The same ability had given him unusual facility with reading and writing, and he began to suspect it also allowed him to absorb the material more quickly and effectively than would otherwise have been possible.

A few weeks after he began, Aleira arrived for a visit. She would have found the atmosphere in the classroom almost crackling with energy. After sitting in the back during a teaching session, she stayed behind for the break. The room soon echoed with laughter as Kylen related a tale involving the twins. Kateren seemed no less captivated than the students.

Aleira was visibly impressed. After a few more weeks, she came to retrieve him.

"We're going to miss you!" Kateren told Kylen with a pat on his cheek. "I'm willing to admit I was entirely wrong about you! I wish all of my students were equally dedicated and determined to learn. And you can be very entertaining when you choose to be!"

Kylen responded by thanking Kateren gratefully and offering warm farewells to the other students.

"You certainly made good use of that opportunity," Aleira told him approvingly as they walked away.

"I learned a lot, and I enjoyed being with Kateren and the others!" he responded. "Much more so than I expected."

"Kateren is our best instructor," she told him. "She can be a bit stern, but she's an expert in her field. And she knows how to teach."

"She was almost as good as Olatiren, my first tutor," he assured her.

When she raised her eyebrows, he added, "Believe me, that's a great compliment!"

ALEIRA SOUGHT him out the next morning. "If you've truly absorbed your basic anatomy, you're ready to observe a bit of healing in action."

Ushering him into the healing rooms, she introduced him to another healer, a woman in late middle age. "Tana, this is Kylen. He has mage touch ability, and he's just spent four weeks learning anatomy."

"Ah, yes. I've heard about you, Kylen," she replied with a smile. "Kateren has good things to say about you, and she doesn't hand out praises lightly."

Feeling color rising in his cheeks, Kylen dipped his head to disguise it.

"Come with me," said Tana. "I'm about to operate on a patient, and it might be possible for you to observe."

Guiding him to a well-lit room, she approached a bed with an elderly male patient lying on it. "I have a student with me. Would you allow him to observe what I'm doing?"

The man nodded his agreement.

"Have you tried to sense internal organs before?" Tana asked Kylen.

He shook his head. "Only my own. The class was theoretical because not all of the students were mages. I've experimented on myself, but that's all."

"Place your hand on his belly," instructed Tana. "You should know where his organs are located. Try to sense them."

Touching the man tentatively, Kylen reached into his body with his mage touch ability. "I can identify his organs," he confirmed. It was somehow different from sensing his own organs. He felt like he was entering a new world filled with wonder.

Then he frowned. "There's a spot in there that doesn't feel right."

"Where?" asked Tana.

"Below his bladder. About where the prostate is."

"Well done!" she enthused. "That's remarkable for a first attempt!"

He shrugged, conscious that it might not be especially remarkable —not when his mage abilities were enhanced by a dragon talisman knitted into his bones.

"You've sensed a cancerous tumor in his body, located in his prostate."

"Are you able to treat it?" he asked curiously.

"We are," she replied. "Can you guess how?"

He thought for a moment. "One way might be to somehow remove the cancer. That sounds complicated. Perhaps you could use mage touch to kill the cells. Maybe some of the cells around the tumor as well, just to be certain you've got it all."

"Those are reasonable guesses, but we have a better way."

She placed her own hand on the man's torso. "Right now I want you to watch while I work. Keep your hand where it is, but don't try to involve yourself in any way."

He nodded, observing in fascination as he sensed power concentrating on the cancer. There seemed to be tiny flashes in other places as well. Then she removed her hand. To his astonishment, he could no longer sense any hint of cancer within the man.

Turning to speak to her, he saw she had lowered herself into a chair. She was breathing heavily, clearly exhausted.

When she had recovered herself a little, she said to the patient, "You can go home now. The cancer is gone."

"Thank you so much!" he breathed, clearly overwhelmed with gratitude.

"A nurse will speak with you on your way out."

Kylen waited impatiently for the man to go. "What did you do?" he asked.

"I identified the cancerous cells, then I sent power throughout his body, killing cells of that type wherever they were lurking. That method is simpler and more effective than other alternatives, and has no real impact on the patient. His body will simply absorb the dead cells."

"How do you learn to kill cells selectively?"

"We begin by practicing on lipomas. A lipoma is a benign fatty growth. It's done under strict supervision, of course. It isn't difficult to find people willing to lose some of their unsightly lumps."

He shook his head in awe. "All of this is astonishing! What else are you capable of?"

She smiled weakly. "Nothing at all until I recover."

IN THE DAYS that followed Aleira revealed many wonders to Kylen. Occasionally she took him to witness Tana carrying out more complex healings, but mostly he observed as she healed people herself.

More than once he spotted Marielle observing them. She didn't look happy about what was happening. But if Kylen ever tried to speak with her, she quickly absented herself.

Recognizing there was little he could do to set things right with Marielle while she wouldn't talk to him, he focused on learning everything he could. He discovered that mage touch allowed an experienced healer to repair torn ligaments, reconnect blood vessels, clear blocked arteries, and carry out countless other operations both major and minor. It required no more than physical touch and intense concentration.

As time passed, Aleira allowed Kylen to try simple tasks. He learned to dull pain, to reset dislocated joints, and even to repair simple cases of broken bones.

His learning took him further afield within the building that housed the healing rooms. Rounding a corner on one visit he found himself face to face with Marielle. Seizing his opportunity, he spoke to her breathlessly. "I'm very sorry for doubting your motives, Marielle. I can see now how hurtful it must have been. Please accept my apologies!"

She clearly wasn't in a conciliatory mood. "Why are you doing all this?" she asked bluntly, waving a hand to encompass the healing rooms generally.

His heart sank. Both her tone and her face made it obvious she wasn't going to forgive him.

Taking a deep breath, he tried to answer her question. "I've benefited so much from the healers here. I'd like to give something back."

She wasn't impressed. "I find myself wondering if that is your only motive." Spinning on her heel, she marched away before he could respond.

He watched her go with something akin to despair. How had it come to this?

He tried to see it through her eyes. He'd doubted her motives, so it wasn't surprising she was doubting his in return. What could he do to show her he was genuine? It seemed a hopeless case.

From time to time Dannah visited to check his progress. She at least had become relaxed with him. And she seemed pleased with him too. Given Aleira's enthusiasm in recounting all he had learned and attempted, he had the impression he was developing much more rapidly than she might have expected.

On one of her visits Dannah took the opportunity to examine his physical condition. "You're healing well!" she told him. "In fact I'm surprised at how well your spleen is recovering." Then she stared at him in surprise. "Have you been trying out your new skills on yourself?"

He flushed red. "I have done a little experimenting," he admitted. "I wanted to try out a few different things, but Aleira felt I wasn't ready."

Dannah examined him more closely. "You haven't limited yourself to your spleen! You've been cleaning up internal scar tissue—some of the adhesions are no longer even detectable!"

"I hope I haven't messed anything up," he said sheepishly. "I feel fine."

She studied him carefully before responding. "You don't appear to have caused any damage. I can't decide whether to congratulate you or to scold you, but you took a fearful risk!"

She turned to Aleira. "Perhaps you could allow him a little more scope." Then she added pointedly, "Provided he restrains his overeagerness!"

AFTER HIS INTERACTION with Dannah the excitement continued to increase for Kylen. He felt like his horizons were expanding more than he could possibly have imagined.

"The main limitation seems to be the energy available to the healer," Kylen suggested on one occasion. He didn't add that nothing he'd attempted so far had remotely exhausted him.

"That's true," Aleira agreed. "A way can be found to do almost anything that's necessary. People are the limiting factor. Most healers are utterly spent at the end of a busy day. Some can only keep it up for an hour or two at a time."

"I have the impression that my own case was more difficult than most."

"That is true. You were so severely injured that almost every part of you required attention, including many of your bones and your organs."

"Were you involved?"

"I was, along with many others. Some of the operations were very complex. Healers worked in teams."

"I don't have words to thank you all!" Kylen told her sincerely.

Aleira dipped her head in a low bow. "It was our pleasure. The more so for me now I've had the opportunity to get to know you a little." She beamed him one of her dazzling smiles.

"It must be difficult to coordinate a complex operation when healers are crowding around a patient."

"It can be. Although healers like Dannah and Marielle don't need to be part of the crowd, of course."

The moment she had said it, Aleira's mouth clamped shut, her eyes going wide.

"Whatever's the matter?" asked Kylen, greatly concerned.

Behind her he noticed Marielle standing in the doorway with a look of fury on her face. It was apparent she had overheard the interaction, and she was not at all happy.

Aleira had gone pale. Hiding her face in her hands, she ran from the room. Marielle immediately set off after her.

He was left totally alone and bemused.

The following day, Dannah reappeared.

"Where is Aleira?" Kylen asked. "Is she well?"

"She is needed elsewhere," Dannah replied, her face expressionless. "But I think you might have worn her out. She needs a break."

"Has she taught me things I wasn't supposed to learn?" he asked anxiously.

"Of course not. You've covered topics familiar to any healer," she assured him.

He stared at her in surprise. "The things we've covered are certainly not familiar to healers in Periton!" he assured her. "People there talk all the time about healers and what they can and can't do. I'm no expert, but I would be astonished if Peritonians are capable of performing one in ten of the healings I have witnessed here!"

It was her turn to be surprised. "Surely that can't be true."

"From the little I know, your skills would transform healing in Periton. You're needed there much more than you are here!"

His words clearly made Dannah very uncomfortable. She left without a further word, and she didn't return.

The following day a different healer approached him, his face grim. "Your training is over, Kylen, at least for the moment," he said.

Kylen's face twisted in puzzlement. "Why?" Something had changed dramatically, and he didn't know the reason.

"Other pressing matters must be attended to," was all the healer would say.

Left alone once more, Kylen tried to make sense of everything that had happened. If Dannah hadn't been concerned by the things he'd learned, it must have been his final interaction with Aleira. She'd appeared horrified about something she let slip, and whatever it was had infuriated Marielle.

He wracked his brains, trying to remember everything she had said. He felt sure it had something to do with Dannah and Marielle not needing to crowd around a patient. What had she meant, and why should it be such a major problem to have said it? Try as he might, he couldn't get to the bottom of it.

That wasn't the worst of it, either. He'd apparently managed to upset Dannah again, and he was further than ever from any reconciliation with Marielle.

Most disheartening of all, his training as a healer appeared to have come to an abrupt halt. What would he do with himself now?

KYLEN WOKE the next morning more alone than ever. Not even the unexpected arrival of Elef'nissar snapped him out of his dismal mood.

The dragon offered no greeting. Eyeing him dispassionately, it announced, "You are needed."

Kylen stared back, unable to comprehend what the creature was saying.

Without waiting for a response, the dragon swiftly reached out a claw and enfolded him in its talons. Then, spreading its wings, it took to the air.

Kylen gasped in alarm as the ground disappeared beneath him. It took several minutes before he was able to think clearly again.

Why had the dragon appeared at that moment, and where was it taking him?

Whatever the answers, he was painfully aware that he had left without saying goodbye—and without resolving anything with Dannah, much less with Marielle.

It was worse than that, though. Much worse. He had just violated a direct instruction from the community elders.

He couldn't begin to guess at the consequences.

CHAPTER 14
TANTEL

Not many days had passed before Lokan found himself summoned before the king once more. Led into a small reception room, he was instructed to wait. He did so with considerable curiosity.

Antilin was abuzz with a confused mixture of information and gossip. Thanks to his sources, Lokan knew that most of it amounted to little more than speculation. One thing was known for certain—the king's forces had taken over the Summer Isles. An invasion of Periton was rumored to be imminent.

He was left wondering what the king could possibly want from him.

Bowing low as King Garneth entered the room, he straightened to find the king eyeing him airily.

"I have a task for you, Lokan. You will be visiting an island. Your ship will leave tomorrow."

Lokan was unable to entirely mask his surprise. "Why me, Your Majesty?" he asked.

"Deemis specifically requested you. You will be sailing with him. You are to treat every aspect of this assignment with the utmost confidence. Do you understand?"

He bowed in acknowledgment.

"One of my aides will provide details of your journey. You are dismissed."

A royal aide appeared as he was leaving. "Your ship sails with the tide an hour after sunrise," he announced. "Deemis will meet you at the entrance to the docks and escort you to the vessel."

Lokan was more apprehensive than curious by the time he arrived at his lodgings. He had no desire to travel to some obscure island. And the king had offered no hint of the purpose of the mission. It made no difference, of course. If the king commanded it he would be going anyway.

More than anything he wanted to confer with Lord Crinholm. But it was too risky. The king had insisted on secrecy, and someone might have been sent to watch him. This was not the moment for a clandestine meeting.

With nothing else to do, Lokan retired to his bed. The hours dragged slowly away. Too much was spinning through his head for him to sleep. The moment the sun rose he set off, feeling anything but prepared for his mysterious assignment.

Deemis was waiting for him at the docks.

"Lokan! I'm so glad to see you again! I do apologize for spending so little time with you! I have been much occupied with His Majesty."

The greeting immediately dispelled any remaining doubt about the access Deemis enjoyed to the king. If he thought it would endear him to his former sponsor, he was mistaken.

Nevertheless, Lokan was careful to hide his reaction. "What is the purpose of our assignment?" he asked evenly.

"We can discuss that further once we're underway," said Deemis, lowering his voice conspiratorially.

He led the way to a three-masted ship that was clearly being prepared for departure. Orders were being shouted, sailors were scurrying about, and barrels were being rolled up the gangplank. As soon as the bustle eased for a moment, Deemis led him aboard.

He immediately sought out the captain. "Captain, this is Lokan, the man I told you about."

"Welcome aboard, Lokan! Have you sailed before?"

"On occasion, Captain," he replied.

"Good! Then you're in for a treat. You're standing on the finest ship in the king's navy!" Someone called, and he bowed respectfully to Deemis. "If you'll excuse me, there are matters I need to attend to."

Deemis nodded graciously. "By all means, Captain!"

Taking Lokan's arm, he led him to the poop deck.

He pointed at a small door. "The captain has kindly arranged for one of his officers to give us his cabin."

Poking his head inside, Lokan saw two hammocks rocking gently with the ship. Between them they took up all the available space. He didn't need to be told that only the captain enjoyed better accommodation.

Deemis smiled, shaking his head. "The captain wanted to give up his own cabin to me. I refused, of course. He needs his sleep more than anyone. I want to believe the man in charge of the vessel is alert and in full possession of his faculties!"

Smiling and nodding in agreement, Lokan returned to the fresh air and openness of the deck. It was very apparent that his access to a cabin owed everything to his association with Deemis.

What had prompted the astonishing rise of Deemis? He had entered Antilin as a nobody.

Lokan himself had precipitated it by bringing the young man to meet the king, braving the king's wrath in doing so. Yet he could not begin to account for the magnitude of the king's change of heart.

Both men stood silently watching as the gangplank was pulled aboard and the ship moved into deeper water. Before many minutes had passed they were clear of the harbor and heading northward under full sail.

Lokan couldn't help but be impressed by the hard work and effectiveness of the sailors in response to a rapid and seemingly endless succession of commands from the officers. He acknowledged to himself he had rarely seen efficiency to match it on land.

Deemis had promised answers once they were underway. "Which island are we heading for? We're heading in the wrong direction for the Summer Isles."

"You're very observant!" Deemis replied. "The island we're heading for is northwest of Periton."

"Why is it of interest to the king?"

"That information will need to wait until we get there. But I can tell you that the island is inhabited, and that the people living there are not going to welcome us."

Lokan frowned. His gut told him that problems were brewing.

His companion seemed anything but concerned. "Have I told you about my first solo sea voyage?" he asked, a mischievous grin lighting up his face. "A local fisherman took me on my very first boat ride. I was about nine years old. After we sailed to a nearby island, he lowered the anchor and threw out his nets. While we were in the area he told me marvelous stories about the island. Supposedly a dragon lived there. If anyone dared to set foot on the island, the dragon would eat them. But if they made it to the highest peak of the island first, the dragon would grant them one wish."

He gazed off into the horizon. "I was captivated! I decided there and then I would go to the island and win a wish from the dragon. I at least had the sense to carefully watch the way the fisherman set his sail and steered the boat. I even asked if he'd let me have a turn at the tiller. He readily did so, and he complimented me on my skills. A couple of days later I waited until the boat was untended. Pushing it into the sea was the biggest challenge, but I somehow managed it. Then, incredibly, I managed to set the sail and steer it toward the island."

Lokan was astonished. "Did you reach the island?"

"I did! As soon as I landed, I raced toward the highest hill on the island. I was exhausted by the time I reached the top." A wry smile came to his face. "You won't be surprised to hear that no dragon appeared to grant me my wish."

"What did you do?"

"I waited hopefully until the sun was sinking low in the sky. Then I made my way back down again. When I arrived at the beach, there was no sign of the boat. The tide had come in and floated it. It drifted away, leaving me stranded."

Lokan was appalled. "How did you come to be rescued?"

"I knew how to make fire, and I built a bonfire on the beach. I kept it going all night in the hope that a passing fisherman might see it. No one came. I eventually went to sleep on the beach as the sun was rising. I woke to voices. The fire had burned down, and it was sending up a thin plume of smoke. A couple of fisherman had seen it. They knew I had gone missing, so they came to investigate. They took me straight home, none the worse for my adventure!"

"It must have been terrifying for you!"

Deemis smiled grimly. "I learned a valuable lesson—don't believe the tales of old fishermen!"

"What happened to the boat?"

"It was never seen again."

"What became of the fisherman?!"

"I have no idea," said Deemis with a shrug. "I made sure I stayed well clear of him after that."

"Did your parents compensate him for the loss of his boat?"

"Certainly not. They couldn't have afforded it, even if they wanted to."

"Didn't you get into trouble?"

"Not at all. My parents were just happy to have me back safe again. Some of the fisherman's friends made a fuss, but my parents made it very clear they held him responsible. If he hadn't spun the tale about the dragon, I would never have taken the boat in the first place."

His companion was beaming. "Isn't that a great story?"

Before Lokan could respond, something abruptly caught Deemis's attention. "Please excuse me. It appears the captain needs me for some reason."

He set off across the deck, leaving Lokan alone with his thoughts.

It was obvious that even at a young age Deemis had possessed remarkable resourcefulness and determination. But Lokan couldn't applaud his adventure as a great story. Not when it stripped a fisherman of his means of earning a livelihood. The fisherman's tall tale seemed to him no worse than a misguided attempt to entertain a young passenger. It didn't absolve Deemis of accountability for what he had done in response.

There was no point dwelling on it. Deemis had been a child at the time. He had hopefully learned to be more responsible in the years that followed.

～

BEGINNING WELL, the voyage had quickly deteriorated. Unaccustomed to sailing in heavy weather, Lokan was soon leaning over the rail emptying his stomach. He retreated to his hammock, hoping it would all be over soon.

Deemis's face appeared in the cabin door, as cheerful as ever. "You had some questions, Lokan. Now that we're close to our destination, it's time to answer them! Come and join me outside. We'll be quite private out there."

Rolling reluctantly out of his hammock, Lokan staggered to the cabin door, trying to steady himself against the energetic rolling and pitching of the deck. Then, pushing down his queasiness, he headed outside.

Emerging into the open, he saw how much the swell had been rising. The waves appeared mountainous, and storm clouds darkened the sky.

"Over here!" called Deemis.

Heading toward his companion, Lokan saw him holding a wheel-shaped object that appeared to be made of wood.

"This is a safety wheel. You put it over your head and hold it under your arms. If you get pitched into the water for some reason, it will keep you afloat. Put it on!" commanded Deemis.

Holding up his arms, Lokan allowed the wheel to settle over his head.

"Where's your safety wheel?" he asked.

Deemis grinned. "I don't need one. I have a feeling I'm more at home with the sea than you."

If he was referring to Lokan's seasickness, it must have been true. He himself showed no trace of it.

Changing the subject, Deemis told him, "We're heading for an island populated by people from another continent. They don't speak our language. They have somehow taken possession of an object that belongs to Tantel. King Garneth is relying on us to get it back."

Lokan peered at him uncertainly. Apart from feeling woefully unequipped to infiltrate an island full of foreigners, it was hard to feel impassioned about retrieving whatever object Deemis was referring to. What difference did it make who had it? In any event, the king had made Deemis responsible for the mission. He was only there to provide support.

"The object in question is a large rock, dark in color, rough to the touch, and a bit bigger than a human head in size. We believe it's located somewhere in the healing rooms of these people."

"What is it? Why is it so important to the king?"

"A priceless jewel is embedded inside it. A dragon gave the rock to the king of Tantel generations ago as a gesture of friendship."

"You mean it's a talisman of some kind?"

A flicker of surprise briefly passed across Deemis's face. Perhaps he hadn't expected Lokan to know anything about dragon talismans. If so, he was underestimating him. Lokan made it his business to possess at least a basic understanding of anything that might affect the kingdom.

"It isn't a talisman. But I believe it has great symbolic value, quite apart from its value as a jewel."

Lokan's face must have shown how little he cared about rocks with jewels, because Deemis was quick to add, "It might not seem significant to us, but it matters a lot to the king! It's the only reason he's gone to the cost and effort of sending us. Especially with everything else that's going on at the moment. If you want to gain favor with the king, there's never been a better opportunity!"

It was hard to argue with Deemis's reasoning. To all appearances, the king was totally engrossed in a foreign adventure. By sending them, he was giving a clear message about the importance of this assignment.

"How are we supposed to get this rock off the island?"

"This ship will stay in the area. Each night, just after sunset, it will sail past the island watching out for us. We will need to light a small fire as a signal. As soon as one of the sailors spots the fire, a boat will be sent to collect us."

It all sounded simple. In practice it was likely to be anything but that.

"I think I can see our destination!" Deemis said excitedly, pointing off to one side.

Moving easily thanks to his sea legs, the younger man made his way to the rail. "Come and join me!" he called before turning to stare into the distance.

Realizing after a moment that Lokan had not followed him, he turned and beckoned. "Come on, Lokan! There's nothing to be frightened about!"

Lokan was old enough and wise enough to ignore taunts. Nevertheless, he found himself swaying off across the deck, barely managing to stay on his feet and feeling foolish as he clutched his safety wheel.

Somehow reaching the side, he peered out across the tossing seas. For a brief moment he thought he caught a glimpse of land nearby. Then it was lost to sight, hidden by the towering waves.

Having risen high on a huge wave, the vessel dipped low into a trough. At the same moment, he felt something hit him hard on the head. A momentary sensation of falling gave way to the terror of the sea rising up to meet him.

Then everything went black.

CHAPTER 15
TANTEL

Chief Master Kharkin sat in the king's reception chamber, waiting for the sovereign to appear. He had no idea why he had been summoned. Weeks had passed since King Garneth had thrown him into a panic by insisting he prepare for an urgent expedition into Ettaran, with the departure date just four weeks away. He had heard nothing further since.

He'd never been a favorite of the king, and recent events had only plunged him lower in the king's estimation. The king had wanted his half-sister Trisanna dead, and Kharkin had delegated the task to Master Pernilla and her team. They failed utterly, succeeding only in inflaming tensions with Periton.

Kharkin knew the king blamed him for the debacle.

It hadn't helped that the chief master had sent Pernilla with a second agenda, one he had carefully concealed from the king. Somehow the king had gotten wind of it, although thankfully he seemed unaware of the details. Kharkin had no idea how he had found out. Even so, it was unreasonable to blame him for whatever disaster had befallen Pernilla and her team. It had happened a long way from Antilin, and primary responsibility for the team lay with the person leading it, not with Kharkin.

Of late the king had even less time than usual for the head mage. Perhaps it wasn't surprising given his preoccupation with Deemis, his newest favorite.

Nevertheless, King Garneth had found time to prepare his army for an invasion of Periton. And he had done it without ever engaging his head mage.

Kharkin could make no sense of that. No king in his right mind would initiate hostilities without the active support of the Compact. It would leave his army unusually vulnerable to magical counter-measures.

Magic could never be used offensively against enemy combatants, of course. The law strictly forbade magical interference against living creatures, human or otherwise. The prohibition was one of the founda-tional principles of magical law, and the long term consequences of flouting it were unthinkable. Nevertheless, a wide array of creative possibilities remained, from weather control to logistical assistance of various kinds.

It was entirely possible, of course, that the king intended to present him with a list of demands at the last possible minute. The more frantic he made people, the better he seemed to like it.

Hearing doors opening, Kharkin hastily pushed himself to his feet, bowing low as the sovereign swept into the room.

King Garneth didn't waste a moment on pleasantries. "Perhaps I might find a use for you after all, Kharkin," he barked, peering down his nose at the head mage.

Kharkin dipped his head in response, unable to trust himself with a proper reply. To the chief master's lasting annoyance, Garneth had never learned that respect needed to run in both directions.

"I am tired of the provocations of the Peritonians," raged the king. "They seem to think they can harbor pretenders to my throne without consequences. And it isn't just one pretender, either—there are two of them! As if that wasn't enough, both of them are mages!"

If the king had expected a response, he would have been disap-pointed. Kharkin had no sympathy for Garneth's posturing. He knew enough of the facts to know his accusations against Periton were without foundation.

"And that's not all," the king continued. "I have learned that a large group of foreigners has established a base on islands to the north of Periton. They are extremely secretive, and act aggressively to hide their presence. But they have hidden designs on both Tantel and Periton. Their resources in their current environment are constrained, and they intend to annex both kingdoms the moment they deem the time is ripe."

Kharkin frowned. This information was entirely new to him.

"Even more alarmingly, the abilities of your mages are pitiful in comparison with theirs, both in function and in power. They must be stopped before they are able to carry out their plans."

"What is the source of this information, Your Majesty?" asked Kharkin bluntly.

The king glowered at him for a moment before deciding to answer.

"A newcomer to our court has had direct contact with them."

"Deemis?" Kharkin asked disbelievingly. "How can you be certain his information is accurate?" He managed to keep the question from sounding mocking, but only with difficulty.

"I have my own ways of assessing the veracity of a report," growled the king. He glared at the chief master. "I have found the boy to be artless. He provides a refreshing change from the sycophants who surround me."

"Would it be possible for me to question Deemis directly about these matters?" asked Kharkin.

The king shook his head dismissively. "He is not currently in Antilin. He is engaged in a mission on my behalf. It is enough for you to know that he learned about these people from an older woman—a mage—who fled one of the islands. She remained in his village for some years. Once she learned to trust him she spoke freely. One day she simply disappeared. He believes the islanders found and removed her."

"What is the nature of the advanced magic possessed by these islanders?"

"Their mage touch ability in particular is exceptionally sophisticated," asserted the king. "It grants them unusual control over every aspect of human physiology."

Kharkin frowned. "I presume you mean they can hurt people, Your Majesty. Members of the Compact are no less capable, except that we are constrained by the vows we take when we become mages. Perhaps these foreigners have fewer inhibitions about the way they use their abilities."

The irony of Kharkin's statement was not entirely lost on him. Having sent an entire team of mages to murder Trisanna, he wasn't exactly qualified to claim the moral high ground. He thrust such considerations from his mind.

"I cannot speak to their scruples," the king replied. "And from what I understand they are vastly more capable of hurting people than any of you. We cannot afford to find ourselves on the receiving end of their powers." His face hardened. "This is your responsibility, Kharkin," he said coolly. "How is it that these foreigners have acquired magical abilities we lack?"

"Without meeting them I can't say."

"Meeting them?" Garneth glared at him disdainfully. "What are you suggesting? Will you knock on their door and ask them to spill all their secrets?"

He bit back a sarcastic response of his own. "What do you propose, Your Majesty?"

"I would have thought it obvious, *Chief Master*. The one thing you seem capable of is research."

The mocking insults were not lost on Kharkin. No doubt Garneth had been sitting back and laughing at the chief master's frantic efforts to find a way to survive in Methesia.

The king was scowling. "It's always been said that the magical abilities of our forebears were vastly greater before the Great Desolation. Now we find out that other mages still possess the abilities of the ancients. It leaves me wondering why Tantel's head mages have for so long accepted mediocrity. Our kingdom might be in a stronger position if its head mage had any fire in his gut."

Kharkin's brows drew together. The king's words, intended to embarrass him, had instead prodded a distant memory. It was undeniable that Kharkin was good at research. It didn't hurt that he had the ability to call to mind precise images of documents he had barely glimpsed. The comment about his gut had brought to his mind an old document—one that talked about activating a talisman by drawing it into the magical gut of a mage.

Could it truly be that simple?

The talisman lay secreted in his robe. Grasping it with one hand, he reached down, deep into the core of his magical being, and drew it in.

His eyes went wide as a flood of power infused him. So much was now clear to him.

The king was looking at him strangely, and he forced himself to remember where he was.

"I will carry out the research you have suggested, Your Majesty," he managed. "If you are willing to release me, I will begin at once."

"You are dismissed!" the king said readily.

After a hastily executed bow, he hurried away, leaving the king staring after him with a puzzled frown on his face.

Free at last, he banished the king from his thoughts. The power he had suddenly acquired placed everything else into an entirely different perspective.

What had just taken place was nothing short of astonishing. The means of activating the talisman had been within his grasp the whole time. It had taken an insult to drag the document into the open.

Why hadn't he been able to access the memory earlier, when he was actively searching for information about activating a talisman? Whatever the reason, it no longer mattered.

As of that moment, he knew he could use his magical abilities continuously, without ever becoming weary. And he could sense the talisman poised within him, ready to offer magical solutions to problems he hadn't yet encountered. It was incredible.

Was this the answer to the missing power of the ancients? Did they have ready access to dragon talismans? Might the same source also be responsible for the supposed abilities of the islanders?

Upon further thought, he decided that talismans could not be the whole answer. A talisman didn't offer new abilities, nor did it increase the sophistication of existing abilities. Even a cursory reading of the achievements of mages before the Great Desolation made it clear that they routinely demonstrated capabilities unseen in later times.

Research was not likely to bridge the gap, either, whatever King Garneth said. As he had already discovered with the issue of activating a talisman, writers of ancient scrolls assumed common knowledge that was not present in their successors.

If it was true that the foreigners had retained such knowledge, there would be a great deal to learn from them. It would depend entirely on their willingness to share their knowledge freely. Such openness seemed completely unrealistic, especially if the king was right about them having designs on Tantel and Periton.

There was a great deal he needed to find out. All of it centered on these mysterious islanders. The king wasn't going to help, and even if Deemis could, he apparently was not available.

Kharkin needed to cultivate connections of his own.

HAVING LEFT THE KING, Kharkin immediately sought out his assistant. "There's work for us to do, Jaizor," he announced.

Jaizor raised his eyebrows questioningly in response. The chief master grinned in appreciation. He was honest enough to acknowledge he would have been less accommodating had the roles been reversed.

"I also have some very good news. I have activated the talisman!"

Jaizor looked both surprised and pleased. "How did you manage that?" he asked.

"The king said something that prodded my memory. I realized I had once read a document that answered the question."

"Is the king still talking about us going to Ettaran?"

He shook his head. "There's been no further mention of it, not that it matters now. I could easily protect us in Methesia."

He waved Jaizor to a chair. "The task ahead of us is something entirely different. According to the king—and I need you to keep this strictly confidential—there is a group of foreigners living on islands to the north of Periton. They supposedly possess much more advanced magical abilities than we do. I want us to find out anything we can about them."

"How long are they supposed to have been there?"

"Many years."

Jaizor's face twisted skeptically. "How is that possible? How could they be there without anyone knowing about them?"

"I have no more idea than you. We'll need to do some digging."

"In the library? It's hard to believe we'll find anything there."

"Not the library. We need to start with sailors. Do you have any contacts?"

Jaizor immediately nodded. "My brother is a sailor on a merchant ship. He's sailed the coastline of both Tantel and Periton many times."

Kharkin released a long sigh of relief. "Where is he now?"

"By a curious chance, he's here in Antilin."

"Could you arrange a meeting?" asked Kharkin eagerly.

Jaizor nodded.

"Set it up while he's still available! Just remember to be very careful what you say."

KHARKIN SAT with Jaizor and his brother Emmri in a private location. After tolerating a few minutes of small talk, he came to the point.

"Have you come across any foreigners in your travels?" he asked.

"Do you mean apart from Peritonians?" the sailor replied.

The head mage nodded.

"Sailing vessels do arrive here occasionally from other continents. But it's very rare. I've seen a foreign vessel only once in my entire life."

"Why is it so rare?"

"The distance, combined with extreme weather conditions, make such voyages extremely hazardous. And when they get here, they discover we have nothing of unusual value to trade. It simply isn't worth the risk."

"Have foreigners ever settled here?"

"Not as far as I know."

"There aren't even rumors about it happening?"

Kharkin tried not to show his disappointment when Emmri shook his head.

Then the sailor's face lit up. "Wait a moment! If you're interested in rumors, there was one person spreading stories. Tall tales more likely. No one believed him."

"What were the tales?"

"He claimed the captain of his ship had sent him to an island in a small boat. Supposedly the captain had a hankering for fresh meat—wild boar or whatever else was available—and he was the best hunter on the ship. The weather quickly began to turn nasty, but he landed safely and headed inland. He supposedly found large numbers of domestic animals, including pigs, goats, sheep, and cows. He also saw houses and tilled land. Then he said he was hit on the head.

"The next thing he remembered was waking up on a beach in Periton with an almighty headache. His little boat was pulled up on the sand. He insisted he'd been knocked out. And that he'd been kept asleep, most likely by a mage. He wasn't allowed to wake up again until after they had returned him to the mainland."

"Why did he think a mage was involved?"

"Because he'd shaved that morning, and when he woke up he had a bit of a beard. It suggested he'd been out for a few days."

"Where was this supposed island?"

"We asked him that, but he claimed he couldn't remember. Maybe it had something to do with being knocked on the head."

"What did his captain say?"

"As soon as they launched his boat, a huge squall came up. The ship almost went onto the rocks. The captain had to leave him to fend for himself. He eventually reconnected with the sailor, of course. But he didn't believe a word of the tales. He was convinced the sailor never made it to the island. He thought he was blown all the way to Periton and was lucky enough to end up on a beach."

"Where is this sailor now?" asked Jaizor.

"That's the most curious thing about his story. He disappeared, not too long after it supposedly happened. No one knows what became of him."

Kharkin exchanged a subtle glance with Jaizor. "It's an entertaining story," he said with a smile. "Talking is thirsty work, though! We've brought some excellent wine—and food, too—and there's plenty to go around. I, for one, have no intention of letting it go to waste!"

CHAPTER 16
ABBETHAR

Confronted by the palpable anger of the community elders, Dannah was doing her best to remain calm. She lifted her voice to be heard over the hubbub. "All we know is that Elef'nissar—the dragon that brought Kylen here—was seen flying away from the healing rooms carrying a person in his talons. It was almost certainly Kylen. It is the most likely explanation for his sudden disappearance."

"We were soft-headed fools! Why did we ever allow him to stay here in the first place?"

"The Peritonian renegade will betray us all!"

"Our position became untenable the moment that fool healer spilled our secrets to him."

"We have no reasonable grounds for such dire conclusions," Dannah interjected. "To begin with, Aleira said nothing even vaguely understandable. It is highly unlikely Kylen made any sense of it. Beyond that, he owes us a debt of gratitude, and he is well aware of it. He has insisted repeatedly he would never betray us. We don't even know if he went with the dragon of his own free will."

"The dragon might have had a purpose of its own in facilitating his escape. We have no reason to trust the creatures! Dragons owe us nothing!"

"He must surely have summoned the dragon. We're facing a conspiracy, and the dragon is almost certainly part of it!"

"You are responsible for this, Dannah! What possessed you to allow a foreigner to learn healing from us?"

Dannah stared at them in consternation. Even if she wanted to reply, there was no longer a way to be heard. Pandemonium had broken out. All of them seemed to be talking at once, some shouting others down. Common sense and reason had dissipated like a morning mist.

A loud clashing sound rose suddenly over the din. Harsh and deafening, it rang out multiple times in quick succession. The elders lapsed into stunned silence.

Every eye in the room moved to a pair of cymbals, held aloft in the hands of Rydel, one of the more senior of the elders. Dannah had noticed him slipping from the room at the height of the chaos. The reason for his sudden departure was now evident.

Rydel's face glowed red with fury as he glared at them. "You dare to call yourselves elders? You're behaving like children! Every one of you should be ashamed!"

Spotting mouths beginning to open, he hoisted his cymbals threateningly. The mouths snapped shut again.

Glancing around the room, Dannah saw a few unrepentant scowls, but many of the elders seemed embarrassed.

Rydel glared sternly at them. "There has been a great deal of wild speculation expressed today," he asserted. "I refuse to subscribe to it! Fear is certainly appropriate at times, but unreasoning fear has no place among us. Perhaps you have forgotten that wisdom has *never* made common cause with panic!"

He turned to Dannah. "Some have claimed you minimize the problems that confront us, Dannah. I am not among them. I see you as pragmatic—someone better able than most to keep your head in troubled times. How do you propose we respond to this situation?"

Dannah dipped her head respectfully. "I don't see myself as solely responsible for the situation that has arisen. Nevertheless, I do acknowledge giving Kylen the benefit of the doubt and therefore a degree of freedom. With that in mind, I believe I should play my part in fixing whatever can be fixed. I propose to go to Periton to seek him out."

After a moment of stunned silence, everyone started talking at once.

Rydel shouted them down. "One at a time! Or I *will* use the cymbals!"

They quickly settled.

"Why you?" asked an elder.

"He knows me, and I believe he trusts me. He won't try to avoid me."

"How can you go to Periton?" another asked. "You won't be able to understand a word they say."

"I have mage hearing ability," she replied. "Language will not be a problem for me."

"You cannot go alone."

"I will ask Aleira to accompany me."

"Isn't she the one who spoke out of turn?" asked one of the elders. When Dannah nodded, he grunted, "Then she deserves it."

"How will you find Kylen?" asked Rydel. "He said he's a renegade, so he will work hard at staying hidden. You won't be able to ask around where to find him."

"Aleira has the ability to detect glimmer. Kylen will be avoiding groups of mages. So we will look for small numbers of mages in out of the way corners of the kingdom."

"What if you are taken in by the authorities and questioned?" she was asked.

"I will say we are from the Summer Isles." Seeing many blank faces, she added, "I have done some research. The Summer Isles are large inhabited islands to the south of Periton. They should be close enough to seem unthreatening and far enough away to be unfamiliar."

Rydel looked uncertain. "Kylen claimed that mages need to be members of the Peritonian Compact, otherwise they are marked for death as renegades. What if you are captured by Compact mages?"

"We will stay well away from such people."

"You could search for months and never find him!" scoffed one of the elders.

"Do you have a better suggestion to offer?" she asked pointedly. "Or would you prefer to simply leave Kylen alone to take whatever action he sees fit?"

The elder subsided, muttering inaudibly.

A great deal more was said before the meeting closed. Not all of the elders were happy with Dannah's proposal. Nevertheless, she left with the one thing she wanted—permission to leave Abbethar in search of Kylen.

She had some preparation to do before she could leave. Aleira would be one of her biggest challenges. The young healer would not be excited about her proposed role in the expedition.

~

PERITON

THE LITTLE BOAT rose and fell alarmingly as it plowed through the swell, leaving Dannah thoroughly disoriented and more than a little queasy. It didn't help that she could see no sign of a horizon. The sea was as dark as the night sky, and the moon was nowhere to be seen. The only hint of illumination came from the few stars not obscured by clouds.

Aleira was huddling face down in the bottom of the boat, wrapped in her hooded cloak and apparently struggling to keep herself from vomiting. She had been more than a little reluctant about her proposed role in this expedition, but she had agreed to come. Dannah had chosen not to play on her guilt. Nevertheless, it was probably the only reason she was there.

They'd brought sufficient supplies to last a few days. After that they'd need to work in exchange for food. Realistically, that meant finding people who would appreciate help from healers.

If Kylen had been right, there would be no shortage of people lining up for help. He had told her that people in Periton's rural areas received little or no support from the crown or the Compact, and that the skill of Dannah and her colleagues far surpassed that of Periton's healers.

His assertions had niggled away at her. If they were true, she couldn't easily ignore them. She hadn't told the elders, but responding to Kylen's disappearance was far from her only reason for going to Periton.

Soon she would have an opportunity to assess the situation for herself. She couldn't wait.

The groans coming from Aleira finally ceased when they came in sight of land. Perhaps by then she had surrendered to sleep. Dannah herself was still alert. It was a good thing, too. She was going to need her wits about her.

The moment the sailors guided the boat to a sandy beach, Aleira stirred. Easing herself over the side of the boat, she splashed ashore, collapsing face down onto the sand once she was well clear of the water.

Dannah thanked the sailors quietly. Then with difficulty she shouldered both packs and waded ashore. She sent a final wave to the sailors as they steered the boat back out to sea.

As soon as they were out of sight, she turned her attention to Aleira.

"It looks like you had a rough passage," she ventured.

"It certainly stank down in the bilges, if that's what you mean," exclaimed her companion, sitting up straight and throwing back her hood.

Her mouth gaping wide, Dannah peered at her in the dim predawn light. "Marielle!" she sputtered, unable to decide between astonishment, alarm, and indignation. "What are you doing here? Where is Aleira?"

Her granddaughter stared back at her calmly. "She didn't want to come, and I did."

"She agreed to this deception?!"

"Not exactly," admitted Marielle. "She was tired, and I helped her get a long sleep."

Dannah couldn't see properly in the dark, but she had the impression Marielle was wincing. As she should be.

"You cannot remain here," said Dannah adamantly.

Marielle waved her head in the direction of the sea. "It's a long swim back to the island."

"There's nothing amusing about this situation! To begin with, Aleira had mage hearing. You do not! How are you going to make sense of a different language?"

"I've been taking lessons. You never know when new skills might become useful."

"Lessons?! From whom?"

"In case you've forgotten, we do have a couple of people in our community who came to us from Periton. We also have a small collection of documents in their language. I told one of them I wanted to be able to read and speak his language. He agreed to help me learn it."

"How long have you been doing that?" demanded Dannah, speaking in the language of Periton.

"For a while. I understand more than I can speak," Marielle replied in the same language.

She had a thick accent, but she was certainly understandable. Dannah was more impressed than she was willing to admit.

"Why are you here?" she demanded. She was known as a person of unusual empathy, but there were times when bluntness was called for.

"Kylen was quick to insist he meant our people no harm. If he has been anything less than truthful, I intend to hold him to account."

"By which you mean you don't trust me to do what's necessary?"

"Can I trust you?" Marielle asked frankly. "You're a very forgiving person, Granny. Much more so than I am. Sometimes you choose to overlook the way people are behaving. I haven't always been convinced it's a good thing."

Dannah didn't hesitate. "For as long as we are in Periton, I am Dannah, and you are my assistant, Marielle." She lowered her tone until it was close to a growl. "But I am still your grandmother. Don't expect you can treat me with the disrespect you showed Aleira. You put her to sleep with neither her knowledge nor her consent, simply because it suited you. I will not overlook such behavior! The community elders entrusted *me* with this task, not you. If you had genuine questions about my willingness to do whatever's needed, you could have raised them with the elders. Instead, you resorted to trickery. You disabled the companion they chose for me and stowed away in her place. I am not about to show you any more respect than you've shown to others!"

The first light of dawn exposed the deep red blush of shame that covered Marielle's face. Turning away without another word, Dannah headed inland, away from the beach.

Never before had Dannah spoken to her granddaughter in such a way. Yet she had no qualms about doing it. There would be a time for a gentle word of affirmation. Now was not that time.

Marielle was gifted, accomplished, and determined. She was also capable of being obstinate and headstrong.

More importantly, in mistaking Dannah's empathy for weakness she had exposed her inexperience. They had set foot in a foreign land with no idea what dangers they would face. When trouble came, Marielle wouldn't instinctively follow Dannah's lead. She would do her own thing.

For both of their sakes she needed to be shaken out of that. That meant confronting her and exposing her to her grandmother's underlying toughness.

Until Marielle learned to follow without hesitation, Dannah intended to be as tough as she needed to be.

DANNAH AND MARIELLE had been wandering aimlessly for three days. In that time they had seen no glimpse of another person and not the slightest hint of habitation.

"You were right. I should never have come here," said Marielle miserably.

A wry smile twisted Dannah's lips. "Did you expect to stumble upon Kylen on your first day?"

"Of course not! But I did expect to find some evidence of human life."

"I never suggested you shouldn't have come, Elle," asserted

Dannah. "I'm actually delighted about the opportunity to spend so much time with you."

"You haven't seemed delighted. You've been very harsh with me," Marielle told her.

"Do you think it was deserved?"

For a moment Marielle looked sullen. Then she raised her hands helplessly. "Very well, if you must know, then yes, it was deserved. I'm ashamed of the way I treated Aleira."

"What about the things you said about me?"

"I thought you overlooked things because you're so forgiving. Little did I know how brutal you can be!"

"I need you to follow my lead. You'll never do it willingly if you think I'm weak. I'm not weak, and you need to understand that."

Marielle nodded tightly.

"If I was too severe on you then I'm sorry."

"I deserved it," Marielle acknowledged with a sigh.

"I'm glad we have that clarified. Our timing was perfect, too. Here comes a farmer!"

A rickety old cart was bumping over the uneven ground, pulled by an aging mare. Neither the horse nor the man on the driver's bench appeared to have much meat on them.

"Well, hello there! Where did you two appear from? We don't get many strangers in these parts."

"We were on a boat..." began Dannah.

"Ahh. Say no more," said the man, nodding wisely. "Boats are dangerous things at the best of times. You'd better come with me, I guess. I've been collecting wood, but there's room in the cart. We don't have much food to share, but my wife will appreciate a bit of company, I'm sure."

Relieved to have human company at last, they climbed into the cart and bumped along behind him.

Before long they spotted a thin trail of smoke. It was coming from the chimney of a ramshackle little house standing in an expanse of open ground. A couple of scrawny chickens pecked around the yard, and a cow stood chewing its cud beside a small barn off to one side.

Climbing down from the cart, they were ushered inside the house.

The farmer's wife greeted them enthusiastically. "You brought visitors! How marvelous!"

"They were shipwrecked!" her husband told her.

She stared at them wide-eyed. "You poor things! We don't have much to offer, but you're welcome to share what we have."

Dannah returned their greetings as warmly as she was able. She didn't correct them about the shipwreck.

She was finding it hard not to stare at them. The farmer's wife was clearly in no better condition than he was. Nor were the two urchins clinging to her skirts.

For her the encounter was unexpectedly confronting, and she was struggling with her own reactions. The simple truth was that she had never seen anyone living in such poverty.

Kylen had claimed that Periton's poor scratched out a hard living. Their very first connection had demonstrated the truth of his words.

CHAPTER 17
PERITON

In spite of their poverty, the Peritonian farmer and his wife had extended a ready welcome to a pair of complete strangers. Grateful to them for their kindness and impressed by their generosity, Dannah decided to do whatever she could in return.

Even with no experience of agriculture, she soon realized that access to water was a major barrier to improving their circumstances. By pooling their mage touch abilities, Dannah and Marielle were able to redirect a stream. Soon it was flowing through a field with vegetables on one side and fruit trees on the other.

"I can't thank you enough!" enthused the farmer. "It will be easy to dig a few little channels to divert some of the water. It'll make all the difference to my plantings!"

Later that day they found him laboriously building up the sides of the stream.

"What are you doing?" asked Dannah curiously.

Leaning on his spade, he took a breather while he surveyed his handiwork. "In the wet season this stream will overflow its banks. I've started work on a small levee to protect the crops. I have other things I need to do now, but I'll continue work on it tomorrow."

He left, taking his spade with him.

Before the sun went down the two mages had completed the task for him. It had taken them a few hours, taking into account the time they needed for rest breaks, but the job was done.

The next morning they led their hosts to the stream. The two of them stared dumbfounded at the solid little levee on either side of the stream. Putting his arm around his wife, the farmer drew her in close. Tears rolled freely down both of their cheeks.

"I don't have words to thank you," managed the woman, wiping at her eyes. She glanced up at her husband. "He never says much, but his back has been real bad the last year or two. Too much hard work and never a proper chance to rest."

Up to that point Marielle had said very little, reluctant to expose her accent. On this occasion she didn't hold back. "Perhaps we can help with that."

Dannah smiled. "May we examine your back?" she asked the farmer.

He nodded mutely.

Positioning themselves on either side of him, the two healers placed their hands on his back and felt up and down his spine.

"Follow my lead, Elle," instructed Dannah as she extended power into the area where a herniated disc had pinched a nerve.

The farmer's eyes went wide. "The pain is gone!" he exclaimed excitedly. "What did you do?"

"We're healers," Dannah told him. She waved a hand across the levee. "We're not very skilled at moving soil, but we do know something about helping people."

They left a couple of days later, intent on connecting with other people. The farmer and his wife waved them off, faces shining with new hope. They pressed eggs and cheese into the hands of the healers as they were leaving. Dannah knew they needed the supplies themselves, but she couldn't find it in herself to deny them a small expression of thanks for what they had done.

Something had changed in Marielle during their time with the family. "I can't believe how cheerful they were when we first met them. Especially considering their situation," she said.

"People can be surprisingly resilient," agreed Dannah. She sighed deeply. "Kylen's words make sense to me now."

Seeing Marielle's eyebrows raised inquiringly, she continued. "I once told him his abilities could be useful on Abbethar. He replied that being useful wasn't the same as being needed. He told me what it was like for people in remote areas of Periton. He said officials did nothing to help them. If it weren't for the renegades, they'd be on their own." She heaved a sigh. "His words troubled me, but I'm not sure I entirely allowed myself to believe them. Not until I saw it for myself."

"That's why you wanted to come here."

"It's certainly one of the reasons."

"I understand, now that I've been here myself," Marielle replied. She shook her head slowly. "I'm beginning to think I never understood Kylen's motivations at all."

Not long after leaving their new friends, they paused for a break.

"I noticed yesterday you're wearing some kind of necklace, Granny. What is it?"

"I've had it for a while. I'm surprised you didn't notice it sooner."

Dannah drew a thin chain from beneath her garments. It supported a locket made of silver. Carefully opening the locket, she spilled its contents into her hand.

Marielle leaned forward, peering down at it. "What is it?"

"It's a piece of dragon claw. From Elef'nissar."

Her granddaughter stared at her in surprise. "Like the one you used to mend Kylen's bones?"

She nodded. "Yes, although it's a bit smaller. The dragon provided two pieces. Initially I thought we might need both, but one was sufficient in the end."

"Why did you keep it?"

"It seemed too valuable to just throw away."

"Is the dragon aware you have it?"

"Of course. I asked permission before deciding to keep it. Elef'nissar didn't seem to mind. Curiously, it said, 'One of you will find it useful.' I asked who apart from me it was referring to, and it replied, 'Your daughter's daughter, of course.'"

Marielle was shocked. "Me?"

Dannah nodded. "It then proceeded to breathe on it. I have no idea why."

"How are we supposed to make use of it?" asked Marielle. "Is there something in particular it's good for?"

"Nothing I'm aware of. I admit I'm not well versed in dragon lore, though."

"I find it fascinating!" said Marielle, examining it closely.

"Would you like to keep it? You already have Elef'nissar's blessing."

Marielle's surprised eyes stared back at her. "Do you mean it?"

"Of course. It's yours if you would like it, Elle. I only have one stipulation. If you ever decide you don't want it anymore, return it to me rather than disposing of it."

"Of course! I can't imagine why I would ever want to dispose of it!"

Removing it from around her neck, Dannah handed it over. With her hands shaking a little, Marielle placed it around her own neck.

Seeing the smile of delight lighting up her face, Dannah was more than content.

DANNAH AND MARIELLE had spent three weeks in Periton without discovering anything about Kylen's whereabouts. They had, however, learned a great deal about the plight of the poor in Periton.

Many people were managing better than the first family they had met. Nevertheless, it became apparent that when times were hard or someone's health declined, the people were on their own. In one large village, they learned that most villagers had never seen a Compact mage. Some of them had occasionally seen renegades, though. The renegades weren't healers, but they were capable in other ways, and they did whatever they could to help.

Dannah was also able to confirm the truth of what Kylen had said about renegades.

When asked about renegades, people had very little to say at first. Once they learned the two women were mages who didn't belong to the Compact, everything changed.

"I hope the mages from Cambrick never catch you. They'll kill you if they do!"

"They've never done a thing for us!" was a common refrain, especially after they had treated the sick.

"We'll need to keep our wits about us," Dannah observed after one such interaction. "It's confronting to know we'll be in serious trouble if we're caught."

"There are things we could do if we get into trouble," ventured Marielle.

"Don't even think such thoughts!" Dannah replied sharply.

Marielle shrugged. "We'll just need to be careful, especially since neither of us can detect glimmer." Her face twisted in a wince. "I imagine Aleira's ability to do that was a big reason you wanted her to accompany you. I am sorry about that, Granny."

"Forget about it, Elle."

Her granddaughter stared absently into the sky. "I think I'm starting to understand what life must be like for Kylen and his friends. It doesn't matter how much you help people, you're still under sentence of death."

Dannah smothered a knowing smile. It came as no surprise to hear that Marielle's thoughts were on Kylen. She often found herself wondering what her granddaughter would do if they did manage to find him.

AFTER SLOWLY MOVING SOUTH they reached a village roughly between Cambrick and Thesmis. Word quickly spread about their arrival, and they spent an entire day treating a stream of sick people that never seemed to end.

Almost at the moment they parted with their final patient, a man and a woman in middle age hurried up to them, looking extremely anxious.

"You're still here!" They seemed relieved.

"How can we help?" asked Dannah.

"It's our daughter."

"What seems to be the problem?"

"She's been sick for a long time. We took her to the mage healers in Cambrick, but they weren't able to help her."

Dannah's ears pricked up. "What did they say was wrong with her?"

"She has a lump inside her skull. They couldn't do anything about it."

The two mages exchanged glances.

"Can you help?" the woman asked plaintively. "We've heard you can heal anything!"

"We can't make promises," Dannah told them. "But we can certainly take a look at her."

They followed the couple to a large residence at one end of the village. It soon became obvious that the family was wealthy. That probably explained how they were able to take their daughter to Cambrick to see the healers.

The parents showed them into the girl's bedroom. She did not look well. A careful examination revealed several tumors inside her brain. Dannah winced as she inspected the end result of a clumsy attempt by the previous healers at opening the girl's skull.

"I take it the best healers were not available," Dannah suggested.

"They were!" the father insisted. "Only the very best of the healers were willing to even try to help her."

"They did try, but as far as we can tell they didn't do any good," said the mother miserably. "Her symptoms are unchanged. And they said there was nothing more anyone could do for her."

"We will see," said Dannah.

After a nod to her granddaughter, the two women began their preparations.

THE TWO HEALERS sat exhausted in the family's living room. Removing the girl's tumors had been a long and grueling process, made considerably more complex by the scar tissue left behind after the earlier bungled attempt.

The parents arrived and handed them fresh milk and newly baked bread.

"Have you finished your work?" the father asked.

Dannah nodded wearily.

"Were you able to help her?" the mother asked nervously.

Dannah nodded again. "The tumors are gone. She will need to rest over the next few days. We will continue to watch her closely and help with pain relief. It will take several months before she fully recovers. We won't be able to stay for long, but we'll tell you what you need to avoid and what you need to do over that period. If you're careful, she should recover well."

"Are the lumps gone for good?"

"We can't promise others won't grow in the future, but it's unlikely."

The parents' response was muted, and Dannah understood perfectly. Their excitement would grow when they witnessed their daughter talking and smiling, and later using her arms, walking, and living life normally. All of that would take time.

The grateful parents gave them a room to sleep in, and they collapsed into it the moment they could do so politely.

"That was horrifying!" exclaimed Marielle. "If that's the best that Periton's healers can offer, it isn't impressive!"

"Kylen was right about that, too," Dannah replied. "He said we far outmatched the skills of the local mages."

"It's encouraging to know that," her granddaughter said with a satisfied smile.

Dannah shook her head miserably. "You're missing the point, Elle! Our community has one overriding priority—to protect and preserve our isolation. It's the reason we were sent to find Kylen! But that also means we've been hiding ourselves away from the people who need us the most."

"What are you suggesting? That we should expose our community to the world?"

"No! That's not what I'm saying. I..." She shook her head helplessly.

"I don't know what I'm trying to say. All I know is we've loved every minute of our time in Periton, difficult as it's been at times. That's been true for you as much as for me. We've loved it because we're needed here! It's exactly what Kylen said to me. We've been able to make a difference—sometimes a huge difference—in peoples' lives. Back home we might be useful, but we're not needed. Not in the way we're needed here."

Marielle had lapsed into silence, a brooding look on her face. Unlike Dannah herself, she didn't seem conflicted. Such perspectives must be new to her, though. She had a big heart. Dannah didn't doubt that in time she would begin to feel uncomfortable as well.

THE CHILD with brain tumors had stabilized almost to the point where Dannah and Marielle could leave her in the care of her parents. With more people than ever arriving for treatment, though, they hadn't been in a position to leave.

After staying in the same location for several days, word about them had clearly spread. Some of their more recent patients had traveled long distances to reach them.

With the new arrivals came updated reports of the looming war with their near neighbor Tantel. Uncertainty about the future affected people in different ways.

One of the women they were treating had been accompanied by two friends. "You have a strange accent," one of them told Marielle bluntly.

"That's because she's from the Summer Isles," interjected Dannah.

"Are you certain she isn't from Tantel?" the woman asked suspiciously. "We've been told to look out for spies now that the Tantellans have invaded our kingdom."

"So far they've only invaded the Summer Isles," asserted another bystander. "Who could blame her for getting out while she could?"

"That's well and good—provided she actually came from there!"

Dannah furrowed her brows. "If we were spies, why would we be treating sick people?"

"To win us over to the other side."

"Well we can stop treating your friend if you like."

"Please don't!" cried the patient and her other friend in unison.

The protester ceased her objections, but only after a dissatisfied grunt.

It was almost dark by the time the three of them left.

Sinking into a chair, Marielle exhaled deeply. "It felt like today would never end!" she exclaimed. "Now that we're on our own, we can finally talk freely. I don't think it's wise for us to stay too much longer. The girl can manage without us."

"I've been having similar thoughts," Dannah replied. "Today's patients came from as far away as Thesmis and Camberton, which means news about us has been spreading. Officials in Cambrick must surely have become aware of us by now. Any mage capable of detecting glimmer will locate us in a moment. We're not safe here anymore. We need to go before it's too late."

"Will we leave in the morning?"

"We'll leave tonight. I've had a chance to look at a map. We'll head south."

"Why south?"

"That's where the trouble seems to be centered. Based on what Kylen told me—and so far everything else he said has been proven to be true—we'll find him and his friends right in the thick of it."

CHAPTER 18
ABBETHAR

You are needed.

Kylen screwed up his face. What was that supposed to mean? How did it justify snatching him away, without even a conversation? And how could the dragon possibly pretend it wasn't the latest example of its interference?

Reminding himself that he owed a great deal—not least his life—to Elef'nissar's interference, Kylen put his annoyance aside.

By then the dragon had been flying long enough for him to have become reconciled to the sensation. Having crossed a wide stretch of water, they were now flying over a mountain range. Unnerving as it was to see the earth so far below him, he decided he would try to appreciate the experience as much as he could. How many people could lay claim to such an adventure?

They were flying swiftly and at a great height. He had spotted birds only twice. On both occasions they had been eagles, flying far below them and soon left behind. The first time he had briefly used his mage sight to borrow the eagle's eyes. The raptor was tracking a mouse scurrying on the ground, and it was beyond strange to witness it from such an altitude.

Trying to remember what he had learned of the geography of Periton, he guessed they were flying a little east of south. After crossing the body of water separating the islands from the mainland, they must have overflown the heights on the southwestern fringes of the Drakkenridge Mountains. The peaks marching ever further away from them to their left must be The Spine, the extensive mountain range that stretched most of the way to Ettaran. An involuntary shudder shook his frame at the reminder of the ruined capital of Methesia.

More peaks loomed ahead. Could they be outliers of the mountain range known as The Ribs?

Before they reached them, the dragon began to descend.

Blood pounded in Kylen's head as the earth rose up alarmingly beneath him. A fertile valley had sprung abruptly from the barrenness of the surrounding countryside, and he was able to make out what appeared to be buildings within it. Then they were gliding ever lower.

Kylen flinched as the dragon's talons neared the ground, although he had no need for concern. Even as they touched down the great claws lifted slightly, releasing him at the very moment Elef'nissar came to a halt.

He stretched awkwardly, then turned to face the dragon, smiling up at it. After the wonder of the flight his earlier exasperation had faded to little more than a memory.

"What am I needed for?" he asked curiously.

A voice reached him. "A dragon has come!"

A girl was running excitedly toward them, and he started as he recognized the face of the phantom he had first encountered in the library in Flaxendell.

She came to a halt before the dragon. "You heard me, and you came!" she said, tears glistening in her eyes.

Another person was hurrying in their direction. He didn't recognize her at first, although there was something familiar about her. Finally he realized who it was. He'd only seen her on a couple of occasions, and they'd never been properly introduced. But it was Inga. He was sure of it. Noticing she was heavily pregnant, his eyebrows rose in surprise.

She glanced wide-eyed at Kylen. "You came!" she said breathlessly.

Then she turned to the dragon and bowed respectfully, speaking to

Kylen as she did so. "Please convey my thanks to the dragon, Kylen, for bringing you after I called for help."

Kylen peered at her in bemusement. First it had been the girl, now Inga. Both of them spoke as if the new arrivals had come in response to their requests.

Inga had turned to face him. She was staring at him, no doubt wondering why he hadn't done anything.

Feeling foolish, he spoke to the dragon. "Inga asked me to thank you," he said. "For bringing me in response to her call for help."

To his astonishment, the dragon dipped its great head solemnly.

Kylen had no idea what to make of it. Was it actually possible that the dragon had heard the calls for help? Could that be the reason he had been snatched away from Abbethar? It made no sense. Not long had passed since Elef'nissar informed him it paid little heed to humans.

The girl was now looking at him as well. "My grandfather had a talisman for most of his life. It has been taken from him. Have you come to heal him?"

"Someone stole a talisman from her grandfather," Kylen told Elef'nissar. "Talismans are dragon business."

"You have a talisman," it replied calmly.

"How does that help? I can't exactly give it to her grandfather!"

"You are needed," the dragon repeated simply.

A quick glance showed all three staring at him.

The situation was ludicrous. He had a sudden urge to break out into mad laughter.

Restraining the impulse with difficulty, he reminded himself that many others, the dragon among them, had made a prodigious effort to save him. Only a short time ago his own case could reasonably have been described as hopeless.

He could at least try to help.

"Can you take me to your grandfather?" he asked the girl.

Her eyes lit up immediately. "Follow me!" she called, hurrying back toward the buildings.

Stiff and uncomfortable after the long dragon flight and not yet fully healed himself, he couldn't keep up with her.

When she reached the building she turned, waiting impatiently for him.

Inga had been plodding along beside him. "We can't stay in this valley," she told him. "Not without her grandfather's talisman to protect us from going mad."

He began to glimpse a reason why the dragon might have seen him as needed. He did at least have a talisman of his own. Reaching inward, he discovered the talisman already presenting solutions. "I can provide protection for everyone in the valley," he told Inga. "Including your baby."

Heaving a sigh of relief, she slowed her pace. "Thank you, Kylen!" she breathed. "You go ahead. Don't wait for me."

Reaching the girl, he gazed at her curiously, comparing her with the images still in his mind from Flaxendell.

"My name is Marigold," she told him. "I already know who you are. You're Kylen."

"It's nice to meet you as a real person, Marigold," he told her with a wry smile.

As she led him inside, he made a start on protecting the valley, including plants and animals along with the humans he was aware of. He ignored Elef'nissar, knowing the dragon was well able to take care of itself.

Marigold led him into a bedroom where a man lay stretched out, unmoving, while a woman sat anxiously at his side. "This is my grand-mother, Vennia, and my grandfather, Sorren," said Marigold, her voice strained with emotion.

"I have a talisman, and you are both protected now, along with everything living in the valley," Kylen assured Vennia.

"Thank you," she said, relief evident on her face. "Are you able to help my husband?"

Sitting down beside her, he placed a hand on the stricken man, checking his vital signs while exploring his veins, his tissues, and his organs for signs of damage. Nothing obvious appeared to be wrong with him physically, but clearly something was not right. Dannah's years of experience would have helped, but she wasn't there.

Yet the dragon had told him he was needed. That suggested he ought to be able to do something to help. The problem had been caused by separation from a talisman, so he reached inwardly for his own talisman. Its magic confirmed that Sorren's ailment was not physical. He sensed that the stolen talisman had settled deeply into Sorren. So much so that the wrench of losing it had done significant damage.

Kylen immediately used his training to relax Sorren's system. To Vennia's great relief, her husband settled visibly. Regrettably, Kylen's limited training as a healer offered no wisdom about what to do next.

His talisman offered an option, though, and he guessed that a talisman's response might be more effective than the best strategy devised by an experienced healer. Carefully deploying the available magic, he nudged and shunted until the proposed solution was achieved. He sensed from the beginning his efforts wouldn't return Sorren to normal. But he'd achieved something.

Sorren opened his eyes. He was greeted by enraptured, if somewhat muted, cries from Vennia and Marigold. His hand instinctively reached for the familiar talisman around his neck, and a puzzled look covered his face. Then he seemed to remember, and his face paled.

Vennia aimed a pleading look at Kylen. The look of pain in her husband's eyes had clearly wrung her heart. When Kylen didn't respond, she got up, taking his arm and leading him outside the room.

"Thank you so much for what you've done already! Is there anything else you can do for him?"

He shook his head slowly. "I'm sorry, but I can't make good the loss of the talisman."

"What will it mean for him?"

He gazed back at her hesitantly. He knew the answer to her question, but she wasn't going to want to hear it.

She squeezed his arm. "Please! I need to know."

Working hard at suppressing a wince, he responded. "Without the power of my own talisman, I'm not sure if anything could have been done for him. As it is, I believe he will be able to live a reasonably normal life. But I don't think it will be safe for him to try to exercise his former mage abilities. Even with a talisman there was nothing I could do to repair the damage to that part of him."

"You mean he'll never be able to be a mage again."

Kylen lowered his head, unwilling to give voice to the appalling truth.

"I understand," she said grimly. "Thank you again for all you've done." Then she returned to her husband, a look of determination on her face.

Feeling suddenly claustrophobic, Kylen pushed through the door of the house into the open air. He found Inga still outside. More surprisingly, the dragon had remained where it landed.

"How is he?" asked Inga anxiously. "His glimmer is so faint I can barely detect it."

Kylen repeated what he had told Vennia.

Inga's face fell. "That will be hard for them both. What are you planning to do, Kylen?" she asked.

"I'll need to stay here. I don't think I have a choice," he told her frankly. "If I leave, the talisman will go with me, and none of you will be protected."

"Thank you," she replied earnestly. "I'm not sure what we would do if we were forced to leave the valley. Not without the help of Dalthinir and Trisanna and the twins."

"They've been here with you?" he asked excitedly. "I wasn't sure if they survived Ettaran!"

"Of course!" she said. "There's so much you couldn't possibly be aware of! All of your friends are well. And Dalthinir and I are married!" She grinned. "He finally came to his senses and asked me to marry him, unlikely as it must seem. I'm carrying our baby."

Kylen felt like his eyes were about to pop out of his head. "That's so much better than anything I could have dreamed of! Congratulations!"

"You must have a story of your own to tell! The others will be just as excited to learn that you're safe. In spite of everything, Trisanna never doubted you were alive and being cared for."

The mention of his friends brought a lump to his throat. "Please excuse me, Inga," he said, dipping his head. "I need to talk to Elef'nissar."

"So the dragon has a name!" she exclaimed, glancing toward it. "Please don't let me detain you!"

Unless he was mistaken, she would have very much liked to

converse with the creature herself. It was another reminder of how fortunate he was.

The great orbs fixed on him impassively as he approached.

"I have done all I could," he reported. "He's had a talisman for most of his adult life, and someone took it from him. Is there any hope for him?"

"Talismans are perilous for humans."

"And yet you donated one to me," he noted ironically.

The dragon continued to eyeball him calmly.

"Would it help if he got his talisman back?" Kylen asked.

When no answer was forthcoming, he added, "What if he were to get a different talisman?"

"You have done all you could," it finally replied, echoing the words he had used himself.

He gritted his teeth. If the dragon had no answer to the question, why didn't it just say so? Then again, it was possible it knew but didn't want to say. Either way, it made little difference, because dragons could never be relied upon for straight answers. Not if this particular creature offered any indication.

The outlook didn't seem promising for Sorren, though. Without his magical abilities life would always seem empty to him.

It had to be better than lying comatose as he was earlier, though. Kylen had his talisman to thank for that. Without it he would have been powerless to help Sorren, even with his training as a healer.

Perhaps his talisman was the reason Elef'nissar brought him to the valley. The dragon hadn't hurried away as it usually did. Had it stayed to find out what he would do with its gift?

It suddenly occurred to him to wonder why the dragon had given him a talisman at all. Had there been a broader purpose beyond helping to knit his bones? The dragon had insisted that interfering in human affairs was forbidden for its kind. Had it found a new way to blur the lines?

There was nothing new about talismans, of course—he knew an evil dragon had somehow been responsible for the Amulet of Zinth. The innovation in this case might have been to embed a talisman in human flesh.

Sorren's talisman had been taken from him by force. It would be a lot less practical to do that in his case. What would happen to the talisman after his death was an open question. Elef'nissar must surely have considered the matter, not least because dragons regarded human life as little more than a breath of vapor.

He faced the creature. "You provided a talisman to be knitted into my body. Are you satisfied with the outcome?" he asked boldly.

The orbed eyes began to whirl, and a plume of smoke spouted from its great nostrils.

"Fare well, Kalmithien," it rumbled, rising to its feet.

"Fare well, Elef'nissar," Kylen replied.

Taking wing, it rose swiftly into the air and was gone.

He watched it go uncertainly. Had he offended the creature? Or had he actually managed to unsettle it?

CHAPTER 19
ABBETHAR

Lokan woke to stillness. He was lying on something soft under a crude shelter. All around him he heard birdsong and the wind in the trees. More faintly he heard a rhythmic crashing. It reminded him of something. Waves pounding against rocks?

Where was he, and how did he get there?

An attempt to move his head left him immediately regretting it. Groaning in pain, he closed his eyes against the pounding headache that suddenly filled his consciousness.

His groans had apparently alerted someone. "So you're awake, are you?"

A face swam into view, bearded and unkempt. "My name is Buck. I fished you out of the water during the storm."

He frowned, trying to make sense of the words.

"My...name...is Lokan." It felt like his thoughts were swirling around in a fog. He paused, trying to remember what he was trying to communicate. "I...fell. From...a ship."

"You're lucky I happened to be looking out to sea when your ship was passing. I could tell it was from Tantel. I was waving and calling out, trying to catch their attention. I saw you fall into the water."

He groaned again. "My head..."

"Hurts a lot? No surprises there—there was a lot of blood!"

"Fell...into the sea." Every word was a struggle.

"Yes, you fell into the sea from a ship. You said that already. There was some kind of wooden thing keeping you afloat. It's the only reason you didn't drown. It was also the only reason I managed to tow you in. Especially in those conditions. The job was left to me, because your ship didn't wait around for you."

Lokan's thoughts were impossibly scrambled. He closed his eyes and rested for a while.

After a pause, he asked, "Who...are you?"

"Buck! My name is Buck."

"Buck..." He grimaced. "I'm...Lokan."

"I know. And you hit your head." The other man snorted. "Clearly I'm not going to get any sense out of you for a while. Try to rest. We'll see how you are in the morning."

DAYLIGHT PENETRATED through the trees around his shelter. Lokan lay still, trying to piece together what he knew. He remembered a storm at sea, talking with Deemis, then falling into the sea. He must have hit his head on the way down.

Vague memories of another voice came to him, someone who had spoken to him since falling from the ship.

Was it the person who had rescued him?

He simply couldn't remember.

As if in response to his thoughts, a scruffy face appeared. He felt like he ought to recognize it.

"Lokan! You're awake again. Do you remember anything from yesterday?"

"Barely. I think you rescued me, but I don't remember your name."

"My name is Buck. You must be thirsty. It might be better if you drink fresh water this time!" He handed over a waterskin.

Unwilling to risk sitting up, Lokan held it up and gulped a few mouthfuls while lying down. It wasn't a sensible plan. The coughing and sputtering that followed set his head pounding again.

Closing his eyes, he resigned himself to enduring the pain. Thankfully, his rescuer left him in peace.

A few hours passed before the other man appeared again to find Lokan sitting up.

"It's good to see you at least partially upright," said Buck with a grin. He handed over the waterskin again. "Are you feeling hungry?"

After taking a couple of cautious sips of water, Lokan slowly released a sigh. "No food, please. My stomach feels queasy. My head will start hammering again if I vomit."

"I'll leave the waterskin with you. Get some more rest."

Another twenty-four hours passed before Lokan felt able to engage with the world again.

After a while Buck arrived. "Thank you for rescuing me!" he said. The acknowledgment was overdue.

"Ah, no need to thank me. I'm glad to have some company again."

"Where are we exactly?"

"Well, the locals call this island Abbethar."

"Who are the locals?"

Buck shrugged. "It's hard to say. They're not from Periton or Tantel —they speak a different language. They refer to themselves as exiles."

"Exiles from where?"

"Somewhere a long way from our continent. Beyond that I don't know."

"How do you come to be here?"

"I'm a fisherman. From Periton. I ended up here as a result of a storm, just like you."

"Did you fall overboard?"

"Sadly, it was a bit worse than that. My ship went down. I was sailing solo, so no one else was affected."

"How long have you been stranded here?"

"About four years, as best I can tell."

"Four years! Do you have anything to do with the locals?"

"Well now, *that's* an interesting question. You see the locals like their privacy and secrecy. They like to think no one else knows they're here."

Lokan hadn't forgotten what Deemis had told him. Their secret had leaked out, whether they knew it or not. "How did you find out they want to stay private?"

"Ah, another good question! I'd been here about six months, barely surviving on whatever I could catch in the sea. It's a harsh shoreline, that's for certain. All of a sudden I spotted a small boat, drifting along with no one steering it, the sail just flapping in the breeze. That boat wasn't built for the open ocean, but that wouldn't have stopped me sailing it home. I didn't hesitate. I dived in and swam for all I was worth. It nearly got away from me, but I was determined! I was almost spent by the time I reached it, but somehow I managed to haul myself aboard."

"Why didn't you sail it home?"

"Ah, why indeed! I quickly discovered I didn't have the boat to myself. The sailor was still on board, lying unconscious in the bilges. I later learned the boom had swung around and knocked him out. Finding him was a surprise. It left me with a bit of a conundrum. I could steer for Periton and let him wake up in his own good time. Or I could go find help for him. One of the toughest choices I've faced."

"What did you do?"

"I went for help. As it turned out, it wasn't the smartest move I've made. But I didn't find that out until later. It didn't take long before I came upon another boat. I jumped up and down and yelled and waved my arms. They saw me soon enough. Their boat was a lot bigger than mine, and the crew was as tough a bunch as I've seen. I soon found out all of them were locals—just like the poor fellow I borrowed the ship from. These geniuses set about putting the pieces together. They weren't gentle with me. That's because they decided I'd somehow sneaked aboard and got the jump on the sailor—knocked him out and stole his ship. I tried to tell them how it was, but they couldn't understand a word I was saying. They wouldn't have believed me anyway."

"What happened?!"

"They took me ashore for questioning. They found someone who spoke our language, and he questioned me. It gave me a chance to put my side of the story, and I think the interpreter believed me. But the others weren't satisfied. I suspect I was about to get a bump on the head myself, except the sailor who'd been unconscious woke up. They'd brought in a healer who did something that fixed him up. He told the others what had actually happened to him. By then I suspect all of them had figured out I was telling the truth, but they weren't about to admit it. The interpreter told me they wanted nothing to do with outsiders. And here I was—not only daring to live on their island, but finding out it was inhabited. It made me a problem."

"How did the interpreter learn our language if they had nothing to do with outsiders?"

"He told me he was from Periton himself. He'd once been in a similar position to me. But while they were deciding what to do with him he got a glimpse of how they lived. He liked it—better than where he'd come from. He also met a girl! She convinced them he was genuine about wanting to stay. I suspect it's the only reason they let him live."

"What about you?"

"My situation was very different. I'd barely been scraping by. I had no desire to be stuck on the island for the rest of my life. Unfortunately, I wasn't smart enough to keep my views to myself. They couldn't let me go back to Periton—not if they wanted to keep their precious secrets.

"The only other alternative was to dispose of me. Before they could settle on that option, I escaped. It was all arranged by the person I'd rescued. He couldn't tell me what he was doing because of the language problem, but I figured it out soon enough. He got me into his boat and brought me here! This part of the island is even more isolated than where I'd been earlier. Then he handed me a pack stuffed full of supplies and pointed at the water. He wanted me to jump out of the boat and swim to shore."

Buck shrugged. "He was bigger than me, but even so he was taking a chance. I could have tried to overpower him and take his boat. I never attempted it, though. He was saving my life and taking a big risk doing it. So I took the supplies, jumped in, and swam to shore. I figured someone would come along sooner or later. Turns out I was right—here you are! Now both of us are stuck here."

"Have you had contact with any other locals since then?"

"Funny you should ask that. Supplies have been left in the area from time to time. Probably I have the sailor to thank for that. Then I had the surprise of my life. A young woman turned up. She'd been learning our language—presumably from my interpreter—and she wanted to test herself out on someone different. I have no idea how she found out about me. She stayed with me for two days. I've never met anyone so determined to learn! She could already speak our language quite well, but she spent every spare minute quizzing me. I was exhausted by the time she left."

"Did you learn anything from her?"

"Only that her name was Elle. She wanted to know everything I could tell her about our customs and culture. She picked me clean! I got nothing in return except a few more supplies. I woke up one morning, and she was gone. I have no idea what became of her."

"It sounds like you haven't been treated badly."

"Not so far. But I'm no fool. If Elle was able to find me, sooner or later, the other lot will as well. That won't be good. Not for either of us!"

Lokan had no intention of staying a minute longer than he had to. The more so now he'd heard Buck's story.

The words of Deemis came to mind. He'd spoken about a jewel hidden inside a rock in the healing rooms. "Have you been to the main settlement on the island?"

"No. Apparently there is one, but they kept me well away from it while they were deciding what to do with me."

With his memory restored, Lokan knew that a boat was supposed to pass by the island each night after dark looking for a signal fire. He wondered if it had already been past a couple of times. As well as rescuing him, the boat might offer Buck his best hope of escaping the island.

He wondered what had become of Deemis. Had he jumped in after Lokan to rescue him? If so, had he survived? The boat wouldn't be coming back if the sailors thought the two of them had drowned. It wasn't a comfortable thought.

Either way, he wasn't going to mention the boat. He couldn't tell Buck about it without revealing he was more than just the victim of a random accident at sea. Quite apart from labeling himself an aspiring thief, he felt certain his fellow castaway would regard Deemis's plan as madness. Buck had witnessed firsthand the attitude of the islanders toward strangers, and Lokan found his account sobering.

From what he'd heard, sneaking into the settlement to steal a priceless artifact seemed anything but sensible.

It left him with a dilemma. What was he going to do?

THE BOAT WAS NOT COMING. There was no other reasonable conclusion.

Seven nights had passed with no sign of it. Each night after sunset Lokan had slipped away from Buck and lit a fire in full view of the sea. The nights had been clear and the sea calm. Any boat on the lookout for a signal would surely have spotted his fire.

After the first night he had come up with a multitude of plausible reasons to explain why the boat had not appeared. As night followed night with no sign of a vessel, his rationalizations began to stretch increasingly thin.

Eventually Lokan abandoned any hope of rescue.

From the beginning he had wondered about the fate of Deemis. Having worked it over and over in his mind, he saw only four possibilities.

The first was that Deemis had followed him into the water to rescue him, intending to tow him to shore and carry out the assignment together as soon as he recovered. If so, Lokan must have been swept out of reach. Whether or not Deemis reached shore, under this scenario he must have been picked up by the boat and continued with the mission on his own.

The second possibility was that Deemis had followed him in and drowned. If so, the tide had carried his body away from the island, because Lokan had thoroughly searched the shoreline without discovering any sign of him.

The third possibility was that from the beginning Deemis had decided it was impractical to rescue him and proceeded with the mission on his own.

That would have required Deemis to put the assignment ahead of rescuing him. Would he do the same if the situations were reversed? Probably not. But he couldn't reasonably criticize Deemis for placing the king's orders ahead of any other priority.

The fourth possibility was that Deemis had called off the mission after deciding nothing could be done to save him.

In the cold light of day, it was obvious that none of these scenarios involved rescuing him.

He was on his own.

CHAPTER 20
PERITON

It didn't take long for Dannah and Marielle to gather their belongings, along with a few supplies for their journey. For the sake of their own safety, they left without saying farewell. They had arrived without fanfare, and it made sense to leave the same way.

Dannah had learned that the road between Thesmis and Cambrick intersected the main road to Sengin, just south of the capital. She planned to head toward Cambrick for a while before cutting southwest across country. That should allow them to join the road to Sengin further from the capital.

A full moon faintly illuminated their way, driving away the darkness of the night. Just ahead of them a farmer was walking along beside a horse and cart. He was probably on his way to market. The road was otherwise deserted.

Rounding a corner she spotted a group of riders not far ahead of them. To her alarm, some of them were clearly soldiers.

"Walk faster!" she hissed. "We're too conspicuous on our own."

Marielle followed her instructions without hesitation. Quickly catching up to the farmer, they trailed along silently behind him.

The riders eyed them curiously as they passed but didn't interfere with them. Several of the men and women in the group wore the garb of mages. Fortunately for the fugitives, none of the party seemed able to detect glimmer.

Unsettled by the encounter, Dannah was considering leaving the road sooner than she had planned. The farmer interrupted her musings.

"Would you like to ride in the wagon?" he asked.

Noticing the hopeful look on Marielle's face, she decided to accept his offer.

"Thank you. We are grateful to you."

Clambering up, they settled down as best they could. Marielle somehow managed to doze as they bumped and bounced along. Sleep eluded Dannah. Through Kylen she had learned she would be regarded as a renegade in Periton. If her identity as a mage become known, she would be hunted down. She had chosen to come anyway.

She sighed. All her life she had lived on Abbethar. Now it felt distant to the point of seeming illusory.

With the first glimmers of dawn lighting the sky, they climbed down from the wagon and thanked the farmer. As soon as he was out of sight, they left the road and headed southwest as near as Dannah could tell it. At first their path led across open fields, and they made good time. The sun came up, spreading a golden glow across the countryside.

After continuing in the sunshine for a couple of hours, they paused to rest.

"I could never have imagined so much open space existed in the world!" Marielle exclaimed. "Abbethar seems impossibly small by comparison."

Dannah smiled grimly. "And I could never have imagined so many sick people living in poverty."

Marielle's brows drew together. "I don't know what's come over you, Granny! I've always seen you as such a cheerful person!"

"Kylen's arrival changed all of our lives," she returned, her mention of his name bringing a frown to Marielle's face.

Dannah didn't fail to notice it. "Have you forgiven him for doubting your motives?" she asked.

"Back on Abbethar, I honestly doubted I ever could," she replied frankly.

"And now?"

Her face twisted in a grimace. "I'm not sure." After ruminating for a few moments, she raised her hands helplessly. "His world is very different from ours. I can see there might be reasons why people here are more suspicious." Then her eyes narrowed. "It doesn't excuse him, though!"

Dannah laughed. "You're certainly a more entertaining companion than Aleira would have been."

Marielle was not impressed. "It isn't kind of you to laugh at me, Granny!"

"I'm not laughing at you, Elle. I'm enjoying you!" she insisted. "In any event, it's time for us to get moving again."

Resuming their journey, they quickly left open fields behind. Their forward progress slowed dramatically as a result. After plodding over rough ground, crossing streams, and climbing hills, they were forced more than once to backtrack. Night fell without them having made it as far as the road to Sengin.

To their relief, the terrain became markedly less challenging the following day. As the sun was rising high they came upon a road. A seemingly continuous stream of people trudged northward toward the capital, overflowing the road and spilling onto the verges. Apart from occasional complaints when someone got in their way, the travelers were mostly silent, no doubt wearied by their long flight from danger.

They had found the road they were seeking.

Dannah didn't doubt that many of the refugees before her would welcome a healer—there would never be any shortage of needy people in the world. But she refused to let herself be diverted. It was time to find Kylen.

Moving against the flow soon proved impossible. There simply wasn't room for a different stream of traffic. "Why would you want to head south?" was a common refrain. "It isn't safe there!"

"We need to wait until nightfall," she told Marielle. "We're attracting too much attention."

Choosing a suitable location, they rested until the sun set once more. Then they traveled south until the sun began to rise.

A motley group of travelers had camped overnight just ahead of them. Eager for news, Dannah chose a place on the fringes of the campsite to settle.

Before long they were joined by a boy and a girl of around fifteen or sixteen years of age.

"You two seem to be heading in the wrong direction," asserted the boy with a grin.

"Only soldiers are going south," added the girl helpfully. "Just in case you hadn't already noticed."

"You must be searching for someone!" they concluded in unison, laughing in delight at their flawless timing.

"Perhaps we can help," the boy offered seriously.

Dannah was too taken aback to respond.

Marielle was a different matter. "Even if we were looking for some-one, what makes you think you would know them?"

"Ah, I detect an accent!" said the girl brightly. "You're not from Periton. Or Tantel, either."

Dannah didn't like where this was going. "Thank you for your offer, but we don't need your help."

The boy turned to her. "And you *don't* have an accent!" he told her. "That makes you a local." He leaned forward conspiratorially. "Unless you're a mage."

"And more particularly, one with mage hearing!" added the girl with a wink.

Dannah's unease must have been obvious, because both of their faces lit up at once. "You *are* a mage!" they said, once more in unison.

"Please! Keep your voices down," whispered Dannah, thoroughly alarmed.

"Follow me," the boy replied in an exaggerated whisper. He led them to a secluded location in a stand of trees. Once there, he eyed them shrewdly. "You're trying to keep your mage identity secret, and you're not wearing a mage's robe. That means you're a renegade!" He didn't give Dannah time to deny it. "But no matter. Please pardon my manners—we haven't introduced ourselves. My name…"

"Is Jonno," Marielle finished for him. "And you must be Bella," she added, turning to the girl.

The astonishment on the faces of the pair brought even Dannah a moment of satisfaction. For a little while she was able to put aside her alarm at being so easily exposed as a mage and a renegade.

"I'm flattered to know our names are spoken of in foreign lands," said Jonno with a theatrical bow.

"More than just your names. Some of your more outrageous exploits have been reported as well," Marielle returned dryly.

That only seemed to please them more. "Your source was clearly an intelligent and knowledgeable person. May I ask who it was?" Bella ventured.

Marielle had divulged too much information already, but Dannah was too late to stop her.

"I heard it from Kylen," she replied.

In a season of surprises, what happened next topped them all. Two people appeared, literally out of nowhere. One was a middle-aged man and the other a young woman.

"When and where did you have contact with Kylen?" the man asked sharply.

Dannah held up her hands. "Enough! Far too much has been said! We are complete strangers. Who are you, and why should we answer your questions?"

"I will gladly introduce myself if you will do the same," he said. When she nodded tightly, he continued. "My name is Dalthinir. And this is Trisanna. We are mages, and renegades, too, thanks to the inflexibility of the Compact. You have already been introduced to the twins."

The information came as no surprise. "My name is Dannah," she told them, "and this is my granddaughter, Marielle. Both of us are mages."

"I am aware that you are mages," he replied. "I am able to detect glimmer."

"And the moment Marielle identified your twins, I knew the two of you would be around somewhere as well," she returned, unwilling to be outdone.

"Where are you from?" he asked.

"Unfortunately I am not at liberty to tell you."

He stared at her for a moment. "I would still very much like to know when and where you connected with Kylen."

"And I would be grateful if you could tell me where he is right now," she retorted.

"If you've been with Kylen, why don't *you* know where he is?"

She stared back at him unyieldingly. It simply wasn't possible to answer his questions without compromising Abbethar's secrets.

He seemed to reach a decision. "Why don't you come with us? Spending time together might help us learn to trust each other. We have a haven where you would be safe."

She shook her head. "I thank you, but we didn't come here to hide away somewhere safe."

"I wonder if you are aware of the extent of your peril. You will be killed without mercy if you are caught."

"I understand the risk. But we've been in the kingdom for quite some time, and no one has interfered with us yet."

He sighed. "Perhaps you see it as a remarkable coincidence that the twins approached you. The truth is that I asked them to find out who you might be. Your glimmer was shining like a beacon."

He whispered to Trisanna, and all of the others abruptly disappeared—not just Dalthinir, Trisanna, and the twins, but Marielle as well. Dannah spun around in a panic, searching for any sign of them. Then, just as suddenly, they were back.

Dalthinir's face was wearing a grim smile. "We don't entirely bury ourselves away in our haven. We have become adept at masking both our physical appearance and our glimmer. It allows us to move about freely without fear of being discovered. Won't you come with us?"

The pleading look on Marielle's face tugged at her resolve, but she shook her head firmly. As she'd already told Dalthinir, they hadn't come to Periton to hide from danger. She'd seen the plight of the disadvantaged herself now, and she couldn't just walk away. Further, they'd been sent there to find Kylen. Wherever he was, it clearly wasn't with Dalthinir and his friends.

Dalthinir didn't hide his disappointment. "If you are intent on searching for Kylen, you won't find him in Sengin."

"How can you know that for certain?"

"His glimmer is well known to me. You will, however, most certainly find Compact mages there. I briefly spoke to one of them myself. I am sure that at least one of his companions will be capable of detecting magical auras."

She shrugged. "We will manage somehow."

"Then I bid you farewell," he said sadly. After a quick nod to Trisanna, the four of them vanished. This time they didn't reappear.

Marielle was staring uncertainly at her. "Are you sure this is the right decision, Granny?"

"We'll discuss it later," she said firmly. "Sometime when we're less likely to have invisible people eavesdropping on our conversation. For now, let's make the most of the opportunity to rest."

Both of them sat quietly, although it wasn't a comfortable silence. For all Dannah's insistence on independence, Dalthinir's visit had shaken her. The situation in Periton was different in ways she hadn't expected. The mages there might have been much less advanced in their healing techniques, but they were clearly capable of things she hadn't imagined. Some of her own mage colleagues would be able to achieve similar tricks with illusion, of course. She was less certain about masking glimmer.

None of it was surprising. The Peritonian renegades had long been under sentence of death, and the kingdom itself was now facing the prospect of invasion. Conflict, or the threat of conflict, had never failed to foster innovation. Her own people had demonstrated that.

MASTER KOTHLAR FROWNED IN IRRITATION. He had sent a message to Adrastas urging him to ride south as a matter of priority to discuss the Tantellan situation. The chief master had been in a foul mood from the moment he reached Kothlar on the road to Sengin.

To be fair, traveling south must have been very challenging, even when accompanied by King Durvaryn's soldiers. Kothlar had long since decided he should have returned to Cambrick before speaking with Adrastas.

"The renegades want us to forgive them in return for their help if it comes to an invasion? Any such suggestion is ridiculous!" growled the head mage. "It's not even worth considering!" He scowled at Kothlar. "And it came from *Dalthinir* of all people! I don't even want to guess what he might do if he was suddenly free to wander the kingdom. Even talking to a renegade is treason! It doesn't say much about your clearheadedness. What were you thinking?"

Kothlar had no intention of pandering to Adrastas. "I was thinking the time has come to reconsider our pointless vendetta against people who've done nothing to harm the kingdom. For years we've spent time and energy trying to track them down, and for what? We never get a glimpse of them unless they allow it to happen! Continuing to waste resources, especially at a time like this, doesn't say much about *your* clearheadedness!"

Adrastas, who had never been entirely predictable, chose to calm down rather than escalate the dispute. "These are trying times, and I'm going to pretend you never said any of that."

"Pretend what you like, Adrastas! All this riding plays havoc with my lower back. I'm going for a walk, even if it means limping. And I'm going on my own!"

CHAPTER 21
ABBETHAR

Lokan was standing on the rocks at the water's edge gazing out to sea when the islanders finally tracked them down. Alerted by a confusion of loud voices from the direction of their crude shelter, he hid himself at once, hoping to avoid them entirely. However, they must have quickly realized that Buck had not been alone, because the hunt was up almost before he could blink.

He quickly saw it would be impossible to elude them for long. And the longer he tried, the more it would be seen as confirmation he had something to hide.

He therefore decided to risk turning himself in. In spite of everything he had heard, he found it hard to believe the islanders would simply kill him out of hand. After all, neither Buck's interpreter nor Buck himself had actually been executed.

With that in mind, he headed boldly back to the shelter. Incredibly, he was able to reach it without being detected. He found Buck sitting there under heavy guard.

Intruders swarmed around him the moment he arrived. Taking a deep breath, he submitted to a search. They made no attempt to be gentle, and he began to wonder if he'd made a mistake. Their continuous flow of harsh interrogation only added to the strain, especially when he couldn't understand a word of it.

Eventually they decided he represented no immediate threat, because they allowed him to join Buck.

With two prisoners now in hand, the islanders' vigilance was increased. Guards armed with swords and heavy sticks took up positions on every side.

They did at least allow the castaways a degree of freedom within the confines of the shelter.

"Apparently we won't be going anywhere for a while," Buck observed. "Are you hungry?"

Lokan stared at him in astonishment. "You seem remarkably unaffected by the situation!"

Buck's brows drew together. "I wouldn't exactly say that. But I *was* ready for a change." He waved a hand around the shelter. "This isn't my idea of home. We can't get away from this island, and I'm tired of hiding."

"Even if we end up dead?"

"Ah, it never helps to be grim. Let's try to stay hopeful!" Smiling genially, he held out some food.

Lokan refused it. The idea of eating held no appeal to him. Not when his insides were twisted in knots.

THEY REMAINED idle for two days, during which time they were given very basic supplies and expected to prepare food for themselves. At the end of that period, they were taken to an open space not far from the water's edge where a large tent had been erected. They discovered a group of eight people waiting for them.

The arrangements baffled him. It seemed inefficient to bring a large group to a remote location. Why hadn't they been taken to wherever the larger group came from?

One particular member of the group was apparently known to Buck, who nodded to him politely. Lokan guessed it was the interpreter he'd met previously.

The group members were seated comfortably. The castaways were not offered seats—they were expected to stand.

One of the group members spoke briefly, and an interpretation was provided immediately by the man recognized by Buck.

"We know a great deal about you already," he told Buck. Nevertheless, they proceeded to question him for the best part of an hour. Most of their questions dealt with the period before Lokan had arrived. Buck had given him a summary of these events. They were now re-examined in excruciating detail.

The most aggressive of the questioners was a man with a prominent double chin. Double Chin regarded Buck as an unlawful intruder, and he didn't hide his animosity toward him. On occasion even the interpreter seemed uncomfortable with the tone and content of the questions.

Curiously, Buck seemed untroubled by it all.

Eventually the questioners redirected their attention to Lokan. "Who are you? What is your purpose in coming here to join this man? And why are you trespassing on our sovereign territory?"

"My name is Lokan. I am from Tantel. We were sailing past the island during a storm, and I fell from the ship." He pointed to Buck. "I only survived because he dived in and rescued me. I knew nothing of him before then."

Double Chin now focused his entire attention on Lokan, staring at him with narrowed eyes. "Why was your ship sailing past this particular island?" he demanded.

"We sailed past many islands," he said with a shrug.

The islanders muttered among themselves for a considerable period. Double Chin in particular had a lot to say. Finally the interpreter said, "They think you are lying."

"About what?" he asked.

"About your presence on this island. They believe you had a purpose in coming here."

Lokan lowered his gaze. They were right, although he didn't dare acknowledge it.

"Who sent you?" demanded Double Chin.

"I wasn't sent here by anyone. I was merely sailing past the island."

"Why didn't your shipmates rescue you?"

There was no need to be evasive this time. "I don't know," he replied despondently. "I've been asking myself the same question."

"Are you a sailor by occupation?"

After pausing momentarily to assess his options, he shook his head. They would almost certainly expose his lie if he pretended to be a sailor.

His hesitation was not lost on Double Chin. "If you are not a sailor, what were you doing on a ship?" he pressed.

"I was accompanying a friend."

"What friend? What was their purpose?"

"He is a sailor, and he was giving me a taste of his daily life." He knew the response sounded feeble, but it was the best he could manage under pressure.

Having steered him into dangerous waters, the interrogator continued pressing. "Why would anyone put the life of a friend at risk in such a way?"

It was a good question, and Lokan had no ready answer.

Double Chin leaned forward eagerly. "If you're not a sailor, then what is your occupation?"

Once again, he couldn't safely tell them the truth. "I am a carpenter by trade." Carpentry was at least a hobby of his. Hopefully that meant he could answer questions with some degree of credibility.

"What kind of carpentry do you do?"

"Cabinet making."

"Do you work for yourself or for someone else?"

"For myself."

"How many items do you make in a typical week?"

"Between five and ten," he replied. He had plucked the numbers from nowhere, hoping they sounded plausible.

Double Chin smirked. "So many! You must be a remarkable worker!"

Lokan kept his face passive, but inside he was squirming. His improvised answers were not compelling, and he knew it.

His heart sank further the longer the interrogation dragged on. Lies had a way of breeding energetically, and his explanations had been slowly but inexorably unraveling under Double Chin's deft questioning.

He felt like his credibility was in tatters by the time the meeting finally broke up. Refreshments were served to the interrogators. Lokan and Buck were led away and given a drink of water.

They were not called back after the break. The interrogators were apparently locked in conference, no doubt deciding what to do with the two intruders.

Lokan did his best not to think about their impending fate. Sitting down, he tried to rest while he had the chance.

Buck was staring fixedly at the sky. "Those clouds look unusually threatening," he observed. "And they're moving in remarkably quickly."

Glancing upward, Lokan was filled with alarm. He was no expert on the weather, but his experience in Brynford told him a major storm was headed in their direction. The wind began to howl, and glancing seaward he saw whitecaps covering the ocean. Drops of rain began falling—big drops that felt unusually heavy when they landed.

"We need to get under shelter! Now!" he shouted to Buck.

He managed only a few steps before guards raced in and threw him to the ground. He lay there unresisting, looking upward anxiously as the storm increased in intensity.

Before long the guards had more to worry about than the prisoners. The ropes mooring the tent briefly resisted the wind, but the strain soon became too great. The structure was doomed the moment one corner of the tent tore loose from its ropes. Filling like a sail, it burst its bonds. In an instant it swept upward and out of sight.

One guard attempted to run inland. Blown off his feet, he collided with a tree before collapsing to the ground senseless. From that moment, no one dared to stand. Escape was out of the question for the prisoners, and the guards focused solely on their own survival.

Hail began to fall, the largest stones exceeding a walnut in size. Lokan and Buck were soon subjected to a series of dangerous and painful blows from the missiles. Guards and interrogators were no less vulnerable.

Huge waves were now thundering in, crashing onto the rocks and hurling spray well beyond the water's edge. Drenched and miserable, the fugitives cowered helplessly, shivering in the gale-force winds. A monstrous wave towered above the rocks before smashing down over them. A second wave quickly followed, then a third. The fourth was the biggest of all.

Crouching beside a large bush, Lokan hung onto its trunk grimly, resisting the backwash sucking him seaward.

Not everyone was so fortunate. Looking on wide-eyed, he saw an islander pulled relentlessly toward the ocean. As the man was swept past, Lokan caught a glimpse of his face. It was Double Chin, his smug self-satisfaction replaced with abject terror.

When all appeared lost for the interrogator, an arm shot out and grabbed him. His unlikely rescuer was Buck. Himself anchored to a sapling that was bending dangerously, the castaway was hanging on grimly as he resisted the pull of the water. Noticing Lokan nearby, he called to him urgently. "Help us!"

Lokan cared nothing for Double Chin, but he owed Buck his life. Diving toward his friend, he grasped his leg with one arm while hooking the other around a small tree. He couldn't have timed it better. Almost at the moment he took a firm grip on Buck, the sapling snapped. His support alone prevented them from being washed away.

Abruptly the pressure eased as the water receded. More waves continued to roll in, but none matched the size or ferocity of the first few breakers. After helping Buck to his feet, he joined him in dragging Double Chin to safety. A couple of guards, themselves disheveled, appeared and took charge of him.

"You need to take him further inland," instructed Buck, waving a hand to illustrate. They must have taken his meaning, because they did it at once.

Lokan couldn't pretend he didn't have mixed feelings about saving the man most set against them. He was honest enough to acknowledge that without Buck's prompting he wouldn't have put himself at risk to do it.

Buck was an enigma. He must surely have known it was Double Chin, yet he acted without hesitation. He seemed to make a habit of rescuing people—he had now been responsible for saving at least three lives, Lokan's included.

The storm continued to rage, but its intensity had diminished. Lokan guessed they could take advantage of the confusion to get away, but where could they go? They had no way to escape from the island, even if it were safe to do so during a storm, and he knew of nowhere they could hide. In the end, he decided the only real option was to wait for events to unfold.

Once the storm had abated, the guards gradually resumed their duties. Their attitude had undergone a transformation. All of them were aware that one of their own had been saved by the prisoners. Their determination to keep their island hidden from the world remained intact, but any trace of personal animosity toward Buck and Lokan had vanished. As a result, the prisoners were offered the same food and drink as the others and treated with consideration.

More than once the interpreter asked Lokan if he had any desire to make his home on the island. It raised a dilemma for him. He knew what the islanders wanted to hear, but he was reluctant to pretend he wanted to stay when he had no such intention.

Barely a day had passed when the situation changed dramatically. Reports from some new arrivals quickly had the other islanders in an uproar.

"What do you think has happened?" Lokan asked Buck.

"Something very bad, you can be sure of it," his companion replied soberly.

"What does it mean for us?"

"Now *that* is a worthy question," Buck replied. "I imagine we'll find out soon enough."

CHAPTER 22
TANTEL

Woken before dawn and ordered to report to the king, Kharkin arrived in the royal reception room to find the king already there, seated beside the young northerner known as Deemis.

"Ah, Kharkin." The king waved him airily to a seat. "What did your search of the archives reveal about the islanders?"

"I found no reference to them in the archives, Your Majesty."

The king snorted. "That's hardly surprising since you didn't spend even a minute in the archives. You've wasted your time listening to sailors and their tall tales!"

After too many years of enduring the king's barbs silently, Kharkin found this latest irritation more than he could endure. "Why bother asking questions if you already know the answers?"

His stomach began to twist the moment he said it. He'd gone too far.

To his astonishment, the king burst out laughing. "Now you can see why I prize our head mage so highly, Deemis. He provides me with my most reliable source of amusement!"

The face of Deemis was unreadable. "Perhaps the head mage used his time wisely, Your Majesty. It's hard to imagine anything being documented about Abbethar. The Artoran exiles are much too careful."

So the island had a name.

Kharkin stared curiously at his unexpected defender. "What can you tell me about the mage abilities of these Artoran exiles?" he asked Deemis.

"Such matters are no longer relevant," interjected the king. "Not now I have leverage. If they refuse to settle with us, it can be used against them."

"May I inquire about the nature of this leverage?"

"We have taken possession of an artifact held by the Artorans," replied Deemis casually. "I understand they stole it when they were fleeing their homeland."

"What is its origin?"

"It is draconic in origin."

"You mean it's a talisman?" Kharkin leaned forward, unable to mask his curiosity.

"It is more than that!" gloated the king. "It is the source of the extraordinary mage powers of the islanders. As of now that power is denied them."

It occurred to Kharkin to wonder how the king could be certain of such statements. He was not a mage, and neither was Deemis. And if the object was a talisman, why had his own talisman failed to reveal it? Was it somehow able to conceal itself? Or did it obey a different set of rules?

He almost licked his lips, so great was his desire to get his hands on it.

"What is my role in these matters, Your Majesty?" he asked, as casually as he was able.

"Look at you, Kharkin!" chortled the king. "You're practically drooling!"

Biting back a retort, Kharkin succeeded this time in holding his peace.

"Don't expect to get your greedy fingers on it," warned the king. "For the moment, giving it to you is going to be nothing more than a threat. That should be enough to keep the Artorans in line."

"What does this have to do with invading Periton?" asked the chief master boldly, sensing an opportunity to discover what had motivated the recent behavior of the king.

"Ah, at last you're beginning to ask questions that matter," the king told him. He waved a hand dismissively. "I have grown increasingly tired of the provocations of the Peritonians. Their supposed kingdom has never been more than a breakaway province. The issue should have been settled long ago! Pernilla and her team were the very best among our mages. Sending them to Periton provided a perfect opportunity to explore the kingdom's weaknesses. Instead, by one means or another the Peritonians managed to dispose of them all. It is an alarming development that cannot be ignored!"

He fixed Kharkin with an angry stare. "You did nothing to prevent her failure! You were a hindrance at best!"

Putting aside his irritation, Garneth nodded toward his new advisor. "Deemis arrived at an opportune time. The information he provided has allowed me to put these matters into a broader perspective. We find ourselves facing a cunningly concealed people group with outrageous ambitions. In confronting the Artorans, we also have the opportunity to settle scores with Periton, thereby righting both an ancient wrong and recent provocations."

He smirked. "The artifact changes everything! Retrieving it was possible only thanks to Deemis." He aimed an indulgent nod in his direction.

"The islanders have just sent two emissaries to negotiate its return. They are undoubtedly mages. I want you to observe them closely. I need to know what powers they have access to."

Kharkin's brows drew together in bafflement. Magical powers could not be detected simply by observing a mage. Was it possible the king didn't understand that? Taking a deep breath, he reminded himself that raising questions would only lead to trouble. He limited himself to a tight nod.

"You will, of course, assemble a team of your most powerful mages and make sure they are ready to intervene at a moment's notice. If these islanders try anything, I want them dealt with immediately. Do you understand?"

Kharkin nodded again.

"Get to work, then! Report back to me by noon. And be aware that this time I will hold you personally accountable if your team fails to do their job!"

USHERED ONCE MORE into the royal reception room, Kharkin was surprised to find himself alone with the king. Deemis was nowhere in sight.

Garneth seemed impatient. "Is your team on hand?"

He nodded. "Eight mages are on high alert outside, Your Majesty. They are led by my deputy, Jaizor. If either one of us calls for assistance, they will be here in an instant."

The king nodded in satisfaction. "Bring in the foreigners," he called to an aide.

Two people were led into the room—a male in older middle age and a slightly younger female, both dressed simply in white garments. Their skin tones were not noticeably different from Tantellans, and he wondered if the effect was natural or the result of illusion. Whether or not they were using mage taste to alter their appearance, hints of magical power flowed about them. Perhaps they were shielding themselves for their own protection.

After all of them were seated, the foreigners introduced themselves.

"I am known as Rydel," said the man. "I have been sent here as senior emissary of our people."

"And I am Tana," said the woman. "I am acting as deputy to my colleague."

Neither of them exhibited the faintest trace of an accent, suggesting that, like him, they were mages with mage hearing ability. It made sense that such people would be chosen as foreign emissaries.

"I am King Garneth, and this is Kharkin, our head mage," replied the king loftily. "You speak of your people. Where are you from?"

"We live on an island," Rydel replied, waving a hand vaguely northward.

The king eyed them smugly. "More precisely, you are Artoran exiles who live on Abbethar," he declared.

Something flashed across the faces of the foreigners before they schooled their expressions. Had it been fear?

"Since you seem insistent on being direct, King Garneth," said Rydel, "we will be direct as well. You have in your possession an object that belongs to us. We have been sent to retrieve it."

"What makes you so certain that I have it?" asked the king indifferently.

"We have been aware of its precise location from the moment we accepted stewardship of it."

"Accepting stewardship sounds noble. I was told you stole it when you fled your homeland."

"Who told you such falsehoods?" demanded Tana, her face flushed with anger.

The king didn't answer. It was becoming clear to Kharkin that his leverage over these people was real.

"Calm yourself, Tana," murmured the man. He spoke in a foreign language, presumably his mother tongue. Kharkin's mage hearing ability allowed him to understand perfectly.

"If you are here to negotiate, then let us not waste time," said the king.

"What is it you want from us?" asked Rydel.

The king's face turned hard. "I understand you have designs over Tantel. And Periton as well."

"You are mistaken," insisted Rydel. "We wish only to live in isolation."

Garneth snorted. "And yet here you are!"

"You have forced this visit upon us by stealing the object we have protected for so long," replied Tana, more calmly this time.

"I understand that this object is the source of your greatest powers," suggested the king.

"You have been misinformed," Rydel replied flatly. He chose not to elaborate. "If you wish to receive a formal undertaking that we will respect the independence and sovereignty of your kingdom, we have been authorized to provide it."

"In return for what?" asked the king.

"In return for the object, of course."

"It's going to take a lot more than that," the king told them bluntly.

"What else?" asked Tana.

"I have a rebellious province that needs to be brought to heel."

"You want us to help you annex Periton?" asked Rydel.

"If you insist on putting it bluntly, then yes," Garneth replied with a sneer.

"We have not been authorized to offer military assistance," the senior emissary returned.

"For your sake, I hope you've been authorized to offer more than words!" exclaimed the king. "I'm not asking for soldiers. I'm interested in arms, materials, and naval transport! I want mages spreading throughout Periton, causing confusion and tying down resources."

"We are willing to offer exchanges of knowledge," the Artoran replied. "We could train your healers in advanced techniques."

The king snorted dismissively. "How do you know these techniques are not already familiar to us?"

The woman glanced at Kharkin. "I'm sure your head mage must have access to Tantel's best healers. Yet he has chronic arthritis. I would say that answers your question."

Kharkin stared at her in surprise. How could she know about his pain?

The king scowled at her. "I'm not interested in having you waste time fixing people with sore backs, even if you could do it. Perhaps I need to arrange for our head mage to spend time with your precious object. He might be able to figure out your techniques for himself."

Alarm registered on the faces of the emissaries. "Don't do that!" they pleaded.

"I'll give you four weeks," the king told them flatly. "Come up with a proposal that has teeth, or it will be the last you see of your toy."

The faces of the emissaries were grim. Nevertheless, as they stood to leave Rydel offered a conciliatory bow to the king. The king turned away without acknowledging the gesture.

At the same time, Tana extended her hand to Kharkin. Seeing no reason to reinforce the king's snub, he took her hand and briefly shook it. She was vulnerable and far from home, and he didn't imagine for a moment she would try to harm him.

She surprised him by gripping his hand firmly and holding it for a lingering moment. Then, with a sigh of weariness, she released him and turned away to follow her colleague from the room.

Stunned speechless, Kharkin stood watching them go. Then slowly he began to move about, testing his limbs with exploratory movements. As far as he could tell she had healed his arthritis completely.

He belatedly noticed the king staring at him.

"Is that an attempt at dancing, Kharkin?" he asked sarcastically.

"I'm testing my back and my limbs. She appears to have just healed my arthritis!"

Garneth rolled his eyes. "Only a fool would trust people like these!" he scoffed. "If you were stupid enough to let her do something to your body, it won't have been anything good. You'll be lucky to be alive in the morning!"

For reasons he couldn't articulate, Kharkin didn't share his cynicism. "Time will tell," he replied evenly.

The king betrayed no further interest in his health. He hadn't quite finished with him, though. "What mage powers do they have?"

"Both of them have mage hearing. Their lack of an accent made that clear. At one point Rydel also spoke to Tana in their own language and told her to calm down. I have mage hearing too, so I understood it. She is also a healer, which means she has mage touch abilities. It is possible one or both of them used mage taste abilities to alter their appearance, although I can't be certain. It's less easy to tell what other abilities they might have."

Garneth seemed satisfied. "Don't go far, Kharkin. I might need you again. You are dismissed!"

The head mage left in a daze. For once the king didn't seem annoyed with him.

More incredibly, his joint pain had vanished entirely. He felt ten years younger.

∼

THE MOMENT they returned to Abbethar, Tana set out with Rydel to meet with the community elders. It was a subdued group that received their report.

"The Tantellan king knows more about us than I would have believed possible," Rydel told them.

"He has the relic, too," added Tana. "He doesn't understand what it is, but that won't help us if he lets his mages play with it."

"What will it take for him to give it back?" asked one of the elders. "The consequences of it being misused could be catastrophic, and not just for us!"

"We offered him goodwill exchanges," Rydel replied. "He had no interest in them. He wants us to help him conquer Periton."

The report was greeted with incredulity. "That's ridiculous!" an elder exclaimed. "Even if we were willing and able to do it, why would this king think he'd be safe? We could go after him next!"

"He thinks he can use the relic to force us to comply with his demands," Tana replied.

"He isn't completely stupid," one of them growled.

The muttering subsided as they absorbed the news. It wasn't long before questions began to flow again.

"Who is it who betrayed us?"

"We have no idea."

"Whoever it is will pay if we catch them!"

"Could it be that boy, Kylen?"

Rydel shook his head. "It can only have been someone intimately connected with us. This king knows far too much about us and our history."

"Could he have captured Dannah?"

"She went to Periton, not to Tantel," Tana replied. "And he strikes me as the kind of person who would have paraded her in front of us if he'd captured her."

"Why did we let her go in the first place?" groaned one. "She could still be captured by the Peritonians!"

"The situation couldn't be worse than it already is!" said another impatiently. "What are we going to do about this king?"

"We could send a team to try to get the relic back."

"That sounds incredibly risky—at every imaginable level!"

"Perhaps we should consider doing what he wants," one of them suggested.

Tana shook her head emphatically. "He is not the kind of person who would return the relic, even if we submitted to his demands," she assured them.

"And make no mistake," added Rydel grimly. "Once he had subdued Periton, we would be next."

Everyone went silent.

"You should let them know what you did at the end of the meeting, Tana," prodded Rydel.

She shrugged. "Their head mage had chronic arthritis, so I healed him."

Several of the elders were incredulous. "What were you thinking?!"

"I was thinking that a bit of goodwill can't hurt," she replied sharply.

"None of us doubt your intentions, but it's hard to predict the consequences of an action like that!"

"The king didn't strike me as a person who would honor an act of goodwill," Rydel told them. "Perhaps the head mage is different."

He sighed. "In any event, the king has given us four weeks to respond to his demands. It took us the best part of a week to get back to Abbethar, so that doesn't leave us a lot of time."

CHAPTER 23
PERITON

Weaving her way among the crowd of refugees, Dannah spotted a man wandering alone on one side of the press of people. From the lines on his face he might have been bearing the troubles of the world on his shoulders. From the way he was limping, he had more immediate problems on his mind.

Normally, Dannah would have hesitated before approaching a lone man in an unfamiliar environment, but with so many people about and Marielle at her side, there seemed little reason to fear for her safety. And something about him stirred her compassion.

She approached him calmly. "I can't help noticing your limp. I might be able to help. Would you allow me to examine your back?"

"It's a kind thought," he replied. "Unfortunately, the best healers in Cambrick have been unable to do anything for me."

"Would you be willing to let me take a look anyway?"

After eyeing her uncertainly for a moment, he shrugged. "Very well. You're not the first refugee to offer me a home-grown remedy, and I don't suppose you can do any harm."

"Thank you," she said with a nod.

"I suppose I should thank you," he replied. A careworn smile came to his face. "For some reason, displaced people seem more ready to help each other."

Positioning herself beside him, she placed a hand on his lower back, closing her eyes to block out distractions. After a couple of minutes she withdrew her hand and stood back, breathing heavily.

He stood wide-eyed for a moment, then he began bending and flexing his leg energetically. "The pain is gone!" he said, a look of complete astonishment on his face. "My leg and my lower back haven't felt like this for years! How did you do that?"

Before she could answer, a large group of people approached, talking loudly and paying little attention to where they were going. Stepping away to avoid them, she found herself separated from him. Seeing no reason to prolong the contact, she grasped Marielle's arm and took the chance to slip away.

Brief as the healing had been, she felt overcome with weariness. She wanted only to find a quiet place to rest.

Spotting the chief master at last among a small group of mages, Kothlar hurried up to him.

"Adrastas! I'm still finding it hard to believe, but my leg pain isn't troubling me anymore!"

Before he could comment further, they were interrupted by Pellistri.

"I'm sorry to intrude, Chief Master," she said. "I've just detected two other mages in the group of people around us. I don't recognize their glimmer! I thought you'd want to know."

Adrastas threw up his hands. "They'll be Tantellan spies," he exclaimed, shaking his head in disgust. "It's just what I needed! I want them brought to me. Kaspra and Ellis and Ramond can take the lead. All of you need to be careful! There's no way of telling what their abilities might be."

As she left to do his bidding, Adrastas glared at Kothlar with narrowed eyes. "Before you say a word about these mages, be aware that I refuse to even consider the possibility that two more renegades are loose in Periton!"

DANNAH KNEW they were in trouble the moment people began surrounding them. It was too late to make any attempt at escape. A glance at Marielle revealed she had seen them too.

A woman not many years older than Marielle approached them.

"She has a magical shield," whispered Marielle.

"I'm aware of it," Dannah returned calmly.

The woman seemed tense and uneasy. "Could you both please come with me?" she asked.

Dannah stared back at her, willing herself to remain calm.

"Who are you?" she returned politely. "My name is Dannah, and this is my granddaughter Marielle."

"My name is Kaspra," the other woman replied tersely, apparently untouched by Dannah's gentle approach. "Please come quietly."

Dannah got to her feet, doing her best to appear non-threatening. A glance at Marielle showed her no more at ease than the other woman. Reaching out, she squeezed her granddaughter's arm reassuringly.

The last thing Dannah wanted was to put them in danger. Perhaps she shouldn't have been so quick to refuse Dalthinir's offer.

She thrust the thought aside. There was no time for regrets.

As they followed Kaspra, she noticed a sizable group of people swinging in around them. All of them seemed alert and on edge. What were they afraid of? Surely they had no knowledge of Abbethar and the capabilities of its mages.

Kaspra led them to two men. One of them was the man whose lumbar pain she had just healed. The other one radiated hostility.

The man she had helped was staring at her intently. He didn't seem to know what to say.

The angry one had no such hesitation. "Who are you, and what is your purpose in Periton?" he demanded, glaring at the two women.

"My name is Dannah, and this is my granddaughter, Marielle."

"Let her answer for herself!" he instructed curtly.

Marielle had never been one to allow such behavior to intimidate her. "My name is Marielle, as my grandmother already told you," she retorted.

Dannah sent her a warning glance. This wasn't the moment to be making points.

"The granddaughter is clearly not from Tantel, which is curious," announced the angry one.

The man she had helped addressed himself to Dannah. "I am Master Kothlar, and I am pleased to meet you both," he said respectfully. "I, too, am interested to hear your answer to our chief master's other question. What has brought you to Periton?"

So the hostile one was the head of the Peritonian mages. Not a good person to have as an enemy. And these people had apparently been expecting to find themselves confronted by Tantellans.

"You will not be surprised to hear that we are healers, Master Kothlar," she replied. "We have no unfriendly intentions toward Periton."

The chief master was slowly nodding, his eyes narrowed. "You match the description of two mages who have been operating without authorization near Thesmis! I sent people to bring you in, but you evaded them!"

"Why should it be illegal to help people who need healing?" Dannah asked reasonably.

"Helping people sounds very altruistic. But where do you come from, and what is your real purpose?" he asked scornfully.

Instead of answering, she turned to Kothlar, her eyebrows raised inquiringly. "How is your limp?" she asked.

"I have no pain at all in my lower back, and I'm able to move my leg freely," he replied, shaking his head in wonder. "I am very grateful to you! How were you able to heal it?"

"It is the result of many years of training and experience," she said simply.

"You might *appear* to be better," said Adrastas. "Time will tell. In any event, these two renegades are under arrest! They have been wandering around using mage abilities without authorization. Who knows what damage they have done?"

"No one I've treated has complained," she said mildly. "Perhaps you have a medical condition of your own, Chief Master. I would be willing to help if I can. Then you can see for yourself if I'm helping or causing damage."

"Do you think I'm stupid?" he retorted. "I won't be letting you anywhere near me!"

"That is your privilege, of course. I have never imposed healing on anyone." She raised her hands helplessly. "Even if I did heal you it might not help. Perhaps I am mistaken, but I doubt there is anything I could do or say to diminish your hostility."

"She has a point," acknowledged Kothlar. "Your mind was made up before you met her."

"It's very simple," growled Adrastas, "We have strict laws in Periton about renegades. Even if she did heal you, it changes nothing." He glared at Kothlar. "Whose side are you on anyway?"

"Why does it have to be about taking sides?" asked Dannah.

Adrastas laughed bitterly. "Perhaps you are not aware that Periton is facing an invasion!"

"I have heard that news. I hope an invasion never eventuates!" She smiled sadly. "But surely there is room for hope when we face the future. Why must the unknown always be something to fear?"

"High sounding words. Hopelessly impractical in my experience." He glared at her. "You still haven't told us where you come from. You're clearly determined to evade the question, and don't think I haven't noticed!"

He was right, of course. She had indeed been working hard to deflect the question.

She couldn't continue to dodge, and nothing would induce her to betray her people. Recognizing she was out of options, she clamped her mouth shut.

～

Kothlar and Adrastas didn't have to wait long before being admitted to King Durvaryn's reception room.

The king seemed restless and preoccupied. "What news do you

have to report?" he asked. "Does anyone have a clear idea what the Tantellans are up to?"

"I am afraid we have very little new information about the Tantellans, Your Majesty," replied Adrastas. "We have, however, taken into custody two foreign mages. They refuse to tell us where they came from."

"Foreign? Do you mean Tantellan?"

"It seems unlikely."

"Why is it unlikely?"

"One of them has an accent that none of us recognizes."

"That's curious! What were they doing? Have they harmed anyone?"

Kothlar decided it was time he injected some reality into the conversation. "They are healers, Your Majesty. A woman and her granddaughter. The granddaughter has an accent. The woman probably has mage hearing, which means she can speak our language as if it were her mother tongue. Before we apprehended them, the woman healed my limp."

"She healed you?" repeated the king. He sounded surprisingly eager.

"She did," he affirmed. "You might have noticed me limping at times. I've experienced pain in my leg and lower back for many years. On occasion it has become debilitating. Now the pain is completely gone."

"It's all very peculiar!" exclaimed the king. "Why did they choose this moment to come to Periton?"

"We have no way of knowing," replied Adrastas, clearly impatient to reinsert himself into the conversation. "But whatever their reasons, they are renegades, and Your Majesty can rest assured that they will be dealt with accordingly."

"You mean you're just going to execute them?" The king sounded alarmed.

"That is what the law requires," asserted the chief master calmly.

"Not until I approve it!" the king insisted. "There could be broader implications. I want to interview them before any action is taken. In fact I would like to see them immediately. Arrange it at once!"

Adrastas clearly wasn't happy, but he dipped his head in acknowledgment.

After they had left the king, Adrastas turned on Kothlar in frustration. "Even the king is going soft on us. And you were no help at all, Kothlar!"

"Perhaps the king simply dislikes executing women who've done nothing to deserve it," he replied evenly.

"The king has no say in it!" growled Adrastas. "By law it's the responsibility of the Compact to deal with rogue mages, foreign or not."

On their way to the holding cells where the two women had been imprisoned they spotted Pellistri. Adrastas told her to locate Kaspra and Ellis and instruct them to report to the prison. She hurried away at once.

They arrived to find Kaspra and Ellis there already. It was apparent to Kothlar that they had been talking with the prisoners. They appeared embarrassed when they saw the chief master. That could only mean their interaction with the prisoners had been friendly.

Adrastas glared at them. "These two are going to be interviewed by the king, and it will be your responsibility to guard them. Entertaining as you might find it to fraternize with them, I'd advise you to remind yourselves that they are renegades. If your negligence results in any harm to the king, you will be in serious trouble!"

The two mages looked suitably chastised. They appeared unusually alert as they escorted the two women to the king.

After they were shown into the royal reception hall, the king wasted no time. "I understand you are both healers."

They both bowed respectfully. "We are, Your Majesty," Dannah replied.

"Are you from Tantel?"

"We are not."

"From somewhere in Periton?"

"No."

"Then from where?"

Neither of them offered an answer.

"In your homeland, is healing more advanced than it is in Periton?"

Dannah glanced expressionlessly at her granddaughter for a moment, but she finally nodded.

"She healed my limp in a couple of minutes," Kothlar offered. "My lower back pain is gone completely. Our best healers were never able to help me."

"Is this true?" the king asked her.

"It is, Your Majesty," Dannah confirmed.

"What are your names?"

"I am Dannah."

"And I am Marielle. I am her granddaughter."

"Are both of you experienced healers?"

"I have many years of experience, Your Majesty," Dannah replied. "My granddaughter is young, but her skills are advanced for her age."

"Very good. Then I want you to heal my son, Crown Prince Firan."

The request provoked a mixed chorus of astonishment and alarm from the Peritonians.

"Your Majesty!" protested Adrastas. "With respect, how can you place your son in the hands of these people?"

"They healed Kothlar, didn't they?" he retorted. "Why should Firan be denied an opportunity?"

Adrastas would have said more, but the king got in first.

"My son will be expected to take the throne one day," he told the two women. "In view of his disability that will be a difficult challenge, perhaps even an impossible one. There will be significant implications for him and for the kingdom. I will be greatly indebted to you if you can help him."

"How old is he, and what is the nature of his disability, Your Majesty?"

"He is nine years old. When he was five, he became sick with a severe fever. His health was normal before the fever—the problems began only after he had recovered. And he isn't getting stronger as he ages. He's getting worse."

"What are his symptoms?" asked Dannah.

"Whenever he's active he becomes short of breath. He can't even climb a flight of steps without a rest. He also suffers from chest pain.

His heart often beats faster than it should, and his feet swell for no reason."

"What have your healers done?"

"Nothing! After examining him, they told us they have no way to help him."

The king's distress was painful to see. Kothlar had known for some years that the prince was not well, but he had never understood the true severity of his condition.

The king must have become desperate indeed to be so willing to put his son in the hands of unknown healers. Could Dannah help the prince as she had helped him? He would like to think so, but Firan's condition sounded considerably worse than his lower back problem.

"Can you help?" asked the king.

"I think I understand what might have happened," Dannah replied. "There may be something we can do, but until we examine the prince we can't say anything with certainty."

The king turned to his aides. "Bring Crown Prince Firan here at once!" he commanded.

Dannah was conversing quietly with her granddaughter, her face betraying no discomfort. By contrast, the younger woman appeared restless and unsettled. Kothlar could draw only one conclusion: both of them knew that healing the boy would be anything but straightforward, and only Dannah was able to conceal her uncertainties.

The look on Adrastas's face made it clear he was indignant about this turn of events. Things would end very badly for the healers if they were unsuccessful. It wouldn't be good for Kothlar, either. His report of his own healing had encouraged the king to place expectations on Dannah.

A tight knot began twisting his stomach as he considered the possible scenarios. Failure wasn't the worst of the potential outcomes. What if their efforts led to a deterioration in the prince's condition, or worse, his death?

The implications were too unsettling to contemplate.

CHAPTER 24
PERITON

Dalthinir reluctantly led his friends away from the two foreign mages. Glancing at Trisanna, he saw her looking as uncomfortable as he felt.

"Shouldn't we stay with them, at least for a while?" she asked. "Just to make sure they don't get into any trouble?"

He shook his head firmly. "Dannah made it clear she didn't want to come with us. And we have no business snooping on them."

"Where to next, then?" asked Jonno.

"I think it's time we returned to the valley. The others will be starting to worry about us."

For all his references to the others, the person uppermost in his mind was Inga. He'd been away from her for too long, especially considering her current state. He set off immediately, his companions trailing along behind him.

"Dalthinir has a spring in his step," observed Jonno. "Could it be he's eager to see someone again?"

"He's been missing getting up to milk the cows before dawn," Bella replied, her voice betraying no hint of irony.

Ignoring them, Dalthinir led them forward. They were following a course parallel to the main road, although thanks to Trisanna they would have been invisible to the travelers trudging wearily northward. He wondered if King Garneth was truly about to invade. If not, the refugees were fleeing for no reason.

His thoughts returned to the two women they had just left. Who were they, and why did they want to see Kylen?

The others were clearly thinking about them as well. "I can't believe Dannah and Marielle had actually heard of us! We're famous!" chortled Bella. "Where do you think they met Kylen?"

"I've been wondering about that," replied Trisanna. "The main thing is that he is alive, wherever they met him!"

"What I want to know is how they managed to lose him," said Jonno.

"It seems he left without telling them," suggested Dalthinir. "I wonder if they parted as friends."

"They must surely be his friends if they know about all of us!" exclaimed Bella.

"I don't think we should assume that," said Dalthinir.

Trisanna was frowning. "Are you suggesting he didn't tell them about us willingly?"

"Or do you think they were friends, but they had a falling out?" added Jonno.

"We can only guess," Dalthinir replied with a shrug. "Dannah and Marielle seemed like nice people, but there are things they're hiding. They weren't willing to answer some of our questions."

"I wonder where they come from," said Jonno. "They're clearly foreigners. Are they from somewhere across the sea?"

"I imagine Kylen could answer these questions," Dalthinir replied. "If he's in Periton, he'll try to find us."

"He won't know where to look!" said Bella.

"No. But we'll find each other somehow."

Having set his face toward home, Dalthinir couldn't get there quickly enough. More than anything, he wanted to be with Inga again. At the same time, all the talk about Kylen had unsettled him. Could he dare to believe that Kylen had not only survived the last few months, but had recovered enough to be wandering around Periton? Such outcomes were more than he had dreamed possible.

If his former apprentice truly had survived, what had become of him? Where was he, and why was he being hunted by Dannah and Marielle? What did they want with him?

Even when Dalthinir had faced crises he'd always managed to find a way forward. At that moment he was conscious only of bewilderment. Perhaps it was because anything involving Kylen still left him paralyzed. Even after all this time he was not entirely free of his guilt.

Until he could draw upon Inga's wisdom, he wouldn't be willing to consider a course of action.

Evening had fallen by the time they crossed the border. Moving to a nearby stand of trees, they ate simply before settling for the night.

"I'm weary, Dalthinir. Do you think we need to worry about staying invisible?" Trisanna asked.

"It's unlikely we'll encounter anyone here," he replied. "I'll continue to hide our glimmer just in case. But I think you can allow yourself some rest. You've earned it."

Dalthinir himself had no difficulty getting to sleep.

He woke to a knee pressing painfully on his chest. Before he could orient himself, he felt something tightening around his neck.

"Hello, Dalthinir," sneered a voice that chilled him to the bone. "I bet you weren't expecting to see me again."

The pressure around his neck almost prevented him from replying. "What do you want, Lars?" he gasped.

"What do I want? I want you to suffer before you die! You made it your life's work to bring me down. Now it's your turn! I'm going to repay you in full."

Dalthinir turned his head in an attempt to locate his companions.

"No use calling for your friends," taunted Lars. "They ran off the moment they saw how things were. Perhaps they're scurrying off to your little valley to get help." He snorted. "They'll soon discover they're wasting their time. If anyone actually was fool enough to stay in the valley, they'll be insane by now."

A wave of panic assaulted Dalthinir. Overcome with fear for Inga and the others, he twisted violently in an attempt to break free. He immediately began to choke. Reaching for his neck, he discovered a noose around it.

"Settle down, Dalthinir! I'm not quite ready for you to die. Not yet!"

Calming himself with an effort, he settled back into his previous position. The pressure eased—enough for him to breathe again.

"Clever little contrivance, isn't it?" offered Lars, no doubt warming to the delights of a truly captive audience. "I was fortunate enough to bump into your friend Agalar a few weeks ago. I found out about the noose from him. He let it slip one night when he was unburdening himself. It was all I could do to endure his self-loathing. It was nause-ating! The fool was no help at all when I started making one. He even tried to stop me! I would have ended his miserable life there and then if he hadn't resorted to illusion. I'm still grateful to him, though, because he left in such a hurry he forgot to take his special cloak—the one that masks glimmer. It's heavy and it's uncomfortable, but I won't deny it's been extremely useful."

Ignoring the ramblings of his captor, Dalthinir focused on his mage touch abilities. He tried to entrap Lars in a shield. The noose immedi-ately began choking him again.

"Don't bother trying to use magic! You're wasting your time," gloated Lars. "Your friend in the valley was very obliging about handing over his talisman. They truly are wondrous relics! I'm sure I don't need to tell you it has seriously boosted my abilities. Your best efforts will be puny by comparison!"

Lars paused in his ranting. "Get on your feet!" he commanded. "I have a nice little place waiting. It will be more than suitable for the entertainment I have planned. Move!"

Pushing himself to his feet, Dalthinir stood motionless. Yanking the noose viciously, Lars propelled him forward.

METHESIA

TRISANNA STOOD by helplessly with the twins as Lars subdued Dalthinir. She had protectively wrapped all three of them in an illusion, hiding both sight and sound.

"So he thinks we've run away. I'm more than willing to correct him!" growled Jonno.

"Don't do anything foolish!" warned Trisanna. "He'll only take it out on Dalthinir."

They exchanged uncomfortable glances as Lars dragged Dalthinir away. "I'll follow them," said Jonno. "We need to know where he's taking Dalthinir!"

"That isn't a good idea!" countered Trisanna. "Sooner or later he'll see you! If he catches you it won't go well either for you or for Dalthinir. I'm the only one who can follow them safely!"

"We need to get back to the valley!" said Bella. "Sorren's in trouble, which means the others are in trouble, especially Inga!"

"Yes, the two of you should go!" agreed Trisanna. "There isn't a lot I can do for them. You will be much more useful."

Jonno hesitated for a moment, but he agreed, if reluctantly. Once he'd made up his mind, he didn't wait around. The twins were out of sight within a few minutes.

Taking a steadying breath, Trisanna set off after Lars and his captive.

KYLEN STOOD GAZING at the horizon beyond the hidden valley. He was so absorbed he completely missed the approach of Inga.

"You seem far away, Kylen," she said gently. "Is there someone in particular on your mind?"

Feeling himself reddening in response, he ran a hand over his face while he recovered himself. "I'm grateful to the dragon for taking me to the one place where I could have been healed. Out of respect for their privacy I can't say any more than that."

She nodded, waiting patiently for him to continue.

"I understand why the dragon brought me here, and I'm not sorry I came, especially after what happened to Sorren."

"You clearly learned a lot about healing while you were away. The change in his condition is beyond remarkable!"

He nodded. "I'm happy I could do something to help."

"You've done a lot more than that. Without the protection of Sorren's amulet we couldn't have remained here. We were frantically preparing to leave, and I'm not sure how we would have managed it. I have no idea where we would have gone."

She gazed at him quietly. "Rescuing us came at a cost to you, didn't it?"

He shrugged helplessly. "My departure wasn't well timed. It was awkward in more ways than one."

"Was there a girl involved?"

He saw no reason to deny it. "She hates me," he said, grimacing.

"So you were friends, but something went wrong?"

He stole a glance at her, but didn't respond.

"It may not be quite what you think." Her mouth quirked up in a wry smile. "My Dalthinir says there are times when women seem as mysterious as dragons."

He stared at her. "Is it worth it?"

She understood what he was asking. "Completely!" she replied emphatically. "The only thing Dalthinir regrets about our relationship is that he left it unresolved for so long. As for me, I've never been more content than I am now."

"I don't think I'll ever figure out how to get beyond my past mistakes," he told her glumly.

"That isn't solely up to you," she told him. "Dalthinir made his share of missteps, but I was prepared to forgive him."

"Why did you?"

"Because I wasn't willing to settle for dull predictability."

Seeing the puzzled look on his face, she continued. "Anyone who embraces love takes a risk. If you love someone you can get hurt. It might not be anyone's fault—even if the person you love never betrays you, death can snatch them away. Life is unpredictable."

"Dragons have a way of snatching people away," he mumbled under his breath.

"There is an alternative, of course. If you close the door entirely on love, you can protect yourself from the pain of loss. Life will be less unpredictable if you lock your heart behind a wall. But there's a price to be paid. Eventually your heart will shrivel up and become hard. I've seen it happen, and it isn't pretty."

He didn't respond.

Her lip curled up in a smile. "If you'll take my advice, Kylen, don't hide behind walls. Be willing to live life to the full, even if it gets painful at times."

THE CONVERSATION with Inga had left Kylen restless. He couldn't go anywhere, though. Not with everyone in the valley depending on his talisman for protection.

If he was honest, he felt trapped. Dalthinir's return wouldn't release him, not when he didn't have a talisman of his own.

He badly wanted to see Dalthinir, though. And the twins and Trisanna. Where were they?

Almost as if his thoughts had summoned them, a shout rang out. "Is that the twins?"

His spirits soared. An age had passed since he last saw them. He hurried toward them.

He arrived to find both of them gasping, their faces red from exertion.

Inga wasn't far behind him. "Is Dalthinir with you?" she asked anxiously.

"He's been captured by another mage!" Jonno eventually managed.

"The one who stole Sorren's talisman!" panted Bella.

"Do you know who has him?" asked Kylen urgently.

"His name is Lars. He's planning to kill Dalthinir," she exclaimed.

Kylen felt the blood drain from his face. He knew what Lars was capable of.

"Trisanna has gone after them," Jonno added.

Kylen couldn't sense Lars's glimmer. Perhaps he'd found a way of masking it. But there was another way of locating him. Closing his eyes for a moment to concentrate, he belatedly sensed the other talisman. He realized it had been niggling away, like an itch somewhere in his magical awareness. Having focused on it, he could sense it flickering like a distant lamp. He knew exactly where it was, although it was slowly becoming fainter.

If he wanted to find Dalthinir, he needed to move quickly.

"I have to go!" he told them. "You'll manage without the talisman for a while. Just make sure none of you goes to sleep!"

With that he was gone.

VOLUME 3—CONSEQUENCES

CHAPTER 25
METHESIA

Dragged along relentlessly, Dalthinir cast about in his mind, desperately trying to assess his options. His current prospects seemed dismal. Now that Lars had stolen Sorren's talisman, he could not expect help from anyone in the hidden valley.

The magically shielded noose around his neck closely resembled the one he had removed from Kylen's neck. However, surreptitious examination had revealed one small difference. The noose designed by Agalar had featured a thick knot in the rope just below the slip knot, too thick to pass through the slip knot's loop. It limited the degree to which the noose could be widened. By contrast, the loop in the slip knot fashioned by Lars was slightly larger than on Agalar's original version. Further, the thick knot in the rope had apparently tightened once Lars began pulling on the rope. It might be possible to pass the knot through the loop, allowing the noose to be removed from his head.

It offered Dalthinir at least some hope of ridding himself of the diabolical contraption. If Lars ever allowed him enough slack on the rope, he would make the attempt. Thus far he had seen no sign of such a lapse.

Of course nothing was stopping him from grabbing the noose with both hands and trying to widen it before Lars could prevent him. Even if he succeeded in removing it, though, it might not help. There had been a time when his magical power exceeded that of Lars. But the talisman would have tilted the balance of power away from him. Every mage took a vow not to use magical power against other creatures, but Lars had long since cast off any such restraint. He would undoubtedly welcome a raw clash of power, knowing his captive would be incapable of overwhelming him.

Dalthinir could only bide his time in the hope that circumstances might change—enough to allow him an opportunity to escape.

They had traveled for a little over an hour when Lars turned aside from the road and headed inland. Hidden away in a wooded dell lay a dilapidated farmhouse, surrounded by spindly pines. Approaching it, Lars opened the door and stepped inside. Tugging on the rope, he forced Dalthinir in after him.

"Sit down!" he said, shoving his captive into the remains of an old armchair.

Making sure the rope attached to the noose never left his hand, Lars discarded his heavy cloak. "Ah, it's a relief to get rid of that! It was a donation from Agalar, not that he was happy about it. I needed it to hide my glimmer from you. But it's a burden I no longer require."

Retrieving food from a pack that lay in a corner of the room, Lars began to eat.

"I'm sure you won't mind waiting," he said, his mouth so full of food Dalthinir could barely understand him. From the noise he was making, he might not have eaten in days.

"It's hungry business waiting," he continued. "I'd offer you some, except it would be a waste considering you won't be around long enough to benefit from it."

He scowled at his captive. "You didn't make it easy for me, Dalthinir! After I located you—I can thank Agalar for leaking that information, too—I had to keep going back to the border to sleep. Until I acquired my new toy, of course." He fingered the talisman he had stolen from Sorren. "Once I had it in my possession, I was well able to protect myself. From Agalar's tales I could visit Ettaran and gaze upon its glittering wonders!" He spread his hands wide before dropping them suddenly. "Whatever's left of them. But no. Nothing matters more than greeting an old friend!"

His twisted smile vanished. "I've been through dark days and difficult times, and all of it thanks to you! And I'm not even referring to the torture of enduring Petria and the royal castoff she likes to think of as her lover. But a single hope sustained me through it all—the anticipation of revenge!" A leer contorted his face. "And here we are! Happy days have come! If only Banadin had lived to see it!"

Desperate as his own situation was, Dalthinir pitied him. "And what will you do next, Lars? It won't only be the Compact chasing you now. You'll be on the run from every renegade you've injured or stolen from. What friends do you have to turn to?" He shook his head grimly. "You should have gone to Ettaran. You'd be safe there. You could eat dust while you search for forgotten loot among the crumbling buildings."

Lars burst out laughing. "Ah, Dalthinir! You missed your calling in life—you should have been a court fool! Why has it taken me this long to see it?" He sobered suddenly. "But your question is a good one. Once I've settled scores with you, I *will* need a new purpose. Perhaps I'll turn my attention to the idiots you call friends hiding away in their cozy little valley. If they've survived. It will be enjoyable to take them down one at a time. They'll soon be watching their backs, but it won't save them."

Dalthinir ground his teeth in helpless fury.

His obvious discomfort filled Lars with delight. "I imagine that will keep me busy for some time! After that, who knows? Maybe I'll give some attention to Adrastas. He's long overdue for it!"

His face set hard. "Enough talk. It's time for some action."

Getting to his feet, he lunged suddenly at Dalthinir, a knife in his hand. He was wasting his energy. Dalthinir's shield turned the knife aside before it could penetrate his skin.

"Well done!" gushed Lars.

At that moment the door swung wildly open, crashing into Lars's back. He must have been anticipating something of the kind, because the door bounced off a shield of his own. It had no more impact on him than his knife had on Dalthinir.

"I can see this is going to be fun," Lars enthused. "I should warn you, though. I've been planning this a long time. And unlike you, I have no scruples." As he was speaking, a large lump of wood flew up and collided with the back of his victim's head.

Even with a shield in place, the force of it momentarily shook Dalthinir. Before he had fully recovered, a second lump of wood pounded against his chest. He dimly became aware that the floor of the little dwelling was littered with such objects. They flew at him in a relentless stream, pummeling every part of his body.

Lars was not content with subjecting Dalthinir to the merciless aerial assault. At the same time he began pulling the noose ever tighter until his victim was struggling to breathe.

Dalthinir did his best to distract his tormentor. He managed to loosen the noose by throwing himself at Lars. The maneuver also resulted in Lars being hit by some of his own missiles. Dalthinir followed it up by causing the rotten floorboards to crumble beneath Lars's feet, sending him tumbling to the ground.

They were minor successes, and they did no more than buy him a little time. Before long he was hurting all over and gasping for breath. If he didn't come up with something soon, the struggle would be over.

Then abruptly the battering stopped. Dazed, he peered at his attacker, barely able to focus.

"Don't go to sleep on me, Dalthinir," chided Lars. "You wouldn't want to miss any of the fun! We're only just getting started!"

KYLEN WAS BARELY OUT of sight of Inga and the twins before it became clear that running was not an option. His body simply hadn't recovered enough to make it possible. Refusing to give in, he put his head down and plodded on determinedly as fast as he was able. An impossibly short time passed before he was forced to stop for a rest. At the rate he was going it would be too late by the time he reached Dalthinir.

"Where are you, Elef'nissar?" he called despairingly.

He shook his head in exasperation. The dragon couldn't hear him, and it wouldn't respond even if it could. Marigold might have been foolish enough to believe the dragon came in response to her call, but he knew better.

He had to press on. Ignoring the protest from his limbs, he set off again, only too aware he would be stopping again soon—long before he could afford to.

The months of recovery on Abbethar had taken a toll. While his bones and his internal organs had slowly been healing, his muscle strength had deteriorated significantly. His fitness had eroded to the point where he was no longer capable of sustained strenuous activity. Even though he knew exactly where to go to find the talisman held by Lars, he was no longer capable of getting there in a reasonable time frame.

It abruptly occurred to him that his mage touch ability might allow him to speed up his journey. Why couldn't magic lighten his body weight and compensate for his weakness?

Drawing upon his earlier experience when lightening a boat, he applied the same technique to his body. He took a small step, then a bigger one. The impact on his body was noticeably lower. Encouraged by the outcome, he launched himself forward in a giant leap. It was exhilarating until he landed. Overbalancing, he crashed to the ground.

Refusing to be deterred, he tried again with ever smaller leaps. The result was always the same. He could shield himself from injury when landing, but he couldn't manage to keep on his feet.

Successive attempts convinced him of two things. First, for a mage with a normal level of fitness, mage touch had astonishing potential to accelerate travel by foot. Second, mastering the technique was out of his reach. With enough time and practice, he might eventually succeed. If ever he did, his talisman would ensure a never-ending supply of magic.

He wasn't optimistic about the prospect of eventual success. Learning to do it would be like learning to walk all over again.

Bowing his head in defeat, he almost failed to notice the giant form gliding down to land beside him.

Elef'nissar had come.

~

HIDDEN FROM SIGHT BY ILLUSION, Trisanna watched the assault on Dalthinir through an outside window. She was so affected by it that her body began to shake uncontrollably. Her every instinct urged her to flee. But she couldn't do it. Not if there was any chance she could find a way to help him.

Dalthinir's shield had kept him alive, even if only just.

It was hard to believe the cruelty with which Lars pressed home his attacks. Dalthinir had been bludgeoned, attacked by clouds of metal needles, crushed by magical shields, and even doused with water from huge tubs. Lars had been unusually creative, to the point where Trisanna could no longer keep track of the range of attacks he had made. Dalthinir had been hard pressed, constantly needing to adjust his defenses in an attempt to protect himself effectively.

Lars's magic was flowing freely, and he showed no sign of tiring. He had the amulet to thank for that.

Dalthinir's magic was not unlimited, and Trisanna felt sure the moment was approaching when it would fail completely.

She could no longer allow herself to watch helplessly. The time had come to act. Wrapping Dalthinir in an illusion, she made him invisible to anyone apart from herself.

The assault paused, and Lars glared angrily around him. Seeing no one, he shifted his attack to the immediate area around the dwelling. Small logs began flying through the air, smashing windows and threatening injury or death to anyone unprotected by a magical shield. Without mage touch, Trisanna had no such barrier to rely on. In an attempt to escape the incessant hail, she threw herself to the ground.

Fearful and distracted, she was unable to sustain her illusion. As a consequence the assault on Dalthinir resumed in full force.

Then suddenly it stopped once more.

Daring to steal a glance through the shattered window, Trisanna saw Lars in confusion. He was groping about the room as though he were blind. Somehow finding the door, he emerged into the open. His blundering was almost comical to watch. He lost his footing wherever the ground was uneven, bumped into trees, and flailed his arms in an attempt to touch what he couldn't see.

In a rage, he initiated a new rain of wooden projectiles, forcing

Trisanna to the ground once more. He himself was occasionally struck by one of his own missiles, although his magical shield easily protected him.

After a few minutes Lars fully regained his senses. He glared about, eager to locate the person responsible for his previous blindness.

Trisanna saw the mage before he did. To her astonishment it was Agalar. He was lying nearby, having apparently been felled by a large log. She hastily wrapped him in a new illusion before Lars spotted him. How he had managed to confuse Lars so successfully was not clear to her, but it was obvious he had done it to protect Dalthinir. That was reason enough to help him.

"No more distractions!" growled Lars. "It's time to finish this!"

She watched in alarm as he strode purposefully back into the cabin.

CHAPTER 26
METHESIA

With Kylen enclosed in its talons, Elef'nissar swept its mighty wings and rose majestically into the air. After remaining airborne for mere moments, they glided down to a small dwelling nestled among pines. The dragon had taken him directly to the stolen talisman.

Kylen sensed magic swirling freely inside the building. A mage was pouring out power, boosted by a talisman. The twins had correctly identified him as Lars. Kylen had first smelled his power when Lars tried to open the forbidden book in the Drakkenridge Mountains.

Dalthinir, too, was using power, and it was dangerously weak.

Bursting through the door, Kylen spotted his mentor and friend huddling on the floor, pounded remorselessly by flying lumps of wood. Immediately strengthening Dalthinir's shields, he turned his attention to the attacker.

The smell of his power was known to Lars, too, but the rogue mage showed no sign of being able to see him. Then Kylen sensed a third source of power, one he recognized as Trisanna's. Realizing she must be hiding him, he wasted no time taking advantage of her protection.

Lifting Lars bodily with mage touch power, Kylen flung him heedlessly out the door. Then, ignoring him completely, he lifted Dalthinir by the same means and bore him carefully from the building. After setting him down behind a tree well clear of the dwelling, he turned to find Lars peering around uncertainly, trying to see his attacker.

The sight of a noose around his mentor's neck had enraged Kylen, and he was in no mood to be gentle. Wrapping a shield around the head of Lars, Kylen sealed it against the passage of air.

Lars lashed out furiously, sending a variety of objects flying about. A couple of them struck Kylen. Heavily shielded, he brushed them aside with contemptuous ease.

Time had run out for Lars. Slowly turning blue in the face, he lapsed into unconsciousness.

Before he could suffocate entirely, Kylen released his head from the shield. Then he moved to the fallen mage, removed the stolen talisman from around his neck, and flung it away in anger.

Hurrying back to Dalthinir, he found Trisanna helping him to a sitting position. The older mage was bruised and battered, but still very much alive.

"Kylen! So it's true. You are alive!" Dalthinir managed.

Tears rolling freely down his cheeks, Kylen embraced his old mentor. "I'm sorry I didn't get here sooner, Dalthinir!"

In response Dalthinir slapped him weakly on the back. He still wasn't ready to stand, and Trisanna and Kylen sat down beside him.

"I see you had some help getting here," said Dalthinir, gazing wonderingly at Elef'nissar.

The dragon had remained, watching the proceedings impassively.

Trisanna nodded toward Lars. "What are we going to do about him?" she asked.

"He does present us with a problem," said Dalthinir quietly. "He'll never quit. I don't think he's capable of leaving the past behind."

"Keep supporting Dalthinir, Kylen," said Trisanna. "I need to check on Agalar."

"Agalar?!" exclaimed both Kylen and Dalthinir simultaneously.

The Tantellan suddenly winked into view. He was sitting up, looking dazed. In his hand was the talisman.

"Don't let him keep that!" Kylen called to Trisanna in alarm.

"I don't think you need to be too concerned about him," she replied calmly. "I hid him for his own protection. He was defending Dalthinir against Lars."

Kylen helped Dalthinir to his feet and they slowly joined her at Agalar's side.

Dalthinir frowned down at him. "You told Lars about the noose," he said accusingly.

"I did," admitted Agalar. "I was a fool for ever mentioning it. I never imagined he would make one, much less that he would use it against you!"

"He told me you tried to stop him," acknowledged Dalthinir.

"I did, and he almost killed me! I only escaped by using illusion. When he left I tailed him. I followed him all the way to your valley. I knew I would bear a large part of the blame if he used the noose against anyone."

"When he was attacking Dalthinir you managed to stop him, at least for a while. How did you do it?" asked Trisanna.

"I wrapped him in an illusion that hid everything from him apart from himself. It was a risky move, but it worked. He couldn't see Dalthinir or anything around him. When he started sending wood flying everywhere, he got lucky. I was using all my available power on the illusion, and without protection the wood knocked me out."

Kylen hadn't forgotten Agalar turning against him in Ettaran. He poked a finger toward the talisman now in Agalar's hand. "That belongs to Sorren," he said pointedly.

"Please return it to him," said Agalar readily, surprising Kylen by handing it to him.

Trisanna interrupted them, pointing. "Lars is up to something!"

Having regained consciousness unnoticed, Lars had gone into the dwelling. He emerged with a burning torch, a vengeful glare in his eye. Kylen couldn't begin to guess what new evil he was about to unleash.

Stepping purposefully toward them, Lars caught sight of the dragon. Coming to an abrupt halt a few paces from the building, he stood rigid, a look of dread on his face. Whether or not he had believed the creatures to be extinct, he wasn't ready to face one.

"Do you dare stand in my presence, lawbreaker?" roared Elef'nissar.

The rogue mage was shaking with terror. Nevertheless, he had enough presence of mind to draw back the torch and throw it mightily in their direction. Then he hurriedly retreated toward the building.

As Kylen set out, too late, to shield himself and his companions, two things happened simultaneously. The torch erupted with a deafening boom, spewing fire at them. At the same instant a shield blocked the flames mid-flight, redirecting them away from the wide-eyed onlookers. The shield could only have come from the dragon.

The barrier created by the shield directed the full force of the blast back to Lars. Knocked from his feet, he fell backward through the open door of the building as rivers of fire showered the little dwelling and splashed over him. Apart from a strangled shriek of agony there was no further sign of him.

Smoke quickly billowed from the windows while flames licked hungrily over the roof. The fire had become a raging inferno. Engulfing the dwelling, it spread to the surrounding trees. The fierceness of the heat forced the little party to move well clear of the area.

The dragon, enigmatic as ever, eyed them dispassionately for a brief moment. Apparently seeing no further reason to remain with them, it called, "Fare well," taking wing before Kylen or Trisanna could respond.

The mages huddled together, watching it disappear into the distance and trying to make sense of everything that had happened.

"It was terrifying when the dragon roared at Lars!" said Agalar.

"It didn't roar," said Kylen in surprise. "It spoke to him."

"It sounded like a roar to me, too," said Dalthinir. "It's what Lars would have heard as well. He didn't have mage hearing any more than I do."

After they had rested for a while, Dalthinir got up. "I'm ready to try to walk now, and I'm eager to get back to Inga."

The others stood as well.

"What are you planning to do, Agalar?" asked Trisanna.

He shrugged helplessly. "I can't say. I have nowhere to go."

"He might as well come with us," said Dalthinir. "He's told us he already knows where the valley is, so there's no benefit to anyone from leaving him behind."

No one objected, so they began the long walk back toward the valley. Kylen could barely manage the slowest of paces, but the others seemed content. All of them offered him an arm to lean on whenever he might need it.

He was left to ponder the dragon's involvement. In addition to transporting him to the scene of the action and terrifying Lars, it had shielded them all at a critical moment.

Why had it responded to his cry for help, and how had it known where he needed to go? Surely it wasn't spending its time monitoring the affairs of a renegade.

Or was it? Did it happen to glance in his direction at the right moment, or was it following an agenda of its own?

Supposedly dragons were prohibited from interfering with humankind. Yet the more he saw of Elef'nissar, the less credible such claims appeared.

Perhaps Elef'nissar would describe its actions as involvement. If so, there was a fine line between involvement and interference.

Waiting for news about Dalthinir had been harrowing for all of them. Vennia was trying to remain hopeful.

Inga was working hard at remaining calm, but the uncertainty had been taking its toll. "How could we have been so careless?" she groaned. "We knew Lars was still out there somewhere! All this time he must have been plotting his revenge on Dalthinir!"

"Dalthinir isn't alone," Vennia reminded her. "Trisanna followed them, and now Kylen has gone to help."

"But will Kylen get there in time? Lars's magical ability was always weaker than Dalthinir's, but he has the talisman now!" She covered her face with her hands.

All of a sudden, Trisanna ran into view. By then Vennia had almost given in to despair herself.

Having reached them, the young mage bent forward with her

hands on her knees, sucking in air. As soon as she was capable of speech, she called, "Dalthinir is safe! All of them are! And Lars won't ever be harming anyone again." She paused for breath before calling, "Jonno, could you please get the donkey cart? Kylen can't walk quickly, and Dalthinir needs to rest."

Tears of relief immediately began rolling down Inga's face. When Jonno brought the cart, she prepared to climb into it, intent on going with Trisanna.

"It won't be at all comfortable, bouncing around in that old thing," Vennia told her. "Think of the baby!"

Inga looked at her uncertainly before reluctantly agreeing.

Before Trisanna left, she leaned down and spoke quietly to Vennia. "We're bringing Agalar with us."

"Agalar! He's got a lot of nerve coming back!" spat Vennia.

"He wasn't helping Lars," Trisanna assured her. "He followed him to try to stop him hurting anyone. He did his best to protect Dalthinir."

"Even so, why would you want to bring him here?!"

"He has nowhere else to go. And he knows where we are now anyway."

Sorren had appeared while they were talking. "Let him come, Vennia. I don't mind."

Vennia stared at him, frowning and shaking her head. When she said nothing further, Trisanna set off with the cart.

"How can you accept him here?" Vennia asked her husband. "He's responsible for what Lars did to you!"

"If he tried to stop Lars, there may be hope for him," Sorren replied. "I'm going to forgive him, and I need you to do it as well."

"Why should either of us forgive him?" she demanded. "He doesn't deserve it!"

"No, he doesn't. But I'm not going to let him and what he's done dominate my thoughts and feelings for the rest of my life. It isn't going to happen! There are better things for me to focus on. There's only one way I can be free, and that's to forgive him. And I want you to do the same."

It was incredible. How could he let go so readily after what had been done to him?

Deep down she knew he was right. She decided she wouldn't be outdone by her husband.

THE WAIT FELT LIKE FOREVER, but eventually Trisanna returned, bringing Dalthinir, Kylen, and Agalar in the cart.

Inga was almost beside herself with relief when Dalthinir arrived, whole and happy if somewhat battered. She thanked each of his companions sincerely, even Agalar. Then she led Dalthinir away, insisting that Kylen join them.

Trisanna headed to the stables with the donkey, mobbed by the twins and Marigold. All three of them were showering her with questions.

Agalar remained. He turned slowly to Sorren. "I'm responsible for what happened to you, and I'm sorry," he said, hanging his head. "Kylen has the talisman now. You can have it back!"

Sorren smiled sadly. "I will never be a mage again, Agalar. My inner being was torn apart when Lars took the talisman. I couldn't function at all before Kylen arrived. He got me back on my feet again, but the damage was too severe to repair. Having a talisman isn't an option now."

Agalar paled. For a few moments he seemed unable to speak. Finally he found his voice. "If there is anything at all I can do to repay you, I will gladly do it."

Sorren nodded. "Thank you," he said simply.

KYLEN HAD BEEN curious to see what kind of reception Agalar might receive. The Tantellan was known to everyone except Inga, and he hadn't endeared himself to any of them by his actions in Flaxendell and Ettaran. Nevertheless, Kylen had witnessed a gradual change in him on the journey to the Methesian capital, and his efforts to protect Dalthinir suggested he had become a different person. Willing to give him another chance, Kylen found himself a little apprehensive about how he would be received by the group.

Trisanna must have told the twins everything that happened, because it quickly became apparent that they regarded Agalar's situation as a challenge worthy of their attention.

"Agalar!" said Bella admiringly. "Trisanna tells us you created an illusion so Lars couldn't see anything except himself."

"Impressive indeed!" agreed Jonno. "If you can do it to Dalthinir whenever we ask, all will be forgiven for my part."

Dalthinir snorted. "My life might be a lot easier if you did it to the twins once in a while," he retorted. "A few unfortunates might get to keep their hard-earned possessions, and I might get to keep a bit of my hair!"

The ensuing laughter did a lot to break the ice.

As soon as he found a private opportunity, Kylen offered the talisman to Sorren.

"It's no good," Sorren told him. "You've already done everything that's possible for me. I've accepted the situation."

"I'm sorry," said Kylen awkwardly.

The outcome didn't surprise him. The dragon had evaded the question when he asked directly if a talisman might restore Sorren. Its reaction hadn't been encouraging, though.

He approached Dalthinir instead. "Would you like this?" he asked, holding it out.

His mentor shook his head. "I don't want it. We'll need to decide as a community who should have it. In the meantime, could you look after it?"

"If you'd like me to," he replied. "I have no interest in it myself. I have a talisman of my own now."

"You do? Could you show it to me?" asked Dalthinir, his eyes wide.

He smiled. "There's nothing to see. It's knitted into my bones."

Dalthinir's jaw was hanging open. "How is that possible?"

"It's a long story," he said. Much as he didn't want to be evasive, he couldn't risk exposing the presence of the Artoran exiles on Abbethar.

Dalthinir was gracious enough to put aside his curiosity. Seeing Trisanna heading their way, he waited for her to arrive and tactfully changed the subject.

"What do you think of the valley, Kylen?" he asked.

"I'm impressed!" he replied. "It's good to see the community thriving. Since becoming a renegade you've never had a safe place to call home. It's exactly what you've needed."

"I agree," Dalthinir replied. "I'm tired of forever wandering the world. We still visit outlying communities every few months. The people there appreciate our help, and when Trisanna and I work together we can travel around safely. But there's nothing like returning home."

Trisanna smiled. "You're about to become a father. That changes everything."

She turned to Kylen. "What are your plans now?"

"My talisman is needed here, at least until the community has decided who will take on Sorren's talisman. Once that's resolved, I won't be staying for long."

Her lip quirked up in a smile. "Is that because of Dannah and Marielle?"

He nodded. There was no point in pretending otherwise. He had been astonished to learn that Dannah and Marielle were in Periton, and disheartened that Dannah had turned down Dalthinir's offer to take them to the hidden valley. He simply had to find them, not least because he couldn't bear to think of them being taken by the Compact.

"It won't be safe for you to go on your own," she said. "I'm willing to go with you. Illusion might be useful at times."

He accepted her offer gratefully. "Thank you!"

"You won't be safe without a way of hiding your glimmer," said Dalthinir. "Even so, I can't promise to accompany you. Not with the baby's arrival getting closer. After everything that's happened, I don't think Inga would forgive me if I left again so soon."

"I wouldn't ask it of you!" Kylen assured him. "Your place is here with your wife and your baby!"

"Lars had a coat that hid glimmer," said Dalthinir. "He stole it from Agalar, who presumably stole it from one of the Compact mages. You might have found it useful. Unfortunately it was destroyed with him in the building."

"I don't need to resolve it immediately," Kylen assured him. "I won't be leaving for a while."

CHAPTER 27
ABBETHAR

The sea had remained calm since the storm that devastated the island. Lokan could not claim to be equally unruffled, but his life had at least settled once more into a predictable rhythm.

In response to the dramatic news from the previous day, all of the islanders had disappeared apart from a few guards left behind with Lokan and Buck. The prisoners were not told what had caused the agitation. Nor did anyone explain the reasons behind the mass exodus.

The remaining guards could not have enlightened them even if they wanted to. They spoke only their own language, and the interpreter had departed with the rest of them.

After a week had dragged by, some of the islanders returned. They wasted no time in calling for the two prisoners. Lokan's heart was pounding as they were led away. Buck seemed as unflustered as ever.

They found Double Chin waiting for them, the interpreter at his side. No tent had been erected, and the two islanders were not even seated. Clearly this was going to be a brief meeting. It wasn't hard to guess at its purpose. Lokan's heart beat faster.

"Circumstances have changed," Double Chin began, speaking through the interpreter. "We have decided to release you—on one condition."

Realizing that his jaw had flopped open, Lokan hastily snapped it shut again.

"What is the condition?" asked Buck.

"That you agree not to speak of what has happened here. You can say you were castaways on an island and that you were rescued by passing fishermen. However, you must agree not to reveal that the island is inhabited."

"You will have no way of knowing whether we keep our word," Buck observed.

Double Chin nodded. "We recognize that. We will be relying upon your integrity. Are you willing to agree to our condition?"

"I am," said Lokan, trying not to sound overeager.

"I am, too," Buck confirmed.

"Why the change of heart?" Lokan asked.

"As I told you, circumstances have changed." Double Chin peered at them uncomfortably. "I wish to apologize for the way you were treated. You risked your own lives to save mine, and I did nothing to deserve such selflessness."

"Think nothing of it," said Buck mildly.

Lokan contented himself with a nod. He was honest enough to acknowledge that their pending release was entirely due to Buck's big-heartedness. His own attitude to Double Chin had not been as generous.

"Each of you will be returned by boat to your own home country," the islander continued. "You will be free to nominate the region where you would like to land. For our own security it will be necessary to blindfold you until you come in sight of your own coastline. I hope that does not prove too distressing."

"I will be glad to return home," said Buck with feeling.

"As will I," agreed Lokan.

Their agreement came as no surprise to Double Chin. "You will be collected later today. A couple of our people will lead you to a place where each of you can safely board your boat."

He left after bidding them both farewell.

The interpreter lingered for a few minutes longer. "In case it isn't obvious, let me make it clear to you that this outcome is unprecedented! I trust you will honor our trust by keeping your promises."

He left with their sincere assurances.

Lokan wasn't quite ready to part from his companion. "I'm deeply indebted to you, Buck! I would have drowned if you hadn't rescued me. And it was entirely your initiative to save our interrogator. That turned out to be a very smart move! I owe you my thanks for that as well."

Buck brushed it off with a wave of his hand. "No need to thank me," he replied. "I was glad to have your company. Four years was an awfully long time to be alone!"

Their conversation was interrupted by their guides. After clapping Buck on the shoulder, Lokan joined him in heading for the boats.

~

TANTEL

SPLASHING ASHORE onto the little beach, Lokan turned to wave a final farewell to the sailors who had conveyed him to Tantel. They had already lost interest in him, their attention wholly focused on returning to their island.

With a shrug of resignation, Lokan headed inland. More than anything he wanted to be home in Brynford, but his responsibilities took priority. He needed to report to the king. He was also anxious to discover what had become of Deemis. He had therefore asked the sailors to take him to the port city of Shelmar, southeast of the capital, Antilin. It was a long voyage, and they had agreed unenthusiastically. He had the feeling they would have gladly deposited him on the first piece of land that belonged to Tantel.

Shelmar was the closest port to Antilin, and Lokan knew a merchant who lived there. If he was fortunate, he might find him at home.

After picking his way overland for a while he found a dirt track heading in the right general direction. It eventually became a road. As soon as he reached the outskirts of the city he asked directions to the house of his friend.

The sun was low in the sky by the time he found his friend's home. It was an imposing mansion set back from the main road. Approaching the front door, he hammered on it with what felt like the last of his energy.

"Who is it?" demanded a harsh voice from within.

When the door was opened by a footman, he asked for his friend. The footman disappeared, shutting the door behind him.

After a short delay the door opened again, and a face peered out. "Lokan?! Is that you?"

"It is! A cold and weary Lokan, at that!"

The door swung wide. "You look terrible! Come in!"

"Thank you, Pindel. I'm in your debt!"

Pindel called for his valet. "Get some fresh clothing for my friend! Hurry, man!" He led him at once to a room that boasted a roaring fire.

Lokan parked himself in front of the fire, soaking in its warmth. Releasing a deep sigh, he allowed his tension to slowly melt away. How long had it been since he could just relax?

"How do you come to be in Shelmar?" Pindel asked. "Especially looking like that!"

"It's a long story," he replied. "In short, I was a castaway on an island until some passing fishermen returned me to the mainland."

"That sounds like quite an adventure! You're fortunate to find me home. I'm heading to the capital first thing in the morning."

"Could I travel with you?" he asked eagerly. "I need to report to the king."

"Of course!"

Pindel lowered his voice. "Maybe you could have a quiet word in the ear of the king when you see him. It's about time somebody did! Wars are not good for business."

"Has something happened while I've been away?"

"We've taken over the Summer Isles! Apparently Periton is next."

Lokan released a sigh. "There isn't anything I can do to stop a war. I might at least be able to find out what's going on."

. . .

AFTER THE HARDSHIPS Lokan had endured on the island, traveling with a prosperous merchant was like being transported to another world. The horses they rode were well bred, and Pindel's retainers were constantly on hand to provide for every need. Whenever they broke their journey, they enjoyed the best available food and the most lavish accommodations. Pindel insisted on paying for everything.

The merchant was one of a rare breed. He seemed larger than life. Riding at his side, Lokan found him to be the best possible company—informed, communicative, and endlessly entertaining. He couldn't remember when he'd laughed so much.

However, it wasn't all smiles and laughter. They rode past almost endless columns of soldiers marching in the opposite direction, toward the port.

"Is the king still building up his army?" asked Lokan.

"Very aggressively!" Pindel confirmed. "He's scooped up all of the youngsters among my retainers." He lowered his voice. "I tried to make...an arrangement, shall we say...with the recruiters. I soon discovered I was wasting my time. The only thing they're concerned about is finding a way to meet the king's quotas."

He raised his eyes heavenward. "I don't understand what the king wants to achieve. He isn't exactly building a dynasty. He has no children. And a war won't make the kingdom more prosperous. The disruption is starting to affect my business significantly."

"My friends in the capital don't understand it, either," Lokan told him.

With nothing useful for either of them to add, the conversation drifted in different directions. Pindel wasn't one to remain glum for long, and he soon had Lokan laughing again.

Lokan didn't part company with the merchant until they had ridden through the city gates. Handing his reins to a retainer, he reached up to grasp Pindel's hand.

"You've been a true friend, and I don't know how to thank you adequately," he said.

Pindel waved a hand dismissively. "No thanks are needed! You're always welcome!"

After watching his friend ride away, Lokan headed toward the royal palace.

Alone once more, his cheerfulness quickly began to dissipate. Memories came surging back. The ill-fated voyage with Deemis and the privations he endured on the island had been followed by the fear of what his captors might decide to do. He hadn't endured it alone, but it was no thanks to any of his countrymen. He wouldn't have survived if it weren't for Buck.

Returning to Antilin gave him nothing to look forward to except a grilling by the king. The thought of it filled him with apprehension. The king wouldn't be happy to see him. He had been sent to the island on a mission, and he had done nothing to further it.

It would take him at least thirty minutes to reach the palace on foot. He discovered he was in no hurry to get there.

By the time the heavy iron gates rose before him at last, he found himself in the grip of a dark mood.

He was challenged brusquely as he approached by a pair of guards who were not known to him.

Then a voice he recognized called out, "Lokan! It really is you!"

Hastily opening the gates, Antone waved him in. After closing them behind him, the guard led him into the grounds.

On his previous arrival in Antilin, he had been greeted with cheerful banter. Not this time.

"I heard you were lost at sea!" Antone told him grimly. "The rumors said you'd drowned!"

"And yet here I am," he said lightly. He had no intention of saying more. Antone's reference to the rumor mill had been a timely reminder that anything he said would swiftly make its way around the palace.

He quickly changed the subject. "What's been happening around here?"

"Nothing good," Antone replied. "The guards you knew are all off with the army now. I'll be joining them in a couple of days. You were lucky to find me here. You wouldn't have found it easy to get past that lot." He jerked his head back toward the gates.

"Is the king here in the palace?" he asked.

Antone nodded.

"What about Deemis?"

The guard rolled his eyes. "He's been strutting about as usual."

Noticing the surprise on Lokan's face, he added, "He came back looking very pleased with himself. It must have been a few days after you left. The king's been in rare good humor ever since."

Enjoying an attentive audience, Antone continued. "That isn't all! A few days ago some foreigners arrived for an interview with the king. They didn't look at all happy when they left!"

Pieces began sliding into place for Lokan. He remembered the consternation of the islanders upon receiving news the day after the huge storm. "Circumstances have changed," Double Chin had said.

It wasn't difficult to guess what must have happened. Deemis had not only survived the storm, he had succeeded in stealing the object and bringing it back to the king. The islanders had wasted no time sending a delegation to get it back. They had apparently gone home disappointed.

If he'd guessed correctly, why hadn't Deemis come looking for him?

His insides were roiling as he left Antone and headed into the palace.

Incredibly, the first person he saw was Deemis. His eyes wide, the king's favorite stared at him in astonishment for a long moment. He quickly recovered himself.

"Lokan! It's such a relief to see you! I thought you were dead!"

Taking his arm, Deemis steered him to a quiet corridor. "You must tell me everything that's happened to you! You hit your head when you went into the water. I jumped in after you almost immediately, but I couldn't reach you! The waves were so big that I only caught brief glimpses of you. Then I lost you completely! I was fortunate to survive myself. The crew somehow kept me in sight, and they threw me a rope. Even then, they were barely able to pull me in."

He exhaled loudly in relief. "It took me a few hours to recover. The captain told me you'd drowned! I was devastated! I decided I wouldn't rest until I'd completed the mission. I wanted to do it for both of us!" He slapped Lokan on the back. "Soon after I made it ashore, a massive storm came up. In the confusion I was able to grab the object. Once the sea calmed down a bit, I was able to make it back to the boat."

He smiled sympathetically at Lokan. "There's no need for you to feel awkward in front of the king. He doesn't hold any of what happened against you!"

Lokan frowned. What more could the king possibly want from him? He had the object he'd wanted. Maybe Lokan hadn't been the one who retrieved it, but he'd almost died trying.

Deemis had become restless. "I can't stop now—I have urgent business for the king to attend to! But we'll catch up soon, and you can tell me everything that happened. And as I said, don't worry about the king! I'll put in a word for you!"

Hurrying away, he called back over his shoulder, "It truly is good to see you alive and well, Lokan!"

Unsettled and bemused, Lokan stood watching him go. He had no idea what to make of the encounter. Was Deemis telling the truth? Either way, he saw little reason to expect the promised catch-up would ever take place.

Given what had happened, it made no sense that the king might hold something against Lokan. It left him more nervous than ever about reporting to him.

Turning on his heel, Lokan walked back through the palace gates and headed into the city. If the king wanted to see him, he could send someone to find him.

Lokan needed to talk to someone with insight into what was going on in the kingdom. Someone he could trust.

He was going to seek out Lord Crinholm.

CHAPTER 28
PERITON

Pale and breathless, Crown Prince Firan walked into the royal reception room, his mother Queen Karolin and his younger sister Princess Layla at his side. Several aides accompanied them. Taking the queen aside, the king conducted a whispered conversation with her. Each of them appeared animated at times.

While they were distracted, Dannah focused on the boy. His obvious distress sent a wave of compassion flooding through her.

Glancing at Marielle, she found her almost as pale as the prince. It wasn't hard to guess what she was thinking. A great deal hung on their efforts to help him.

For her own part she was hopeful. Normally, she would have a large and experienced team at her side for complex cases, but if the kingdom's healers were willing to work with her it might still be possible to do what was needed.

Just as the king was concluding his whispered interaction with the queen, two other people entered the room.

"Master Gerrar," acknowledged the king, nodding warmly to a tall man who must have been at least as old as Dannah.

"Your Majesty," he replied with a bow, a smile on his weathered face.

The other person was a woman who looked anything but happy. "Master Frezaya," said the king, eyeing her coolly.

For the sake of the foreigners, he offered an introduction. "Master Gerrar is our senior healer, and Master Frezaya is his deputy," he told Dannah.

He addressed the two Peritonian healers. "It seems we have been presented with a new opportunity to do what our best healers have failed to do."

Gerrar colored slightly. Frezaya radiated defiance.

Dannah winced. The king wasn't going to make her task easier by turning it into a competition.

"What credentials have these foreign renegades presented, Your Majesty?" Frezaya asked icily.

The king's eyes narrowed. "They healed Kothlar," he replied. "I understand that none of our healers were able to help him."

"It doesn't count as a healing when the so-called problem exists only in the mind of the sufferer," said Frezaya breezily.

Kothlar looked furious.

The chief master interjected before he could speak. "Hold your tongue, Frezaya!" he growled. "You go too far!"

She stared back at him unrepentantly, but she said no more.

"Enough!" exclaimed the king. "Our guests asked to examine Firan, and he is here. It is time to proceed!"

With Marielle at her side, Dannah stepped forward with a confidence she didn't feel. Her earlier hopefulness had vanished. It was impossible to imagine any help coming from the Peritonian healers. The two of them were on their own.

"May we take your hands?" she asked the prince.

He looked uncertain, but he nodded. She took one hand while Marielle took the other.

His obvious frailty steadied her. Thrusting from her mind the posturing of Frezaya, she focused her attention solely on the boy that so desperately needed her help.

Using her mage touch abilities, she examined his internal organs.

"Valves," murmured Marielle.

She nodded. As she had suspected, the problem lay with valves in his heart. Two of them were permitting blood to flow in the wrong direction. The issue had almost certainly resulted from the fever he contracted when he was five years old.

Smiling at the prince, she released his hand. "Thank you," she said gently.

Ignoring Frezaya, she addressed Gerrar. "The problem lies with two of the valves in his heart," she said.

"Every healer in Periton is aware of that," interjected Frezaya mockingly. "You clearly overheard someone speaking of it."

Gerrar ignored his colleague. "Your diagnosis is accurate," he said. "We have not been able to correct the problem. Do you think you are able to do so?"

"I have carried out similar healings in the past, but only with the active assistance of other colleagues," she told him frankly.

Frezaya's mouth began to open, no doubt for another sarcastic remark. Seeing it, Gerrar cut her off. "There is no reason for further discourtesy!" he told her firmly.

"Well said!" growled Kothlar.

Her eyes narrowed at the rebuke of the two senior mages. Aiming a poisonous glare in the direction of Dannah and Marielle, she turned on her heel and stormed out of the room.

"I apologize for my colleague," said Gerrar.

She nodded an acknowledgment. "Would you be able to help us?" Dannah asked him.

"In what way?" he asked.

"Do you work as a team when carrying out healings?" she asked.

He frowned in puzzlement. "I'm not sure what you mean. We freely share knowledge and techniques, but we work individually."

"I see," she replied, completely deflated. She had never imagined their methods could be so primitive. Kylen's assessment had now been thoroughly vindicated.

The king had been listening impatiently. "Can you heal our son?" he demanded.

After a moment's hesitation, she replied. "We can try."

"Is there a risk you will leave him worse than before?"

"Not if we are careful."

He paused for a moment to exchange a significant glance with the queen. What he saw in her eyes seemed to satisfy him. "Then do it!" he ordered.

"We will need time to prepare ourselves, Your Majesty. We can begin tomorrow morning."

SLEEP PROVED ELUSIVE FOR DANNAH. The child's condition would not have been hopeless on Abbethar, not with an experienced team of healers working together. But Peritonian healers did not work together. Even if they had all been supportive, they could do nothing to help.

It should be possible to teach them to heal as a team, but that would take time and patience. And practicing on the crown prince would be out of the question.

The problem was the lack of raw power. Dannah and Marielle were both more powerful than many mages, but even together their power would not be enough. She wondered if she should have told the king they couldn't heal his son. But they had to at least try. She wasn't solely concerned about the implications for them. She couldn't ignore the plight of the boy. The whole kingdom expected him to take the throne one day. Even if he survived to adulthood, he would never be effective as king. Not in his current condition.

When she eventually managed to sleep, she dreamed.

SHE FOUND herself standing on the shoreline where she had first arrived in Periton. A huge winged shape wheeled overhead before dropping from the sky and landing immediately before her. Looking up, she peered into the whirling orbs that were Elef'nissar's eyes.

"She must reach deep into her being," said the dragon.

Her brows drew together in confusion. "Who?" she asked.

"Your daughter's daughter. She must draw it in."

"Draw what in?"

The question was never answered, because the dragon was gone.

• • •

Waking with a start, Dannah tried to make sense of the dream. Elef'nissar must have been talking about Marielle. It had referred to her as Dannah's daughter's daughter on one other occasion. At the time it had been talking about the tiny piece of its claw she had kept. It had said that one of them might find it useful.

Was it saying that Marielle should reach deep into her being and draw in the piece of claw? What did that mean?

Unwilling to wait for the dawn, she woke her granddaughter and told her what had happened.

After hearing her out, Marielle went quiet for a moment. Then her eyes went wide.

"It's incredible!" she said. "I just did it, and it's giving me access to incredible power. I feel like I'm only seeing the smallest glimpse of what it's capable of."

"Do you mean your mage touch ability has been enhanced?"

"Yes! And that is only the beginning. There is so much more that the claw can allow me to do."

"Do you think you've gained enough extra power for us to heal the prince?"

"It's hard to believe the power is actually unlimited, but I feel like anything is possible!"

"Well, I imagine we will find out very soon."

A couple of hours after dawn, Dannah and Marielle were taken to the bedchamber of Crown Prince Firan. King Durvaryn and his wife Queen Karolin stood at the foot of the bed, along with Chief Master Adrastas and Master Kothlar.

Master Gerrar was also present. To Dannah's relief, there was no sign of Master Frezaya.

The king and queen both looked decidedly uneasy.

"Are you sure you want to go through with this, Your Majesties?" asked the chief master.

"Can you offer our son hope from any other source, Adrastas?" asked the king.

The chief master reluctantly shook his head.

With his expectation confirmed, the king turned his full attention on Dannah and Marielle. "Before you begin, I must warn you!" the king told them. "Most of my advisors have strongly urged me not to place our son in your hands. Chief Master Adrastas and Master Kothlar are present for a reason. If you play us false they have been instructed to show you no mercy! Do you understand?"

Dannah swallowed. "We do, Your Majesty."

His voice softened. "In saying that, it is not my desire to make you unduly fearful, especially when you are willing to attempt what others believe to be impossible. If it helps, both the queen and I trust you, although neither of us can entirely explain why." He exchanged a glance with the queen. Both of them looked tense. "You may begin as soon as you are ready."

Dannah bowed. "Thank you, Your Majesties. You honor us with your trust. Let me assure you that your son's welfare is our sole concern now."

Before approaching the prince she locked eyes with Periton's senior healer. "Master Gerrar, you are very welcome to join us," she told him.

"What did you have in mind?" he asked uncertainly.

"If you place a hand on the prince, will you be able to observe his internal organs?"

"Of course," he replied.

"Then please feel free to monitor what we are doing."

After a moment's hesitation, Gerrar nodded.

All three of them approached the prince, who was lying on his bed. Dannah positioned herself on one side of the bed, with Gerrar beside her. Marielle stood opposite them. The prince flinched when they placed their hands on him.

"We are going to put you to sleep, Your Highness," Dannah told him.

He nodded at once. He seemed relieved.

Marielle had accumulated a great deal of experience during her time in the healing rooms, and Dannah knew she was more than capable of safely putting the prince to sleep. "Marielle, could you please make the crown prince comfortable?"

Nodding once, the younger mage quickly did what was necessary. His eyes closed as he sank deeply into unconsciousness.

Witnessing the young mage in action, Gerrar raised his eyebrows in surprise. "I am impressed," he murmured.

His response encouraged Dannah. They had undertaken to heal the prince. Somehow they would find a way.

Delving in carefully with her magic, she sought the two heart valves she had identified the previous day. Then she began a complex process of reconstruction. It involved far more than repair. The valves could not be rebuilt without new cells being produced at an unusually rapid rate. Magical stimulation of a very precise nature would be required to achieve it.

Quickly reaching the limit of her power, Dannah began to draw freely on what Marielle had to offer. Even before she began she knew it wouldn't be anywhere near enough. Yet to her astonishment power continued to flow from Marielle, however liberally she consumed it.

It could only be the gift of the dragon's claw. Newly energized, she continued her efforts.

Time passed. Had they been working for two hours, three? It didn't matter, because the end was in sight. One of the valves, newly reconstructed, was now operating normally. Her work on the second was nearing completion.

As soon as it was done, she heaved a sigh of exhausted relief. Nodding to Marielle, she watched as her granddaughter awakened the prince from his slumber.

Master Gerrar was staring at her, his eyes glistening. She smiled at him, and he smiled back, barely able to contain his emotion.

"How do you feel, Prince Firan?" she asked.

Before the boy could answer, Master Frezaya burst into the room. "I demand to know what you have done to the prince!"

Dannah swallowed her irritation. "Come and see for yourself," she offered, pointing to the prince. Still lying on his bed, he was now alert and had color in his cheeks.

Frezaya strode to the bed. Instead of joining Marielle on the other side of the bed, she shoved in beside Gerrar, squeezing him between herself and Dannah. Joining the others in placing a hand on the boy, she concentrated her attention on him.

Her face twisted in a sudden frown. "What have you done to him?" she demanded angrily, leaning forward to glare at Dannah around Gerrar. "Tell the king what they have done to his son!" she commanded Gerrar imperiously.

He stared back at her. First bemusement then anger gathered on his brow. As he opened his mouth to speak, he abruptly collapsed on the floor.

"*She* has incapacitated Master Gerrar!" shouted Frezaya, jabbing a finger at Dannah. "She did it to prevent him exposing the harm she has done to the crown prince!"

Dannah was too shocked to respond.

Marielle glared at Frezaya. "You were the one who disabled him! Master Gerrar was about to confirm the prince's healing!"

"I'll disable *you*, you young upstart!" Striking out furiously at Marielle, Frezaya almost fell forward onto the prince.

"Enough!" roared Adrastas. "Step back at once before you injure the prince, Frezaya!"

Seeing her hesitate, he shouted, "Do it now!"

Eyes narrowed, she glared at the chief master before moving reluctantly away from the bed.

"I insist on the two of you moving back as well!" Adrastas told Dannah and Marielle. "Now!"

Shaking her head in disbelief, Dannah complied, waving Marielle back as well.

"What you have done to the prince will be thoroughly investigated," Adrastas told them sternly. "The king warned that your actions would have consequences."

Kothlar was clearly appalled by what was happening. "It was apparent to me that Master Gerrar was nothing but supportive of what these women were doing. There was no problem until Master Frezaya appeared!" He turned to the prince. "How are you feeling, Your Highness?"

Adrastas cut him off. "This is not the time to preempt a formal inquiry, Kothlar. These women came without credentials, and as foreigners they owe no allegiance to our king. Far too much license has already been granted to them. Master Frezaya has accused them of harming the prince and incapacitating Master Gerrar. These are serious charges, and they will be properly investigated."

Opening the door to the prince's bedchamber, the chief master called in a group of royal guards. Several mages had also been positioned outside the room, and they joined the guards in the room.

"Escort these two women to a secure lockup," ordered Adrastas. "Ensure that they are well guarded!"

CHAPTER 29
PERITON

Pacing restlessly on the battlements of the royal castle, Kothlar tried to come to terms with what he had witnessed in the prince's bedchamber. Every indication suggested that the two foreigners had been treated appallingly. Kothlar had himself sensed no alarm of any kind from Master Gerrar. Unless he had been reading the situation completely wrongly, the old healer's reaction had been more akin to awe.

Perhaps he was unable to be objective, especially now his own back problems seemed a thing of the past.

His attention was diverted to a slight figure in a hooded gown climbing slowly up the stairs that led to the battlements. He paused, waiting for the person to reveal themselves. Upon reaching him, the visitor immediately pulled back her hood. To his surprise, he found himself facing Queen Karolin.

She peered anxiously up at him. "Do you know what has become of the two healers, Master Kothlar?" she asked.

He frowned. "Adrastas won't let me anywhere near them."

"The king insists the matter must be left to the Compact to resolve," she sighed. "By law mages must be allowed to deal with all matters involving other mages."

"What of your son, Your Majesty? How does he seem?"

"He is well! I can scarcely believe it!" she replied fervently. "His health seems no different from any normal boy of his age. That has never been the case—not since his fever!"

He shook his head slowly. "You're only confirming my suspicions, Your Majesty. We're treating Dannah and her granddaughter like criminals when we should be honoring them!"

"None of this would have happened if that Frezaya woman hadn't interfered! The king says I shouldn't say such things, but I don't care!" She peered up at him anxiously. "Has Master Gerrar recovered?"

"He has regained consciousness, but his wits appear addled. I doubt we'll get much sense out of him for another day or two."

"Who did it to him?"

"I can't say with any certainty, but I don't believe for a minute that Dannah did it."

The queen shook her head. "All of this is such foolishness. With the Tantellans on our doorstep, the king has more than enough else to worry about!"

He nodded helplessly.

"I know you have reason to be grateful to Dannah as well. If you get a chance to speak to her, please tell her how much we appreciate what she and her granddaughter did for our son. They've changed his life, and ours as well!"

DANNAH STARED into an empty corridor through the bars on the door of their cell. Their quarters offered little by way of comfort, and although they had been fed regularly, the food was indifferent at best.

They had been locked up as if they were dangerous criminals. She smiled wryly at the thought. It would have been much worse if the Peritonians had any real idea what they were capable of.

"What will become of us, Granny?" asked Marielle. She had been working hard at staying positive, but with limited success.

"I have no idea," she replied with a helpless shrug. "I'm so sorry I got you into this, Elle. Now that I've witnessed the size of Cambrick and its population, I can see I underestimated the challenge we would be facing. I should have accepted Dalthinir's offer of help."

"And what would have happened to the young prince if we'd done that?"

Dannah gazed at her affectionately. Marielle had matured a lot since they first arrived in Periton. The suffering she had witnessed quickly stirred her compassion, and her focus now was firmly on the welfare of others, even with the cost to herself so high. Staying positive or not, she was coping better than Dannah might have expected.

"Do you ever wonder what Kylen is doing right now?" Marielle asked wistfully. "I wonder if he would do something to help us if he knew of our situation."

Before Dannah could respond, she heard the echoes of many feet marching down the corridor toward their cell. Both of them moved to the door to get a better look.

The face of Kaspra appeared before them. "The inquiry is about to commence, and your presence is required. Are you willing to come peaceably?"

Dannah nodded.

The door was opened, and the two were led away with a large group of soldiers and mages positioned before and behind them.

They were led into a large room filled with men and women. Based on the distinctive broad crimson fringe on their robes, every person present was a mage. Glancing around, Dannah spotted faces she recognized, including Chief Master Adrastas, Master Kothlar, Master Gerrar and Master Frezaya. Kothlar sent her a grim smile.

The head mage introduced the proceedings. "We have in our midst two women of unknown origin. They tell us that they are known as Dannah and Marielle. Marielle is supposedly Dannah's granddaughter." He pointed to each of them in turn as he said their names. "Both of them are mages, and I have no need to tell you that they are not members of our Compact. Nor do they come with references from any other kingdom."

Muttering broke out at his words. Dannah glanced around the

room, noting the frowns and pointed dark looks sent in their direction. The obvious other kingdom was Tantel, and it made sense that no visit from Tantellan mages would be welcome in the current climate, with or without references.

"Nor are they from Tantel," continued Adrastas. "The accent of the granddaughter is unrecognizable. It has been suggested that the older woman has mage hearing, which would account for her facility with our language."

The murmuring increased further at his words. It was apparent that not all of them had heard this news.

"They claim to be healers, and they have been working as such in the northern and western regions of Periton without authorization. They were taken into custody on the road from Cambrick to Sengin. They have refused to say either where they came from or why they are here."

The muttering had become louder, and Adrastas held up his hands for silence.

"The first matter we must examine relates to the crown prince. I will call Master Frezaya, the deputy to our senior healer, to give evidence."

Master Frezaya got up and sauntered to the head mage's side. "Astonishing as it will no doubt seem to you all, the king and queen consented to these *women*,"—she sneered in their direction—"operating on their son, our beloved Crown Prince Firan. We can thank *him*, for that," she added coolly, jabbing a finger in the direction of Master Kothlar. "He claimed that the older one healed a little twinge he imagined was troubling him."

An uproar threatened at her words. She shouted them down. "I did not consent to this folly," she yelled. "The moment I learned that an operation was underway, I forced my way into the room. I found that the prince had been grievously harmed by the women. For reasons known best to himself, our senior healer was present. When I invited him to expose what they had done, the old woman struck him down to prevent him!"

Many voices were raised in anger. When the din showed no sign of abating, the chief mage was forced to call repeatedly for order.

"Thank you for your calm and measured words, Master Frezaya," Adrastas said sarcastically. "You may resume your seat. I call upon Master Gerrar to testify."

The senior healer looked a little unsteady as he got to his feet, and a wave of sympathetic murmurs swept the building. Nevertheless, he was unwavering as he faced the gathered mages. "I was indeed present at the bedside of Crown Prince Firan. You are all aware of the seriousness of his health condition. The king and queen must have been desperate indeed to allow unknown healers to tend to him."

A new round of murmuring arose at his words, and he waited for it to die away before continuing. "My hands were on the prince throughout, allowing me to monitor his internal organs. I witnessed a remarkable healing. No healer in this kingdom is capable of performing the operation I witnessed. I visited the prince before I came to this meeting and questioned him closely. I also examined him internally, with particular focus on the heart valves that were always the main cause of his problem. I can testify that he has been fully restored to normal health."

A stunned silence greeted his pronouncement. "Why then, did that woman strike you down?" interjected someone from the audience. Other voices rose in support of the question.

"I cannot say exactly what happened," he replied. "But Dannah had no reason to disable me. I was opening my mouth to affirm her actions, not to expose them."

Adrastas rose quickly to his feet again, mostly likely intent on forestalling further interruptions. "Thank you, Master Gerrar. I call on Master Kothlar to present evidence."

It was obvious to Dannah that the head mage was less than enthusiastic about calling this latest witness. Knowing that Kothlar was not prejudiced against her, she was relieved that he had been given a chance to speak.

"First, I must congratulate Master Frezaya on the way she so effortlessly diminished the condition that plagued me for many years. Many of you would have seen me limping at times. I need hardly say that if her own attempts at treatment had been as effective as her words in dismissing my pain, I would never have needed help from a foreign healer." Raucous laughter greeted his words. It was becoming obvious that Master Frezaya was not well liked by many of the mages.

His tone became serious. "For myself, I am grateful—and no less awed—to have experienced firsthand the astonishing potency of a genuinely skilled healer." He paused to let his words sink in before continuing. "I was present throughout the operation on the prince. The two foreigners knew before they began that none of our healers saw any hope for the prince to ever be healed. They also understood that their attempts would likely lead to their own deaths if they failed. Yet they didn't hesitate to give their best efforts on his behalf." He bowed in their direction. "The queen has personally asked me to convey to them the full extent of her gratitude."

A hush had come over the gathering. Frezaya's face was red, either with anger or embarrassment—Dannah couldn't tell. But she didn't try to interrupt.

One of the mages raised a hand. "You may speak," Adrastas told him.

"We all know that the human body possesses a remarkable ability to heal. Is it possible that the prince's condition has been naturally improving over the course of time? What if his apparent healing was no more than a coincidence? And who was responsible for striking down Master Gerrar? We can't simply overlook such an attack. It must be taken seriously!"

"These are important questions," agreed Adrastas. "Unfortunately, I do not think it likely that answers will ever be found."

Dannah could remain silent no longer. "Does your system of justice allow the accused an opportunity to speak?" she interjected.

The chief master glowered at her, but he answered her evenly. "Of course. We are not barbarians."

"And we are not criminals," she replied calmly.

He ignored her remark. "What do you have to say in your own defense?" he asked.

"I wanted to respond to your earlier assertion. Is it true that you have no way to answer the questions raised earlier?" She nodded toward the mage from the audience who had spoken up.

His brows furrowed. "What are you suggesting? Do you know of a way to prove who incapacitated Master Gerrar?"

"I do," she replied. "Any magical action performed on a living being leaves behind a characteristic smell that identifies the mage responsible for the action." Seeing the blank looks on their faces, she added, "Is it possible that you are not aware of this?"

Master Kothlar got to his feet. "All of us are able to detect the use of power, and also to smell who used the power. But none of us are capable of detecting the smell on a creature after the event. Do you mean that if someone killed Adrastas's dog, for example, it would be possible to determine who did it?"

Adrastas started at the question. She had no idea why.

"Of course," she said. "Every mage is capable of doing what I have described, provided they are properly taught, although healers tend to find it easier than others. I am willing to demonstrate the technique if you like."

"I am willing to volunteer as a subject," said Kothlar without hesitation, stepping forward.

"Are there healers willing to learn the technique?" asked Dannah.

Two younger mages, both women, got up immediately and came forward. They introduced themselves as Masters Faliba and Reza. They were joined by Master Gerrar. Master Frezaya didn't move a muscle.

"As you have heard, I healed the lumbar condition of Master Kothlar here. Please examine him. You will be looking for a distinctive smell that still lingers at the site of the healing."

Faliba reached a hand toward Kothlar's lower back.

"Don't touch him there!" warned Dannah. "Your own scent will confuse your magical senses. Touch him somewhere else. His hand, for example."

The two younger healers took one hand each. Master Gerrar knelt and touched his ankle.

"Explore his back," she instructed, "in his lower lumbar region. Look for a scent that doesn't belong to his body."

"I sense it!" said Faliba excitedly. "How is it that I have never noticed such traces before?"

"I sense it, too," confirmed Master Gerrar.

It took Reza a moment longer, but she too was able to detect the scent.

"We are not familiar with your scent," observed Faliba.

"Once you witness me using power it will be easy to confirm the scents are the same. To demonstrate I am going to throw a small shield around my right foot."

She did as she promised, and all three faces lit up.

"You did heal his lower back!" said Faliba. "And the scent is spread over a considerable area, which suggests it was a significant healing."

"I can confirm it, too," said Gerrar.

"Me, too," added Reza.

The healers nodded their thanks to Kothlar as he stepped away.

"Now take one of Master Gerrar's hands," she instructed Reza and Faliba. "I don't know exactly how he was disabled, but I suggest you examine his heart."

The whole room went quiet for a few moments as they did as she suggested.

"You're right. It was his heart," said Faliba, her voice trembling. "And it was a major attack! It's fortunate his heart wasn't stopped permanently."

"The scent isn't yours," Reza told Dannah.

"No, it isn't," she replied. "I did not attack him. Do you recognize who the scent belongs to?"

The two of them exchanged glances. Then their eyes sought out Master Frezaya.

"How dare you!" she spat. "This is nothing more than sorcery!"

"Call it what you will," retorted Faliba, "a scent can't lie."

Master Gerrar turned to Frezaya, shaking his head in disbelief. "You were the only one with reason to silence me," he said. "Both of you must have known I was about to affirm what she had done. But even so, I never suspected you of attacking me. I never imagined you could stoop so low!"

"You left me no choice!" she hissed. "You are too stupid to see how dangerous these people are!"

The chief master's brow darkened. He signaled to a couple of aides.

"Take Master Frezaya to the lockup! In light of what she has done, she will face an inquiry of her own."

After the sensation of Frezaya's arrest, the room descended into complete disorder. Adrastas was forced to shout for order three times before the proceedings could continue.

He addressed Dannah and Marielle. "I am delighted to learn that the prince is now well. However, if you think you have been cleared as a result, I must assure you that you still have a case to answer! The key question of motive remains. We need to understand your purpose in coming here."

Dannah offered no response.

"Why did you come to Periton?" he demanded.

"There are people here who need healing," she replied. "In remote areas of the kingdom, some live their entire lives without laying eyes on a member of the Compact. We have tried to offer them help. It has also become obvious to us that some of the skills available to us as healers are not known here. It is satisfying to have been able to apply those skills to benefit Master Kothlar and the crown prince."

She gazed at the head mage calmly. "We have no desire to withhold knowledge from you. I have willingly transferred some of our forensic skills to your healers, and I didn't do it solely to prevent an injustice. I believe our behavior demonstrates that our motives are in no way sinister."

"It isn't quite that simple. If your goal was to ingratiate yourself to the royal family so you could gain influence over them, you have every reason to feel satisfied. Where do you come from?"

Dannah remained silent. She had answered his previous question honestly, even if she had been sparing with the truth. They had come to Periton to find Kylen, and she had no intention of revealing that.

This latest question could not be answered, though, not even in part. She would never expose their origins.

"Were you sent here, and if so by whom?"

Once more she held her peace.

"You do yourselves no favors by refusing to answer. We can only conclude you know your answers will incriminate you."

Still she remained silent.

"Return them to their cells," ordered the chief master. "A panel will be appointed to decide their fate."

With that, they were marched away, their heads low.

Dannah harbored no illusions about the likely outcome. In spite of their efforts on behalf of the prince, their current situation seemed hopeless.

CHAPTER 30
METHESIA

A few days after Dalthinir's rescue, the residents of the hidden valley met to discuss their future. Kylen was invited to attend, even though he wasn't formally part of the community.

Agalar had absented himself. Guessing that he would be one of the topics for discussion, he had headed to the barn to do a few chores.

"We need to decide about the talisman," Vennia began. "We also need to decide about Agalar. I want you to know that Sorren has forgiven him, and so have I. Agalar has told me he would be grateful for the opportunity to join our community. He is also aware that his past actions count against him."

Every person present appeared thoughtful, but no one responded.

"Let's discuss the talisman first." She nodded in Kylen's direction. "All of us are grateful to Kylen for his help. I can't imagine what we would have done without him. But I think we can safely excuse him from consideration. Even if he ever calls this community home, he already has a talisman of his own. I know he also has other things he needs to do, and he intends to leave as soon as he can."

Seeing him nodding in agreement, she turned her attention to the others. "It isn't possible for Sorren to take the talisman again, and I don't think more needs to be said on that topic. I don't want it, either. I would feel uncomfortable taking it when Sorren can't, although that's by no means my only reason. I think it's time it went to someone younger. Marigold isn't a mage yet, so she isn't an option. That means it won't remain in our family's hands, and I have a feeling that might be healthy. Does anyone have suggestions about who should take it?"

"I don't want it," said Dalthinir immediately. "Whoever takes the talisman will need to stay in this valley. Although I'm delighted to be based here, I'm conscious that visiting the wider world from time to time seems part of my destiny."

Trisanna wasn't far behind him. "I don't want it, either. I've had enough of talismans to last me a lifetime! And I'm like Dalthinir—I suspect I might want to leave the valley from time to time."

All eyes turned to Inga.

"Please don't ask me to take it!" she said. "I need to focus on my baby. I can easily see myself ending my days here, but I also have ties to Sengin I can't entirely ignore. I might want to visit my relatives there from time to time in the future." She glanced around the group. "I know he hasn't even been accepted into the community yet, but have any of you considered Agalar?"

Kylen noted with interest that no one seemed particularly taken aback by the question.

"It's clearly time to decide whether Agalar has a future with us," Vennia said. "All of us know his history. We've also seen how he has behaved since he came here. I'd like to invite comment."

"Do you feel you can trust him?" Kylen asked them all.

Trisanna shrugged. "We don't have a choice. He knows about this valley, and we can't undo that. Whatever we decide about him joining us, we'll need to trust him."

"I agree," said Dalthinir. "What do you think, Kylen? You suffered directly at his hands."

Kylen didn't hesitate. "I've spent time with him over the last few days, and I'm confident he isn't the same person who put the noose around me in Flaxendell."

"Inga's good at reading people," suggested Jonno.

"She is!" agreed Bella. "What do you think, Inga?"

"He freely owns his past mistakes, which is a good sign," Inga replied. "It's also encouraging that he took responsibility for having told Lars about the noose. He went to a lot of effort to tail him. And he did what he could to protect Dalthinir."

"You've been talking to him, Marigold," said Vennia. "What do you think?"

"I think he's been learning a lot," she said. "He told me he lost his parents when he was young, and he thought of Pernilla and her team as his family. But he said he never witnessed how family was supposed to work until he came here."

Vennia glanced at her husband. "You haven't said anything, Sorren."

He responded, speaking slowly. "Agalar sought me out when he first arrived. That can't have been easy. He told me he knows he's responsible for my condition, and that he's sorry."

"What do you think we should do?" Trisanna asked him.

Sorren smiled. "We should give him a chance. Both with us and with the talisman."

Heads everywhere nodded in agreement.

"Does anyone object?" asked Vennia.

All of them remained silent.

"I think I should be the one to offer it to him," said Sorren quietly.

No one disagreed.

After handing him the talisman, Kylen went out to find Agalar. They returned together.

Sorren greeted Agalar solemnly. "You told me you were willing to do anything you could to repay me for what happened when Lars took the amulet. Did you mean it?"

Agalar flushed brightly, but he didn't hesitate. "I meant it, Sorren. I'll do whatever you ask me to do."

Sorren held out the talisman. "Then take this. Use it for good and for the benefit of this community."

Overcome with emotion, Agalar swallowed hard as he stared at him. When he had recovered himself sufficiently, he glanced around at the others. He saw only welcome and acceptance.

Sorren thrust out the talisman once more, nodding an encouragement.

Agalar opened his mouth, then clamped it shut again. Finally, he reached out a trembling hand and took the talisman.

It took him a moment before he could speak. "I won't let you down," he told them, his voice breaking with emotion.

AFTER TRACKING DOWN HIS MENTOR, Kylen drew him aside to question him.

"There's nothing preventing me from leaving the valley now," he said. "I need to find Dannah and Marielle! Trisanna is coming with me, so we'll be able to stay out of sight. But we won't be safe unless I can mask both our use of magic and our glimmer."

"You can't do it?" asked Dalthinir.

Kylen frowned. "I've been trying, but it's no good. I've always relied on you to do it for me."

"Not always. You were doing both when I first met you. I was astonished! You somehow managed it without understanding what you were doing. Once I explained it all you tried again and weren't able to repeat it."

"I'd forgotten that," Kylen told him.

"When we were heading into the Drakkenridge Mountains, after your accident on the river, you were briefly able to mask the use of magical power again. For both of us."

"I do remember that. I felt like I was overflowing with power the closer we came to the mountains. I'm not sure how I did it. It just happened." He frowned. "Why can't I do it now?"

"It's a good question. Perhaps it's my fault. It was easy for me to do it for you, so I did. But it also meant you never needed to learn to do it yourself."

"Whatever the reason, it isn't working." Kylen threw up his hands in frustration. "I'm definitely not capable of it anymore!"

"That isn't true. You *are* capable—you've proven it. If you've convinced yourself otherwise, that's the problem."

"What does that mean?"

Dalthinir gazed at him. "Let me tell you a story. Many years ago I knew a man who'd lost both hands in an accident. At first, whenever I was with him I tried to anticipate his needs and do things for him. He made it clear he wasn't interested in my help. I soon discovered he'd become proficient at a wide range of tasks, even without hands. His creativity and his determination constantly astonished me."

Seeing Kylen's eyebrows raised, he added, "That's a true story in case you're wondering."

He smiled. "A second incident might help illustrate the point. Before I became a renegade, my quarters in Cambrick were serviced by a woman employed by the Compact. Among other routine tasks, she regularly polished the silverware using a special paste. She was too short to reach the high cupboard where the paste was stored, so I always got it down for her. If I knew I wouldn't be at home when she came, I left it out for her. If I ever forgot, the silverware missed out.

"Later, she left, and the Compact employed a different woman called Millie. She was no taller than her predecessor. On one occasion, after forgetting to get the paste down in preparation for her visit, I was surprised when I returned home to find Millie polishing the silver. I asked her how she reached the paste, and she told me she stood on a stool."

He locked eyes with Kylen. "Both stories illustrate the same life lesson. It's important to understand your limitations. But it's a mistake to allow your limitations to define you!"

"So you're saying I'm like the first woman who cleaned your silver. I've become so used to you masking my glimmer that I can't even imagine doing it myself."

"I wasn't trying to be quite so blunt. But you've grasped the general idea."

"Perhaps you're right. Do you have any suggestions about how I can get past the barrier?"

Dalthinir thought for a while. "Maybe it helps to be desperate. The first time I was able to mask my glimmer I was about to be captured. If I hadn't succeeded I would have been caught and killed. Somehow I managed it. From that moment I was always able to mask my own glimmer, and also the glimmer of other mages."

He shook his head. "I still have no idea how it happened, except that I was thinking of a dragon at the time. I know that must sound strange, because back then I thought dragons were extinct. But I'd seen a dragon in a vision. It was golden in color with blue streaks on its wings and it was huge. It was lying asleep in a giant cavern hidden in the cliffs beside Cambrick. Much later I had a dream where I was riding on the back of the same dragon."

He shrugged. "Now that I've seen a living dragon, I've often wondered if the golden dragon might be real. Whether it is or not, when I first began masking my glimmer my thoughts were full of the magic that surrounded the sleeping dragon, and I was remembering that dragons had supposedly been able to mask their glimmer."

Kylen's brows furrowed. Dalthinir had said it might help to be desperate. He was certainly more than eager to find Marielle and Dannah, and without mastering this ability he couldn't safely leave the valley. Did that count?

Dragons clearly had the ability to mask their glimmer. From the beginning his farsense had allowed him to smell the glimmer of mages from a great distance, yet he had failed to detect the glimmer of Elef'nissar during their first encounter in the Drakkenridge Mountains —even when the dragon had been close enough to touch.

Why couldn't he do it, too? The magic he was using had been awakened by Elef'nissar, and he had a piece of the dragon's claw embedded in his bones.

Almost without thinking, he surrounded himself with a shield.

"You're doing it!" exclaimed Dalthinir excitedly.

"Doing what?"

"Masking your glimmer! Examine your shield! Do you sense anything different about it?"

He eagerly did as Dalthinir suggested. There *was* something unfamiliar about it—a new component of some kind. He quickly removed the shield and reestablished it again.

"Is it still there?" he asked nervously.

"Yes, it is!"

Upon further examination he could still detect the strangeness. It was incredible. The new component to his shield magic was already beginning to feel familiar. He was sure he could call upon it again.

"Let's find Trisanna!" he said excitedly. "I want to know if I'm able to mask her glimmer as well."

He hurried away in search of her, his mentor not far behind him. Even before reaching her, he wrapped her glimmer in a shield.

With his heart pounding with excitement, he turned back to Dalthinir. "Is it working for her as well?"

"It is," the mage confirmed with a smile.

Trisanna was peering at them quizzically.

"Kylen has figured out how to mask glimmer," Dalthinir explained.

She was clearly impressed.

"Can you please create an illusion, Trisanna?" Kylen asked.

She immediately disappeared.

"Were you able to detect her use of power?" Kylen asked his mentor.

"No," he replied. "Well done, Kylen! You're successfully masking both her glimmer and her use of power."

Trisanna winked into sight again. "I imagine you'll want to leave now, Kylen," she said with a grin.

"As soon as you're ready," he confirmed, trying not to sound too eager.

"I'll get started on my preparation," she promised.

"I'll do the same," he replied, immediately hurrying away to make a start.

His thoughts were focused on Dannah and Marielle as he placed a few essentials into a small pack. He owed Dannah a huge debt of gratitude. She had played a key role in his healing, and she had trusted him enough to allow him to be trained as a healer himself. After leaving Abbethar in direct contravention of the orders of the community elders, he badly wanted to find her and assure her he hadn't done so by his own choice.

It was less straightforward with Marielle. He wanted to see her more than he could express, but he hadn't forgotten the anger in her eyes. At the time he left, she hadn't been able to bear the sight of him, and the idea of being with her again filled him with apprehension.

All that aside, the thought of them being found and executed was more than he could bear. He was desperate to find them before the Compact did.

What had prompted Marielle to come to Periton? Why had either of them come? They knew what would happen to renegades there. He'd told them plainly enough.

He would face a new dilemma once he found them. They would be safe in the hidden valley, but they might not be willing to go there. Even if they agreed, they probably wouldn't stay for long.

And what would he do if they insisted he return with them to Abbethar?

He sighed. Reconnecting with them was likely to be complicated in ways he couldn't predict.

Pushing uncertainties from his mind, he slung the pack onto his back and headed for the kitchen to gather supplies for the journey.

His questions could wait until he found them.

Leaving the valley proved to be anything but a quick and easy operation. Vennia insisted on preparing food to send with them, and everyone else stopped whatever they were doing to give them a proper farewell.

"We're coming with you, of course," said Jonno.

"We need to get to know your girlfriend better," added Bella.

Seeing the color rising to his face, both of them chortled with delight.

"Marielle isn't my girlfriend," he said, working hard at keeping his poise.

"I was actually referring to Dannah," said Bella with a twinkle in her eyes.

"I can see why you'd be interested in Marielle," said Jonno. "She is unusually attractive. And it helps that she's clearly besotted with you!"

"She has no interest in me!" insisted Kylen.

"That isn't what her voice said when she crooned your name," said Bella.

"To say nothing of the pitiful sigh that followed," added Jonno.

Kylen frowned at them, sending both of them into fits of laughter.

"Leave the poor boy alone!" chided Vennia. "If you keep it up for much longer he'll be incapable of speech when he sees her."

"This kind of nonsense is the exact reason why you're *not* coming with us!" Trisanna told them sternly.

"Perhaps the real reason is that Trisanna wants Kylen all to herself," suggested Jonno with a cheeky grin.

"That's enough!" exclaimed Inga. "If there's another word, the pair of you will be milking the cows at dawn for the next two weeks!"

The twins finally subsided, although the cheeky grins didn't leave their faces. They had at least accepted they would be staying behind.

After embraces all round, Kylen and Trisanna sent a parting wave and headed out of the valley.

Given Kylen's condition, Sorren had offered to drive them in the donkey cart, at least until they reached the border. Dalthinir joined them in case Sorren needed help on the return journey. Trisanna hid them, cart and all, and this time it was Kylen who masked the mages' glimmer. In the end, they traveled some distance beyond the border before Sorren and Dalthinir left them and headed back to the valley. After they had gone, Trisanna ensured the cart remained hidden for as long as she could.

The gravity of their situation didn't fully hit Kylen until they were alone. His mentor had always been at his side to provide guidance and protection when situations escalated. Now he and Trisanna were on their own. The time had come for him to stand on his own two feet.

"After what happened with Lars, I think it might be wise to remain hidden as much as possible," suggested Kylen. "I'll continue to mask our glimmer, and I'll mask our use of magic as well."

"I have an illusion in place," Trisanna assured him. "Onlookers won't be able to see, hear, or smell us. Where would you like to begin our search?"

"I've been giving that some thought. You met Dannah and Marielle on the main road between Sengin and Cambrick. Which direction were they heading?"

"They were heading south toward Sengin, and we were heading north. That's the only reason we met them. They said they were looking for you, and Dalthinir told them they wouldn't find you in Sengin."

Dalthinir had given Kylen similar information. "Did they say why they were looking for me?" he asked, not at all certain he was going to like the answer.

Trisanna shook her head. "They didn't say."

"If they took Dalthinir seriously, they might have changed direction and headed north," said Kylen.

"I agree."

He nodded grimly. "They can't hide their glimmer, which means others are going to find them, just like you did. Sooner or later they'll end up in Cambrick, if they're not there already."

"Then let's go straight to the capital," she said. "What will we do when we get there?"

Kylen remembered what they'd done when they visited the capital to retrieve Bella. It felt like an eternity had passed since then. "We'll go where the Compact mages are, and we'll listen in on their conversation. If two foreign mages have been found and brought in, people are sure to be talking about it."

She seemed satisfied. "Are you sure you can cope with all this walking?"

Recalling his abortive attempts to walk faster using magic, he allowed a wry smile to curl his lip. "I'll manage somehow. Just keep an eye out for any carts heading in the right direction."

She nodded. "I'll let you set the pace."

Their progress was slow enough that Kylen was tempted to despair. Thankfully, his wish was granted the following day when a farmer with a cart approached them, heading in the same direction. After they had hurried behind a tree, Trisanna ended the illusion. They then stepped back onto the road and Trisanna asked the farmer for a ride. He agreed without hesitation and waved them into the back.

The farmer seemed pleased to have company, and as the hours passed they heard plenty about his sick cow, the challenges caused by the unseasonal weather, and his largely futile attempts to improve the yield of his crops. That wasn't all. The kingdom's troubles provided a constant backdrop to everything he said.

"Everyone's talking about the Tantellans—and cursing their king," the farmer told them. "Our king hasn't been idle, either. We're a long way from Cambrick, but a band of soldiers showed up last week. They drafted my oldest son into the army. The missus was inconsolable. It's been a heavy blow. I need him around the farm!"

He was trying to put a good face on it. "I told my wife to calm herself," he said. "There's no good reason for Tantel and Periton to fight each other. It'll all blow over, and our son will be back soon enough."

Both Trisanna and Kylen earnestly expressed their sympathy. They asked plenty of questions about what was happening, but neither of them offered opinions.

When the farmer stopped the cart to water the horse, the farmer eyed Kylen appraisingly. "The minute these army types clap eyes on you, young fella, you'll be in uniform! They'll recruit you before you can blink!"

Alarmed as Trisanna was by the prediction, Kylen made light of it. Nevertheless, it did give him plenty to think about during the long hours of travel.

In the end, they bumped along in the back of the cart all the way to Cambrick. They reached the gates a couple of hours after dawn. Climbing down from the cart, they thanked the farmer gratefully for his kindness.

CHAPTER 31
TANTEL

Kharkin slipped down a dark alley and through the side entrance of the house where he was meeting Lord Crinholm. Based on the roundabout path taken by his guide, it seemed very unlikely he had been followed.

"Thank you for agreeing to meet with me, Your Lordship."

The nobleman dipped his head in response. "Chief Master. I am curious to learn what has prompted this meeting."

"I wish to explore the attitude of the Conclave to the current situation that confronts the kingdom."

"There is no single attitude to report. The Conclave is an informal association of nobles. It is not like the Compact, where one mage speaks for all."

"I am aware of that. I am also aware that you are unusually well connected, and that many of the nobles follow your lead."

"You flatter me, Chief Master. I make no such claim on my own behalf."

"Be that as it may, I would be glad to speak with you—on one condition. It must remain strictly confidential! Are you willing to engage in discussion on those terms?"

"I am," the noble replied.

"Should anything that passes between us leak out, I will, of course, deny that the conversation ever took place."

Crinholm dipped his head in acknowledgment.

"Very well. We find ourselves on the brink of war. Yet we have established an adversarial relationship with a foreign power of unknown capabilities. Are you and your peers aware of this information?"

"I cannot speak for others. However, I am aware that we have taken possession of an object that belongs to the islanders. I am also aware that they sent a delegation to the king, presumably to get it back."

Kharkin was impressed, and he didn't try to hide it. Crinholm was living up to his reputation.

"I sincerely hope that events will not spiral out of control," he said. "Should those hopes be disappointed, though, I would like to think that like-minded individuals with influence could work together for the good of the kingdom."

"Are we like-minded, Chief Master? What is your agenda in all this?"

"You speak frankly, and I welcome that. I will be frank in return. I attended the meeting with the delegation sent by the islanders, as you are no doubt aware."

Crinholm dipped his head in acknowledgment.

"Then you should also know that a member of the delegation healed my arthritis as she was leaving."

The nobleman's brows rose in surprise.

"Whatever her motive might have been, two things have changed as a result. First, I find my own attitude to life has become unexpectedly hopeful. And second, I do not wish to see us provoke a war with the islanders. Or with Periton, for that matter."

"I believe you to be sincere, Chief Master."

Kharkin sighed in relief. Crinholm's ability to accurately read people encouraged him enormously.

"We appear to be like-minded, on these matters at least," the nobleman continued. "I will look forward to working constructively with you, should the need ever arise."

After they had shaken hands on it, Kharkin allowed himself to be guided away from the meeting place. He left considerably more relaxed than when he had arrived.

~

HAVING REACHED Lord Crinholm's mansion, instinct guided Lokan to the side entrance used by retainers. When he knocked on the door, he was recognized by the footman who opened it. Ushering him inside, the footman called for Lord Crinholm.

When the nobleman appeared, he immediately hurried Lokan to his study, telling his valet he did not wish to be disturbed.

"Lokan! You're alive!" Crinholm shook his head in wonder.

"I seem to be getting that reaction a lot since I returned to Antilin," Lokan told him wryly.

"What happened to you? Tell me everything!"

Lokan hesitated. He was bursting to confide in Crinholm. But the king had told him everything about his assignment was to be treated in the strictest confidence, and the islanders had sworn him to secrecy.

Crinholm was shaking his head. "I know what you're thinking. The king undoubtedly insisted on secrecy in this particular matter. Let me assure you that you're wasting your time if you honor his wishes. And I strongly suspect that your loyalty is badly misplaced."

He sighed. "Let me tell you what I already know. I can't tell you how, but I learned of your mission before you set out, and I managed to place a sailor loyal to me on board your ship. It took enormous effort, especially given the limited time. I instructed him not to take any kind of action—he was there only to observe. I did tell him to keep an eye out for you, though. When he eventually reported back to me, I greatly regretted having restricted him so severely. But by then it was too late."

Lokan's jaw was hanging open. He didn't care.

"He kept track of where you sailed. After you reached the island, he saw Deemis place the wheel around your waist, hit you on the head, and throw you in."

"He hit me on the head?" Lokan stared at him in astonishment. "Was he certain?"

"He was! Immediately after he did it, Deemis glanced around to see if anyone had noticed. My man barely averted his eyes in time. But he had no doubt about what he saw. The ship sailed away from the island, but it remained in the area for several days. He noticed that someone had lit a fire onshore, and he guessed it was you sending a signal. Deemis ignored it. Eventually, they moved to the other side of the island. Deemis left the ship and went ashore. Then a full scale hurricane blew up. The vessel almost sank! After the storm died down, Deemis reappeared with a large object wrapped in a blanket. After putting it in his cabin and locking the door, he instructed the captain to return to Tantel."

Crinholm ran a hand across his face. "I was horrified when I eventually heard all this. It took me vastly longer than I had hoped, but I managed to send a small ship to the location, guided by my sailor. They found the place, and he went ashore. He found the remains of a crude shelter and signs that people had been there in the recent past. But no one was there. He only returned two days ago."

"Your man probably followed me all the way back to Tantel," said Lokan. "And to think I was worried about what became of Deemis!" he said bitterly. "He knew I was there all along, and he did nothing to help me!" He clasped the nobleman's arm. "Thank you! You were the only one who actually tried to do something."

"I wouldn't be much of a friend if I did anything less," Crinholm told him. "I'm sure you can understand why I was so astonished to find you at my door! But it's your turn now. Tell me what happened to you!"

Lokan didn't hold back. He spoke openly of the mission and its purpose, of his rescue by Buck and what he learned from him. Then, after swearing Crinholm to secrecy, he broke his promise and described the arrival of the islanders, the interrogation, the storm, and the eventual decision to send the two prisoners home. Finally, he described his recent meeting with Deemis.

"So circumstances had changed," mused Crinholm. "It isn't hard to guess what that meant. When they discovered that the object had been stolen, they must have realized their isolation was over. And they decided not to kill you, perhaps because you'd saved their interrogator."

"That all makes sense," agreed Lokan.

"They must have somehow found out the king had their object," continued Crinholm, "so they sent a delegation to ask for it back. They met with the king and Kharkin."

"I heard about the delegation from one of the guards."

"Kharkin positioned a large group of mages outside the room where they met the delegation. It was most likely a precaution in case something went wrong. According to an informed source, Kharkin has been a different person since the meeting. It seems he was healed by one of the delegation members. I can't guess why, because I understand the two members of the delegation weren't happy when they left."

"The guard said the same thing."

"As for the object, we can only guess at its significance," said the nobleman.

"According to Deemis, it came from a dragon, although he claimed it isn't a talisman. Supposedly it has a priceless jewel inside it. That's if you can believe anything Deemis says."

Crinholm shrugged. "What I don't understand is why the king cares about it. From all reports, he's been incredibly pleased with himself since he got it. How does it help him win his war? Rumor has it that he's planning to invade Periton in a week, or two at the outside."

"Is it possible he thinks the islanders can help his invasion?" asked Lokan.

"How? Do they have a lot of soldiers?"

Lokan shook his head helplessly. "I have no idea."

The nobleman frowned. "We have too many questions and not enough answers. The biggest question is how to stop this war. Apart from the king, I don't know anyone who wants it."

"Do you have any thoughts?"

"I'm at a complete loss. There was a time when I wondered if your Deemis might somehow be able to help. I've long since abandoned any such notion. I was already feeling uneasy about him before this latest incident."

"I'm beginning to regret ever bringing him to the capital," said Lokan miserably.

"All we can do is stay alert and hope for an opportunity we can exploit. What are you going to do, Lokan?"

"Deemis will no doubt report my return to the capital. The king might want to see me, although I can't see any point in it. According to Deemis, he might not be happy with me. He claimed he was going to put in a word on my behalf."

"The king already sees me as a complainer," Crinholm told him. "It might be wise if we're not seen together. I know an inn where you'll be comfortable. I'll arrange it."

"Thank you! I appreciate everything you've done. More than I can say."

Leaving by the same side door, Lokan set off for the tavern.

A couple of idle bystanders saw him leave. Their studied indifference wasn't convincing, and he hurried away feeling very uneasy. He decided he would let Lord Crinholm know at the earliest opportunity.

Late the following morning, one of the king's aides was shown to his room at the inn.

"The king wishes to meet with you. Be at the palace in one hour," he was told. The aide left after delivering his message. Lokan was left to guess how he knew where to find him.

Having always suspected he wouldn't escape an interview with the king, Lokan wasn't surprised. Nevertheless, he became increasingly nervous as he waited outside the king's reception room. Three hours passed before the king finally arrived. If the king's purpose had been to discompose him, he achieved his goal.

As soon as King Garneth arrived, an aide ushered Lokan into the room, closing the door behind him as he left.

"Ah, Lokan," said the king dispassionately. "I see you somehow survived your little adventure."

He didn't exactly sound disappointed, but Lokan was left with the impression that he didn't particularly care.

"Deemis seemed to think you were worried about meeting me. I can't imagine why. I wanted the relic, and now I have it."

It was galling to discover that Deemis had misrepresented them both. Lokan said nothing.

"Did the exiles treat you well? And how are your friends?" asked the king dryly.

Seeing his blank look at the latter question, the king added, "I'm referring to Pindel and Crinholm, of course."

Anger rose within Lokan, sweeping away his anxiety. After everything he had suffered on the king's behalf, the monarch's dismissive questions had been provoking enough. The final stroke was the casual revelation that royal agents had spied on him and the only two people who had bothered to help him.

He stared back at the king unflinching. "The exiles did not treat me well, Your Majesty. I am glad to have friends willing to help in a time of need."

To his astonishment the king burst out laughing. "Your unexpected resilience is your greatest asset, Lokan! You have disarmed me entirely." Then his eyes narrowed. "That does not mean I will overlook treason," he growled.

"Perhaps I haven't always succeeded at the tasks you have set me, but I have never hesitated to attempt them," said Lokan steadfastly. "I am sure Your Majesty can find no grounds for complaint when it comes to my loyalty."

The king calmed down. "You speak the truth, Lokan. And I have not forgotten the great good you did me in bringing young Deemis to my attention. Or that you risked my wrath to do it."

Lokan dipped his head.

"You have earned yourself a short break," the king told him. "Take a rest from further demands, at least for the moment. You are dismissed!"

Too relieved to speak, Lokan bowed low and left the room.

～

THAT NIGHT LOKAN sat at a small table in the inn enjoying a mug of ale as he reflected on the events of the day. The patrons crowding the inn were becoming noisier with every passing minute. The scene was no different from a typical evening at an inn back home at Brynford.

His eye restlessly roamed about the room, observing the customers and their demeanor. He'd done it for years, and he saw no reason to stop now.

A man he recognized as a retainer of Crinholm entered the inn. Sitting down with an ale, he briefly locked eyes with Lokan before casually looking away. After slowly sipping the ale for several minutes, he directed another glance in Lokan's direction. Then he drained the mug in a few gulps and left the inn.

Lokan remained on his stool for several more minutes before calmly getting up and leaving the inn himself. Moving into the shadows at the side of the building, he glimpsed a dark figure leaning against the wall.

Bending forward, the man addressed him quietly. "His Lordship is waiting. Follow me!"

Without waiting for a response, the speaker slipped down a side alley. Lokan hurried after him. The two of them wound their way through dark streets and alleys, sometimes sprinting and sometimes pausing to check for possible pursuit.

Eventually they arrived at a small house with a side door opening onto a shadowy alley. Stepping through the door, Lokan crossed a narrow corridor and entered an adjoining room dimly illuminated by candlelight. He found Lord Crinholm reclining in an armchair sipping a port.

The retainer approached the noble and bent low for a whispered conversation. Then he left the room.

"Thank you for coming," said the nobleman, waving him to a seat. "I heard that the king had called you in, and I wanted to be certain you emerged unscathed."

"Nothing happened to me," Lokan assured him. "We're being watched, though."

"You were followed here?" asked Crinholm in surprise.

He shook his head. "When I left your mansion yesterday I noticed a couple of men watching the place. They definitely saw me leave. Then the king asked about my friends, and he named you as one of them. Later he made a veiled threat about treason. He calmed down after I assured him of my loyalty."

Crinholm was frowning. "You mean he accused me of disloyalty?"

"Not directly. He must have known I would pass on to you what he said. I suspect he intended his remarks as a warning."

"We need to be careful," said his friend. "It's the reason this meeting is clandestine. What else did he tell you?"

Lokan grimaced. "He told me he hadn't forgotten the service I did him in bringing Deemis to his attention."

"Deemis certainly gets a great deal of his attention," Crinholm replied. "I can't begin to guess what games the king is playing. Tomorrow afternoon's proclamation will be very interesting."

"Proclamation?"

"I'm sure you'll receive an invitation if you haven't already. Anyone of significance has been invited to the palace to hear a proclamation. No details are on offer. It must be important, though. I'm told it's gone out to royal officials, the Conclave of Nobles, the mages of the Compact, the senior merchants, and the guildmasters from the Guild Council."

Lokan's eyebrows went up. "Do you think the proclamation might have something to do with the war?"

Crinholm shook his head. "I suspect not. But I can only guess. I've already heard any number of wild theories, and none of them sound vaguely plausible to me. Whatever the proclamation is about, the king has managed to keep it extremely quiet. My sources have nothing to offer beyond speculation."

The nobleman settled back in his armchair with a sigh. "What are you planning to do, Lokan?"

"I'm going to lie low for a while. The king told me to take some time off."

Crinholm's eyebrows went up. "That doesn't sound like him! He must be in an unusually good mood."

"It took me by surprise too."

"Since you seem to have time on your hands, I'd like you to join me after the proclamation. I'm planning to meet with one or two others, and it would be useful to include you in the conversation."

"Is that wise?"

"As long as we're careful it shouldn't be a problem. Further to that, I'll make sure my man is doubly careful when he takes you back to your inn."

As Crinholm had predicted, Lokan found a packet waiting for him in his room at the inn.

Opening it, he found a card stamped with the royal seal. It read:

His Majesty King Garneth
Commands
The presence of Lokan
To receive a
Proclamation from the king

Invitees should present themselves
In the palace courtyard
Two hours after noon tomorrow

What could the proclamation be about? How would it affect him?

His life had changed more than he could have believed possible since his encounter with Deemis at the inn in Brynford. Stranded in the capital, he was at his leisure awaiting a new assignment from the king after barely surviving the last one. More alarmingly, he was secretly meeting with highly placed individuals who questioned the priorities of the king.

He lay down for the night more uncertain about the future than ever. Several hours passed before he managed to get to sleep.

CHAPTER 32
PERITON

Kylen and Trisanna stood for many minutes observing the entrance to Cambrick. Although people were freely entering and leaving, the gates of the city were guarded as never before, with officers and armed soldiers on the alert at each side of the road.

As they watched, two young men were pulled aside and questioned. In one case the youth was allowed to rejoin his companions and go on his way.

The other youth, dejected and with his head down, was sent into the city with a soldier gripping each arm. He had been traveling with what appeared to be his parents and a sister. The noisy protests of the parents were ignored.

"The farmer was right," murmured Trisanna. "They're pressing young men into service, willing or not."

Kylen nodded. "It doesn't look like I'll have any chance of making it into the city without your help."

"I've activated an illusion," Trisanna replied. "We can go whenever you're ready. Don't forget that I don't know my way around. I've never been here before."

For a time it seemed that the stream of people and their animals would never end. However, eventually the flow did ease briefly.

Seizing the opportunity, Kylen grabbed Trisanna's hand and led her through the gates. None of the soldiers betrayed any awareness of them.

Once inside, he moved purposefully forward along the main road.

Being invisible to other people had its complexities, especially on busy city streets. Pedestrians could change direction in an instant and collide with them. More than once someone headed directly for them, believing the way ahead was clear. Kylen needed to be doubly alert to make sure he didn't lose contact with Trisanna.

After a few minutes Trisanna pulled him out of the flow of people. "Unless you particularly want to be invisible, I can change our appearance so no one will recognize us."

"Will that make it easier for you?"

"It will require the same amount of power. But at least people will see us coming."

"Let's do it, then."

To his astonishment, Trisanna instantly disappeared, replaced by an older woman with her gray hair tied in a bun. He chortled before he could stop himself.

"You wouldn't be laughing if you could see what you looked like!" she assured him.

Glancing down, he saw his hands weathered and wrinkled. He shrugged. He might as well be an old man considering his walking pace. A self-conscious grin twisted his lips as he set off again.

With other people able to consciously avoid them, the journey became much less stressful. After a while he led his companion off the main road into less frequented streets and alleys. Pausing gratefully for a rest, he remembered ruefully that he had once clambered about on roofs and leaped between buildings. Such feats were beyond him now. Perhaps one day he might fully recover—in the meantime he needed to accept his limitations.

Eventually they arrived in a city slum that had once been very familiar to him. Reaching the derelict building where he had so often slept, Kylen released Trisanna's hand at last. Before he met Dalthinir, Kylen had sheltered here, along with Jonno and Bella.

Other street urchins had also called the crumbling structure their home. The worst among them had been Raff, a bully and snitch who had occasionally caused considerable trouble for Kylen. The reminder of Raff prompted his brows to draw together in a frown. He fingered the stub of his missing little finger restlessly.

No one was in sight.

Entering the structure, he peered around, on the lookout for the subtle hints that people still sheltered there. He saw nothing. The building appeared to be abandoned.

What had become of Raff and his cronies?

"This is where I once lived," he told Trisanna.

Seeing the astonishment on her face, he shrugged. "I was an orphan living on the streets before I met Dalthinir."

"I'm sorry," she said sincerely. "I can't imagine what life must have been like for you."

"Don't be sorry," he replied. "For the most part it wasn't a bad life. And it's how I met the twins."

She could only shake her head.

He decided to change the subject. "I can only walk slowly, but I think there's still enough day left for us to go to the part of the city where the mages tend to congregate. Shall we see if we can hear anything about Dannah and Marielle?"

"That sounds like a good idea," she replied. "I am starting to feel a little weary, though, and I imagine it will be wise to be invisible when we get there. Do you think it would be safe for me to drop the illusion for a while so I can take a break?"

"I'm sure we can manage. Provided you can hide us completely at short notice if something goes wrong."

"I should be able to do that. I've dropped the illusion, so as of now we need to be careful."

Kylen led them away. "I know my way around these parts," he told her, "and I would normally stick to alleys and back streets. Keeping out of trouble often requires lightning quick responses, though, and my body isn't up to that yet. So I'm going to take us back to the main road. As well as the usual dangers, we'll need to be particularly on the lookout for army recruiters."

"Lead the way," she replied. "Just be aware that I didn't grow up in a city, so I have no idea what counts as usual dangers."

He nodded. "Let's go."

At Kylen's slower pace it took time to return to the road. They reached it without incident, though, and it did at least offer the most direct route to their destination.

Stopping frequently for rests, Kylen led them deeper into the city. The first time he spotted soldiers, he instinctively shrunk back out of sight. He soon discovered he had no need to worry. Patrolling soldiers appeared no more interested in him than in anyone else. Perhaps specific officers had been tasked with finding recruits. If so, they were the only ones Kylen needed to avoid. After a while he ignored the soldiers entirely.

It was a mistake.

A loud shout sounded over the din of the city, and a small group of soldiers suddenly converged on Kylen, swarming around him.

"Well, here's a surprise!" drawled a once-familiar voice. "Look who's appeared out of nowhere!"

Kylen looked up into the leering face of Raff. He was surrounded by his old cronies, all of them now in uniform.

A few of the passersby glanced at them, but none tried to intervene. Lowering their heads, they kept moving. Such scenes had undoubtedly become familiar, and no one was willing to invite trouble without a good reason.

"So the army decided to take a chance on you, Raff," he said coolly. "Nice to see you benefiting someone other than yourself for a change."

Raff's face flushed with anger. Drawing back his arm to strike Kylen, he hesitated. Perhaps he was recalling what happened during their last encounter, just before Kylen left Cambrick with the twins.

"We can't have riffraff like you wandering the streets, Kylen," he sneered. "I'll have you enlisted before the day is out. Then I'll take care of you myself." He pointed to the colored strip of fabric sewn onto each shoulder of his uniform. "I'm a corporal now! That means you'll do whatever I say!"

He waved to two of his companions. "Grab hold of him! He's coming with us."

At that moment all of them gasped. "Where did he go?"

Alerted to the commotion, an officer strode toward them. "What's going on here?"

"There's a street rat...to be enlisted, sir," sputtered Raff.

The officer glanced around. "I don't see anyone! Where is he?" he demanded.

"He...he seems to have disappeared, sir," mumbled Raff, his head down.

"Are you mocking me?" roared the officer.

"No, sir," Raff managed.

"Latrine duty for the next week, Corporal! Now get back to base, all of you! If I see you aimlessly meandering around the streets again, disciplinary action will take on a whole new meaning for you!"

Kylen watched them slink away, a satisfied grin on his face. "Thanks for rescuing me, Trisanna! You can drop the illusion now."

She shook her head. "It's too risky! Look what just happened!"

He eyed her doubtfully, but she insisted. "I've had a bit of a rest. I can manage."

He could only take her at her word. Resuming their journey, he reminded himself he needed to keep out of the way of other travelers.

An hour had passed before they reached the main concentration of Compact mages. Glimmer now surrounded them on every side. By then walking had become a major problem for Kylen, and Trisanna was also clearly spent. In the past he would have climbed onto a roof to watch and listen. That simply wasn't possible for him now.

With both of them needing to lie low, he invested his last reserves of energy in hunting for a place where they could rest unseen. A memory came to his mind of a small park, not far from the building used by the Compact for large meetings. Inga had gone there after her trial, and Kylen and his friends had followed her in hope of finding the missing Bella. They had not been disappointed.

Seeking it out, he searched among the trees until he found a small space surrounded on all sides by bushes where the two of them could sit with some degree of comfort.

"We should be able to rest here without being seen or disturbed," he told Trisanna. "We shouldn't need the illusion anymore."

She heaved a sigh of relief. "I've dropped it."

Aware that his voice was no longer masked, Kylen lowered his voice. "I'll continue to shield us. I can keep it up indefinitely now I have a talisman."

There was just enough room for both of them to stretch out, and they did so immediately. Kylen wasn't planning to sleep, but he was so weary he drifted off anyway.

His eyes opened to the fading light of dusk. Trisanna's movements had woken him.

"I left to buy some food," she told him. "I didn't want to wake you, especially because you were the one most likely to be recognized."

He grunted. It didn't sit well with him to allow her to take all the risks. He could hardly argue, though. She'd returned safely, and with something for them to eat.

He soon discovered she'd returned with more than food.

"I overheard a couple of mages talking. They mentioned two foreigners detained by the chief master."

"If the chief master detained them, they must be mages," he replied.

She nodded. "And while I was at the market buying supplies, I caught a glimpse of one of the friends of your bully boy Raff. He was hanging around, trying to look inconspicuous. Not doing a very good job of it, either!"

"I don't care about Raff. He's like a gnat. He can be annoying, but he can't do any real harm. Your other news is important, though. We must have come to the right place. You did well, Trisanna!"

After eating, both of them lay down for a well-earned sleep.

ONCE MORE ELEF'NISSAR visited him in his dreams.

"Zin'thelestar has new schemes," the dragon told him. "As ever, it is intent on destruction!"

"Zin'thelestar?" he asked in bafflement.

"Your companion knows it as the Destroyer—the dragon responsible for the Amulet of Zinth. It has haunted your dreams before."

Memories flooded into his mind—gliding across an underground lake in a boat, ascending a hill in the dark, finding a staff shaped like a dragon at rest. He had grasped the staff, and the world had been utterly destroyed.

Even in his dream state he shuddered, dismayed by the reminder of what he had witnessed.

"I see you recognize the creature of which I speak," Elef'nissar told him. "Never forget that I have successfully resisted its purposes."

The dragon had not resisted alone. Images flashed through his mind—mages struggling in the Great Library in Ettaran, dark magic writhing in a glowing orb, the building's destruction. They had prevailed at great cost.

"You must prevent disaster. You and the girl."

"Trisanna?"

The dragon's eyes whirled. "The healer's daughter's daughter."

He closed his eyes, trying to figure it out. Daughter's daughter must mean granddaughter, and the healer must be Dannah. With a start he realized the dragon was referring to Marielle. In what way was she supposed to be involved?

THE DREAM ENDED as he woke with the dawn. Elef'nissar was gone.

He lay still, grappling with the meaning of what he had heard. It left him with a new set of unanswered questions. What was Zin'thelestar planning now? And how were he and Marielle expected to prevent it?

For all the uncertainties, if he understood correctly, the message of the dream boiled down to something very simple: Zin'thelestar hadn't given up on its ambitions to destroy humankind, and once more it fell to him to do something about it.

This time Marielle had been assigned a key role. He felt a flush traveling up his face. Had he imagined that part of it?

He rolled his eyes. The dream—every element of it—could only be attributed to Elef'nissar. His own imagination had played no part.

It underscored the importance of finding Dannah and Marielle. He fervently hoped they were beginning their search in the right place.

He released a heavy sigh. How had he become caught up in these events?

Dragons were continuing to interfere. Apparently the evil creature known as Zin'thelestar was doing so in every way it could, and Elef'nissar seemed determined to match it.

Their interference was becoming an oppressive burden. As far as he could tell, the weight of interference had fallen heaviest on him.

CHAPTER 33
PERITON

Both Kylen and Trisanna had woken refreshed and renewed. Kylen debated with himself whether or not to tell her about his dream. If Elef'nissar had spoken of a role for her it would have been an easy decision. As it was, he wasn't sure how she might feel about it.

In the end, he decided to tell her about the dream while being sparing with the details.

"Could you please hide what we're saying?" he asked.

"Certainly," she replied. "Anyone observing us will think we're sitting here silently."

He nodded. "I had a dream yesterday," he began.

"So did I!" she said excitedly. "I was wondering how to tell you about it! The dragon spoke to me—the one who brought you to rescue Dalthinir. It spoke to me before, when we were in Methesia. I always thought of it as the Preserver. It said that the Destroyer—the dragon that empowered the Amulet of Zinth—hasn't given up on destroying humankind. It has to be stopped. It said you will be involved, and that I need to support you in whatever way I can."

He felt relieved. There had clearly been no reason to hold back on his dream.

She seemed suddenly tentative. "There was more it said about you." Then she seemed to recover herself. "It said you and the healer's girl need to prevent the evil from happening. The healer's girl has to be Marielle."

There was something about him she wasn't saying, but she didn't elaborate. She just stared at him, concern in her eyes. "All of this is a big responsibility, Kylen."

What could he say? Trisanna's report had only reinforced his irritation about the lofty way the dragon assigned responsibility to him. Some years previously he had watched a puppet show from a distance.

"Do you ever feel like a puppet, with the dragon being the one who pulls the strings?" he asked her.

Her brows drew together. "What's a puppet?"

He shrugged helplessly. "Never mind. It doesn't matter. What does matter is that my dream was very similar. The dragon didn't say what this Destroyer is planning, though, or how I'm supposed to prevent it. Do you know?" Before she could reply he added self-consciously, "I suppose I should have said how Marielle and I are supposed to prevent it."

Seeing his discomfort at mentioning Marielle, a grin flashed across her face. Then she became serious. "I don't know any more than you do. Except I do know that freeing Dannah and Marielle has become more important than ever."

"Are you sure you have the energy?" he asked. She'd been hiding their speech instead of resting.

"I'll manage," she assured him. "What I've been doing doesn't take much energy. As of now I'm masking our visibility as well as our sound."

He led them away from the park and toward a bright cluster of glimmer. After a few minutes hunting they found a perfect location. Positioning themselves against a wall, they were far enough from the mages to make it unlikely they would be approached, but close enough to hear everything being said.

They were in time to witness a conversation initiated by a mage who had just returned to the capital after spending time in Sengin.

"What's happening about the two foreign mages in custody?" she asked.

"The chief master has chaired a panel tasked with deciding their fate," she was told. "A full gathering of the Compact has been called for tomorrow morning. The decision will be announced at the gathering."

"I've heard they'll be executed," said another mage.

"That would be harsh, especially after they healed the crown prince!" said another.

"Yes, but what was their motive for doing it? And why were they here in the first place? Periton is effectively at war with Tantel. It's a strange time for foreigners to appear here."

"Where are they from? Their king might not take it kindly if we kill them, especially when they've broken no laws."

"They *have* broken the law! Mages can't just wander around in another kingdom without permission! They must be stupid if they thought there wouldn't be consequences."

The debate rambled on without reaching a conclusion. But the likely outcomes were not at all encouraging. Kylen was becoming increasingly alarmed. He needed to free his friends.

A frown was twisting Trisanna's brow. "What do you think we should do?" she asked.

"We need to find out where they're being held," he replied. "We also need to find out what will happen if the panel decides to execute them."

"How do we do that?"

He shook his head. "I have no idea."

The daylight was almost gone by the time they gave up and returned to their hiding place in the park. Kylen was troubled and weary. Trisanna was almost ready to drop. They had no food, but neither of them cared. Throwing themselves down, they yielded to sleep.

KYLEN WOKE TO A SUDDEN NOISE. To his astonishment, he looked up to see a spear plunging directly toward his gut. Behind it a young soldier stared down at him. Startled almost out of his wits, he spun out of the way, avoiding the thrust by the narrowest of margins. Belatedly, he threw up a shield to protect himself.

To his astonishment, the soldier acted as though he hadn't seen him. Turning aside, he headed in a different direction.

"I'm so sorry," winced Trisanna. "I had no idea the spear would go so close! I hid you the moment I woke up. There wasn't time to warn you!"

Kylen exhaled in relief. "No damage done," he assured her.

The young soldier had moved on. Glancing around, he saw half a dozen others moving through the park, systematically stabbing the ground, and even thin air, with their spears. He knew them. It was Raff and his friends.

"That was a nice trick acting dumb at the market yesterday," said a voice not far from them. "All her attention was on you. She didn't even notice I was watching her!"

So that was how they'd done it. They'd spotted Trisanna buying food the previous evening and recognized her. They must have tried to follow her and lost sight of her near the park.

Raff's voice rang out. "They're here somewhere! According to that mage I spoke to, we should still be able to hear and smell them. And being invisible won't protect them against a spear in the guts! Put some energy into it!"

They had rightly concluded that Kylen's earlier disappearance was the result of illusion.

"Raff is smarter than I thought!" said Kylen with a grim smile. "Latrine duty must be good for him."

He picked up a small fallen branch. "Can you hide this for me as well?" he asked. "Sight but not sound?"

When Trisanna nodded, he tossed it across the park into some bushes.

"Did you hear that?" called a voice. "They're over here!"

Kylen's ploy had worked perfectly. The intruders ran toward the sound and surrounded the bushes, stabbing into them fiercely.

"Time for us to get out of here," he exclaimed. "Sooner or later they might realize you can hide sound and smell as well!"

Picking their way through the foliage, they hurried from the park.

They soon discovered men and women with distinctive crimson strips on their black robes heading in the same direction.

Kylen and Trisanna set off after them.

The mages were heading into a building Kylen remembered from Inga's trial. The last of them were about to go in. On impulse, he grabbed Trisanna's hand and hurried inside, clearing the doors a moment before they were closed. Once inside, they stood side by side along the wall near the exit.

"Can you keep the illusion going?" he asked.

She nodded.

Redirecting his attention to the meeting, he spotted Dannah and Marielle sitting at the front of the gathering. They were positioned at one side, allowing them to see and be seen by both the gathered mages as well as the person at the podium.

The room wasn't entirely full. Most likely, some Compact mages had been sent to Sengin or elsewhere to help guard against invasion.

As they watched, a small group of mages filed in from a door at the back of the building. One of their number stepped forward and addressed the assembly.

"All of you will have received the notification about this meeting. Thank you for attending. I would like to turn this meeting over to Chief Master Adrastas. He will speak on behalf of the panel that has considered the matters before us."

The chief master strode to the podium, acknowledging the facilitator with a brief nod. Then he turned to the assembled mages.

"As you know, we have been considering our options and obligations in light of the unprecedented, and, more importantly, unsanctioned arrival of the two foreign mages before you. The panel of review has carefully considered the case, but before final conclusions can be reached, the mages in question will be offered an opportunity to answer some key questions and make any statement they might wish to make."

He addressed the two women. "Will you tell us where are you from?"

Neither of them responded.

"Who sent you here, and for what purpose?"

Once more they remained silent.

"Why did you exercise mage abilities in Periton without first requesting permission from the Compact?"

Still they said nothing.

The head mage shook his head in frustration. "Do you wish to make a statement before I present the findings of the panel?"

His offer finally drew a response.

"I am willing to speak on behalf of us both," said Dannah. "Since arriving in Periton my granddaughter and I have sought to use our mage abilities for the good of any who might benefit from our help. We have labored without distinction, serving the poorest of the poor as well as the crown prince of your kingdom. Where people offered food and lodging along the way we gratefully accepted it, but we never asked for payment. We felt more than compensated by the warm appreciation we received from the people we worked with."

She faced Adrastas. "You have warned of dire consequences for us if we fail to answer your questions. We have not responded for a simple reason—we are not at liberty to do so. Like you, we answer to higher authorities, and it is not our place to speak on their behalf. Impartial observers might well ask how any kingdom can reasonably claim to be civilized if it condemns people to death on such slight provocation. If I had opportunity, I would tell such observers that the fault does not lie with the rulers of the kingdom. I know your monarchs have no desire to see us punished in that way. The Compact alone must bear the responsibility for any action you take. I can only hope that those we answer to in our homeland will show more restraint and humanity than the Compact when they learn of our fate."

Exclamations broke out throughout the room.

Adrastas shouted over it. "Are you threatening us?" he demanded, his face flushed with anger.

"I am hardly in a position to threaten you," she replied. "And I have already told you I cannot speak for anyone else."

Kylen smiled wryly to himself. Even after living among the

Artorans, he had no idea what force they might be capable of wielding. Nevertheless, Dannah had reminded the mages that their actions would be seen and assessed by foreigners of unknown might. And the consternation caused by her remarks gave Kylen hope.

Adrastas wasn't moved by such considerations.

"Are foreigners allowed to wander freely and without permission in your homeland?" he demanded.

She paused before shaking her head. "They are not," she told him honestly.

Kylen groaned. Dannah was incriminating herself unnecessarily. Why wasn't she simply refusing to answer these questions as well?

Adrastas pressed his advantage. "Do the authorities take action if such intrusions occur?"

"They do," she acknowledged frankly.

"Stern action?" he pressed.

"Yes," she replied after a brief hesitation.

Muttering broke out anew.

"Is it possible they might decide to take the sternest action possible?"

She responded, although reluctantly. "It is possible."

"Then it is no more legal in your homeland than it is in Periton for foreigners to wander about doing whatever they like. Whomever you answer to must therefore have been well aware of the possible implications of sending you here. You have refused to be direct about your motives. That refusal forces us to draw our own conclusions. The panel has decided how to respond if you proved unwilling to be candid with us."

Not so much as a murmur interrupted him.

"All of you are aware of the background to this situation. You know that these women carried out unauthorized medical procedures in the region between Thesmis and the capital. You are aware that before we took them into custody, they performed a healing on Master Kothlar." He frowned briefly at a mage who was not among the panel. "You also know they were later permitted to operate on the crown prince, who, to all appearances, has been healed. Time alone will confirm it. All of us also know that in defending herself against false accusations from one of our own, Dannah revealed a useful forensic technique that will in future be taught to all of our healers."

His face became stern. "Admirable as these actions might seem, we can only guess at their real purpose since the motives that prompted them are hidden from us. What we do now know for certain is that in coming here they flouted their own laws as well as ours. Either their leaders sent them covertly, knowing their presence here would be illegal, or they came with an agenda of their own, without the permission or approval of their leaders. Either way, their refusal to say why they are here can mean only one thing—they are well aware that the truth will incriminate them."

He glared remorselessly at the two women. "The panel decided that clemency would not be appropriate if you refused to answer legitimate questions. Therefore, according to the rights and responsibilities delegated to the Compact, you are sentenced to death. The appointed mages will reconvene at Bagot's Rise, where the sentence will be carried out immediately."

A stunned silence greeted his words.

Kothlar's voice rang out in anger. "This isn't justice! It's a travesty!"

The chief master stared him down. "I am aware of your very personal reasons for being sympathetic to these women, Master Kothlar, and it could be argued that these reasons make it impossible for you to be objective. But it should not be necessary to remind you that, in a situation of this nature, the appropriate sentence is not a matter for discussion. The law of the kingdom offers no flexibility."

Adrastas threw up his hands helplessly. "None of us want this outcome! A stay of execution might have been possible if the prisoners had been willing to provide clear and direct answers to a few simple questions. They have stubbornly refused to say a word! In view of that, our hands are tied!"

Kothlar was visibly unhappy, but he offered no rebuttal of the head mage's reasoning.

"I declare this meeting closed!" cried the chief master.

Kylen leaned toward Trisanna, raising his voice to be heard over the rising din. "I know where Bagot's Rise is. If we leave this building, can you make it appear that the doors haven't moved?"

She nodded readily.

"Then we should go! At the pace I travel, it's going to take us a very long time to get there!"

Hurrying to the main doors, he briefly held one open while they slipped outside.

CHAPTER 34
TANTEL

Intensely curious about King Garneth's forthcoming proclamation, Lokan set out for the palace at noon, allowing himself plenty of time to get inside the palace grounds and onto the main courtyard before the event began. If Lord Crinholm was right about the invitees, the event would be unique. Lokan was not aware of any royal gathering that equaled it in size or in the breadth of its reach across the kingdom's institutions.

From his previous experience of royal events, Lokan expected it would take time to get everyone into position. The security precautions would reflect the size of the gathering. Royal guards would be everywhere, checking credentials and making themselves generally intrusive. Their involvement was certain to destroy any hope of the preparation running smoothly.

A public proclamation was itself almost unprecedented, which only added to the uncertainty. Lokan could not remember the last time the king made such a proclamation. He still couldn't begin to guess at its purpose.

He emerged into the open to be confronted with lowering clouds and strong winds. Even if rain didn't eventuate, the weather promised to be unpleasant. The king must surely be regretting his choice of a date and time, especially in view of the mild weather in the recent past.

Feeling increasingly cold and miserable, he arrived at the palace gates to find a restless crowd of people waiting impatiently to be admitted. From the way the guards were examining invitations, anyone would think they expected forgeries. When combined with the cold wind and the threatening skies, the officiousness of the guards was guaranteed to heighten tension.

An hour passed with little change in the numbers queued outside the palace gates. By then people were openly voicing their anger. Lokan was himself struggling to master his impatience. A senior official finally arrived, and a steady stream of people soon began flowing into the palace grounds.

Lokan reached the main palace courtyard to find a huge crowd assembled. The time for the king's proclamation must have been drawing near. Stamping their feet in the cold, people glanced expectantly up at a balcony overlooking the area. Officials in royal livery made brief appearances on the balcony, presumably preparing for the king's arrival.

The wind continued to pick up. Glancing up, Lokan saw clouds that had become darker and more menacing than ever. Transferring his attention to the balcony, he frowned, willing the king to get it done before the sky decided to empty itself onto the exposed attendees.

An official appeared on the balcony, clad in a lavish gown and holding an important-looking parchment. The moment had finally arrived. The official watched on as the king himself emerged, richly attired and flanked by none other than Deemis.

Lokan stared up at the balcony in bemusement. Deemis might have become the king's favorite, but what was he doing at his side on such an important occasion?

After a bow, the official faced the crowd once more. Stepping forward purposefully, he was immediately exposed to the full force of the wind.

Perched on his head was a woolen hat with an upturned brim, adorned with a large feather. As he opened his mouth to speak, a gust of wind swept it from his head. Reaching up with one hand, he somehow managed to ensnare it. The episode was quickly repeated multiple times. Each time he placed the hat back in position, a new gust swept it away. Undeterred, he persevered against the odds.

The unexpected entertainment brought a spark of life to the shivering crowd. Each new defeat prompted louder bursts of laughter from the crowd. Finally, the strongest gust of all blew the hat out of his reach.

Lokan caught his breath as Deemis, leaping high with a hand outstretched, seized the hat.

Energetic cheering and applause greeted the feat. In response, he offered an extravagant bow to the crowd while holding the hat aloft. Then, with a theatrical flourish, he presented the hat, now minus its feather, to the official. The crowd erupted, whooping and laughing noisily.

The king's patience had reached an end. Leaning forward, he spoke sharply to the flustered official.

Facing the crowd again, this time without his hat, the man introduced the sovereign, plodding his way through every one of King Garneth's many titles. After solemnly instructing the assembled multitude to pay close and respectful attention to the pending proclamation, he scuttled away, yielding the balcony to the king and Deemis.

Stepping forward, the king took a deep breath and began addressing the crowd.

"Some among my loyal subjects have raised the issue of the royal succession. This matter is important, and I intend to address it once and for all."

As he spoke, the wind began to howl so loudly his voice could barely be heard.

Lokan noticed Deemis looking up at the clouds, a worried frown on his face. He had reason to worry.

Up to that point the wind had done nothing worse than toy with the official and his hat. Now it began to fiercely buffet both of the men still on the balcony. Cries rose up from the crowd as a mighty gust drove them both to the very edge. Bracing themselves against the wind, they hugged the stone lip of the balcony, their faces white.

For a moment neither of them moved. Then the sovereign, his robes billowing, decided on a bid for safety. Bending low, he began backing away toward the building.

Releasing his grip on the solid stone proved to be his undoing. To the horror of the gathered throng, the fiercest squall of all scooped him up and tipped him over the brink.

Quick as lightning, Deemis thrust out a hand, somehow grasping the end of the king's gown before it could disappear entirely. Dragged sideways, he managed to hook his leg around something solid.

Lokan watched breathless as Deemis leaned precariously into the void, struggling to prevent the monarch from plunging to his death. With the full weight of the king dangling ominously below him, it seemed certain that both of them would soon be lost.

Then, with a terrible sound of ripping fabric, the king's gown tore apart. A collective gasp rose from the lips of the multitude as he fell heavily to the pavement below.

Every voice fell silent. Only the howling of the wind remained.

Rising on tiptoes, Lokan tried to peer over the heads of the crowd, waiting against all expectation for the king to clamber to his feet and send a cheery wave to his subjects.

No one moved. Everyone around him stood rigid, as if frozen in place.

Murmurs of dismay slowly became cries of horror until a single voice silenced the crowd. "Guards! Attend to your king!" bellowed Deemis, his cry rising above the wind and the noise of the multitude. Having spoken, he began inching his way around the edge of the balcony, never for a moment releasing his grip.

As he disappeared inside the building, guards sprang into action at last. Forming a solid line, they cordoned off the place where the king had fallen. Then they began pushing people back, away from the area.

Eager to leave the crowd behind, Lokan headed for the small garden located at the back of the palace. He discovered that someone else had followed a similar instinct. To his amazement, he found himself staring into the drawn features of Deemis.

"I don't like looking at dead bodies," said Deemis.

Unsure how to respond, he remained silent.

"He could be a bully, and a lot of the time he was arrogant and demanding," the young man continued, "but he was good to me. He didn't deserve to die like that."

Lokan found his voice. "What was the proclamation going to be about?"

Deemis shrugged. "I have no idea. He never as much as hinted at it."

"Yet he had you there on the balcony with him."

"He insisted on it for some reason. Maybe he was hoping to embarrass me."

Seeing Lokan's frown, he added, "I'm well aware that people have seen me as his favorite and resented me for it. Having me up there with him was only going to make it worse."

After the events of the voyage Lokan had no sympathy for Deemis, although he hid his reaction carefully. "What are you going to do now?"

Gazing into the sky, Deemis seemed not to have heard him. "It is strange, don't you think? The wind has died down significantly, and even the clouds are beginning to clear. He chose the worst possible moment to make his announcement, whatever it was about."

It was true. The sun had poked through a gap in the clouds, and Lokan was no longer suffering from the cold.

"I don't know what I'll do," Deemis conceded. "I won't be constantly running around on his errands anymore. Perhaps I'll go home again. I won't decide anything in a hurry."

Glancing past Lokan, he concluded, "I'll leave you in peace now. Someone seems to be looking for you. Thank you for all you've done for me."

With that, he was gone.

Lord Crinholm strode up. "I thought I saw you heading this way," he told Lokan. He threw a curious glance in the direction of Deemis, who at that moment was disappearing around the side of a building. Then he added, "That meeting I told you about has been brought forward. A few people will be joining us here."

Even before he finished speaking, Chief Master Kharkin arrived in the company of several other nobles.

"Was that Deemis I saw leaving?" he asked.

"It was," Crinholm confirmed. He turned to Lokan. "What did he say to you?" he asked.

Seeing no reason to dissemble, Lokan reported everything that had passed between them.

"I'm not sure I believe him," said Kharkin.

"What are you referring to?" asked Crinholm.

"The part about him not knowing what the king was planning to say."

"What difference does it make?" asked a noble Lokan knew to be Lord Burnleigh. "What matters is that we're faced with a constitutional crisis! The king has left us without an heir!"

"The situation is not entirely without precedent," Crinholm replied evenly. "A constitutional council will need to be formed to address the issue."

"Our state of affairs would be easier to manage if we weren't on the brink of war with Periton," said Lady Tolmer, another of the senior nobles.

"And at loggerheads with an almost completely unknown foreign power," added Kharkin grimly.

The conversation sputtered on, achieving little apart from exposing the frustrations of the kingdom's senior figures. Aware that every one of them outranked him, Lokan said nothing.

"Look who's coming!" said Lady Tolmer abruptly.

Glancing back toward the palace, Lokan saw a man hurrying in their direction. It was the harried official who had preceded the king onto the balcony. His head was bare of the hat that had earlier caused such merriment.

"There you all are!" he panted. "I've been searching for you everywhere! It is necessary for me to convey to senior members of the Compact and the Conclave what the king intended to proclaim!" He waved a parchment before them.

The official then paused, throwing a pointed glance in Lokan's direction.

"Lokan has every right to be here," Crinholm assured him. "He has for many years acted as the king's most senior official in the northern provinces of the kingdom."

"I know who he is," the official replied testily. "I am also aware that he is the person who introduced *Deemis* to the court. Does he have a conflict of interest?"

"Can I suggest you simply share the king's proposed proclamation with us?" Crinholm retorted. "I say proposed, because its status must be regarded as questionable at best."

"Why do you say that?" asked the official sharply.

"Simply because the king never actually proclaimed it."

The official considered Crinholm's words. The suggestion that the proclamation might not be valid didn't seem to trouble him at all.

"I will read it to you," he said. "You may draw your own conclusions."

> In the matter of the succession to the throne of Tantel,
> I, Garneth, by birthright king of Tantel, recognize as my
> rightful successor my half-brother—the man generally known
> as Deemis. I am resolved, and my decision is final.

STEADFASTLY IGNORING the consternation caused by these words, the official raised his voice and continued reading.

> This decision addresses once and for all the oft-stated
> concern that, having failed to father an heir, I will one day
> leave the kingdom without a successor.
> I command you to join with me in acknowledging Crown
> Prince Deemis, heir to the throne of Tantel.

THE OFFICIAL HELD up the parchment for their inspection. "As you can see, the king applied his seal to the document."

He faced Lord Crinholm. "Due process requires the formation of a council to decide the succession." He produced a second parchment that also bore the king's seal. It remained unopened. "The king commanded that this document should be made available to the succession council in the event of his death."

He thrust both parchments into Lord Crinholm's hand. "All of you are witnesses that I have entrusted these documents to Lord Crinholm."

He exhaled with relief. "These matters are no longer my problem!"

So saying, he turned on his heel and left them.

Every one of them stood speechless, staring after him.

CHAPTER 35
PERITON

Dannah was bound and bundled into a cart, Marielle at her side. After rumbling through the city streets, they turned off onto a narrow road that headed toward the cliff face that formed the most formidable section of the city's defensive wall. Leaving the last of the dwellings behind, they rolled through a narrow entrance onto a bare patch of ground. In the shadow of the cliff, a small hill, presumably Bagot's Rise, overlooked the area. A group of mages had encompassed the cart on every side. Master Kothlar did not appear to have been included in their number.

The Compact's death sentence had confirmed Dannah's worst fears. She was still struggling to understand how it had come to this.

A single issue dominated her thinking: Marielle's death would be on her hands. While he was still on Abbethar, Kylen had warned her about the implacability of the Compact. Then, against the odds, she had connected with his mentor, Dalthinir. He had offered them safety, and Dannah had turned him down.

At the time they had been able to avoid the authorities, and she had hoped and expected they would somehow manage to remain free. If they did ever encounter the authorities, she imagined they could reach an understanding, especially in light of the good they had done during their time in Periton. Never had she imagined they would be subjected to such a heavy-handed response. The stubbornness and inflexibility of the chief master took her breath away.

Yet she could not pretend the leaders of her own people were any less implacable. She had witnessed it herself.

With the wisdom of hindsight she had been a fool, and Marielle would pay the price of her folly. It was more than she could bear.

"We could defend ourselves, Granny," suggested Marielle, speaking in their native language.

"By striking them down?" She shook her head. "I couldn't do it." She threw up her hands helplessly. "None of this makes any sense. Elef'nissar came to me in a dream last night. You and Kylen are supposed to prevent some kind of evil from happening."

"I had a dream, too," Marielle told her. "The dragon didn't speak to me—I don't have mage hearing. But I had a similar impression."

Stealing a glance at her granddaughter, Dannah saw her face flushed. What had she seen in the dream, and how had it involved Kylen?

"It looks like Kylen will have to save the world on his own," concluded Marielle bitterly.

She faced her grandmother. "How are they planning to execute us?"

"I've been wondering the same thing," she replied. "I've read about such executions in the past. There do seem to be ways of doing it," she said vaguely. She had no intention of giving details.

"Well I have mage touch abilities supported by a talisman," said Marielle stubbornly. "I could easily take quite a few of them with us."

Seeing the alarmed look on Dannah's face, she returned a grim smile. "Don't worry. I'm not actually going to do it. But I can't pretend the thought isn't appealing!" Her face set in determination. "What I am going to do is protect us both with a shield. They'll have to break through it first if they want to kill us."

"I will add my power to yours, at least until it runs out," Dannah assured her. "They don't seem to have learned how to draw upon another mage's magic in the way we can. Perhaps we can hold out for a while."

Reaching the brow of the hill, the cart stopped and the two of them were bundled out. They stood hand in hand as their escorts withdrew. The Peritonian mages soon surrounded the crest of the hill, a stone's throw from the condemned women.

"I will give you one final chance," called the chief master. "Will you answer our questions?"

Neither of them gave him a response.

"My shield is in place," murmured Marielle.

"And my power is available to you," she replied. "It's there whenever you need it."

The chief master was shaking his head in what might have been regret. "It seems I have no choice but to call for the sentence to be carried out," he cried.

He raised a hand, and Dannah at once felt power pressing around her. However, the nature of the attack wasn't immediately obvious. A glance at Marielle showed she was none the wiser.

She first realized their intent when she began to feel a little light-headed. "They're starving us of air!" she gasped.

Marielle's eyes went wide with surprise, then she frowned in concentration. Dannah sensed a surge of power. Catching a whiff of fresh air, she eagerly filled her lungs. Marielle had punched a hole in the suffocating shield.

"Well done!" she exclaimed admiringly.

No more than a couple of minutes seemed to pass before her breathing again became labored. Once more Marielle responded, and once more fresh air rushed in. Then it happened all over again.

The Peritonians were closing the holes as quickly as Marielle opened them.

The other mages were increasing the pressure, because there came a time when Dannah felt power being drawn out of her. Once more the Peritonian shield was breached, but that hole, too, was closed before long.

How long could they keep this up? It was so tempting to strike back. Either of them could easily do it. They could pick off their tormentors one at a time. If the Peritonians had any idea what the two women were capable of, they would flee for their lives.

It was no use. She couldn't do it, even in her own defense. That meant the end could not be long delayed.

Then, to her astonishment, a mighty surge of power erupted nearby and the atmosphere cleared completely. The Peritonian mages were peering about them in disarray, trying to understand what had happened.

Then two figures appeared out of nowhere, invoking memories of her first meeting with Dalthinir.

Kylen and Trisanna had arrived.

Although the chief master and his mages showed no reaction to the appearance of the two mages, they began calling out in alarm and pointing toward Dannah and Marielle.

"I've ruptured the shield they wrapped around you, at least for the moment," called Kylen. "Trisanna has also added you to our illusion. They can't see any of us, and I'm masking our glimmer. It's time we got you away from here! Follow me! We'll need to hurry! The way you came in is the only way to get clear of this area."

Dannah and Marielle hurried over to them, and together they headed down the hill, picking their way around any mages who blundered into their way.

The Peritonians must have guessed what had happened. A few of them had rushed to the crest of the hill, groping about in an effort to connect with the missing women. Others were wandering randomly around the hill slope doing the same thing. Dannah's quick glance didn't account for all of the mages, but she had enough else to think about.

Thanks to Kylen and Trisanna's help, they made it to the bottom of the hill without incident. Dannah was under no delusion, though. Escaping the city was likely to be an entirely different matter.

Even so, she could never have imagined how quickly their situation could deteriorate.

"I'm becoming weary, Kylen," said Trisanna suddenly. "Maintaining the illusion is tiring—I can't keep it going for much longer!"

❧

IT TOOK NO MORE than a glance for Kylen to see the severity of the strain Trisanna was under. Without a talisman to replenish her power, he'd been asking far too much of her.

"We need to find somewhere safe for you to rest!" he said. "The area around Bagot's Rise is very exposed. Do you think you can keep it going long enough for us to get clear? Unfortunately I can't walk quickly, as you know."

She looked uncertain. "I can try. We'll need to do it quickly, though!"

Attempting to move forward, Kylen was alarmed to find his way blocked by a strong shield.

The magical barrier was no surprise—the atmosphere was almost buzzing with power. Taking the simplest approach, he attempted to go around it.

It quickly became obvious there was no way forward. Something solid lay on either side of the path. Something invisible.

At that crucial moment, Trisanna reached the limit of her endurance. "I can't keep it up any longer!" she groaned.

Cries of triumph from their enemies confirmed the terrible truth—their invisibility had come to an abrupt end.

"Emmela and team! You can end your illusion now!" called the chief master's voice.

Kylen stared in shock as the truth was laid bare. Before him stood a solid mass of mages, Adrastas at their head. Between them they formed the shield that had blocked their progress and the illusion that blinded them to what was happening. Behind and on either side of the mages, wagons had been dragged across the road. Soldiers brandishing spears filled the wagons.

Standing to one side just behind Chief Master Adrastas stood a figure Kylen knew only too well.

"That's him," gloated Raff, pointing directly at him. "That's Kylen! I told you he'd be here!"

"You've done very well, young soldier! Very well indeed!" Adrastas replied. "And I suppose that's Trisanna beside him. We've waited far too long to run these renegades to ground! No doubt Dalthinir is lurking somewhere nearby. Whether he is or not, he'll be next!"

Kylen gritted his teeth. Once again he'd underestimated Raff. He'd been far too ready to dismiss his old nemesis. Raff was one of the few people in Cambrick who could readily identify him, and he must have guessed at Kylen's purpose in returning to Cambrick.

The head mage sneered at Dannah and Marielle. "It's no wonder you refused to answer our questions! You were never going to admit you'd made common cause with our renegades!"

Catching movement out of the corner of his eye, Kylen saw that the mages left behind at Bagot's Rise had come up behind them. They were now completely surrounded.

Kylen's shield was still in place, and with a talisman supporting him he wasn't about to run out of power. But even though there was no immediate risk of them being overwhelmed, he could see no way to break free.

"There's no hope for you, Kylen!" called Adrastas. "It's time for you to give yourself up."

Before he could respond, faces everywhere turned upward and voices cried out in terror. Leaping from their carts, the soldiers scrambled beneath them. Mages everywhere cowered in fear.

A huge dragon was gliding earthward, its wings spread wide. Stretching its talons to the earth, the fearsome creature touched down directly behind Kylen, scattering the frantic mages who occupied the location.

Kylen watched as people everywhere drew back in fear. He wasn't surprised. With dragons absent from the skies for generations, people had concluded the creatures were extinct. He had made the same mistake himself. It had taken a confrontation with the very real and very intimidating Elef'nissar to open his eyes.

Now he looked back on his own reasoning as incomprehensible. Proof relied on evidence. But how could people decide that the absence of evidence proved anything?

Spinning around to face the creature, Kylen bowed his head respectfully. "Greetings, mighty Elef'nissar," he said.

The dragon dipped its head in return. "Well met, Kalmithien," it replied.

"We seem to have reached an impasse," said Kylen calmly. "Would you be willing to extract us?"

"That is my purpose," acknowledged the creature. "I will carry the healer and your father's daughter. The bearers of my talismans can ride on my back."

His brows knitted together as he tried to make sense of Elef'nissar's choice of words.

He dimly heard Dannah passing on the dragon's instructions to Marielle, the only one of them without mage hearing. Then she raised her voice insistently. "Kylen!"

Snapped out of his musing by the urgency in her voice, he set out to find a way onto the creature's back. Marielle was way ahead of him. Having already clambered onto its scaled front leg, she was ready to scramble onto its back. Witnessing his clumsy efforts to follow her, she reached down a hand for him. Awkward as he felt, he took her hand. Between them they reached Elef'nissar's back. Kylen positioned himself just ahead of the great wings with Marielle sitting immediately behind him.

The moment they were in place, the dragon grasped the two women, protecting them in its talons, and launched itself into the air.

Throughout it all, the human audience looked on in stunned silence. As they left the ground, Kylen caught sight of Raff. The snitch was bent almost double, hiding his face in dread. Kylen tried not to gloat too much.

The ground fell rapidly away. At first worried about the risk of falling off, Kylen soon realized he had no need for concern. A pocket of power cushioned the two mounted passengers so securely that he felt confident he could stand on his head in perfect safety if he were able to do it.

The experience was beyond exhilarating.

At one point Marielle leaned forward, gripping his waist. "Isn't it incredible?" she called into his ear.

Turning his head, he grinned back at her in pure delight.

With time at last to think, he continued to ponder the dragon's words. He had been astonished to learn that Marielle was the bearer of a talisman from Elef'nissar. When had that happened? Was that how they were supposed to prevent the disaster planned by Zin'thelestar, the evil dragon?

And why had it referred to Trisanna as his father's daughter?

All too soon, the ground grew closer again as Elef'nissar swooped low, coming to rest in a familiar valley.

Excited voices reached them. Dalthinir, Inga, and the others appeared, pulling Kylen and Trisanna into a shared embrace.

"For those you who haven't met them, these are my friends Dannah and Marielle," Kylen announced happily. "They're a long way from home, but I know you'll make them welcome!"

Once introductions were completed, Vennia called for their attention. "We've just finished preparing a meal, and there's plenty to go around. Come inside, everyone—it's time for a celebration!"

Each person with mage hearing thanked Elef'nissar warmly before following Vennia inside.

Kylen lingered until the dragon departed. Then, feeling suddenly exhausted, he set off after the others.

They had found Dannah and Marielle and saved them from certain death. And they had escaped—solely thanks to the intervention of a dragon.

KOTHLAR BOWED low as King Durvaryn entered the royal reception room. The head mage followed him in.

"What's he doing here?" asked Adrastas bluntly, pointing in Kothlar's direction.

"Master Kothlar is here at my invitation," replied the king evenly.

Adrastas chose not to comment, although his grunt said plenty.

"I have been given to understand that a momentous event took place earlier today," prompted the king.

"It was an unmitigated disaster!" growled the chief master. "We had two renegades almost within our grasp, and they escaped! Worse, it has become apparent that the two foreigners are in league with our renegades. And if that wasn't enough, all of them have allied themselves with a dragon! I can scarcely believe the magnitude of this disaster!"

"Why should the appearance of a dragon be such a disaster?"

"Your Majesty cannot be serious! You know the histories. Periton and Tantel were ravaged by dragons! And in our folly we believed them to be extinct!"

"Did this dragon destroy anyone or anything?" asked the king reasonably.

"It did not, astonishing as that seems!" Adrastas returned. "We were fortunate—this time."

"Unless, of course, we've been wrong about the dragons," interjected Kothlar. "We've been wrong about plenty else," he muttered loudly.

Adrastas rounded on him. "You weren't there!" he protested.

"I wasn't invited," corrected Kothlar. "That doesn't mean I wasn't there."

He continued before Adrastas could respond. "The dragon seemed to be on friendly terms with all four of your intended victims."

The chief master was outraged. "*My* intended victims? What are you talking about? Our law prescribes that every renegade is worthy of death!"

The king stared at him pointedly. "Then it is time the law was changed."

"Perhaps Your Majesty has forgotten that this law was enacted by your predecessor!" sputtered Adrastas. "It reflects the wishes of the crown!"

"The statutes in question were established for a particular purpose after a single devastating incident," returned the king. "We have inherited them with all their inflexibility, and they have plagued us for years."

A steely calm had come over the head mage. "You seem to be suggesting that the law has outlived its purpose. Are you proposing that mages no longer need to be answerable to anyone except themselves?"

"I am proposing no such thing. My understanding is that some renegades would willingly come under the authority of the Compact if they were offered an opportunity."

"I presume you are referring to Dalthinir."

"And to Kylen and Trisanna. Unless I have been misinformed, neither of them became renegades by choice. It happened solely by virtue of events over which they had no control."

"Dalthinir became a renegade by his own choice! He did it because he was unwilling to submit to clear directives issued by the Compact."

Kothlar couldn't remain silent any longer. "That was because the Compact leadership made a colossal error of judgment, as later events demonstrated spectacularly! Dalthinir's fears were completely justified. All of us owe our continued existence to his stubborn insistence on protecting us from our own folly. He has never been thanked for the enormous price he paid to save us all. The fact that he was right and we were wrong has never even been acknowledged!"

Adrastas was slowly turning red.

"Condemning the two healers to death was another significant error of judgment," said the king emphatically.

Seeing the look on Adrastas's face, the king continued. "I am well aware of the reasoning you applied to their case, Chief Master. You point to their refusal to answer key questions, and you present it as unassailable proof of their evil intent. Their silence proves no such thing! In your discussions with your king you routinely refuse to divulge the tiniest detail of internal Compact discussions, even when I ask direct questions. I acknowledge, of course, that your silence is consistent with long-established protocol. Nevertheless, based on your own logic, it also proves that internal Compact discussions are evil in intent!"

Kothlar stared at the king in astonishment. He had seen the monarch as patient and forbearing to the point of timidity. His words and his tone on this occasion were unyielding.

Adrastas seemed equally taken aback.

The king had one further thing to say. "You have invested a great deal of energy enforcing the law against renegades, Chief Master. As you have already pointed out, that law was established by a past king.

You'd better get used to the idea that the current king is about to change it!"

CHAPTER 36
TANTEL

Lokan sat quietly as the terms of reference of the constitutional council were presented to its twelve members. Even with his seniority, it had come as a surprise to find himself included in their number. He suspected he largely owed his inclusion to the influence of Lord Crinholm. His friend's maneuvering probably hadn't been the only reason, though. Deemis might well emerge as King Garneth's successor, and Lokan had been the royal official responsible for introducing him to the king.

He wasn't at all sure how he felt about the prospect of Deemis being elevated to the most powerful position in the kingdom. He hoped and expected the proceedings of the council would offer an opportunity to find clarity, one way or another.

Lady Tolmer had agreed to facilitate the proceedings. Rising to her feet, she held up a hand for silence before addressing them.

"All of you are familiar with the proclamation the king intended to issue on the day of his death. However, since it provides important context to our discussion, I will refresh your memories." Selecting the original copy from the papers before her, she read it aloud.

When no one commented, she continued. "With that behind us, the first order of business is to examine a second document written by the king. He commanded that it be delivered to this council in the event of his death. The document was given over to Lord Crinholm for safe-keeping. I call upon him to read it now. After he has done so, our task will be to examine the legal standing of the proclamation."

Crinholm stood up, the parchment in his hand. "This document bears the king's seal, as did the proclamation parchment. It should be apparent that the seal remains unbroken."

Passing it around the group, he allowed each member to examine the seal for themselves. As soon as it was returned to him, he broke the seal, opened the document, and began reading.

This document has been a source of considerable irritation to me! I have chosen my successor and issued a decree, and that ought to be the end of the matter! From the time I became king, no individual dared to question my decisions. Only a coward would wait until after my death to challenge me.

Nevertheless, one of the more pedantic of my officials had the temerity to remind me—repeatedly—that our law requires every royal succession to be confirmed by a constitutional council. That law applies even in the most straightforward of cases. Since I have no direct heir, he insisted that the succession in my case will be anything but straightforward.

For that reason alone, I decided to suspend my irritation long enough to document the process that led to my choice of a successor.

After learning of the existence and the lineage of my half-sister—the traitorous renegade mage known as Trisanna—I urgently commissioned an investigation to discover whether the dalliances of my late father might have resulted in other illegitimate offspring.

The investigators subsequently made me aware of a boy, also born to a mother who was a mage. Unlike his half-sister, who was secretly raised in a quiet corner of Tantel under our noses, he had been shipped off to Periton as an infant. It appears that he is also a renegade mage, known as Kylen. He remains in Periton to this day.

It is intolerable that the Peritonian pretender who calls himself 'King' Durvaryn continues to shield such renegades. But I will not digress.

The law of Tantel makes it clear that no mage can have any claim to the throne. These two renegades are therefore forever precluded. Nevertheless, if they have not already joined forces with malicious intent, they might do so in the future. It will be the responsibility of my successor, Deemis, to safeguard the kingdom against any threat they might pose.

One final revelation related to a servant girl from the far north of the kingdom. My father is known to have impregnated her during a brief visit to the region more than twenty years ago. This indiscretion preceded the other two, and unlike them, did not involve a mage. The girl was given access to a considerable sum of money and left to bring up the child in her own village. It was made clear to her that no further assistance would be forthcoming, and that any attempt on her part to contact the king would lead to serious consequences. For reasons known only to himself, my father also gifted her with a physical token of her child's royal ancestry— a signet ring that had long belonged to the royal family. The investigators were able to determine that she later gave birth to a son. They found no further trace of her.

Then Deemis arrived in Antilin, purportedly to reveal information he believed would be of value to me. He more than fulfilled that purpose, because I saw at once that his information had the potential to further the interests of the kingdom significantly.

He said nothing to me of his heritage, although when asked he freely revealed the location where he had grown up. I immediately sent investigators to that village to learn what they could of him. They reported that he had indeed lived there, along with his mother who had died a few months previously. They learned that throughout her life she and her son had benefited from a substantial gift by a mysterious benefactor, although the legacy had apparently been fully consumed by the time of her death. This information, along with a number of other telling indications, left them confident they had found the missing servant girl, and that her illegitimate son was therefore my half-brother. They learned that her son had left the village not long before their visit to seek his fortune.

After returning to the palace and observing Deemis surreptitiously, my investigators were also able to confirm that the signet ring given to the servant girl was now in his possession.

This information shed new light on his possible purposes in coming to Antilin. I at once became suspicious of his motives. I decided to set him a test. I wrote a letter and sent it to him anonymously. The letter stated that the king had become aware of his lineage. It asserted, entirely accurately, that the king despised weak-minded individuals, and it concluded he would be best served if he boldly claimed King Nolan as his father and demanded to be recognized as the current king's successor.

Deemis subsequently came to me and openly showed me the letter, making it clear he refused to do any such thing. He told me he had never intended to reveal his heritage to me. Everything he knew of me had led him to believe I would regard any such revelation with great suspicion. More impor-

tantly, it might distract my attention from the information he came to convey. Consequently, he had worked hard to conceal the truth from me.

He admitted he had sensed a weight of destiny upon him from his earliest years, but not because of any awareness of his heritage. His mother had hidden his father's identity from him until he came of age.

However, witnessing me at work had given him new perspective. He now understood why kings must be groomed from childhood, which he had not been. Further, observing me had shown him both the complexity of the role and the importance to the kingdom of doing it well.

He said that if he truly was my brother, even if only in part, then it was a privilege he had neither earned nor deserved. He concluded by saying he had always been taught that brothers were strongest when they supported each other. He therefore stood ready to help me in whatever way he could.

Deemis's response to my test was not what I expected. Nevertheless, I found it satisfying—surprisingly so. It is undeniably true that he is ill equipped to follow me as king. However, I intend to remedy that. I expect others to work unceasingly toward the same end.

Garneth, by birthright king of Tantel.

CRINHOLM SAT DOWN ABRUPTLY, sucking in a deep breath and exhaling loudly.

Everyone immediately began speaking at once. Lady Tolmer was forced to yell to restore order.

"Deemis's response to the king's test was telling," Lord Burnleigh asserted.

"Yes, it spoke well of his humility," suggested another committee member.

Burnleigh saw it differently. "Are you serious? He flattered the king shamelessly!"

Every aspect of the two documents was energetically examined, but hours passed with the committee unable to reach a unanimous view.

"Lokan has had more exposure to Deemis than any of us," said Crinholm. "What can you tell us about him?"

Lokan took a deep breath while he marshaled his thoughts. He recognized that a substantial response was called for. At the same time, he had no intention of exposing Crinholm. That meant he needed to remain silent about Deemis's actions during the voyage. He began with the positives.

"I have seen him show compassion in practical ways toward vulnerable people on more than one occasion. At times of crisis he has willingly put his life at risk for the sake of others. We all witnessed his efforts to save the king on the balcony. He could easily have died as a result." Heads were nodding around the table.

"He risked himself to save my life in a similar way when we were traveling to Antilin," Lokan continued.

He decided it might be prudent to be vague about the negatives. "At the same time, his choices have left me confused at times."

A question loomed in his mind. "Does anyone know the location of the village where Deemis grew up?"

None of them had any idea.

The discussion continued until Lady Tolmer drew it to a close. "We need to interview Deemis next. That will need to wait until tomorrow."

She concluded by offering her own summary of the situation. "We have not specifically resolved the question of the legal standing of the king's intended proclamation. Nevertheless, I believe we have found our way to the core of the central issue. The king had no legitimate siblings, and his father before him was an only child. Assuming he told the truth about his investigations, Deemis has a very strong claim to the throne. No other potential candidate comes close."

No one disagreed with her.

~

"Thank you for joining us, Deemis," said Lady Tolmer respectfully. "With your permission we would like to ask you some questions."

"Of course," he replied with a smile.

"Were you aware that the king was about to anoint you as his successor?"

He shook his head firmly. "I only learned of it later. I was astonished, as you might imagine."

"Why should you have been astonished? You are King Garneth's half-brother, are you not?"

"I believe that to be the case, yes. Even so, I was not seeking such an honor." A self-conscious grin twisted his lips. "To be honest, I never witnessed the king honoring anyone."

His understatement was greeted with wry chuckles. The king was known only for criticizing and belittling others.

"We understand that you came to Antilin to share important information with the king," said Lord Burnleigh. "What was the nature of that information?"

"It related to a potential threat to the kingdom," Deemis replied. "I hope you will pardon me if I am a little vague, but the details are sensitive. I will, of course, convey them in full to the next monarch."

Burnleigh seemed disappointed, but he accepted the response.

Deemis was asked about his early years.

"I grew up as an only child," he told them. "It was not an easy life, especially without a father, although I was fortunate to be part of a tight-knit community. We lived in a village in the north of Tantel."

"Was it a fishing community?" he was asked.

He shook his head. "It was a farming community. The village was situated inland. The river was the only major source of water nearby."

Lokan started. Deemis's answer was not consistent with the story he had told about his first solo sea voyage. If Deemis truly grew up where he was claiming, the earlier story must have been an invention. Yet at the time Lokan had sensed a ring of truth about it. Inexplicable as the discrepancy was, he told himself there must be some kind of explanation.

The conversation had moved on. "Your attempt to save the king was unusually bold," Deemis was told. "We very nearly lost you as well!"

Deemis winced. "There wasn't time to think about it—I reacted instinctively. I'm only sorry I wasn't able to save him."

"You modeled unselfishness at its best," acknowledged Crinholm. "It was inspiring."

"You are too kind, my lord," Deemis replied modestly.

Lady Tolmer asked a question that must have loomed large in every mind. "If you were king, would you continue to pursue hostilities against Periton?"

Deemis did not hesitate. "I would not! Much as I respected the king, I was never able to understand how a war would benefit this kingdom. I would prefer to see Tantel and Periton working together in harmony."

His response was greeted with open delight.

"What about the Summer Isles? Would you evacuate our forces?"

"Not entirely. I believe a close association between Tantel and the Summer Isles would be mutually advantageous. However, I would prefer the tone to be one of cooperation rather than a military imposition. That means the majority of our troops would come home."

Audible sighs of relief greeted his statement.

"What about the foreigners?" Lord Burnleigh asked.

For a moment Deemis seemed discomposed. He quickly recovered himself. "We know very little about these people, which makes it more important than ever to work on resolving misunderstandings," he replied. "I would address this matter personally in an effort to find common ground."

This answer did not satisfy Lokan, especially with his firsthand knowledge of Deemis's theft. Shooting a glance at Crinholm, he saw he was not convinced either. He didn't risk a glance in Kharkin's direction.

Many other questions were asked, but none of greater significance.

The enthusiasm in the room was palpable. King Garneth's passion for a war with Periton had never been popular, and from the moment Deemis revealed he would call a halt to it, he had most of the committee members eating out of his hand.

Lady Tolmer got to her feet. "I think we can release you now, Deemis. Thank you for joining us. We have very much appreciated your candor."

Dipping his head respectfully, Deemis left the room.

In spite of his mistrust, Lokan watched him go with awe. For a young man untrained in statecraft, he had delivered an impressive performance.

"All of us recognize the strength of Deemis's claim to the throne. Was there anything in our interview that would preclude him from taking it?"

The reaction was immediate.

"On the contrary!"

"The sooner the better!"

"Then I will put it to each of you in turn. A two-thirds majority is required to approve the succession, but it would clearly be helpful to be able to make a stronger statement if possible. I will begin with Chief Master Kharkin. Do you approve?"

"I do," he replied. If he had reservations, he wasn't owning them.

As she went around the room she received the same response, in some cases with considerable enthusiasm. She was about halfway through when she reached Crinholm. He gave his approval with barely a hesitation.

Lokan understood. The mood of the meeting made it clear that approving Deemis was a foregone conclusion. Once the new king was installed, there could be repercussions for anyone seen as opposing his succession.

When his turn came, he gave his approval too. Deemis's claim was undeniably strong, and he could come up with no convincing argument for opposing it.

Although Deemis had treated him badly, Lokan told himself it would be foolish to take it personally. Thankfully, Deemis was not aware that his deceptions had been exposed, so he had no reason to be see Lokan as a threat.

"The king's choice of successor is hereby approved unanimously!" Lady Tolmer announced importantly. "Our new king will have a great deal to learn, and he will need our wholehearted support."

Deemis was escorted back into the room, and the committee members congratulated him exuberantly.

Although Lokan joined in the acclaim, his enthusiasm was a pretense. He was not at peace when he left the meeting.

However much he tried to reassure himself, his efforts were in vain. A nagging sense of doom hung over their decision, and nothing would dispel it.

EPILOGUE

ABBETHAR

Making her way into one of Abbethar's private conference rooms, Tana took a seat among the other community elders. The grim look on Rydel's face suggested they had not been called together to hear good news.

"We have just received a communication from Tantel. It seems their reigning monarch, King Garneth, has died in an accident. A new king, known as Deemis, has taken his place."

Seeing the hopeful looks on a number of faces, he added, "I need to make one thing clear. The ease with which the Tantellans contacted us makes it clear that our long isolation is over. We must come to terms with that, whether we like it or not. It is remarkable we were able to preserve it for so long."

Before anyone could comment, he opened the Tantellan dispatch and began reading aloud.

Having recently been invested as king of Tantel, I wish to inform you that a delegation will be sent to Abbethar to resume the discussions you began with my predecessor, King Garneth. In the meantime, let me make it clear that Artorans are not welcome in Tantel. Should any of your people appear anywhere within the borders of my kingdom, for any reason whatever, I will regard it as an act of war. You have been warned!

"THE DOCUMENT BEARS the seal of the Tantellan king," he concluded.

The communication was greeted with dismay. "What will we do?"

"We will tread very carefully," replied Rydel.

"Are you suggesting we should meekly submit to his wishes? After Tantel has stolen the relic?"

"That is not what I meant and not what I said! I see no reason for us to bow to his demands."

"What are you proposing, then?"

"To begin with, this is what I have in mind..." Rydel told them.

~

PERITON

KOTHLAR HAD JOINED Adrastas and several senior nobles in one of King Durvaryn's royal reception rooms.

"King Garneth has died in Antilin," King Durvaryn told them. "Our agents have confirmed it. The new monarch, King Deemis, has officially informed us that Tantel holds no animosity toward Periton and wishes to normalize relations. He regrets any misunderstandings that might have resulted from the actions of his predecessor."

The nobles reacted with delight. "Does that mean the war is over?" one of them asked.

"It is too early to say anything with certainty," the king replied.

"Surely we won't be standing down our troops!" exclaimed Adrastas. "This could be a ploy to get us to lower our guard!"

"Our troops will stay on the highest alert until our agents confirm that the Tantellan army has demobilized," the king assured him.

Adrastas nodded in satisfaction. "What do we know of this King Deemis?"

"Very little at this point, although we are working to rectify that," the king replied. "If he is truly sincere about normalizing relations, it is good news. However, there is another problem. We have also received a dispatch from a group of people describing themselves as Artoran exiles. They claim to inhabit islands to the north of Periton. If they can be believed, they have done so for generations. Their dispatch offers no more detail than that. They propose to establish diplomatic relations with us. They have retrospectively granted envoy status to a person who has arrived in our kingdom. While their new envoy will be unable to speak on their behalf until instructions have been forwarded, they invite us to use the contact to begin conveying our own views and priorities."

All of them looked astonished at this news.

"Why should that be a problem?" asked Adrastas.

The king glared at him. "Because the envoy they are referring to is a senior healer named Dannah who has been traveling in our kingdom with her granddaughter Marielle, conducting peaceful business of their own."

Adrastas stared at the king. "You mean...?"

"Yes! They want to establish friendly relations, and they want to do it through a woman you condemned to death, Chief Master! Even if we had a way of making contact with the two women, they could hardly be expected to trust us. They barely escaped with their lives, and that was thanks only to two renegades and a dragon!"

Kothlar snorted. "Someone will need to explain to these Artorans why we did our best to execute not only their envoy, but her granddaughter as well!"

Leaning forward, he lowered his voice so only the chief master could hear. "Are you planning to volunteer, Adrastas?" he asked dryly.

~

METHESIA

Since leaving Tantel, Trisanna's life had been anything but dull. If the visit to Ettaran had not been challenging enough, her latest adventure would have ended in disaster were it not for the unprecedented appearance in Cambrick of a dragon.

After returning to the hidden valley, the pace of life had slowed dramatically, and Trisanna's tension had slowly ebbed away.

The same could not be said for Kylen. He didn't seem even vaguely at peace.

She knew about his unfinished business with the Artorans, and that the two women had come to Periton in search of him after he left their island without permission. They at least now understood that leaving had not been his choice. Even so, coming to an understanding with them didn't seem to have resolved his awkwardness around Marielle.

Marielle wasn't the only problem, though. Something else was troubling him.

Seeing him standing alone beside a building, she moved to join him.

"Hello, brother," she said self-consciously. "Something's bothering you."

He managed a wry smile in return. "It's the dragon."

"Elef'nissar?"

He nodded. "It might not be here with us in the valley, but that doesn't mean I'm free of its interference. I know it's spoken to you in your dreams, and it keeps doing that with me. It says I need to act before it's too late!"

"I know. It told me I should support you. What does it want you to do?"

"That's the problem! I have no idea! No one could ever accuse it of being straightforward in its communication." He grimaced. "It's alarmed, though. Very alarmed. Another dragon has been interfering, and not with good intent. Elef'nissar said something about all the pieces now being in place. I've seen enough in the past to guess at what will happen if we do nothing except stand back and watch."

He ran a hand across his face. "The images it's been showing me are terrifying! They're beyond description—death and the destruction of everything."

"And it's up to you to do something about it."

"Yes. Not just me, though—Marielle as well. I have no idea why it has to be us!"

"Oh, Kylen!" Throwing her arms around him, she held him tightly. "It seems like you're never allowed to rest!"

At that moment, Marielle appeared around the side of the building, almost colliding with them.

Kylen hurriedly broke away from the embrace, flushing red with embarrassment.

"My apologies," said Marielle, her tone aloof. "I didn't mean to interrupt you."

"It isn't like that!" said Kylen.

Her head went up proudly. "You don't have to explain yourself to me," she sniffed.

"You don't understand!" he blurted. "I need you!"

Her eyes narrowed.

Trisanna decided it was time to help Kylen out. "You might not be aware, Marielle," she said, "but I'm his sister. His half-sister to be more accurate. We have the same father."

Marielle stared back at her skeptically. "Kylen told me he didn't know who his parents were."

"We found out quite recently—from Elef'nissar," she replied. "While it was rescuing us. Your grandmother has mage hearing. She can confirm it."

Marielle eyed them uncertainly. "She did say the dragon mentioned a 'father's daughter'. I didn't know what it meant." She peered at Trisanna. "Who was your father?"

"King Nolan of Tantel."

She gaped first at Trisanna, then at Kylen.

He found his voice at last. "When I said I need you, I meant there's something both of us have to do. The dragon made it clear what will happen if we fail, and it's terrible!"

"I know. The dragon showed me in my dreams." The reminder clearly unsettled her, although she tried to put on a bold face. "So disaster is looming and we're supposed to somehow save the world."

He nodded.

"And the dragon expects us to do it together."

He nodded again.

She raised her arms heavenward. "It doesn't sound very realistic to me."

When he didn't respond, she fixed her eyes on him with a look hinting at an intense inner debate.

Kylen submitted silently to her scrutiny, his cheeks flushed.

After a while she spoke. "Whether we succeed in saving the world or not, it seems like we'll be spending a lot of time together." She sounded less than excited.

After staring at him for a few moments more, she shook her head in resignation. "I suppose I can't dodge it any longer." A sigh escaped her lips. "It looks like I'm going to have to forgive you."

~

TANTEL

Deemis, by birthright king of Tantel, stood alone on the balcony—the same balcony from which King Garneth had fallen—smiling indulgently down at the jubilant throng. Occasionally he waved a hand to them, provoking a new outburst of cheering.

After his coronation the masses had been admitted to the palace courtyard. They crowded in, eager to gaze up in awed wonder at their new sovereign. He was in no hurry to disperse them.

His first act as king had been to announce that preparations for military activity were at an end. All recent draftees were therefore released with immediate effect. The move had been wildly popular.

Men had cheered, and women wept as they blew him kisses. He had made a strong start.

Eager for more adulation, he raised his hand in another wave. The crowd did not disappoint him.

He had taken fearful risks to get there. Throughout his short life he had always been a risk taker, and too often it had gotten him into trouble. This time the risks had a purpose.

He couldn't have reached the king without Lokan's help. As an unusually good judge of character, Lokan hadn't been easy to win over. He shook his head remembering the lengths he went to in earning the official's trust and support—his frantic labor at the collapsed house in Brynford and later the rescue of Lokan himself on the brink of the cliff near Howling Pass.

As for grabbing the king's gown as he disappeared over the balcony, even now his heart pounded when recalling it. It had been beyond reckless. But it had won him admiration and respect from the high and mighty of the kingdom as they looked on with mouths agape.

High risk behavior was behind him now. He had no intention of losing his life in an act of stupidity. He was, after all, 'King Deemis.'

His actual name was not Deemis, of course. The real Deemis—the true half-brother of the late King Garneth—had recently drowned in a swollen river. Watching it had not been pleasant. But it was for the best. The poor fool would not have survived long in Antilin once Garneth figured out who he was.

Once deceased, he no longer needed his name. Having adopted it, the new Deemis had already elevated it to great heights.

Reflecting on all that had happened, he acknowledged that the previous weeks had been nothing short of remarkable.

Meeting the real Deemis had been perfectly timed. The young innocent had just left his village to seek opportunities at the side of his royal half-brother. He had been pathetically easy to draw out. He had talked for hours about his mother, his life in the village, and his hopes and plans for the future. Such background information was vital for the man who took his place.

Next, the mighty storm in Brynford had given him the opportunity to meet Lokan and win his trust.

Then he had arrived in Antilin at a time when the king needed leverage against Periton.

The timing of each event might have seemed fortuitous to an outside observer. In fact, there was nothing accidental about any of it. Every step had been carefully planned in advance by the mysterious creature that had guided him every step of the way.

As a child on Abbethar his dreams had frequently been filled with images of great deeds. Upon his magical awakening there, those dreams had suddenly included a Voice. It used words he understood perfectly thanks to his new mage hearing ability.

He had been enthusiastic when the Voice instructed him to leave Abbethar. During his youth on the island he had been branded a troublemaker. It was hardly his fault. The exiles had become so insular he felt like he was being suffocated. His energies needed new outlets.

The Voice had directed him to a foreign beach. There he found a dragon talisman waiting for him, embedded in a broken coconut shell discarded by a juvenile robber crab. Next it sent him to find the original Deemis, then to Brynford, and later to Antilin. The timing of each move had been perfect. He reached his final destination a few weeks before Garneth planned to unleash his army on Periton.

Once he had acquired the talisman, the Voice explained how to activate it. He had been taught how to use it to hide his glimmer and mask his use of magic. These steps were crucial to his future plans. If his new subjects had known he was a mage, they would never have allowed him to take the throne.

The Voice might have guided his steps, but the talisman allowed him to fend for himself. It readily boosted his other, more modest mage abilities. Before long he was able to manipulate the weather at will. He could swell the flow of a river to drown the hapless Deemis while he was crossing. It became easy for him to call up a huge storm to devastate a major town like Brynford. He could cause the wind to shriek like a demon in Howling Pass. He could even summon a squall strong enough to blow a king from a balcony.

Stealing the relic from the Artorans had probably been his greatest achievement. After throwing Lokan into the sea off the coast of Abbethar, he had kept the ship in the area until he saw Lokan's signal fire. Then he had waited until a patrol boat spotted it, knowing the intrusion would be reported to the Artoran authorities. He knew that fretting over a new incursion, they would send their best people to interrogate the intruder. While they were thus distracted, he sailed to the other side of the island and called up a storm. It had given him the ideal opportunity to slip in and steal the relic.

He had made mistakes along the way. Telling Lokan about the solo sea voyage in his youth had been an error of judgment. The northerner had noticed the inconsistency—he was certain of it. He would need to have Lokan watched closely. It was a shame, because he owed the man a lot. However, Lokan wasn't the kind of person he needed around him. King Deemis would benefit most from people whose values were a little more flexible.

Lord Crinholm would also need to be watched. The noble struck him as a little too astute for his own good.

These men were far from the only possible threats. Deemis's talisman had revealed to him that Chief Master Kharkin also possessed a dragon talisman. Thankfully, Kharkin had seemed no more able to detect his talisman than to sense his glimmer or use of magic. Even so, Kharkin would warrant close attention.

It was the Artorans who now represented his biggest threat. He couldn't allow himself to be seen by any of them. Too many among them knew who he really was. They would need to be dealt with decisively. He had significant military force to call upon now, and he wouldn't hesitate to use it if the need arose.

Even so, there would be no further need of soldiers and sailors once he fulfilled his obligations to the owner of the voice that had guided him. He could not be certain what manner of creature it was, although he was able to hazard a guess. Whatever it was, it had delivered in full on its initial promises. They had only been the beginning. It pledged power beyond measure once he made good on his commitments. The stolen relic would empower him to fulfill his end of the bargain.

There was no reason for undue haste, though. Before attempting anything it would be necessary to consolidate his power. After that he intended to savor his new situation. That wasn't something that could be hurried.

Returning his focus to the crowd below, he obligingly raised a hand to them once more. Cheered by their response, he sighed in pleasure.

This was his moment of triumph, and he refused to allow anything to spoil it.

∽

The End

∽

The saga continues and concludes with

Waking the Dragon
Book 4 of Allan N. Packer's
The Ruptured Kingdom series

LIST OF CHARACTERS

- *Adrastas* - Chief Master (head mage) of the Peritonian Compact
- *Agalar* - Tantellan mage with mage taste (illusion) abilities as well as moderate mage touch abilities
- *Aleira* - young Artoran healer
- *Antone* - palace guard at Antilin
- *Arestor* - young Tantellan and sometime spy in the employ of Lord Crinholm
- *Banadin* - Peritonian mage who died some years previously, and who was a key factor in Dalthinir becoming a renegade
- *Bella* - twin of Jonno and companion of Dalthinir and Kylen
- *Buck* - Peritonian castaway
- *Burnleigh* - senior Tantellan nobleman
- *Crinholm* - senior Tantellan nobleman
- *Dalthinir* - renegade Peritonian mage
- *Dannah* - senior Artoran healer
- *Deemis* - stranger from the far north of Tantel
- *Durvaryn* - king of Periton; middle-aged, married to Karolin with two children: Firan, a son, and Layla, a daughter

- *Emmela* - Peritonian mage with illusionary magic ability; friend of Inga
- Emmri - sailor, brother of Tantellan mage Jaizor
- *Ellis* - Peritonian mage
- *Faliba* - Peritonian mage, healer
- *Felicia* - cousin of Inga, daughter of Jemilla; lives in the town of Sengin in the southeastern corner of Periton
- *Frezaya* - Peritonian mage, deputy to the senior healer
- *Garneth* - king of Tantel; son of King Nolan
- *Gerrar* - Peritonian mage, senior healer
- *Inga* - mage with the Compact's strongest farsense ability; friend of Dalthinir prior to him becoming a renegade
- *Jaizor* - Tantellan mage
- *Jemilla* - aunt of Master Inga; lives in the town of Sengin in the southeastern corner of Periton
- *Jonno* - twin of Bella and companion of Dalthinir and Kylen
- *Kalmithien* - the name given to Kylen by the dragon
- *Karolin* - queen of Periton; middle-aged, married to Durvaryn with two children: Firan, a son, and Layla, a daughter
- *Kaspra* - Peritonian mage
- *Kateren* - Artoran healer and instructor
- *Kharkin* - chief master of the Tantellan Compact
- *Kothlar* - Peritonian mage
- *Kylen* - renegade mage and companion of Dalthinir and the twins
- *Lars* - Peritonian mage who has become a renegade
- *Lokan* - senior official for King Garneth in the northern region of Tantel
- *Marielle* - Artoran; apprentice healer; granddaughter of Dannah
- *Marigold* - granddaughter of Sorren and Vennia
- *Nolan* - previous king of Tantel; father of Garneth
- *Olatiren* - Kylen's tutor in his early years on the streets.
- *Petria* - Peritonian mage with has become a renegade

- *Pernilla* - Tantellan mage (female); head of special mage group
- *Pellistri* - Peritonian mage
- *Pindel* - wealthy Tantellan merchant based in Shelmar
- *Ramond* - mercenary leader; childhood friend of Adrastas
- *Reza* - Peritonian mage, healer
- *Rydel* - Artoran mage and senior elder
- *Sorren* - Methesian mage; husband to Vennia
- *Tana* - senior Artoran healer
- *Tolmer* - senior Tantellan noblewoman
- *Trisanna* - Tantellan mage fleeing her home country
- *Tunney* - Tantellan official, appointed governor in Brynford
- *Vennia* - Methesian mage; wife to Sorren
- *Zeke* - Tantellan fisherman

RESEARCH NOTES

Rheumatic Heart Disease

The symptoms of Crown Prince Firan before his healing were consistent with rheumatic heart disease. See the following World Health Organization website for more information: https://www.who.int/news-room/fact-sheets/detail/rheumatic-heart-disease.

Key facts (from that website)

• Rheumatic heart disease is the most commonly acquired heart disease in people under age 25.

• Rheumatic heart disease affects an estimated 55 million people worldwide and claims approximately 360,000 lives each year – the large majority in low- or middle-income countries.

• The disease results from damage to heart valves caused by one or several episodes of rheumatic fever, an autoimmune inflammatory reaction to throat infection caused by group A streptococci (streptococcal pharyngitis or strep throat).

• It most commonly occurs in childhood and can lead to death or life-long disability.

• Rheumatic heart disease can be prevented by preventing streptococcal infections through addressing poverty and improving living and housing standards, or prompt treatment of streptococcal infections with antibiotics when they do occur.

Traumatic Brain Injury

Kylen suffered from a range of traumas after the calamitous collapse of the library in Ettaran, traumatic brain injury among them.

See   https://en.wikipedia.org/wiki/Traumatic_brain_injury   for more information.

From that website:

Traumatic brain injury is defined as damage to the brain resulting from external mechanical force, such as rapid acceleration or deceleration, impact, blast waves, or penetration by a projectile. Brain function is temporarily or permanently impaired and structural damage may or may not be detectable with current technology.

NOTE FROM THE AUTHOR

Thank you for reading *The Weight of Interference*—I hope you enjoyed it. Please consider leaving a review. Reviews make a huge difference to me as well as benefiting other readers.

I also very much appreciate feedback from my readers. I'd love to hear from you—please feel free to send me an email.

The saga of the Ruptured Kingdom will continue and conclude in *Waking the Dragon (The Ruptured Kingdom Book 4)*.

To be kept up to date on new releases, sign up to my newsletter mailing list at *www.allanpacker.com*. New subscribers will receive an exclusive bonus novelette—a prequel to *The Hard Edge of Magic*. The novelette, *The Renegade*, provides important background to the wider story, revealing the beginnings of Dalthinir's relationship with Inga and portraying the process that led to him becoming a renegade. The novelette is described below.

A second exclusive bonus novelette is also available to subscribers —a prequel to *The Cost of Knowing* from my first epic fantasy series, *The Stone Cycle*. The novelette, *The Rending*, is a complete story that can be read independently from other books in the series.

~

Is anything worth being hunted and despised?

Dalthinir's life quickly unravels when he acts on suspicions about a fellow mage. After desperately using magic to escape an attempt on his life, he finds himself on trial for murder.

But more is at stake than his reputation. In their greed for power, reckless mages are willing to risk a release of magic so powerful it will destroy the kingdom. He alone recognizes the peril.

Prohibited from taking action, Dalthinir must decide what he is prepared to lose for the sake of the kingdom. Can he sacrifice everything he cares about to become a scorned and hunted renegade?

The Renegade is also available in print and audiobook editions at online bookstores.

ACKNOWLEDGMENTS

I rely heavily on the feedback of my wife, Merilyn, and she once again offered valuable insights on the alpha draft.

I'm indebted to my beta readers, Deborah, Alison George, Roly Edwardes, and Graeme Cellier. Their critiques significantly improved the final story. I also greatly appreciate Arpenny Hart's feedback on the audiobook draft.

Special thanks to my new developmental editor, Adrian Herber, who proved his worth with a range of very helpful insights. And thanks once more to James for his usual meticulous proofread.

My appreciation to Brian Plush, who made some additional tweaks to his wonderful map to accommodate this story. And thanks to 100 Covers for their great cover.

Last, but by no means least, I am grateful to God, who graciously offers strength and hope while guiding me through the shoals of life.

ABOUT THE AUTHOR

Allan Packer writes epic fantasy. *The Ruptured Kingdom* is his second series, following *The Stone of Knowing* and later stories in *The Stone Cycle* series.

Allan grew up surrounded by books and became an avid reader during his childhood. In his university years fantasy displaced science fiction as his favorite genre, thanks primarily to J. R. R. Tolkien. He later shared this love with his four children by reading *The Lord of the Rings* to them aloud—a three-month marathon he completed twice during their formative years.

Born in Australia, Allan has lived and worked on three continents, and spent one quarter of his working years abroad. Having worked as an IT professional throughout his career, he was first published as a technical author.

Today he lives with his wife in Adelaide, South Australia, at the heart of a growing and geographically distributed extended family.

Allan is currently working on the final installment in his series *The Ruptured Kingdom*.

www.ingramcontent.com/pod-product-compliance
Lightning Source LLC
Chambersburg PA
CBHW030553170726
48283CB00002B/311